Mortzeel's Lost & Found

Found

꩜ ☉ ꩜

The One-armed Wizard

By
Nick Cennamo-Smith

ISBN-13: 9798440542679

Cover design by: Nick Cennamo-Smith
Font, Draconis, design by: Neale Davidson of pixelsaga.com
Library of Congress Control Number: 2018675309
Printed in the United States of America

Acknowledgements

To my wife, who has always supported me;
Thank you for indulging your nerdy husband.

To my daughter, who slept on my shoulder;
Thank you for keeping me company at night.

To my mother, who proofread all my work;
Thank you for not making me an accountant.

To my cat, who supervised my desk;
Meow mew mew meow purr.

None of this would have been possible without you all.

Shimmervale

Lakeshire

Coldash
Mountains

Patter's
Port

Bentwood

Cavish

Valley
Peak

Vallameria

Descemb

Ulama

Belgar

Splinterwood
Forest

Kalbasha Sea

Rothwood

Twinbank
Forest

Gables Glebe

Messmire
Wood

Taverish

Tristfall

The Country of
Escana

miles 50 100 150

PROLOGUE

The world of Aldera, a spec floating through the infinite void of the astral sea. Aeons ago the gods roamed this world, and all was well and good. Until it wasn't. A world created by gods and demons, then destroyed by them. A great war between the gods known only as the Cataclysm that nearly destroyed everything they had created, and shattered the realms into their elemental planes. In an effort to save it, and the mortal creatures that called this spec home, the gods chose to abandon it. They created the divine gate, locking themselves away from the world, and trapping the demonic gods in the depths of the nine hells.

Thus the mortal world was left to guide itself, the interference of the divine and infernal kept at bay, for the most part.

Left alone with no gifts from the gods, save the few devoted worshippers, the mortals discovered their own power in the form of arcane magics. This began the age of arcanum, where powerful mages and sorcerers crafted spells to twist the world to their whim.

At the height of this age, four great kings and masters of the arcane made a choice that would change the world forever. Confronted with their own mortality these wizard-kings sought power through the arcane arts of necromancy, the magic of life and death. Sacrificing vast scores of their subjects, these four kings gained immortality through the path of lichdom, becoming the most powerful wizards in history. They became known as the Lords of Ash, leaving nothing but death and desolation in their wake.

Their reign passed for generations, their kingdoms dark and forsaken with little hope for their people as the hunger of the lich-kings grew year upon year. Separating the land out, the kings locked themselves away, ever fearful and suspicious of their once companions, each attempting to gain more power to maintain their control.

In the twelfth century of the Age of Arcanum, nine adventures emerged. Great heroes as the stories go, who risked their lives to end the dominion of the lich-kings. One by one the liches fell to the blades of these heroes, the reign of the Lords of Ash and the age of arcanum came to an end.

In the aftermath of the devastation left behind the world began to recover, though the scars of the past continued to remain. Wishing to leave behind that corrupting power created during the age of arcanum the surviving kingdom, the city of Halanheim, imposed strict laws to constrain this immeasurable power.

Tomes of higher magics, the libraries of the Lords of Ash, and all remains of necromancy were destroyed. Great pyres of scrolls and spellbooks burned for days, illuminating the night skies.

And the world moved on, a new era beginning, rising from the ashes. The heroes that saved the world from eternal death and decay faded back into myth and legend, their memories preserved in great statues and monuments. The Lords of Ash became ghost stories, cautionary tales of the corrupting power of magic.

It is here that our story begins, in Belgar. A coastal city in the country of Escana, where adventure and coin awaits those who wish to find it. Under the light of the moons Aras and her two smaller sisters, Elle and Banna, where a young elven woman sleeps in the streets of Belgar. Her life about to take an unexpected turn down a path twisted by chance and fate. The sun rises on a new day, and a new adventure.

CHAPTER 1

Belgar isn't the most exciting of places, not the dullest either. Sitting on the western coast of Escana looking out towards the Kalbasha Ocean, it does a good business in exotic wines and foreign spices. It is also the city of choice for the up-and-coming adventurer. With the Coldash Mountains to the north and the Splinterwood forest to the east, there was always work to be found for those looking to make a name for themselves, and today was no different.

The streets were a bustle with vendors, shoppers, travellers, and locals. The sound of seagulls and roaring merchants filled the air, the aroma of cooked meats and fresh spices covering the stench of the unwashed masses.

Making her way through the crowds, ignoring the unmissable deals and bargains being offered to her at every turn, Tal'avera was an elf on a mission. A tall woman, long blond hair with more colourful threads woven in than a Wintervail tree, long ears jingling all the way with silver hoops, and stern yet cheerful features. Her emerald green robes ruffled and wrinkled from a hard night's sleep, the hems caked with mud and dust from her journeys. But she didn't have time to be concerned with that now, it wasn't anything a simple prestidigitation couldn't fix. If only she was able to cast any spells.

Tal'avera was not local to Belgar, in fact she'd only arrived in the city the day before, and had already received such a warm welcome. Her backpack containing the majority of her possessions had been swept from her shoulder by a couple of teenagers offering her directions to the nearest tavern, and then things only got worse.

Having been turned around enough already this morning she finally found the entrance to the guardhouse. Dusting herself off as best she could, Tal took a deep breath and strode inside.

The building itself was surprisingly empty, the bare stone walls keeping the room fresh and cool in contrast to the warm summer day outside. A single guard sitting behind a booth was doing his best to look busy, and a young boy pinned notices to a board by the entrance.

Despite herself, and knowing the luck she'd had lately, Tal took a few steps over to the boy and in a hushed voice asked, "Excuse me, sorry, but I don't suppose this is the guardhouse, is it?"

The boy looked up at her with a toothy smile. "Well if it isn't Miss, then I'm gonna be real late for work." He smiled again and went back to pinning notices of what appeared to be wanted posters.

Tal smiled back at him, happy to be in the right place, but took no notice of the posters. She didn't know anyone who lived here or have the time to go bounty hunting. The duty guard was her next target. Standing before his booth as he thumbed over paperwork, she smiled and cleared her throat to announce her presence.

With the heavy sigh of a man who had been hoping for a quiet morning, the guard sat back and looked up at her. "Good morning Miss, and how can I help you?"

"Good morning, and I do indeed hope so. You see, I'd like to report a theft." Tal tried her best to maintain a cheerful disposition after her trying morning.

The guard shuffled through to a blank sheet of parchment. "Ok, can you please provide details on the item or items that have been stolen and the location where you saw it or them last." He rattled off this well practiced line with all the enthusiasm he was able.

"Just one item," Tal said, beginning to feel flustered, "my hand, and the last place I saw it was here, on my wrist."

The guard looked up from his notes in confusion to see Tal holding up her right forearm and pointing with her left hand to the stump where it ended.

The guard's mouth opened and closed a number of times while he carefully chose the right words for the situation. "What?"

Tal sighed. "My arcane prosthetic, an engraved brass cuff with a permanent enchantment. When I woke up this morning it was gone. My backpack was also stolen by some street kids yesterday."

The guard made a note, trying his hardest not to stare. "Okay Miss, and could you tell me where you were staying last night and who else had access to your room?"

Tal's cheeks flushed slightly. "Well you see, as I mentioned my backpack was also stolen yesterday..."

The guard nodded, his ink pen hovering over the parchment.

"...and my coin purse was inside it, so I couldn't pay for lodgings."

"So can I ask where you were staying?"

Tal took a deep pouty breath. "I'm not sure. Do you know the marketplace by the east gate?" The guard nodded. "There's a statue of some old guy there, I slept next to that."

"I see," the guard scribbled some more notes, "and do you..er.. remove your prosthetic to sleep?"

"No, I usually need two hands when I wake up and I've gotten used to it over the years." Tal absentmindedly rubbed her stump. "And to answer your next question, yes someone took it off my arm in my sleep, and no I didn't wake up, I'm a pretty heavy sleeper."

The guard chuckled, "You'd have to be to sleep through losing a hand." He finished making his notes, ignoring the glare coming from the elven woman in front of him. "Okay. I think I've got everything I need. If anyone hands it in...sorry...we shall contact you, where can we reach you?"

Tal raised an eyebrow. "Sorry, what do you mean 'if anyone hands it in'? You're not going to investigate?"

The guard sighed. "In all honesty, we've got more serious things to be looking into, and the chances of your prosthetic still being in the city are lower than my pay. But if it turns up, we'll get it back to you, we just need to know where you'll be staying."

"So you're saying I've lost my hand? For the second time? What am I supposed to do?" She began pacing and gesturing wildly, which was only half as effective as it used to be. "I've got nothing! No coin, no change of clothes, not even my books! What am I supposed to do?"

The guard had pushed his chair back a few feet, putting him out of arm's reach from the flailing woman. "Look, there's every chance it could turn up. We'll put a note out to the enchanters to be aware it's stolen goods. But that's about the best we can do, okay?"

It wasn't okay, but arguing about it wasn't going to get her anywhere. After giving a detailed description of her cuff, she would have provided a sketch but unfortunately she was a righty, and giving as good an account of the two teens that had made off with her bag, there was nothing more Tal could do. The guard was kind enough to give her a small pouch of copper and a change of clothes from their charity box. It wasn't enough for her to get far but it was enough for a warm meal and a bed for a night. He'd even suggested, although implying that it was more of a last resort, a place she could stay for cheap.

This was a last resort situation. Without her spellbooks or her hand she couldn't get work, and without work she'd be on the streets again in a matter of days. Now was not the time to be picky.

So with a determined head she made her way through the more impoverished district of Belgar to The Troll's Den, a tavern for those on a budget, where she'd been told she could find a place to stay for a night or two at least. As she walked through the streets Tal couldn't help but wonder if this trip had been a bad idea. Sure her life back home had been relatively dull, and she'd hunted down enough giant rats and forest bandits to last a lifetime, but leaving everything behind to hit the big city might have been a mistake. Master Brum, the librarian and her tutor had told her things would be difficult, but he'd neglected to mention she'd be mugged and stranded. Then again, he'd never specifically said she wouldn't be. Master Brum was crafty like that.

6

Leaving her thoughts of home behind, Tal took in the peculiar sight of the tavern as she approached. Rickety wasn't really the word for it, patchwork maybe. It looked like the owners had made repair after repair, just enough to keep it from being condemned. A towering three storey building held together with scaffolding and prayers, with architectural design ranging from decades to centuries. If it was in a nicer part of town Tal ventured the property would be worth a fortune, if only for the eccentricity of it all. Though her favourite part was the surprisingly artistic sign that hung above the door, a picturesque hovel with 'The Troll's Den' carved beneath.

With a deep breath, preparing for the worst, Tal walked into the tavern, and gasped.

Inside was cosy, warmly decorated like an old hunting lodge, with mismatched furniture draped with all manner of furs, a large open smoldering fireplace sat beneath a variety of horns and tusks, some of which Tal recognised as troll tusks. A few patrons sat staring into their tankards, though none of them seemed to notice or care that someone had entered.

The only head that turned in her direction was the tavern keeper, who with a brief nod to an empty bar stool returned to cleaning mugs.

Tal took up the stool looking at the collection of barrels that sat behind the bar, none of which were labeled. She smiled at the tavern keeper, a tall, grey-skinned, burly troll-orc woman, with matted dreadlocked hair and tusks long enough that she could have passed for a troll herself if the light were less favourable.

Leaning against the bar so hard the heavy wood creaked, the keeper looked Tal up and down. "What can I get you sweetie?"

"I need a room and some food...and some wine. I really need some wine."

The troll-orc smirked, "Rough day sweetie?" She pushed off the bar and grabbed a goblet from the back shelves. Pulling a lever with one hand a small bell rang in the distance, while she turned the tap on a barrel with the other, a dark red liquid flowing into the goblet.

"You don't know the half of it." Tal dropped her face into her hand.

"Well tell me about it," she placed the goblet in front of Tal, "it's been pretty quiet here lately, I could do with some gossip."

Tal didn't know how she felt about her recent tragedy being referred to as 'gossip', but she had little else to do. "Sure, I got... oh, how much do I owe you?" She took a sip from her goblet, having made a second grab for it with her existing hand, her nose twinging at the taste.

"Well one meal is included with the room, so that plus the drink, ten copper."

Tal reached for the coin purse she'd been given, swallowing the strange liquid. "That's fair. What am I drinking by the way? It's quite unusual." Looking into the purse she inwardly cursed, there was only forty copper inside, maybe she shouldn't have ordered the 'wine'.

"Red-barrel ale. The barrel was used to make wine, so that's the closest I've got." The keeper smiled a tusky smile as she held out her hand for the coin.

Tal paid the few copper, which was immediately pocketed. "Thank you kindly," she smiled, "The name's Tess by the way, welcome to the Troll's Den." She held out her hand.

Tal shook it, and quite the firm shake it was. Tess's eyes widening slightly in surprise as Tal placed her stump in Tess's calloused palm. "Tal'avera, and thank you, it's quite a charming place you've got here."

Tess poured herself a drink, something dark and thick, trying not to glance at Tal's arm. "Thanks, been in the family for generations, now it's all mine." She leaned back against the wall of barrels. "So then, what's gone wrong in your life that you've ended up here?"

Whether it was the wine-ale, the stress, or just Tess's friendly demeanor, Tal didn't care, she regurgitated the story of her last two days like a torrent, exploding from deep within and eager to be out on the surface. Tess was a good listener, or at least seemed to be, not interrupting the story once, just sipping her ale and letting Tal vent her frustration, like a therapist with an open bar.

When the exhausted young elven woman had finally finished Tess took the mostly empty goblet from her, refilled it, and handed it back to her. "I think you've earned this one sweetie. Who steals a person's hand for god's sake?"

A small bell rang and Tess walked over to a panel, lifting it and retrieving a steaming bowl of something, which she also placed in front of Tal.

"I know, it's been quite inconvenient. Thank you," she picked up the spoon and began stirring the food she'd been given, only now realising she hadn't seen a menu or been given a choice. "What is this if you don't mind me asking?"

"Troll Stew," Tess smiled, "The house special, and the only thing we make. Meat, veg, and a broth that'll put hair on your chest."

Tal hesitantly and shakily took a spoonful. She wasn't too keen on the idea of a hairy chest, but it was warm and tasty, and right now that's all that mattered.

"You a righty?" Tess asked as she watched the elf eat. Tal nodded and Tess shook her head once more. "Some people, no respect. You take your time sweetie."

Tal smiled through a mouthful of stew, letting the warmth fill her and the tension drain from her body. After this a warm bath would not go a miss she thought to herself, now wondering if there were baths in this place.

"You know, I'm not one for getting into other people's business," Tess began as she leaned in towards Tal, "But I might know someone who could help you with your problem."

The way she spoke made Tal feel like they were about to discuss an assassination.

"There's someone who stays here, runs a sort of detective agency out of their room. Doesn't bother me too much and they pay monthly, it's even good for getting a few more butts on seats, but that's not the point. Still, I think they might be able to give you a hand...sorry." Tess made an awkward apologetic face.

Tal ignored the comment. "A detective agency? Are they any good?"

Tess shrugged. "Well it's not the best detective agency, I mean their office is a room in a tavern, but I've not heard many complaints. Still probably a better shot than waiting for the City Watch to get things done."

That Tal had to agree with. After all, what did she have to lose, she'd already been mugged twice in as many days. "Thanks, I guess I could try at least. Which room?"

"Room nine, on the second floor, they've got a little sign hanging on the door." Tess chuckled. "They'll be paying to repair that if they ever leave."

Tal washed down the last of her stew with the wine-ale, dabbing her lips with the sleeve of her robe. "Thank you. I'll head on up."

"Sure, no problem." Tess took the plate and handed her an iron key with an engraved tooth pendant. "You're in room seven, second floor as well. They should still be up there, not seen them leave and a young couple headed up to see them not ten minutes before you walked through the door."

Tal thanked her again and headed up the creaky stairs, feeling with each step like the boards might snap beneath her. As she made her way up to the second floor she stopped, suddenly remembering the state of the building she was in, and feeling as though she could feel the walls rock slowly from her additional weight. Tal shook her head, that wasn't possible, just her mind playing tricks. Though even after telling herself this, she continued much slower up the stairs than before.

After what seemed like an age Tal reached the second floor, checking the number on her key again just to be sure, and walked to her room. For cheap digs the room wasn't as bad as she was expecting, a large firm bed, vanity table with some rustic mirrors, and a basin in the corner. All of which looked like it had been rescued from the street many moons ago, but it matched the charm of the rest of the place.

Tal threw the bag of clothes onto the bed and looked herself over in the mirror. She'd looked worse, her hair needed a good brush and a more comfortable night's sleep would fix the bags under her eyes. She didn't like the idea of wearing someone else's clothes, and her robes weren't all that bad, a quick dust off and she would be presentable. Tal began the motions for her casting out of habit before shooting herself a look in the mirror. With a sigh she smoothed out the creases in her dress with her hand as best she could and headed back out.

The detective agency, as Tess had called it, seemed, at least from the outside, like a normal tavern room, apart from the crude sign that hung from the door. 'Mortzeel's Lost & Found'. Tal shrugged, this seemed more like a child's secret hideout than a reputable detective, but as they say, 'any port in a storm'. She rapped against the door and waited.

"Just a moment if you'd be so kind!" a voice called from the other side. The sound of chairs scraping followed by some more muffled voices, then footsteps. Tal stepped back just in time as the door swung open, and two armed and armoured adventures stepped out.

"Thank you again," the first said. A dark-skinned girl, human Tal guessed by the ears, dressed in worn leather armour with a bow and quiver slung over her shoulder. Tal could tell by the slightly smeared eye makeup that the girl had been crying.

"Yes, anything you can do to help would be greatly appreciated," the second added. A stocky half-elf in jangly chainmail with a broad sword belted to his hip. He turned and shook the hand of the well dressed tiefling that followed.

"It is my pleasure, I shall inform you as soon as I have any information." As the couple walked away the tiefling turned to Tal, "Welcome my dear, please, come, come, come," they gestured through the door. "Clients today, they are like carriages, nothing for weeks and now two at once!"

Tal was hurried into the room, and the door shut behind her, her host sweeping past her to the desk.

The room was larger than hers, dimly lit by a variety of scattered candles balanced on any available surface, the window mostly obscured by a chest of drawers with piles of scrolls stacked on top. A room divider, of a style Tal did not recognise, separated the 'office' from the 'bedroom', though not so much that she couldn't see the unmade bed and clothes strewn about the floor. The office was slightly tidier, two comfortable chairs sat in front of a tidy desk, a neat pile of parchments on one side and an ink well and pens on the other.

The tiefling, however, seemed very out of place. Crimson-purple skin, black and brown patched horns sweeping from their forehead to the back of the skull, where their long dark-silver hair was held in a messy bun with two carved wooden hair pins. They dressed in a slightly dated three-piece suit, sleeves rolled up to the elbows and the top button undone, very business casual. The flickering candle light gave their face an almost gaunt look, making their chiseled features seem too large. Tal would have considered the tiefling to be gangly if they had been much taller than her, their slim frame moving rather elegantly as they pulled out their chair.

As they sat a cheerful smile spread across their face, yellow eyes glittering in the flickering candle light. "Welcome to Mortzeel's Lost and Found, I am Kaivel Mortzeel, how can I be of service?" Tal couldn't quite place the accent, it was faint, but still seemed like the common tongue was not their first language.

Tal sat down and cleared her throat. "Tal'avera, and Tess downstairs recommended your services," she pulled her sleeve back, revealing her stump and raising the immaculate eyebrows of Kaivel. "My hand was stolen, by which I mean my arcane prosthetic."

"I was about to ask," their smile intensified. Kaivel picked up a pen and a fresh piece of parchment. "Why don't you start from the beginning, spare no details."

Tal recounted, for the third time today, her recent nightmare of a life since she got to Belgar. All the while Kaivel took notes, maintained a straight face, and added the occasional, "I see." When she finished Tal slumped back into her chair and waited for Kaivel to finish with their notes.

With a final flourish of their pen, Kaivel looked up with a beaming smile. "Well you have had quite the welcome to this fair city."

"I'd argue with the 'fair' comment, but other than that yes," Tal smiled despite herself, Kaivel's friendly attitude was quite infectious.

Kaivel cleared their throat, "Well to get down to the business side, I charge two gold pieces a day and guarantee results in two weeks or your coin back." Kaivel looked down at the notes and back up to Tal. "But since you've pretty much been beaten over the head from the moment you got here I'll give you the friends and family discount, one gold piece a day. How does that sound?"

It was reasonable enough, and if her backpack wasn't recovered she wouldn't have to, or be able to, pay them anyway. "Sounds fair to me."

"Perfect!" Standing up from the desk, Kaivel grabbed a small satchel from the back of their armchair. "I've got a few places I can try, and as luck would have it, it suits both my cases. I shall inform you as soon as I have any information, where can I find you?"

Tal tucked her chair under the desk, "Well I know no one and have nothing to do so..."

Kaivel smiled and grabbed her by the shoulders. "Perfect, I could do with some company!" They headed for the door and gestured for Tal, "Shall we?"

CHAPTER 2

Out in the streets the pair were on their way at a fast pace, but to where Tal had no idea. "Do you mind if I ask where we're going Mister...Miss...?"

"Kaivel," they smiled at her, "Or Kai, since we're friends. And we're heading to Botan's by way of The Phoenix." Kai rummaged through their satchel and pulled out a dry piece of jerky. "Would you like a piece? And do you mind if I call you Tally? Tal'avera sounds far too formal."

"No thank you, and I prefer Tal, or Vera," though the only person who ever called her Vera was Master Brum, and only then when she was slacking off. Tal didn't know why she thought of that, maybe homesickness was a real thing.

"Vera doesn't suit you. Tal it is." Kai smiled and took a bite of the jerky. "It's nice having someone else to talk to, I look less crazy that way."

They moved through the streets at a brisk pace, Tal hardly knew where she was to begin with, but now she was utterly lost. "Are they friends of yours or places?"

"Both, kind of." The pair had reached one of the market places, so their pace had slowed enough to have more of a conversation, though the clammer of the crowd made it harder to hear. "The Phoenix is where that poor lad was murdered, and Botan's is-"

"Wait a second, who was murdered?" Tal stopped in the middle of the street.

Kai turned and stared at her for a moment in confusion, before slapping their forehead. "I forgot you weren't there. Sorry, but come, we walk and talk," Kai pushed on, not waiting to see if she followed. Tal double stepped to keep up, she was clearly missing some vital information.

"The couple that I saw before you, their friend was murdered in his sleep and his family sword stolen," Kai shook their head. "Some people have no honour."

"So we're going to see a dead body?" Tal asked as she began to rethink her plans for the day.

Kai laughed. "Hopefully not, The Phoenix has excellent room service, I'm sure they've cleaned it up by now." Looking back at the shocked expression on Tal's face, Kai cleared their throat. "I'm joking. We're going to speak to the keeper and see if they saw anything. Botan's a shopkeeper and a friend, she deals in magical items and adventuring gear." Kai smiled. "So the family sword and your hand. Two stones with one bird."

"I think it's 'two birds with one stone'," Tal corrected.

Kai turned and blinked at her. "Hmm, that would be more impressive," they said before pushing on through the crowd.

After more winding through streets their first stop was in sight. The Phoenix Down Tavern and Inn stood at the north end of the East Gate Market, a spot Tal remembered well. She looked towards the statue in the centre of the market. "Do you know who that's a statue of?" she asked Kai, who was already heading inside the tavern.

Kai turned and stared out into the market. "Huh, I've never noticed that before," and they stepped into the tavern. Tal blinked. How could they have not noticed a statue before? Shaking her head she followed them inside.

The Phoenix, as Kai had shortened it, was more of what Tal had had in mind when she thought of a city tavern. Busy tables full of people talking and drinking. Adventurers huddled together making plans and splitting up loot, all looking and smelling like they'd climbed out of the sewers. Tal sighed, it made her nostalgic for her time back home, but it wasn't a life she was cut out for.

15

The two of them made their way to the bar where a grey-haired man stood pouring what seemed like a full cask of ales into various mugs and tankards. Pushing them across the bar to the two patiently waiting dwarves, he turned to Kai and Tal. "What can I do for you?"

"Two mugs of the Roc," Kai said, placing a few copper coins on the bar, "and we've got some questions about the adventurer who died here the other night." Kai slid two more silver pieces across the counter.

Looking back and forth across the bar, the barkeep pocketed the coin and leant across the bar. "What do you want to know?"

Tal leaned in as well, feeling like this was the thing to do. Kai just stood there. "Well first of all I was serious about those drinks."

The barkeep grunted and went off to pour the mugs. "Why are you acting so secretive?" they asked, turning to Tal.

She opened her mouth, then shook her head. "Well you're asking about dead people and the barkeep leaned in all hush-hush. I thought we were trying to keep it quiet."

"Well he might be, probably not good for business having adventurers dying in your establishment." Kai looked around the room. "I personally don't care that much, I'd never stay in such a crowded place."

The barkeep returned, "Your drinks, Now, what do you wanna know?"

Kai took the mugs, handing one to Tal. "The adventurer that died here, what do you know about him?"

The old man wiped his nose across his forearm. "Seemed fancier than most of the types we get round here. Well made armour, nice sword, flashed his coin about a bit much, but I'm not one to say no to a paying customer."

Tal sipped her ale, sweet with a hint of spice, and took a moment to look around the bar. Most of the patrons did look more like working folk, those who had armour were covered in dents and the odd bit of rust, weathered skin and tired eyes, not the kind of people that came from money.

"Did you see anyone with him? Maybe take someone up to his room?" Kai asked.

"That was days ago, I get a lot of people in and out of here. A lot of faces, can't be keeping an eye on all of them."

Now Kai did lean in, running a finger around the rim of their mug. "But a customer like that? Drawing attention to themselves, throwing coin around, you didn't perhaps see anyone getting too close?"

The barkeep bit his lip, casting his mind back and tapping against the bar. After a moment he snapped his fingers and jabbed one towards Kai. "I think there was a redhead. Elven or half or something like that, I can't really tell the difference." Tal raised an eyebrow. "Real pretty girl though, didn't look to be the adventuring type."

"How could you tell?" Tal asked. She'd often heard the same said about herself.

Turning to Tal the barkeep continued. "She dressed nice, all dolled up with some fancy jewellery. Looked more like a working girl, but I'm not one to judge."

Kai had a strange smirk on their face. "Did you see if our rich adventurer took her up to his room?"

The barkeep shook his head. "Can't say. That time of night I would have been sorting out the barrels in the cellar."

"Maybe..." Tal started then looked over to Kai, who was still smirking. They nodded and she continued, "Maybe we could have a look at the room? If there's no one else staying in there that is?"

Stepping away from the conversation, waving a hand to a couple at the other end of the bar, the keeper returned with a key. "Knock yourselves out."

"I don't know if we'll do that, but thank you." Kai took the key and downed their mug in one, their body shivering. "Shall we?" They continued to smirk.

"Thank you," Tal said to the barkeep, who had already moved on, and the pair headed upstairs to the rooms. "Why are you smiling like that?" she asked Kai as they walked, "It's kind of creepy."

"You are enjoying this, no?" Kai smirked towards her, "You ask questions, make suggestions. You are curious."

17

"Of course I'm curious. A guy dies in a tavern and no one knows anything? You don't find that curious?"

Kai stopped outside the door to the room they'd been headed towards, turning to face Tal. "Of course I do, but this is my job. You are just a tourist. Would you like the honours?" They held the key out to Tal.

"Tourist?" Tal snatched the key from them and opened the door. "Tourist?" she huffed and went inside. Kai, and their smirk, followed her in.

The room seemed normal; a simple bed, a desk with a chair, and a wash basin in the corner. Nothing destroyed, no blood covering the walls, just a plain, normal tavern room.

"Huh," Kai said as the two of them looked about the room.

"What's wrong?" Tal tried to follow Kai's eye line, but it seemed to be wandering.

Kai sighed. "Everything. There's nothing here. No Blood, no signs of a struggle, no footprints..." Kai suddenly dropped to the floor with a heavy thud, startling Tal. "No," they said after a moment, "no footprints at all. This is the cleanest room I've ever seen."

Judging by the state of Kai's room back at the Troll's Den, Tal didn't doubt that, "So what now?" she asked, trying not to sound like a tourist.

Kai stood up, dusting off their trousers. "Now I have to actually do some work," they sighed. "I was hoping this was going to be easy."

Tal flicked her tongue. "Well the fact that there's nothing here kind of is something isn't it?"

Turning the chair around to face the room, Kai sat down, "Please, explain."

"Well," Tal began walking in small circles around the room, "if the furniture was damaged we'd know there'd been a fight. And if there was blood we'd know he...?" Tal looked over to Kai, who nodded. "Then we'd know he'd been attacked somehow."

"What about the lack of footprints?" Kai asked.

Tal shrugged. "Whoever killed him had clean feet." Tal furrowed her face as she saw once again that Kai was smirking. "What now?"

"Points to the tourist," Kai stood up and gave a slow clap. "You are quite good at this." They paced the room again, their eyes focused on each little detail. "I think we're done here," Kai smiled at Tal, "Maybe we'll have better luck finding the redhead."

As the pair made their way back to the bar, Tal couldn't help but keep wondering. "So how did this guy die then?"

With a thoughtful scratch of their chin Kai pondered along with her. "Hmm. I think we can rule out old age."

"I'm not kidding," Tal growled. She was going to have to find some way of knowing when, or if, Kai was being serious.

"Neither am I," Kai continued down the stairs, "The more possibilities we eliminate the fewer possibilities there can be."

They headed back to the bar and waved to the barkeep. "Excuse me," Kai slapped the key on the bar, "but what rooms were our departed friend's friends staying in? In case we need to talk to them."

"The rooms on either side," he replied without looking up from the drink he was serving.

"Wonderful, let's go." Kai patted Tal on the shoulder and headed to the door.

ঌ☉৯

Back out in the bright noonday streets Kai stood for a moment, taking in the sun and waiting for Tal to catch up. "So," they said smiling back to the increasingly frustrated elf, "What kills you but doesn't make a mess?"

Tal stretched out and let out a huff. "Magic? There are a number of spells that can kill without the target bleeding out." She thought for a further moment. "But only something very powerful would do it before he had a chance to fight back."

Kai nodded, taking yet another piece of dried meat out of their satchel. "And how common is that sort of magic?"

"Not very," she admitted, "and I don't know why someone would use such powerful magic just to kill an adventurer."

"Maybe it's not because he was an adventurer," Kai took a bite, "the barkeep said he looked like he came from money. Maybe it was personal. Do you want some?" Kai took out another piece of jerky, holding it out to Tal.

"How long has that been in your bag?" she cocked an eyebrow at Kai, who shrugged. "I think I'll pass, thank you. What do we know about this guy then? Who was his family?"

"Not a clue. We can ask his friends later. Come on, we have places to be," Kai put away the jerky and walked off into the crowd. With a groan Tal followed after them. She was beginning to regret joining this expedition, but curiosity was also getting the better of her, and she still needed her hand back.

The two continued their musings as they walked through the city, drawing a few eyes as they casually discussed methods of murder.

"What about poison?" Tal suggested, "Or a drug? The redheaded woman could have been trying to drug him to rob him, and given him too much by mistake?"

"Or on purpose," Kai said, "A dead man can't hunt you down to get his money back."

A morbid thought, but one Tal couldn't argue with. "So killing him for coin, is that our theory right now?"

"Our theory?" Kai laughed and began grinning again. "Okay. It is one theory, but let's keep thinking, it is good exercise." They stopped suddenly as the pair entered an open square, a temple Maival towering high before them. "I can never remember if it's this street or the next," Kai tapped their foot against the ground. "It's this way," they declared, heading confidently up the north-east street. Tal began to follow, but no sooner had they entered the street did Kai about-face. "No, wrong way."

Shortly after this navigational blunder, the pair were halfway up the north-west street when Kai pointed to a rather conspicuous building. It bore no sign, nor anything at all that made it stand out, which, on a street lined with shops, made it stand out all the more. That and the white painted brickwork made it look almost

20

out of place. Whatever the case, Kai strode confidently towards it, and Tal followed closely behind. This city really was starting to surprise her, in a good way.

They pushed open the door, a small bell ringing pleasantly above, and Tal was slightly less than amazed to see that the entrance was just as bare as the outside, just a simple white staircase leading up to another floor. A voice called down, "Just one moment darlings, I will be right with you."

Tal looked around, trying to find some little detail to show what type of establishment this was. "What is this place?" she finally gave up and asked.

"This is Botan's. Botan's Boutique," Kai announced as if that explained everything. When Tal continued to stare blankly at them, they opened their mouth to respond.

"Botan's Boutique," the voice from above declared, "Purveyor of bespoke magical items and fashionable adventuring gear." The two looked up the stairs as a gnome dressed in an elegant white robe floated down the stairs on a silver disc, dark shoulder length hair framing her bespectacled face, making her eyes look larger than her head could hold. "And I, my dears, am Botan." She hovered towards Kai, holding out a tiny hand. "Wonderful to see you again darling, it's been some time."

Kai leaned forward, kissing Botan's outstretched hand. "Yes it has, but I brought a friend this time."

Botan turned to face Tal, her disc floating slightly higher to keep her at eye level with the elf. "Yes you have darling, and I see she is in desperate need of my assistance! Come, come, come, there is no time to waste!" Botan's disc turned and she began floating back up the stairs.

Kai followed with their usual smirk, leaving Tal standing in confused frustration. "What do you mean 'in desperate need'?!" she fumed, storming up after them.

The main floor, as it seemed to be, was much more impressive. Shelves floated freely along each wall, holding glass cases containing all manner of weapons, jewellery, and headwear. Suits of armour, robes and garments hung from floating hooks, everything spiralling up and down the high ceiling, and from somewhere ethereal music subtly echoed against the silence.

"Now darling," Botan hovered next to a small plinth in the centre of the room, "stand here for me, let me see you."

Tal shot a look towards Kai, who gestured towards the plinth and began perusing the many shelves. Reluctantly she stepped up onto the plinth and looked down at Botan, who floated up to meet her gaze.

"Now, darling, let me see what I have to work with." She began slowly orbiting Tal, looking her up and down, her large eyes narrowing as she seemed to be inspecting every thread in Tal's soiled robes. She'd never felt quite so observed, and the fact that she could see Kai peering over at her, with that smirk that she was now sure was permanently stuck on their face, wasn't helping her to feel otherwise.

"These clothes have seen better days, darling," Botan mused as she spun, "and green is not your colour, darling, it clashes with your eyes. No, no, no, this will not do!" The bespectacled gnome flew up to meet her gaze, a small hand lifting her chin in what was meant to be a reassuring manner. "But do not fear, Botan is here and she knows what you need."

"On the subject of things we need," Kai finally interjected, putting down a rather flamboyant hat they'd been trying on, "we are in the market for information."

Botan hovered around the room, her arms folded as she looked at Kai through her thick glasses. "Information is not something I trade in, darling, but if I can help, you know I would be happy to." With a flurry of her hand a small tea cup appeared before her, which she took a sip from. "Oh, much too hot."

"I'm sure you will be of immeasurable help," Kai flattered, "we would love to know if any of your customers have tried to sell you an arcane cuff," they looked over to Tal, "or an enchanted sword marked with a family crest."

Botan blew on her tea. "You know I would love to help you, darling, I really would, but my customers' business is confidential. I couldn't possibly break that trust." She looked over the rim of her glasses.

Kai leaned in close to Botan, lowering their voice despite no one else being present. "Of course. But these items would have been acquired by less than honourable means."

Botan shot a glare towards the tiefling. "I do not deal in stolen goods, darling," her voice not quite as hushed as Kai's. "I have a reputation to consider."

Tal stepped down from the plinth, about to open her mouth to speak.

"I understand, and I would never suggest you were anything but the best," Kai looked over to Tal, "but should anyone come by looking to part with such goods I thought you should be warned."

Botan smiled, her glasses rising as her cheeks glowed. "You are too kind darling, really, you are." She sipped her tea. "So, please tell me, and do not skip on the details, about what it is I need to keep my eyes open for."

Kai pulled a piece of parchment from their satchel, and as Tal wandered over to join the two of them she saw the hastily written notes Kai had made. "Well the first is an enchanted longsword, rose-gold dragon maw guard, with a crest engraved into the pommel. The...er..." Kai squinted at their notes, "House of Vaskar, a thorned rose." They looked up at Botan. "As for the cuff," they gestured to Tal, who cleared her throat.

"It's a brass cuff, engraved with elvish and draconic arcane runes, a mage hand enchantment built in," she pulled up her sleeve, "and it fits right here."

Shattering porcelain echoed in the otherwise quiet room, as a teacup fell from Botan's grasp, scattering itself and it's still too hot contents across the floor. "*Gudin mor!*" Botan swore, looking down at the mess below her, then back up to the stump before her. "My darling, I will do all that I can to see that you and your hand are reunited once more." She shook her head, waving her hand in a simple incantation as the spilled tea cleaned itself up. "I do not know what this city is coming to when a person can have their hand stolen."

Kai smirked as Tal pulled her sleeve down once again, her cheeks reddening.

"Indeed," Kai added, shaking their head, "but thank you for your time, my friend, anything you can do would be appreciated."

"Yes, yes, yes, do not worry darlings, when Botan knows, you shall know, I promise this!" The gnome hovered with them as the pair made their way back down the stairs. "And don't you worry darling, I shall have your new robes ready in a day or so, so you come back to see Botan. I will be waiting for you."

"My what?" Tal asked, stopping mid step before being pulled forward by Kai.

"Much appreciated," Kai added as they opened the door, pushing Tal through, "I count the moments until I see you again." Closing the door behind them Kai turned to answer the puzzled look they were receiving from their new elven friend.

"I didn't ask for, or order new robes," Tal said, her puzzled look turning to worry as she began to wonder if she was expected to pay for something she didn't ask for with money she didn't have.

Kai shrugged. "I didn't order a three-piece suit," they said, "but I needed to know how I might track down a sending stone, and now I own five of them in different shades of grey." Pre-empting the 'why' that was about to exit Tal's lips, Kai continued, "Botan enjoys making clothing, it was a hobby that turned into a business, but she's never stopped and I doubt she ever will."

Tal had to admire that. There were few people who got such joy out of their line of work, and Botan was clearly one of those few. "Will I have to buy them, even if I don't want them?" she asked.

Kai shook their head. "Not at all, unless you don't wish to offend her." They ran their hands through some loose locks of hair. "It's getting late, shall we get a bite to eat?" Without waiting for a response they began walking away from the store and Tal had to double step to catch up.

The day had seemingly gotten away from them. Although it was still quite light out, the shadows were growing longer and the merchant stalls were all but packed away. The few people that were left in the streets were heading home or to the taverns, though where Kai was heading towards Tal could only guess. "Is this your first visit to Belgar?" Kai asked while they wandered seemingly aimlessly through the streets.

"Yes," Tal replied, "though it's also my first visit to any city."

Kai raised an eyebrow, "You've never travelled?" Kai slowed pace for a moment as they came to a fork in the street. "This way," they said, moving on once again, but this time a half step slower.

Tal shook her head. "Not really, I've spent most of my life in a library." She smiled, the memories of home briefly passing through her mind. "I explored around my local area, doing odd jobs here and there for people and traders passing by, but this is the first time I've been so far from home."

"What sort of odd jobs did you do?" Kai asked, seemingly torn between listening to Tal's story and trying not to get lost. "It would be good to know more about who I'm working with, yes?" They flashed her a smile.

Tal made a note to press that subject later, but continued her story. "Mostly exterminating oversized rodents and scaring bandits away from trade caravans. I'm an arcanist, so mostly something big and flashy, enough to get the job done. I came here to become an enchanter." She looked down at her stump. "Which is why it would be wonderful to get my hand back."

"You cannot enchant with one hand?" The pair rounded a corner, walking along the walled bank of the river that separated most of the city from the Island district, where the nobles kept themselves behind guarded gates.

"I could," Tal admitted, "but I'd rather do it with two hands." Kai nodded. "I guess it would take twice as long. Ah, we're here." Kai picked up the pace, "Trust me you're going to enjoy this."

Tal watched as Kai almost skipped towards a smoking cart with a grumpy mule tied up to the wall. As they got closer the smells that wafted from the cart began to overpower the stench of the river. Warm, aromatic spices drifted around her. If Tal hadn't been hungry before she certainly was now. Through the smoke she could make out a stout figure with burly arms and matted

25

hair silhouetted in busy movement as sizzling and clattering accompanied the conversations of folk gathered nearby.

"What is this?" Tal asked as they approached, walking quicker to catch up with Kai who was already greeting the figure.

"Only the best meal in town," Kai smirked, slapping their palm down on the cart's makeshift counter. "Davros, my good sir! Two of the house specials, with everything."

The smoke and grease-stained Dwarf looked down at Kai and Tal, a broad smile poking through his matted beard. "Ah, ya hook-horned tart, can't ya see I'm rushed off me arse 'ere?" Davros gestured with a large knife to the people gathered at the nearby tables, which were just barrels with wooden planks balanced on top.

"By the looks of your arse you need the exercise," Kai shot back with their usual smirk. "Now come on, I told my new friend here that this was the best meal in town, and you best not make me a liar."

Davros wiped a greasy wrist across his chin. "Aye, I wouldn't dream of it. Pull up a wall and I'll see ya true." With a chuckle the Dwarf returned to his stove, his knives hacking and scraping against the hot iron.

Kai gestured to Tal and the pair took a spot against the wall, away from the pluming smoke, and looked out across the river.

"So, how are you liking your second day in the city?" Kai leaned against the low wall, stretching out before slumping into a more relaxed pose.

Tal brushed some loose grit from the wall, not wishing to ruin her dress any further, and took a deep breath, releasing it in a heavy sigh. "It's certainly better than my first, though that's hardly a fair contest." She smiled at Kai, her remaining fingers twiddling through the colourful strands in her hair.

Kai laughed, a short burst before clapping their hands together. "True, but we should all be happy for any improvement in our lives." They ran their own fingers through their hair, tightening the two hair pins holding the bun in place.

Tal smiled to herself. They made a good point in some respects, but on the other hand she was still missing her other hand. "How did you get into this then?"

Kai shrugged. "I was walking by one night and heard a noise. Then once I tried it I was hooked."

Tal blinked away the confusion, and with a slow, measured breath tried again. "No, not this. Investigating."

"That makes more sense," Kai chuckled, "though Davros' cooking is also a life changing experience." They took another piece of dried jerky from their satchel and chewed on it, more out of habit now it seemed, as they looked up into the evening sky. "Things just seemed to happen. I helped a guy one time, then he told a friend, who told a friend, and before I knew it I needed a sign on my door." They smiled at Tal. "Life takes us to strange places, might as well make the best of it."

Tal was about to press them further when a call of, "Order up!" interrupted her.

"Perfect!" Kai tossed the remains of their jerky into the river and headed back to the cart, with Tal following after. "Since this is your first time, it's my treat," Kai slapped a handful of coppers into Davros' greasy palm and retrieved what appeared to be two very large bread rolls. They handed one to Tal, who gasped, not expecting the bread to be as hot as it was.

"Bread?" Tal raised an eyebrow. "The best meal in town is bread?"

Kai was already digging into their own roll and did nothing more than wave hand at her. With an apathetic sigh Tal took a bite.

"Dwarven ale-soaked beef," Kai began as the flavours tickled Tal's senses. "Spiced vegetables," they continued as the elves' eyes nearly rolled back in her skull. "Baked inside sourdough in a portable Dwarven forge."

Tal wasn't even listening any more, the warmth of her meal flowing through her body, the tiny hairs on the back of her neck standing to attention, and the bitter-sweetness filling every sense with delight. Kai was indeed correct, this was without a doubt the best meal in town.

The pair walked in silence back through the darkening city streets, enjoying their food and the company enough, and allowing Tal to take in more of her surroundings.

As rough and dishevelled as the southern district of the city had seemed on her first dash through, now that Tal had a moment to sightsee there was a certain charm to it. It had character, the aging architecture a monument to the city's early construction and times past. In a way it reminded her of home, where buildings stood until they didn't, not destroyed to make way for something newer or bolder, family homes that held history and memories. The homesickness was setting in again, and Tal desperately sought to distract herself from the tears she felt pooling behind her eyes. Fortunately Kai seemed prepared.

"Where are you staying tonight?" They asked, swallowing the last piece of bread. "We are nearly back at the Troll and I just realised I never asked."

Tal cleared her throat, mostly to give herself a second for collection. "Don't worry," she smiled, "I'm staying at the Troll's Den as well. I have a room just down from your office."

"Wonderful, then would you like to join me again in the morning? If it helps to persuade you, I have enjoyed your company."

With a smile and not a second thought Tal nodded, "Yes, as it happens I would. Surprisingly I've enjoyed yours also."

Kai's face fell momentarily into a hurt expression. "Surprisingly?" But with a chuckle they put a hand on Tal's shoulder. "I see we are going to get on well."

The pair continued down the street to the Troll's Den, where the usual quiet regulars paid no attention to their entrance, and Tess gave them a tusked grin, gesturing them towards the bar.

"What's the news?" She asked, grabbing a couple of mugs from under the bar. "You find your hand yet?"

Tal held up her right arm and shook her head. "Not yet," she sighed, "but I didn't lose the other one." Tal cracked an awkward smile, pulling up a stool as the pair sat down at the bar.

"Good," laughed Tess, "cause I ain't feeding you if you do. Get you anything else?"

"That'll do," Kai raised their mug to her, "put it on my tab?"

Tess frowned and kissed her tusks at them. "Do you plan on paying that off any time soon?"

"In due time, Tessy, in due time."

"Let me know when you do," Tess rolled her eyes, "I'll be taking a vacation with that sum." She gave the bar a quick wipe and returned to tending her tavern.

Tal and Kai tapped their mugs together and sipped at the hoppy brew within. Still not wine, but Tal was learning to roll with the punches. With a belly full of food, and the ale working its magic, Tal relaxed against the bar, propping her head up on her stump. "What's the plan for tomorrow then?" she asked Kai, who had adopted a similar pose.

Kai scratched at their chin. "Well, I'd like to have another chat with Samara and Kirtin before we head anywhere else, to see if they know more about this red-headed woman." Kai took a moment to register the look of confusion on Tal's face. "Ah, my other clients, the ones that came in before you." They smiled, "Forgive me, I still feel like you've been with me from the start." Kai cleared their throat and continued, "If they remember anything about her that might give us a good start."

Tal sipped her drink, nodding in agreement. "And if they don't remember her?"

Kai frowned, "Then tomorrow is going to be a long day." With a sigh they dropped down onto the bar with a heavy thud, the mugs bouncing and startling the patrons in the otherwise quiet tavern.

Tal looked around waving an apologetic hand, her cheeks turning a similar colour to Kai. Feeling very observed and awkward, Tal sat in silence, trying not to look at anyone, or move, or do anything that would draw more attention to the pair of them. She just sat and waited for Kai to move, or speak, or do something that would let her know they were still alive.

"Get off the bar," Tess growled as she poured a tankard of water over Kai's head, "you're making the place look untidy."

Kai shot up, shaking their head like a wet dog. "I needed that, thanks."

"Whatever," Tess was already walking away.

29

Kai stood and stretched, dripping all over the floor. "Well now that I'm showered I think it's time to call it a night." They patted Tal on the shoulder, "See you in the morning?"

Tal smiled, "Sure, shall I wait for you down here?"

"I'll find you," Kai said with a wave as they headed up the rickety stairs.

"Be afraid," Tess whispered across the bar, "be very afraid."

Chapter 3

Her second night in the city was much more comfortable than the first. The wool stuffed mattress softer than the stone steps of a statue, the cotton blanket warmer than the cold night breeze. Yes, this was definitely a better place to spend the night.

Light seeped in through the shuttered window at just the right angle to catch Tal's eyes, doing its job in rousing the sleepy elf. Tal stretched out and rubbed at her eyes. Eye. With a groan her left hand did the work of two, rubbing the crust out of her right eye too. Taking the time to find the energy and will to get out of bed, Tal made her way to the mirror and basin.

"You look terrible," she informed her reflection and began washing, letting the cold water remove the last remnants of sleep from her mind. Tal had attempted to wash her robe the night before, with some success, however it remained unwearably damp this morning, and the idea of wearing the donated clothes from the guardhouse did not thrill her.

"How do people get by without magic," she muttered, pulling on the itchy woollen trousers and simple linen top. Tal took a step back so she could properly see herself in the mirror, and with a sigh she declared that it would have to do.

Making her way down to the tavern below Tal was surprised to see Tess sitting at one of the tables with her boots up reading a book. The grey-skinned troll-orc gave her a wave and pointed to the bar. "There's a brew on, help yourself."

Tal did just that, pouring the warm coffee into what she hoped was a clean mug, and went to join Tess at her table. "Thanks," she sipped her smouldering brew, feeling the rush of caffeine invigorate her body.

"Not a problem," Tess folded down the corner of the page she was reading, which received a look of disapproval from Tal, and put it cover side down on the table. "You sleep ok? Hope it was better than the streets is all," she laughed and picked up her own mug.

"Yes, it was," Tal managed a smile, still fixated on the desecration of the book before her, "What are you reading, if you don't mind me asking?"

Tess's cheeks slightly reddened, "Oh just something I found lying about the place, just something to pass the time." She looked over towards the window where the light was beginning to shine in. "Speaking of time, I should probably get the place ready," Tess pushed herself up off the table, taking the book with her, keeping the cover hidden from Tal's view.

This only made her more curious, but she'd learned to be patient. "Have you seen Kai this morning?" she called over, "They were meant to meet me down here."

Tess laughed as she shifted barrels around, with an almost scary ease. "If you were expecting them to be down this early, you're in for a long wait." She leant across the bar, holding a key out towards Tal. "If you're feeling brave, you can try and wake them yourself?" Tess dangled the key, swaying it back and forth as if she were trying to hypnotise Tal into doing her bidding. Whether that was her intent or not, it seemed to work.

Tal took the key from her, ignoring the wry tusky smile Tess was giving her, and with a deep and determined breath made her way up the rickety staircase.

"How bad could it be?" Tal asked herself as she approached Kai's door. Sliding the key into the lock the door rocked open with a creak, Tal cautiously pushed it wider, poking her face into the darkened room. There was no sign of Kai anywhere in the chaos that was their chambers.

"Kai?" she called out, stepping inside and closing the door behind her. Her eyes adjusting to the darkness within, Tal carefully stepped through what could be called the office area of

Kai's room, trying her hardest not to step on a scroll or knock over a pile of books. The way literature was treated in this inn was something that required serious attention, but that was a job for another day.

Moving the partition that divided Kai's room, Tal edged slowly towards the bed, staring at the mound of clothes and blankets for any signs of life.

"Kai?" she called out in a hushed voice. Prodding at the mound with her stump it felt soft. Tal began pulling the pile apart, tossing things left and right. The room was already a mess, so what did it matter?

"What are you doing?" Kai's voice came from behind, startling Tal into an incantation she couldn't complete.

"Don't do that!" She half cried, her hand on the chest. "You scared me half to death!"

Kai smiled awkwardly. "Then I'll not do that twice in a row." They held up a small parcel, pulling out a pastry. "I went to get us breakfast." Kai walked towards her, sitting down on the laundry pile that was their bed, and began eating something that smelt very strongly of cheese. They held one out to Tal. "Hungry?" they asked mid-chew.

Tal turned her nose up, more at Kai's manner's than the smell of what they were eating. "I thought you were sleeping?" She took the pastry from Kai and took a small bite. Tal didn't know why, but she'd always been dubious about people handing her unknown foods. It may have been something to do with the rat skewers she'd accidentally eaten from a travelling vendor back home.

"I was," Kai said, swallowing their mouthful, "Then I got hungry so I went to get breakfast. The first pastry of the day is always the best."

Opening her mouth to say something, Tal instead took a bite of the breakfast Kai had been so eager to acquire, not being able to find anything against their logic.

"What happened to your wonderful robe?" Kai asked after a brief silence. "Please don't tell me someone stole it in your sleep."

33

A chuckle and some pastry flakes escaped Tal's lips. "I washed it," she explained, "but it's still soaked through, so I've got to do with these." she gestured to the second-hand clothing she wore.

Kai shook their head. "Thank the gods we're not seeing Botan today. You'd give her a heart attack dressed like that." Licking their fingers clean, Kai pushed off the bed and began rummaging through their office. Tal watched as Kai stuffed blank parchment and quills into their satchel, before turning to smile at her. "Shall we be going? Since you're awake I assume you're ready?"

Moments later the pair were out in the fresh air of the summer's morning, the streets waking up, ready for a new day. Kai and Tal strolled through the busy market square as the vendors prepared their stalls for the days' trade, and tavern cooks argued over the freshest produce.

Retracing their steps from the day before, the unusual pair entered the doors of The Phoenix Down once again.

Not as busy as their previous visit, but still bustling with geared up adventures enjoying a hearty breakfast before a day of chasing honour and glory. Those at the table Kai headed towards, however, looked less excited for the day ahead.

Tal recognised two of the table's occupants, Samara and Kirtan, but the third she'd never seen before, nor had Kai mentioned them. Looking less than happy to be here, was a grouchy looking halfling, his shaved head a maze of tattoos and scars. He didn't look to be that old, but he'd certainly led a hard life. Tal began to open her mouth to greet them, when the scraping of wood cut her off.

Kai spun the chair they'd just dragged along the floor round and sat down at the table, leaning forward as if they'd been part of the conversation the whole time.

"How are we all doing?" Kai beamed at the three of them. "I don't believe we've had the pleasure," they held a hand out to the tattooed figure, "Kaivel Mortzeel, private detective."

The halfling stared straight passed Kai. "Charmed," was all they said before hunching back over the table.

Samara cleared her throat. "This is Galen," she gestured to the halfling, "he's another member of our party." She turned herself to face Kai. "Do you have news for us? Do you know what happened to Patrice?"

Kai shook their head. "I'm good, but not that good," they smiled at Samara, "but I have made some progress and we," Kai gestured to Tal, "my assistant, Tal'avera and I, are looking into some very promising leads."

Tal didn't know how she felt about being called an assistant, or about lying to these people about promising leads. They had one lead and they weren't even sure if there was a dog at the end of it.

"That's great," Kirtan slapped a meaty hand on the table, "so what are these leads, maybe we can help."

Kai quickly waved that notion off. "No, no, please, this is what you pay me for. And these things require a delicate touch. If I need a great beast slain I promise you'll be the first I come to." Kai's already broad smile seemed to grow wider, the tips of their sharp canines making the smile seem more like a threat to Tal. "I do have some questions for you though that would greatly aid our investigation."

"Certainly," Samara looked to her party for confirmation, "anything we can do to help find out what happened to Patrice."

Tal stepped away from the table to find a chair, this looked to be more than just a brief conversation.

"We have spoken to some witnesses that claim to have seen your friend with a very beautiful red-haired woman. Do you recall such a person?"

Kai's eyes darted from face to face as both Samara and Kirtan's brows furrowed with thought. Galen was focused heavily on something stuck under his fingernail.

"I do recall a girl that was hanging around the bar," Samara said after a moment. "She didn't seem to be with anyone in particular."

Kirtan jumped in, "Yes, the one that spent the night decorating the bar." He nodded at his own words. "Yeah, I remember her. Do you think she had something to do with this?"

Kai had begun making notes on a scrap of parchment. "Too soon to tell, but she may have seen something that could help."

"I don't want to join you," Tal's angry voice came from across the room, "I just want the chair." Kai looked over to see the elven woman arguing with two men who were clinging to the chair she was trying to walk away with.

Samara shook her head, "Those arseholes again." She drew a small dagger from her hip and walked towards the confrontation.

"You going to tell this devil detective or am I?" Galen spoke when Samara was out of ear shot.

Kirtan suddenly looked nervous. "I don't want to cause any more problems!" he said in a hushed voice.

"You realise I'm still here?" Kai cocked an eyebrow.

With a sidelong glare at the scared halfling, Kirtan gave a heavy sigh and turned to Kai. "Right, but don't say anything to Samara, ok? She kinda had a thing for Patrice and I don't wanna damage the memory of him for her."

Galen snorted and rolled his eyes.

"Whatever you tell me will be in complete confidence as much as it can be." Kai gave a slight bow of their head.

Biting his lower lip, Kirtan leaned forward. "So we were celebrating, we were back from a big score. Hunted down this big devil frog thing-,"

"A friend of yours, I'm sure," Galen smirked at Kai.

"-that had been taking folk from this village two days south of here." Kirtan continued without seeming to notice Galen's slight. "Real messed up this place was, stuff growing out of everything, bits of bodies just rotting in corners."

"And you found the red-haired woman there?" Kai had been making notes as they listened, though their gaze was firmly locked on the Halfling.

"What? No!" Kirtan shook his head. "Like I said we were celebrating. Samara came back here to get our rooms sorted while Patrice, Galen, and I picked up the bounty from the guild."

He looked over to where Samara and Tal stood talking at the bar. "Anyway, there was a bit of a bonus, so we stopped off at the Dancing Dryad." His cheeks began to flush, while Galen just smiled and nodded, staring into space, probably enjoying the memory.

Kai made a note, sighing heavily. "So the girl worked there, a dancer?"

Both men nodded. "And damn could she dance," Galen smiled.

Kai folded the parchment and slipped it into a pocket. "This might get us somewhere, thank you Kirtan."

As he went to open his mouth Samara and Tal re-joined the table, pulling Tal's chair with them. "Everything ok?" Samara asked as the two women sat.

Kai nodded, beaming their smile once more. "Yes, in fact they have been very helpful. Galen remembered a similar looking woman working at the guild," Kai felt Kirtan's tension release as they spoke, "so we're going to head over there to see if anyone there remembers her."

"But I just sat down," Tal groaned to herself.

"Wonderful," Samara smiled almost hopefully, "if there's anything more you need you can find us here for the next few days at least."

Kai stood, adjusting their waistcoat and satchel. "Of course, information is always helpful. After all," Kai shot a look towards Galen, letting their eyes flare briefly, "the devil is in the detail."

࿐☉࿐

Back out on the streets, Kai chewing on a piece of satchel jerky as Tal had decided to call it, they began wandering.

"What was that about?" Tal asked when they were far enough away from the tavern.

"Questioning witnesses," Kai said with a shrug. "Did you get anything out of Samara? Very clever idea by the way. Pretending to need a chair, excellent."

"What?" Tal squinted at Kai, not sure if they were mad or she was. "No, I meant the eyes, and the devil comment?"

Kai rolled their eyes to the sky. "Oh that," again they shrugged, "little man's not a fan of infernal blood." They said it so casually that it caught Tal off guard. "To each their own. I'm not a fan of arseholes so we're even I'd say." They smiled at Tal, quickly returning to their previous question. "So, did you get anything out of Samara?"

Tal looped a strand of hair around her finger. "She seems to be the most concerned about what happened to Patrice. She's intent on getting his family sword back before they ship his body back to the family."

Kai raised an eyebrow at that comment. "They're sending him home? Must be an important man." They chewed on the jerky again, looking around to see where exactly they were.

"He had a family sword with a crest, so they must be pretty influential," Tal bit her lip, racking her brain, "though I can't say that I've ever heard of them."

"Can't be that important then," Kai had now stopped walking and was staring up and down the streets.

Tal followed their eye line, to what end she didn't know. She had no idea where they were going or what they were looking for. Even if she did, it wouldn't have done her much good, since she still barely knew her way around the city. "What are you looking for?" Tal eventually asked after moments of awkward silence.

"Jasper." Kai said the name as if that explained everything, still looking around the street. "He's usually out by this time of day." They started moving again, and as the pair turned the next corner, Tal realised they had been walking in circles since they had left the tavern.

As Kai led her around another corner, Tal stepped faster to catch up with them. "Perhaps if you told me what this Jasper looked like I'd be able to help?"

"Look for a pile of rags with a beard," Kai said flatly, their attention focused elsewhere as their eyes darted around the streets.

Tal opened her mouth to speak, but nothing made it past her lips, she just watched as Kai wandered like they were searching for a lost button.

After passing the same street for a third time Tal was beginning to get bored, not to mention sweaty as the sun was getting higher and warmer over the city, and the idea of lunch kept interrupting her thoughts.

"Tsk, tsk, tsk. Calls theirself a detective, do they?" A gruff raspy voice came from just behind Tal, making her jump and nearly trip over her own feet.

A hoarse laugh followed as she turned to see nearly exactly what Kai had described. Matted hair moved into an thick unkempt bread, two piercing green eyes gleaming through the follicle shrubbery, all sitting on top of layers upon layers of ragged patchwork cloaks. Tal took one look and nearly fainted with heatstroke on their behalf.

"No harm, girlie, no harm," the figure's tone was friendly and calming, two dirty hands appearing from beneath the layers. "I've been following you for nearly an hour, it was just too much fun."

"Jasper, I presume?" Tal raised a suspicious eyebrow, at who she hoped they'd been looking for, and not just a very conspicuous stalker.

Discoloured teeth appeared in the beard in the shape of a wide smile. "That's what they call me," Jasper gave a bow, "how may I be of service?"

"You can start by not wasting my time!" Kai shouted from across the street as they stormed towards Tal. "What do you think you're playing at, eh?"

"I believe the youngins call it '*hide and seek*'," Jasper chuckled, "and I believe I won again."

"You knew we were coming?" Tal looked over to Kai who was still glaring at Jasper.

The hairy man laughed again. "No, I saw this one coming a mile off," Jasper clapped Kai on the shoulder, "and thought I'd have a bit of fun." With surprising force Jasper pulled Kai into a tight embrace. "It's good to see you, my friend."

Kai struggled free, pushing away from Jasper and brushing the newly acquired dirt from their suit. "Well now you've had your fun," Kai groaned and sighed, "I've got some favours to ask."

Now was Jasper's turn to groan. "Ayyy, favours, favours, favours. All you ever ask of me is favours. Never, 'how was your day Jasper?', 'can I buy you a drink Jasper?'." With a chuckle the ragged man gently nudged Kai's cheek. "Ah, but how can I say no to this face, huh? What do you need, my friend?"

Kai gestured to Tal, who was once again beginning to feel very awkward. "My dear associate, Tal'avera, was relieved of her belongings...and her hand."

Tal waved her stump as Jasper's eyes went from confusion to shock, before that toothy smile appeared again.

"How do you lose a hand?" Jasper chuckled. "I mean apart from the obvious way, but that doesn't look fresh enough."

"It's my prosthetic that's been stolen," Tal was beginning to tire of explaining it, "a brass enchanted cuff."

"Can't be too many of those knocking around," Kai fiddled with their hair pins, "think you could ruffle some collars and see what you can find?"

Jasper threw his arms wide and chuckled. "Ruffling collars is what I do, my friend." He bowed down to Tal, "If I can be of service, my dear, then I'm happy to help." For a filthy looking man, Tal thought he was surprisingly charming. "I believe you mentioned some belongings as well?"

Tal nodded. "Yes, some kids made off with my backpack. It had a few changes of clothes, my books, and my coin."

Jasper tousled his own matted hair, and Tal could have sworn she saw something moving in there. "The coin is probably gone by now, so you can probably forget that. But the rest of the stuff might have hit the markets."

Tal's heart sank. "Do the vendors here all deal in stolen goods?" she groaned into her hand.

"Not if they know it's stolen," Kai gave a supportive, yet somehow patronising, pat on the shoulder, "but clothes and books aren't the sort of thing that'd raise an eyebrow. And you can replace them easily enough."

Tal shook her head. "The clothes, yes, but my spellbooks will take days, no, months to replace. Not to mention how expensive it'd be." Her head fell again.

Jasper snapped his fingers. "Why didn't you say," his matted shrubbery almost bristled with the excitement in his voice. "Spellbooks are much harder to shift. I'll poke around and see if anyone's looking to move some."

With renewed hope, Tal almost bounced with joy. "Are you serious? Oh Jasper, you have no idea how much that would mean to me!"

The multi-layered man gave an overly flamboyant bow, "Anything to be of service, my lady." He straightened up, clearing his throat. "If I can get any information for you, you know where to find me."

"In the last place I look, yeah, yeah," Kai rolled their eyes, "now be off with you." They gave Jasper a final pat on the back before spinning on their heel and walking off down the street.

Jasper gave Tal another bow and made his way to wherever it was he came from.

"Next time I'll buy you that drink!" Tal called after him as she quickstepped after Kai. "What a lovely man" Tal smiled as she caught up with the tiefling. "Is he your contact on the streets then? Your homeless spy?" Tal's mind skipped back to the novels she'd read back in Master Brum's tower.

"Jasper's not homeless," Kai laughed, "he's a fence."

"A what?" Tal blinked away the rosy fantasy in her mind.

"A fence," Kai repeated. "A dealer. A middleman. A pusher. A trafficker of illicit acquisitions." They laughed again at the look of disappointment on Tal's face. "Chances are whoever stole your hand is going to use Jasper to try and move it." They patted Tal on the back. "But don't worry, he's a crook, but an honest crook. If someone brings it to him you'll get it back."

That gave Tal more hope, and once again moved her mind to the romantic ideals of her novels. "So where to next?"

Kai had begun chewing on a piece of their never-ending jerky. "Well, while you were off wrestling with chairs," they smirked, "the two fine gentlemen told me a lovely story about a little side trip they made to the Dancing Dryad..." Kai sighed heavily. "Adventurers...too much coin and not enough sense."

"Is that another tavern?" Tal's stomach began to grumble as she watched Kai chew.

"Of sorts…"

"So we're going there?" Tal sensed a hint of reluctance in Kai's voice.

Kai sighed again. "As much as I wish we weren't, it looks like we have to. But not now," Kai looked Tal up and down, "they don't open until later in the evening and we wouldn't get past the door looking like this." They scratched their chin. "No, right now we should head back to the office. Maybe Tess has something that'll fit you."

As they turned back in the direction the Troll's Den, Tal cleared her throat, almost raising her hand as she asked, "Can we please get something to eat?"

Chapter 4

No," Tal groaned with disappointment for the tenth time, throwing the dress back at Tess. "They're all too...too..." She bit into her lip, trying to find the safest word.

Tess glowered as she re-hung her snakeskin dress, "Too what? Go on, say it."

Tal's cheeks were burning under the gaze of Tess' dark eyes. "Big!" she finally blurted out. "Ok, big! Tess, your shoulders are nearly twice the size of me!" She stepped up to Tess, "And you're nearly a foot taller than me!"

It wasn't too much of an overstatement. As feminine as some of her features were, even with her troll-orc heritage, she was an imposing figure. Add to that the troll blood that had survived many generations, and it left her with a lithe figure, broad shoulders, and limbs only slightly longer than they should be. As opposed to Tal'avera, a petite elven woman who could, and has, fit inside an ale barrel with room to spare.

Tess's face relaxed into a smile, "What did you expect? I run a tavern, not a haberdashery."

"Can't we just trim one of them down?" Kai, who was sitting cross-legged on Tess's large fur covered bed, suggested as they looked up from one of the many books they'd surrounded themselves with.

Tess pointed a finger, which may as well have been a fist, over at Kai. "You try such a thing and I'll trim you down!" She muttered something else under her breath, that Tal recognised as orcish, before heading over to a chest of draws.

"What are you doing here anyway?" Tal looked over to Kai.

"Research," they replied without looking up, "It's always important to know things you don't already." They closed the large leather tomb and picked up another.

Tal wandered over to a mirror, holding her hair up in a high ponytail before letting it fall down her back again. "But why are you doing it here? Isn't that why you have an office?"

An evil sounding cackle slipped through Kai's lips. "And miss this?" they gestured from Tal to Tess. "Not a chance."

"What about this?" Tess said after rummaging through her drawers, handing a deep green silk to Tal.

Holding it up against her body in the mirror Tal's cheeks flushed. It was a lovely colour, the material was soft and smooth, it was even a nice length, coming down just below her knees. But one thing about it concerned her.

"Is...is this a nightgown?" her voice shook as she asked the question.

Tess laughed. "Well you did say you were going to the Dancing Dryad, didn't you?" She looked over to Kai, who seemed more focused on their book than the conversation.

Tal's cheeks grew redder. "What's that supposed to mean?"

Tess's eyes widened, her tusked smile growing wide as her jaw almost fell open, and a hearty laugh rolled from deep within her. "You don't know?" She turned to face Kai. "You've not told her?"

A book slammed shut as Kai rolled from the bed and was at the door in the blink of an eye. "I should probably get ready too," they said as the door closed behind them.

Now Tal was really getting nervous. "It's a tavern, right? Just a fancy tavern?" She was almost pleading against the voice in her head that told her she was wrong.

Stepping closer to the small elven woman, Tess wrapped her arms around Tal's body and held her close. "Oh sweetie," she stroked Tal's hair like a child, "don't worry, Kai'll take care of you." She pushed back and Tal saw a ferocity in the troll-orc's eyes. "If they don't you just tell me, and I'll give 'em hell."

A gentle rapping at the door interrupted the moment, and Tess flipped like a switch. "What?" she barked at whoever was there.

The door opened slowly and an elderly gnomish face poked inside. "My apologies miss," the wrinkled face said, "but I was told to deliver this immediately, and your patrons told me you'd be back here." The door pushed open and the gnome carried a large box in, placing it on the ground just inside. "Again, my apologies." The door closed as the elderly gnome disappeared, hurried footsteps fading away.

Tess lifted the box, which now looked much smaller to Tal. "Huh, it's for you, and there's a note."

Sitting down on the edge of Tess's bed, Tal turned her attention away from the array of books Kai had left behind. "For me? What does it say?"

Clearing her throat for dramatic effect, Tess read the note aloud in an attempt at a posh accent. "Darling, the thought of you in those rags kept me up all night. This will keep you going until I am finished. B."

The word 'darling' alone triggered the memory of Botan hovering around her, and as Tess unrolled the fabric within, Tal's jaw nearly fell from its hinge.

The material shone with a silk-like glaze, but as Tal ran her fingers down it she could feel the cotton weave. Beautiful gold and silver embroidered arcane symbols decorated the deep crimson fabric, the sides cut away with a delicate lace. It looked very elegant and far too expensive. Tal hoped against hope that she and Kai were able to find her belongings, so maybe she could sell them to pay for this robe.

A whistle was all that came from Tess' lips. "How about that, eh?" She watched as Tal continued to run her fingers over every thread. "Well don't just stand there, put it on!"

Tal snapped out of her daze, looking up at Tess with eager anticipation.

≈⊙≈

"Kai, are you ready?" Tal asked, kicking their office door. She was carrying the books they'd left behind, which Tess insisted be removed or destroyed.

As she'd piled the books atop one another, Tal had been surprised by the range of subjects; anthropology, demonology, botany, religious texts, and folklore. It was like Kai had raided a library in a hurry, grabbing whatever they could on their way through.

When no response came Tal kicked again. "Are you in there?" she shouted through the door.

A distant voice called back, "I'm coming, I'm coming." As the door opened Tal panicked as the figure standing before her was not what she expected to see. It was Kai alright, but not as she'd ever expected to see them. Wearing an elegant black robe, adorned with silver and pearlescent needlework, dark eyeshadow and lipstick standing out from the soft red skin. Their horns and fingers adorned with silver and gold rings, and their hair, no longer held in place by the pins, tumbling in waves over their shoulders. Tal didn't know whether to be shocked or impressed.

"You had a robe like that lying around, and you sent me to get something from Tess?!" she growled at them, opting for annoyed over shocked or impressed.

Kai blinked, giving a half shrug. "Well yes, this is mine." They looked down at the pile of books in Tal's hands. "As are these, thank you." They took the books and went back into their room.

Following them in, Tal continued her outrage. "You have other clothes though, couldn't you have worn something else?"

Kai dropped the books down next to their desk. "I could have worn one of my other robes, I guess, but this one's my favourite." They looked Tal up and down, giving an approving nod and a smile. "You look lovely."

Tal puffed out her cheeks. "Don't change the subject. Others? You have other dress robes?"

"Yes," Kai said as they slung a small bag over their shoulder, "and you do look lovely. Shall we go?" Without waiting for a reply, Kai was out the door, leaving Tal pouting in their office.

"I don't look *lovely*," she muttered to herself as she followed, "I look amazing."

46

Tal'avera was not very comfortable with people, especially people she didn't know. Especially with people she didn't know watching her as she walked by. Right now, Tal'avera was very, very uncomfortable. As she and Kai walked through the streets of Belgar, the number of eyes that followed them made her wish she'd had a frumpy looking cloak, or that she had accepted one of Tess's oversized dresses.

"How much further is this place?" This was the fourth time Tal had asked this, and she didn't expect a different answer, but she hoped.

"I told you," Kai repeated, "we're almost there."

There was something about seeing Kai in a dress that made Tal smile. She'd never had many friends growing up, and never had she gotten dressed up to go to a fancy tavern for a girl's night out. Maybe living in the city was going to be good for her after all. But still, she had to ask.

"Why are you dressed like that? You look so different," Tal smiled in a way she hoped told Kai that was meant as a compliment.

Kai smiled back, their dark make-up making their previously cheeky expression look somewhat menacing. "That's the point, I'm in disguise." They winked at Tal. "Who do you think this girl would be more likely to talk to? A detective," they bumped Tal with their hip, "or a woman of class looking for some gossip?"

After a short while longer on the early evening streets of Belgar, as people were returning to their homes or claiming their spot in the nearest tavern, Kai pointed to a tall building nestled between a winery and a jewellers. Tal could see that the proprietor was leaning heavily into their dryad theme. Thick ivy climbed up the exterior of the building, a variety of beautiful, colourful flowers breaking up the tones of green, and a thick tree branch held the ornate sign.

"It's kind of inconspicuous, don't you think?", Tal joked.

Kai blinked at her. "Really? Seems quite conspicuous to me." They took a moment to adjust theirself. "Come on, let's go." With a deep breath Kai set their shoulders and strode forward through the large oak door.

Tal followed quickly, not wanting to be left alone in the street. As she stepped through the doorway, pushing aside a pair of heavy velvet curtains, it was as if she'd stepped into another world. Dim candles flickered from ornate chandeliers giving just enough light to see where you were going, as elegantly dressed patrons, and seductively dressed staff lounged across the soft furniture and scattered cushions. Everything looked very comfortable, if not too cosy for Tal's liking. Her eyes were wide, taking in everything she was seeing, while her jaw wobbled.

"Good evening ladies," a soft voice addressed them as a very handsome elven man approached them, his open silk shirt displaying a muscular body beneath. "Welcome to the Dancing Dryad," he continued, "may I get you a drink and escort you to a table?"

Tal's mouth and throat instantly dried up, as if all the moisture was suddenly drawn from her body, a strange rasping sound was all she managed as she tried and failed to look into the man's eyes.

"That would be quite delightful," Kai replied in a soft elegant accent, "my dear friend here is in desperate need of something to help her relax." Kai ran a finger softly down Tal's reddening cheek, smiling as they watched the embarrassment take over her entire body until she was so red she could have passed for a rare subrace of hornless tiefling. "Now, why don't we follow this lovely gentleman?" Kai stepped forward, linking their arm with the elven man, who held out the other for Tal.

"Right this way, my lady," the elf smiled at Tal, which did nothing to help her current condition. However she managed to step forward enough to link her arm with his, feeling the hard bicep beneath, and be led through the tavern in search of an empty table.

Tal looked around as they made their way across the floor, her eyes drawn to the small stage in the middle of the room where another woman danced sultrily to the soft piano music being played by a hulking goliath. You didn't see many goliaths this far south, and never wearing such a fine suit. It was possibly the most confusing part of this entire experience.

"What can I offer you ladies this evening?" their host asked as they arrived at a low curved sofa in the corner of the room. "We have a fine selection of Galvarian wines. Or perhaps you'd care to sample some of our finer spirits?"

"A bottle of something red and fruity," Kai said as they relaxed into the cushions, "something from the Sydair region." Kai patted the sofa next to them, locking eyes with Tal.

In her daze Tal hadn't realised she was still holding on to the elven man's arm. "Oh, yes, thank you," she almost curtsied as she released her grip and joined Kai on the sofa, sitting perfectly straight like she was trying to balance a wine glass on her head.

The elven man gave a low bow. "An excellent choice my lady, is there anything else I can get you?"

With an exaggerated thinking expression as they tapped their finger to their pouting lips, Kai pondered for a moment. Snapping their fingers suddenly as if remembering something Kai looked up to the elf. "Ah yes," they smiled their broad cheeky smile, "As it happens a friend of mine was here the other night, and recommended a girl. Oh what was her name," Kai closed their eyes and snapped their fingers again, pretending to recall a memory. "Ah, it escapes me. But he said she was a wonderful dancer, with flaming red hair. I don't suppose you know who he could have been referring to?"

Their host scratched his chin as he looked around the tavern. "That could have been Jenah," he said after a moment, "she was working a few nights ago, but I'm not sure if she's here tonight."

Kai pouted, giving a hurt-puppy look of disappointment. "Oh that is such a shame, I was so looking forward to seeing her perform."

"I'll see what I can do," the elven man said with a slight bow. "I shall return momentarily with your drinks. Ladies." He gave another sweeping bow before turning around and walking towards the bar.

Tal shuffled closer to Kai, shaking the image of the elf walking away from her mind. "What is this place!" Though her voice was

49

lowered, the frustration carried through, which was only met by Kai's usual smirk.

"It's an establishment for those with an excess of coin and a lack of morals." Kai whispered too, dropping the facade of their character. "Just follow my lead, you're doing wonderfully."

"And what is all this?" Tal gestured up and down Kai, "who are you supposed to be?"

With a smile Kai returned to their accented voice. "Why I'm your oldest friend, Baroness Lutresa of the Smouldering Isles."

"Baroness who, of the what now?" Tal was getting more and more confused by the moment.

Kai held up a finger. "My dear, a good backstory is a key part of any good disguise. We'll work on that later." Clearing their throat they fluttered their eyelashes as the elven host returned with a tall thin bottle and two beautiful crystal wine glasses.

"I have spoken to management," he said, pouring the wine out, "and unfortunately Jenah is unavailable tonight. But we have many other very beautiful dancers that I'm sure would please you."

Kai feigned disappointment as they took the offered wine glass. "Well I am sorry to hear that, I do hope she's alright."

The elf gave a gentle nod. "Of course. I'm sure if you visit us again she'll be more than happy to see you."

Tal took a slow deep breath, biting her lip as she built up the courage to join in with Kai's charade. "Oh but I so had my heart set on seeing her perform this evening," she looked from the host to Kai, "since we're leaving for Vallameria in the morning, and who knows when we'll be back."

"I'm sorry my love," Kai took Tal's hand stroking it gently, "tonight was going to be so special."

Not wanting to lose steam Tal turned back to the host. "Isn't there anything you could do?" She took his hand in her own with her stump pressed into his palm, "We'd be ever so grateful, and I'm sure my lady could make it worth your while."

The elf looked down into Tal's pleading eyes, absently stroking her wrist. With a smile and another gentle bow the host replied, "I shall speak with management, maybe if they know she's being specially requested they may be able to help."

"Thank you," Tal called after him as he walked away, her eyes dropping once again. As she lifted the wine glass, Tal took a deep sigh of relief, sinking back into the cushions with Kai.

"Bravo," Kai smiled, giving a gentle applause. "That was impressive. You're becoming a natural at this Tal." They held their glass out to her.

"No," Tal smiled as she tapped her glass against theirs, "my name is Lady Monique, consort to the Baroness of the Smouldering Islands."

Kai's smile broadened further. "Close enough," they sipped their wine and settled in.

The atmosphere within the Dancing Dryad was surprisingly very relaxing once Tal managed to calm her anxiety, with the aid of a very fine wine. Though this was clearly a place where, as Kai said, those with coin to spare came to indulge themselves, she found that compared to most taverns it was a place one could unwind in peace. Ethereal piano, played so delicately by such an imposing figure, gave a wonderful backdrop to the hypnotic movements of the dancers performing. All together it made for a fabulously enjoyable evening.

"Do you do this sort of thing a lot?" Tal asked Kai as she refilled her glass. She'd kicked off her boots and made herself more comfortable, tucking her feet up onto the soft sofa.

Kai shook their head. "No, I don't really enjoy places like this." They held their glass out to Tal.

"No," she gave a small chuckle as she topped off Kai's wine. "I mean put on disguises and play different characters."

Kai sipped and nodded. "Ah," they nestled back into the cushions, "that would depend on the case. It has been a while though."

"Do you enjoy it?" Now that they had some time alone, and in such a laid back environment, Tal thought she'd take the opportunity to get to know her peculiar new friend.

"I don't hate it," Kai swirled the wine in their glass. "It's just a part of the job. Though I wish this dress had pockets."

Tal smiled at Kai, rolling her eyes as once again they'd misunderstood her. "Being a detective. An investigator. Helping people in need."

"Hmm," Kai examined their already chipped nail polish as they contemplated. "I suppose I do. I enjoy the puzzle," they sipped their wine, "and it's better than the alternative." Their face took on a subtle but serious look, not the kind Tal would have associated with the near-constantly smirking detective.

"The alternative?"

Kai's cheeky smile returned as they slipped back into their persona. "We have company," they whispered over the lip of the wine glass.

Tal followed their eye-line across the tavern as a slim figure walked gracefully down the stairs. As she stepped into the candle light, the shining red hair that tumbled down her body was unmissable. Tal watched as the woman walked towards them, her long jewelled ears and sharp angled features identifying her elven heritage. Her long emerald green dress hugged her slender frame, with a vine-like necklace that hung down her torso, if she were in a forest Tal thought she could have been mistaken for a dryad herself.

She smiled at the two of them as she reached their table, sliding onto the sofa with friendly grace, as if she were joining old friends. "Good evening," her tone was relaxed and welcoming, "I understand you asked to see me personally. I am Jenah, and I don't believe we've had the pleasure."

"No we haven't," Kai held out their hand, "Baroness Lutresa." Jenah shook it softly. "And my friend, the lady Monique," they gestured to Tal.

"Lovely to meet you both," Jenah smiled. "Now how may I be of service to you this evening?"

Kai swirled their wine in the glass. "A dear friend of ours," they began, taking on a casual offhand tone, "the young Lord Vaskar, Patrice, recommended you most highly."

"Yes," Tal leaned in across the table, "he said we simply had to visit and see you for ourselves."

Jenah's relaxed posture noticeably stiffened. "I'm not sure I know who that is," she pushed her hair over her ear, glancing over her shoulder.

Kai waved the subject away. "Well that's not important," they said, with a flutter of eyelashes. "We would very much enjoy seeing you dance though. Perhaps we could move to somewhere more private?"

Jenah gave a gentle nod, brushing the creases out of her dress as she stood up. "If you'd like to follow me," she held her hand out to Kai, "I'd be more than happy to."

Kai took the offered hand, holding their own out to Tal, "Come, my love."

Together, the three of them weaved their way towards the stairs where Jenah had first descended. As they climbed to the floor above the music faded away to a dull hum, with Jenah leading them down a corridor to a curtained off room. She gestured for Kai and Tal to enter, drawing the curtain behind them.

Kai and Tal settled down on the pile of cushions that had been gathered against the opposite wall as Jenah opened a small ornate wooden box that sat on a shelf. A small crystal floated up from within, and with a little spin it began to sing with faint twinkling music.

"Now, just relax," Jenah smiled, "and enjoy."

As Jenah began to sway, Kai sat up. "Actually my dear," they patted the ground next to them. "We'd really like to talk about Lord Vaskar."

The sultry elf slowed her movements, "I really don't know who that is." She began to move towards the curtain, but Kai was quicker, rising up and sliding past her, blocking the exit.

"Let's not play this game," they smiled, eyes narrowing with a glint of flame.

"Please," Tal stood up and moved closer to Jenah, "we just want to find out what happened to him."

The dancer shook her head, a look of panic on her face. "I can't help you," she said, her voice almost pleading. "I think you should leave."

"A man was murdered," Kai said in a low voice, "you were the last person to see him alive," they moved in closer, "I'm sure you can appreciate how this looks."

"Please," Jenah's lip began to wobble, "you need to leave. Both of you."

Tal shot a look over Kai's shoulder, just a second too late as the tiefling turned just in time to see the large grey hand reach forward and grasp hold of their face.

"Mo mit," Kai mumbled into the palm as they grasped at the thick muscled wrist of a suited goliath.

"Let go," Tal ran forward, pushing Jenah into the wall as she tried to pry the meaty fingers away from Kai's face.

A second hand reached out, grabbing her shortened arm and lifting her from the ground.

In a deep rumbling voice, the goliath politely said, "If you would please come with me," he backed out of the room pulling the pair with him, "my master will see you now."

CHAPTER 5

Struggling hadn't done any good, and to begin with Tal had struggled like her life depended on it, which it probably did. She'd kicked, thumped, screamed and yelled, all to no avail. Either nobody could hear her or nobody cared.

Kai on the other hand, and in the other hand, had stood patiently with their face in a palm. Not fighting back. Not shouting their lungs out. Just standing and waiting for Tal to finish making a scene.

Once she'd settled down, the hulking goliath had taken them, one under each arm as if he were carrying sacks of grain, through a door at the far end of the corridor. From there they were carried down a long flight of spiralling stairs, much longer than those they'd taken with Jenah.

Now the two of them sat in silence on battered wooden armchairs in what looked to be some kind of store room, with the goliath watching over them and Jenah huddled in the corner. She looked far more frightened than either Tal or Kai, which was not making their situation seem any less grave.

Kai, for that matter, had been taking this all in their stride. Tal didn't know whether this calm attitude in the face of what she thought was quite a dangerous situation came from years of experience, or if Kai had some ingenious plan to free them from their captor.

With her hand and her spellbooks this would have been a breeze, even against someone twice her size in every dimension. But right now she was powerless, and she didn't like it one bit.

"What do we do?" Tal whispered to Kai, who sat with their arms folded and legs crossed looking like they were waiting for a carriage.

The goliath grunted at her, the suit he wore somehow making him seem more threatening than the tribal attire associated with goliaths that she'd heard and read about. Though the deep red tattoos that peaked out from his collar and sleeves told Tal that he was no stranger to the wilds.

Kai said nothing, their gaze fixed on Jenah in the corner. The elven girl hadn't looked them in the eye the entire walk down to this dingy store room.

"Psst!" Tal hissed, "I said, what do we do?"

The goliath grunted again, louder this time as he puffed out his chest, testing the strength of his shirt buttons and making an intimidating point.

Kai turned to the goliath and smiled before lolling their head in Tal's direction. "You heard the man," Kai grinned, "we *hrrrrr.*"

Turning their attention back to Jenah, Kai swept their hair up and knotted it into a makeshift bun. "You know," they'd dropped the charade of the Baroness's sultry voice, "if you're in need of some help, I have some very competitive rates." They tilted their head lower, trying to catch the elf's eye. "And you do seem to need help."

Jenah looked up, and for the first time Kai saw the panic in her eyes. She began to open her mouth when a gentle rapping against the door sent a visible shiver up her spine and she once again stared at the floor.

Tal trembled slightly as the door opened, though Kai kept their attention on Jenah, as if they knew what was coming.

For a moment Tal could have sworn a ghost stepped into the room. Then her surprise changed tune as an albino tiefling walked gracefully inside, short silver hair trimmed around ivory horns that were decorated with gold bands and jewels. Dressed in a brilliant white doublet and slacks, he seemed to almost glow in the darkened room. In the dim light the tiefling looked to be several years older than Kai or Tal, his pale skin slightly wrinkled around the eyes and forehead.

"Thank you, Bao," the tiefling patted the goliath on the arm as the door closed. He took a moment to examine his two captives, a sharp toothed grin spreading across his face as he stepped closer to Kai. A deep chuckle came from his chest as with the tip of his pointed tail he turned Kai's chin to face him.

"Kaivel, Kaivel, Kaivel," the tiefling laughed, "what in the name of the gods are you wearing?" A flick of the tail pushed Kai's face aside. "If you were looking for work there are easier ways my friend."

Kai snorted. "When I need work that badly, Malachai, I'll be sure to jump off a bridge first."

The pale tiefling pouted and grinned. "Words hurt, Kaivel, and I was so happy to see you once again." Malachai turned to Tal. "I see you've brought a friend," he stepped closer to her, reaching out and touching her chin, "and a pretty one at that."

Tal went to slap him, but his tail was just a touch too fast, looping around her wrist like a whip.

"She's feisty," Malachai laughed as he released her chin and wrist. "So tell me, to what do I owe the pleasure of a visit after all these years?"

Kai levelled their gaze on Malachai, their smile broadening like a suit of armour. "To be honest I forgot you were here," they gestured to Jenah, "we were just here to enjoy the company of this lovely woman."

"They were asking about that kid," Jenah nearly shouted at them. "They were asking questions, sir, but I swear I didn't say anything."

Malachai walked over to her and ran a gentle finger down her cheek. "Of course you didn't, my sweet," he kissed her on the forehead, "you've done so well."

Jenah's body fell, as if a great weight had been lifted from her shoulders. Looking towards Kai and Tal her expression changed to sympathy, her gaze returning to the floor as Malachai walked back.

"Still playing the detective, I see," Malachai smiled at Kai. He took the small bag Kai had brought with them, examining the contents with interest. "Not even a knife," he said with a disappointing tone, pushing the bag into Boa's meaty hands. "Times really have changed." He cleared his throat. "Now tell me, what is your interest in the demise of Patrice Vaskar?"

"He was murdered," Tal swallowed her fear and spoke up.

Malachai raised an eyebrow. "Yes, that's what demise means." He turned to Kai. "I hope you're a better detective than you are a tutor."

Tal's fear quickly turned to anger. "She was that last person to see him alive," Tal pointed an accusatory finger at Jenah.

"Well she certainly didn't kill him, did you my sweet?" Malachai locked eyes with Tal as he spoke, his gaze burrowing into her.

"No, sir," Jenah's voice quivered.

"See," Malachai clapped his hands together, "my dear Jenah is innocent, you have my word."

Tal scoffed. "And we should just trust you?"

"Yes," Kai interrupted Tal's interrogation. "Malachai is many things. Many horrible, terrible things," they glared at the tiefling, "but a liar is not one of them."

Malachai smiled, their gaze narrowing with a look of sweet victory. "You should learn to control that temper, my dear. It is far easier to make enemies than friends."

"In her defence," Kai scratched their chin, "you did have us kidnapped."

Malachai shrugged, "Well how else was I going to see my old friend?" He turned back to Tal. "It was nothing personal, my dear, just business." Malachai nodded to Boa, the goliath returning the gesture and opening the door. "Now if there is nothing else, I suggest you leave while I'm feeling charitable."

Tal stood instantly.

"Actually," Kai hadn't moved an inch, "since we're all friends here, I do have some questions." They gave Malachai an intense stare. "You said you were feeling charitable."

With a scoff and a grin Malachai nodded to the goliath again, the door closing as Boa stepped in front of it.

"You always were meddlesome," Malachai grinned, "but since we're all friends, and it is strangely nice to see you again, go ahead. Jenah?" He beckoned the elven girl forward.

58

With reluctant obedience Jenah emerged from her corner of safety to stand by Malachai's side. He put an arm around her shoulder, holding her in place next to him.

Kai nodded to Tal, standing up to face both Malachai and Jenah. "If you'd be so kind?" They gestured to Bao.

With a grunt the goliath held out the bag, Tal taking it from him and handing it to Kai. She moved behind Kai, her eyes still locked on Malachai.

Kai took out a folded sheet of parchment and an inkpen, scribbling in the corner to get the ink flowing. "So you didn't kill him," they began in a soft tone, "can you tell us what happened that night?"

Jenah looked at Malachai.

"Go on my dear," the imposing tiefling gently squeezed her shoulder, "we have nothing to hide, do we?"

She shook her head. "He, the Lord Vaskar I mean, and his friends came in a few nights ago." A little smile raised the corner of her lips. "They were polite, charming even, and Patrice invited me to join him at a tavern later that evening." She looked again at Malachai.

"It's not unheard of," the snow skinned tiefling said as he ran his fingers through Jenah's flaming hair. "And the boy had excellent taste. Not to mention a heavy coin purse."

"What happened when you got to the tavern?" Kai did their best to ignore Malachai as they made notes.

Jenah continued. "He met me at the bar, brought me a drink," she smiled at the memory, "and told me to wait five minutes after his friends went up stairs. Before joining him."

Kai scribbled down every word she spoke. "And when you went up?"

She looked once again at Malachai, who nodded.

"When I got to the room the door was unlocked, and I found him slumped down on the bed." Jenah looked at Kai. "I thought he was sleeping at first," she said, "thought the ale had hit him. But when I touched his shoulder he fell to the ground..." Her eyes lost focus, staring off into space as she continued. "His eyes. I'll never forget those eyes. So empty."

59

Tal spoke over Kai's shoulder. "So what did you do?"

Wiping a tear from her cheek, managing to avoid smearing her makeup, she shrugged. "I didn't know what to do. I just grabbed his coin purse and left."

"That's my girl," Malachai gave her a squeeze.

"You didn't perhaps see a sword while you were there?" Kai looked up from their notes.

Jenah nodded. "Yes. He'd left his armour and a sword at the end of the bed. Why?"

"Did you take any of it?" Kai continued, ignoring her question.

Jenah shook her head. "No, I just wanted to get out of there as fast as possible."

"You did well my sweet," Malachai kissed her on the forehead again. "Now off you go, take the rest of the night off."

"Yes sir," she gave a gentle bow, turning to Kai and Tal with a look of guilt, before leaving the room.

"Are you satisfied?" Malachai smiled at Kai as Boa closed the door behind Jenah.

Making a final note before folding the parchment and putting it back inside their bag, Kai turned to Tal. "I think we've got enough to go on with," they said. "Thank you for your hospitality." Kai held a hand out to Malachai.

Taking it with a firm shake, Malachai's voice took on a thick roar. "*Pu aoyrzi wuqfy yl euy.*" Tal recognised the language to be infernal, though she'd never heard it spoken before. It sent a shiver down her spine.

Kai sighed heavily. "Not if I can help it." They released their grip and stepped past Malachai.

Tal followed close behind, avoiding eye contact with either the tiefling or goliath before they left.

"Don't be a stranger," Malachai said as he stepped out into the corridor, watching them walk away.

Moving quickly Kai led the way back through the corridor. They'd clearly been paying more attention than Tal during their kidnapping, as none of this looked familiar.

Back onto the tavern floor a few heads turned as the pair hurried from the establishment, pushing the doors open and stepping out into the late evening air.

Once the two were in the middle of the street Kai doubled over, breathing like they'd just run a marathon. Tal gently stroked their back, waving awkwardly at the few people staring at them as they walked past.

Collecting theirself after a moment had passed Kai straightened up and gave a deep sigh, the panicked expression on their face quickly shifting back to their trademark smile. "Well that could have gone worse," they said with a chuckle.

"Are you ok?" Tal stroked Kai's arm.

"Of course," Kai cleared their throat. "Let's get back home, my feet are killing me." Kai gave Tal's hand a gentle squeeze and began the long walk home.

The evening air was cool, and Tal wished she'd brought a cloak with her. Small braziers were being lit by guards, illuminating the streets and giving an almost magical look to the city that she'd not yet seen.

"Who was that tiefling?" Tal asked as they walked. She couldn't quite shake the uncomfortable feeling she'd had when he touched her face.

Kai sighed. "Malachai Vorikz, or at least that's the name he gave me." They gave Tal a look filled with deep concern. "You are either very brave or very stupid," they softened the blow with a chuckle. "I've seen him kill people for less."

Tal took a moment to think back on their encounter. Stupid might have been the correct assumption. Tal had had no idea who she was talking to, who this white tiefling was, yet she'd provoked and tried to slap him. No doubt he deserved it, and probably much more, but things could have gone much worse.

She laughed despite herself, making a mental note to keep herself in check. After all Kai hadn't panicked, so maybe it was best to follow their lead.

"How do you know him?" she asked when the silence had begun to get uncomfortable. "Was he a client of yours? A friend?"

Kai gave a snort of a laugh. "To call us 'friends' would be a stretch of the word. No, nothing like that." They looked up at the darkening sky and took a deep breath. "When you come to a new place, and you're alone and don't know anyone, you seek out your own kind." They gave a laugh and shook their head. "Comfort in the familiar, no matter how uncomfortable that familiarity may be. But when you're offered a bed and the promise of work, how can you say no?"

Tal chewed on her lip. Though she was a stranger to this city she didn't feel out of place or the need to seek out other elves. "I guess it's strange not seeing many of your kind," she touched their shoulder.

Kai shrugged. "You get used to it pretty quick. When you're one of a handful in a place it allows you to be more memorable. And there are those like Malachai who enjoy the infamy of it."

"So you worked for him?" Tal took the segue back to Malachai. "What did you do?"

"For a time," Kai frowned at the memories, "and I was in acquisitions." When Tal gave them a look like she was expecting more Kai continued. "Acquiring items for those who wanted them from those who owned them. Usually without their consent." They shrugged. "It wasn't the most honest work, but it kept me fed and dry, and at that time that's all I cared about."

"How did you come to be doing this? From what I know that line of work is hard to get out of." Tal's knowledge came predominantly from Master Brum's novels and stories. She'd never actually met anyone who had worked as a thief. At least not that she knew.

"I broke into the wrong house," Kai smiled, "or that right house depending on your perspective. I was given a choice, owe the man a favour or spend my days in the Belgar gaol. I naturally chose the former."

Tal walked silently while they spoke, now more curious about Kai than before.

"As it turns out the favour was quite profitable and I managed to buy my way out from under Malachai." They spread their arms wide as if presenting theirself. "And here we are. It all worked out quite well I'd say."

Again Tal had no frame of reference but her novels and this ending to the tale was significantly better than most.

"What got you interested in magic, if you don't mind me asking?" It was Kai's turn to interview, and they still had a ways to go before they made it back to the Troll's Den.

"I like books," Tal said with a nonchalant tone, "always have. There was a small library in my hometown run by a grumpy old man and I would spend every day there going from shelf to shelf."

The pair turned a corner into the open market square. Mostly empty but for a few drunks bumbling along.

"One day the old man slammed a book down in front of me, an old dusty tome that had seen better days, and told me to read it if I could." Her lips curled into a slight smile, remembering the feel of the worn leather and fragile parchments. "It was his spellbook. Without knowing it I accidentally set fire to a pile of scrolls. I thought he was going to scold me, drag me home to my parents by my ear, but he just said 'again'."

"He sounds rather insane," Kai smirked, "I like him."

Tal nodded, the fond memories of her time in the library dancing through her mind. "Yes, he is. And from then on I was hooked. Old Man Brum became Master Brum to me. He tutored me every day in the seven schools of magic, it was amazing and exhausting and wonderful."

Kai scratched their cheek as the pair turned the final corner. "Aren't there eight schools of magic?"

"Well yes," Tal rocked her head back and forth, "but necromancy is illegal, and I want nothing to do with death magic."

ↂⓄↂ

"You're back," Tess greeted them with a cheer, the few other patrons in the tavern not so much as raised a hair at the intrusion. "How did it go? You cracked the case yet? Are you going to pay your rent?" She began filling mugs with a dark brown ale.

"I think we've hit a dead end," Tal said with a sigh as they approached the bar.

Kai shook their head. "There's no such thing as a dead end," they said as if quoting some sacred text, "there are only-"

"Walls to be climbed," Tess finished the quote with a roll of her eyes, "yeah, yeah."

Tall blinked at the two of them as she took the offered mug. "Who said that?"

"I did," Kai took the mug and drank from it. "Weren't you listening?"

Tess leaned across the bar. "Did you at least have a good night? Find lots of attractive rich nobles to whisk you away to a life of luxury?"

"Pfft," Tal scoffed, "hardly. Just one arrogant jerk with too much power and not enough manners." Tal continued to mutter a string of elvish curses into her mug.

"We had a meeting with Malachai," Kai answered the expression of curiosity on Tess's face. "All in all it was quite the evening."

Tess's eyes grew wide and her jaw dropped. "You met Malachai? *The* Malachai?"

Tal simply nodded.

Slapping her palm down against the bar, making no one but Tal jump, Tess swept the mugs off the bar. "We're going to need something stronger." She marched into the back room, which Tal knew now to be Tess's private quarters, and returned moments later with a bottle bound in dark leather.

Grabbing three fresh mugs on her way back to the pair, Tess poured out a small amount of the shimmering blue liquor. "Tell me everything."

And she did. Tal narrated the night's events, with only a few embellishments, of their time inside the Dancing Dryad, making sure to explain exactly how gorgeous the elven host was. Kai seemed happy to listen, sipping away at the liquor without complaint or comment.

Tess continued pouring out shots as Tal moved on to the red-haired Jenah, how she'd led them into a trap where they were kidnapped by a hulking goliath.

After her third shot Tal couldn't remember how much she'd told Tess, or even how the night had ended. All she knew for sure was that she was on the floor next to her bed, with light streaming through the window, and what felt like a team of experienced dwarven miners digging through her skull with their sharpest pickaxes.

She rolled onto her back, licking her lips to try and find some moisture in the desert that was her throat. "Why..." she groaned to herself as she carefully sat up, the movement causing the miners to work double time.

"Good morning sleepy head," Kai's voice scraped against the inside of her skull, "sleep well?"

Tal looked up to see Kai, laying in her bed, hair a mess, with a smile that said more than words could.

As she collapsed back down to the floor the only sounds that escaped her lips were, "oh no..."

CHAPTER 6

Tal clutched at the sheet that was draped over her body, realising now why the floor felt so cold. She shuffled back against the wall as her mind raced trying to recall any shred of memories from the night before. Her jaw opened and closed as noises escaped but failed to form coherent words.

"Are you ok Tally?" Kai smiled at her as they lay across her bed wrapped in their own sheet, propping their head up with their bare arm. "You're looking redder than I am."

Tal continued to flounder, the dry mouth not helping the words escape. Clearing her throat a few times she eventually managed to find two words to string together. "Did we...?"

A pouty expression dragged Kai's face down, their dark eyes growing wide like a puppy. "You don't remember? Well that hurts my feelings..."

The elven woman's mouth began opening and closing again as her cheeks grew hotter and hotter, the embarrassment beginning to flood down her body.

"For what it's worth," Kai said when Tal remained silent for too long, "you were very gentle." Tal's eyes grew wider. "You made me feel very safe and comfortable," Kai continued as the panic set into Tal's face. "And that thing you did with your stump, my gods!"

Tal threw her head into her arms. "Oh god, oh god, oh god," there was a quiver in her voice. "I'm sorry, I'm so sorry, I didn't know...I mean I was drunk and I..." she looked up as a small chuckle from the bed grew louder into a full bellowing laugh.

"I... I couldn't... I couldn't resist!" Kai sat up throwing the sheet aside to reveal their fully dressed body, their sleeve rolled up to the elbow and their jacket folded behind them. "That was more fun than I expected," they continued to giggle as they stood up.

Tal grabbed a boot and flung it as hard as she could at Kai. "Really? Really!" The boot thudded against the wall. "You think that was funny?!"

"Evidently," Kai sighed as they composed theirself. "So you don't remember what happened last night?" Tal shook her head. "Oooh. Probably for the best," they pushed off of the bed. "I'll meet you downstairs, get ready, it's already past lunch."

Taking slow careful steps, Tal made her way to the tavern bar where both Kai and Tess watched with cruel smiles as she struggled towards them. Climbing onto the stool she dropped her head onto the bar with a heavy groan. "What did you do to me…?" She lifted her head up just enough to see their still smiling faces. "And why aren't you two suffering?"

"Troll blood," Tess shrugged.

"Infernal constitution," Kai followed up.

Tal dropped her head again and began muttering curses in elvish. A patronising stroke on the head helped to sooth the throbbing. She tilted enough to see Kai looking down on her with a smile. "What were we drinking last night?" she managed to groan with her face smooshed against the bartop.

"I'm not really sure," Tess retrieved the empty bottle from the back of the bar. "I got a case of it delivered by mistake, tried some, thought it was too good to sell. So I just keep it for special occasions." She placed the leather-bound bottle on the bar. There was no label, no brand. Nothing to identify what it was or where it came from. "I just call it the Blue Stuff."

"I'm going to be sick," Tal groaned, pressing her face back into the bar.

Kai patted her on the back, which didn't help. "You've got time for that later, right now we need to get going. We're not getting paid to hold the bar up."

"I'm the one paying you," her muffled voice replied.

Kai patted Tal again. "Exactly, and wouldn't you want me to be out there working my tail off?" They smiled their cheekiest of smiles. "Now let's go!"

⇜ ☉ ⇝

Tess had been kind enough to fill a wineskin with water for Tal to take with her, and by the gods did she need it. As if intentionally taunting her, today was an exceptionally beautiful day. Clear blue skies gave way only to the hot sun that was beating down on the city, and Tal in particular.

"I'm guessing you're not much of a drinker?" Kai chuckled as they strolled casually through the city.

Scowling as best she could, furrowing her brow made the headache worse, Tal mustered as much sarcasm as she could gather. "Wow, you must be some kind of detective."

Kai blinked at her. "You're very grumpy in the mornings, aren't you?" They smiled, "And after you were so caring last night. I need to keep an eye on you my Tal'avera."

Tal's face reddened further. She took a long drink of water to steady her mind and cool herself down. "And another thing," she began, "did you really think that was funny? Making me think we'd slept together after getting me drunk?"

Reaching into their satchel as the two of them turned a corner Kai pulled out a piece of dried jerky, pointing it at Tal. "First of all, yes. It was hilarious." Kai took a bite. "And second of all, you got you drunk. Tess and I were the ones to drag you up to your room when you couldn't stand up. That was shortly after you tried to conjure something using a fork and a piece of stale bread."

Tal's face reddened further. She'd not questioned how she'd even gotten to her room or what had happened the night before. Though the shock of waking up with Kai and her head splitting in two had been quite the distraction.

As these thoughts went through her mind Kai's hand gripping her shoulder stirred her back into the world. "We are friends, Tal'avera, you and I. We take care of our friends. But we also

68

play jokes on them." They chuckled and patted her on the cheek. "Now drink your water, we have work to do."

She took a long drink as they continued. "Where are we heading to?" she asked looking around at the buildings for a frame of reference.

"The Adventurers Lodge," Kai replied as they finished their jerky. "I want to know more about what our dear departed lord was up to." They looked over at Tal. "And there's a small market just around the corner from the lodge that deals in adventuring gear. I thought you might have some luck finding your spellbooks there."

The pair continued through the city streets, with Kai leading the way, until they stood before a building that could only be described as a renovated barn. The wooden exterior decorated with banners for Belgar, a silver sword with a glowing pommel on a deep blue cloth, and Escana, a vibrant green tree on a royal purple, as well as its own flag bearing a one-eyed dragon skull.

"It's not what I expected," Tal said with a hint of disappointment in her voice.

"Well it seems to be doing alright for itself." Kai pointed down the street. "If you take the next right you'll be at the quick-market. I'll come and find you there, hopefully this won't take long." Kai fished around inside their satchel and pulled out a small coin purse. Counting out a few silver coins they handed them to Tal with a smile. "Take this. If you manage to find your books, try to haggle until I get back." With a pat on the shoulder Kai turned and made their way through the large wooden doors.

Left alone in the streets Tal took another drink from her wineskin and wandered off down the street.

The quick-market, as Kai had called it, wasn't as busy as the market square they'd previously trundled through. The stalls were made up of stacked crates with sheets thrown over them, the wares cluttered on top in a very haphazard way.

Rusted weapons, bloodstained clothes, broken trinkets and pieces of jewellery were being offered around as she passed, and Tal quickly came to realise that these stalls dealt with the leftovers from adventuring.

Having spent a brief time as an adventurer herself, Tal knew that they could be hoarders, desperate to hang on to every little item for no reason whatsoever. But eventually your pack gets heavy or your arms get tired and not everyone wants to buy a broken sword that you used to open a lockbox.

Except here. Here it seems people were happy to buy anything and everything in the hopes of shifting it on to someone with lower standards.

"Excuse me?" Tal asked in shocked disbelief of the offer the vendor had made her.

"Half price, it's a fair deal, ain't it?" The vendor of the stall Tal had stopped to browse at gestured kindly to her as she inspected a pair of slightly bloodied leather gloves. "I mean you're only going to use one of them."

He made no further comments after both gloves were thrown into his face as Tal stormed away from his stall to continue her search.

Stopping a couple more times to admire some pieces of jewellery, Tal eventually found a stall piled with sodden books and scrolls. And like a starving man at a banquet she dove in.

It had become a habit of hers during her time spent with Master Brum to examine every piece of parchment she came across, and thanks to this Tal had become a bit of a speed reader.

It would have been quicker with two hands, but with the one and a stump Tal managed to unroll each scroll and give it a glance before moving on to the next.

The books were easier to discern as she knew the covers of her spellbooks very well, but her inquisitive side made her open and read each one in turn.

An elderly halfling woman, who Tal assumed was minding the stall, smiled at her. "Take your time dear, they're not going to run away," she patted her own legs, "and neither am I." She gave a soft little chuckle.

"Sorry," Tal returned a guilty smile, "I'm looking for something in particular."

"Well if you find it let me know," the old woman settled back down into her blanketed chair.

Tal shuffled through a few more books before something caught her eye. Not something on the stall though. She'd looked up to ask the elderly woman a question when a familiar face poked around a corner before disappearing in a blur down an alley.

Dropping the book onto the stall Tal darted down the street towards the alley Galen, the scared halfling, had rushed towards. She made it to the entrance just in time to see him pull up a dark hood before pushing back out into the street.

Galen to Tal's mind looked like a person who was trying not to be seen, and people trying not to be seen rarely had good intentions. Trying to blend in to the crowd herself, Tal followed the halfling as best she could as he took left turn after right turn, seemingly moving aimlessly but with a determined stride.

They moved through streets she didn't recognise, but the worry of finding her way back was pushed out of her mind by the need to know where this sneaky halfling was headed.

After nearly a half-hour of hiding behind corners and taller citizens, Galen turned down another shadowed alleyway off the main street. Taking a quick look around Tal moved to the edge of the building and poked her head around the corner. She blinked a few times to adjust her eyes to the shadow, and the silhouette of Galen shuffled down to the dead end of the alley.

She ducked behind the wall again when she saw Galen throw his hood back. Tal counted to ten, breathing slowly, before looking back down the alley. A second silhouette now stood looming over the halfling. Not in a menacing way, but the difference in their size made it appear as if Galen was about to be crushed.

Tal cursed silently while she watched the encounter. She was too far away to hear what was being said over the chatter from the street, and it was too dark to make out their expressions. The one thing she did know was that nothing good came from meetings in dark alleyways.

Whatever Galen and the tall dark figure were discussing they were definitely cautious of anyone overhearing. Tal caught glimpses of Galen's face as he continually checked over his shoulder, but she was sure she'd hidden herself well enough. There was a handshake, which consumed most of Galen's forearm, and the halfling handed over a pouch. After opening and inspecting the contents the larger figure nodded, tucking it under their large cloak.

Tal quickly ducked back behind the wall as Galen turned and made his way back up the alley towards her. Scurrying into a nearby shop Tal peeked out through the doorway, watching Galen step back onto the street and look both ways. Pulling his hood up he began making his way back in the direction she'd followed him from.

"Can I help you, lass?" A voice interrupted her spying.

Tal turned to see a crowded butcher's shop, the dozen or so occupants staring at her as she lurked in the doorway. Her cheeks flushed as she smiled awkwardly at each person in turn. "Oh no, sorry, I'm a vegetarian," an odd chuckle escaped her lips before she rushed out and away from her embarrassment.

"What a strange girl," was the last thing she heard before the door closed behind her and she was back out onto the street.

She looked around to see if there was any sign of Galen, but he'd slipped away into the crowd. Moving carefully Tal went back to her spot against the wall and peeked around the corner once more. The large figure was gone. They certainly hadn't walked out of the alley, and as far as Tal could tell there was no other way out.

After a very brief debate between her fear and curiosity a winner was declared and Tal began walking cautiously into the alley, her eyes darting around for any signs of movement.

The alley, as far as Tal could tell, was completely empty apart from the odd rat that scurried away as she approached. She tried all the usual things. Tapping against parts of the walls. Moving a crate to find a hidden path. Pushing odd looking bricks to see it a secret door opened. But nothing. In fact she was starting to feel pretty silly imagining how this looked to anyone that might be observing her. With a sigh and a pout Tal accepted defeat and made her way back up the alley. Now she had a new challenge ahead of her, finding out where she was and how to get back to Kai.

"Did you find anything?" a familiar gruff voice greeted Tal as she stepped out into the open street.

Tal half jumped out of her skin as she spun on the spot to see a tall man leaning against the wall. Clean shaven, with neat combed back blonde hair, and battleworn leather armour, this was certainly a face Tal had never laid eyes on before. But that voice was terribly familiar.

"Who..what? Er I'm sorry, can I help you?" Tal flustered trying to get a grasp of the voice in her memory.

The man stepped towards her, his hands adjusting his belt which held an impressive array of daggers. Tal backed away slowly as he approached, wishing again and again that she had some way to protect herself.

"It's not nice to spy on people," he said in an almost jovial tone, which combined with the roughness of his voice seemed more threatening than playful. "But I can be persuaded to overlook it this one time," he smiled broadly at her, "if you buy me that drink you promised?"

Like a ripped purse, coins began to drop in Tal's mind as she released the breath she'd been holding. "Jasper?"

The smile broadened as Jasper threw his arms open. "That's what they call me."

Tal looked the man up and down again. She almost couldn't believe that this was the same man beneath those mounds of cloaks and the shrubbery of a beard. She poked his chest a couple of times to see if there was some kind of illusion in play, but the hard leather met her finger each time.

"Are you done? People are starting to stare..." Jasper brushed away the prodding finger as he looked around the street.

Tal followed his gaze, and there were indeed people slowing down as they passed giving the two of them very peculiar looks.

"Sorry," Tal retrieved her hand, blushing under the eyes of so many strangers. "I didn't recognise you. You look so...so…"

73

Jasper smoothly slid his arm around Tal's shoulders and began walking her down the street. "Let's find somewhere quieter we can talk, my dear," Jasper looked over his shoulder, "it's far too crowded out here."

≈⊙≈

On their cosy walk neither Tal nor Jasper spoke a word. Jasper clearly not wanting to be overheard in public, and Tal simply being trapped in a state of shock and embarrassment as she was escorted by her surprisingly handsome chaperone.

Jasper led her to a small tavern nestled by the North-East Gate, a sign with a timid mouse hanging above the door. Inside was dimly lit by shaded candles, no windows or other doors apart from the one they'd entered through, and in place of tables a few small booths held up the wall.

"This place doesn't look very cheery," Tal noted quietly as she and Jasper sat down in an unoccupied booth. Not that any of the booths were occupied.

"It has a subtle charm," Jasper winked at her, "besides, I come here more for the peace and quiet." He stretched his long arms out across the back of his side of the cushioned booth, nearly filling the width of the seat. With a quick look towards the bar, where a pale skinned dwarf sat drinking, Jasper held up two fingers. The dwarf nodded and made his way to the other side of the bar and began pouring.

Jasper didn't utter a single word until the drinks arrived at their table, he just sat and stared with a frightening intensity at Tal. As the tankards were set down before them, Tal fished out a silver piece from the coins Kai had given her and the dwarf returned to his stool.

"To your health," Jasper tapped his tankard against Tal's and took a heavy gulp of ale. Wiping his lips clean with his thumb, Jasper steepled his fingers and fixed his gaze upon Tal. "Now, what were you doing snooping around alleyways?"

Tal sipped her ale. Slightly too bitter for her liking, but she'd not been given a choice. "I wasn't snooping," she said after a moment's thought, "I was investigating."

A raised eyebrow was Jasper's first response, followed by a chuckle. "Isn't that just a fancy word for snooping?"

"What were you doing there anyway?" Tal decided flipping the question was better than arguing semantics. She folded her arms and straightened her posture, hoping it gave her a more professional and authoritative look.

Jasper smiled into his ale. "Working," he said after a sip, "and before you ask I won't tell you with whom or at what."

That wasn't the main question bouncing around in Tal's mind. What she really wanted to ask came out next, but in a much less eloquent way than she'd intended. "What happened to your beard?"

Her question seemed to catch Jasper off guard, as he coughed and spat ale across the table, sprinkling Tal, before crumpling into hoarse laughter. Taking his time to recover, patting the table a few times as he caught his breath, Jasper eventually sat back with a deep sigh.

"You are a wonderful person, Miss Tal'avera," he said with a smile while the damp elf finished wiping her face with the edge of her sleeve. "The beard and the cloaks are what I wear when I'm transporting goods."

"So all that stuff was to hide the things you were carrying?" Tal pretended to take a sip of ale, just letting the liquid touch her lips. It really wasn't pleasant, plus she'd had more than enough to drink the night before.

Jasper shook his head. "Not at all, I was only carrying..." He caught himself at the last moment, clearing his throat before continuing. "The items I was carrying we're quite small."

Confusion settled in on Tal's face. "Then why the costume?"

With a cheerful smile Jasper relaxed back against the booth. "Isn't it obvious? No one mugs a tramp." He said it like a well-rehearsed line. Clearly this was a question he'd been asked many times before.

Tal couldn't fault the logic though, mugging a tramp would very rarely pay well.

"Anyway, back onto the matter of you skulking around dark alleyways. What were you doing? And where the devil," Jasper chuckled to himself, "is your devil?"

She scrunched up her face. Tal hadn't met many tieflings in her life, and those she had met had only been in the last few days, but somehow she felt calling them 'devils' isn't something she should condone. "Kai," she said sternly, "is following up a lead."

"So you have joined their little brigade."

"And I was tracking down another," she ignored his comment. "I was following a person of interest."

Jasper nodded. "And how interesting was this person?"

"Quite. I think he might be the one we're looking for."

With a loud clap of his hands Jasper sat forward, leaning across the table towards Tal. "On the matter of looking for people. I was in fact looking for you." He pulled a rolled up piece of parchment out of his pocket, placing it on the table and pushing it slowly towards her. "I have set up a meeting for you. A couple of young lads looking to part with some expensive spellbooks."

Tal's eyes widened. She grabbed the parchment, with Jasper's hand still wrapped around it. "You've found my things? My hand too?"

"I believe so," he wrestled his hand back, "but I don't know about your hand. They said they were looking to move some spellbooks. I'm guessing the rest of your belongings have already been sold or disposed of if they weren't worth selling."

Tal sighed. "I had some really nice robes in that bag." She shook her head. The important thing was she'd get her spellbooks back. Besides her hand they would have been the most expensive to replace. Tal unrolled the parchment and gave it a quick glance. A date and time for this evening, and a location she wasn't familiar with. She folded it back up and tucked it away. "Thank you Jasper, this really means so much to me."

Jasper tapped his tankers against hers again. "You're welcome, maybe one day you can repay the favour."

"Of course," she looked up at him, "but if I could ask you one more favour."

"It'll cost you one more drink," he smiled.

Tal pushed her nearly untouched tankard towards him. "Could you take me back to the Adventurers Lodge? I have no idea where we are."

∽☉∾

"Where the hells have you been!" Kai yelled as Tal and Jasper approached the Adventurers Lodge. "I've been looking everywhere for you!"

"I'm sorry," Tal flushed suddenly feeling terribly guilty. She'd not given a thought to Kai as she'd gone off on her own. She'd also never imagined Kai would have been so worried about her.

"That's my fault," Jasper spoke up while Tal was still searching for words. "I saw her wandering around and invited her for a drink." He put an arm around her shoulders once more and gave her a squeeze. "Thank you for a wonderful afternoon my dear, I'll see you both very soon." He gave Kai a wink and walked off into the crowd of passing folk.

"Wait right there you...!" Kai began. But Jasper was gone, leaving the frustrated tiefling cursing in infernal. Spinning on their heel Kai turned to their elven companion. "What happened?"

Tal proceeded to recite the events of her afternoon, spotting Galen whilst browsing the market, following him to a dark alley, and going for drinks with Jasper. "And he gave me this." Tal handed Kai the rolled up parchment Jasper had given to her.

Kai took the parchment and gave it a quick read before handing it back to her. They looked up at the sky for a moment before nodding to Tal. "Well we've got a few hours left until sundown. So let's grab something to eat and head back. I'll tell you what you missed out on."

CHAPTER 7

After a short trip to Davros' food cart, Kai and Tal returned to the Troll's Den where they took what were quickly becoming their usual stools by the bar. Tal had chosen to sample something different from Davros' surprisingly diverse menu; a flatbread stuffed with pigeon, roasted apricots, and cabbage. Not something she would normally have gone for, but the greasy dwarf had insisted she'd enjoy it. He wasn't wrong.

On the journey back Kai had regaled Tal with their findings from the Adventurer's Lodge. Mostly things they already knew, but 'confirmation was useful information' Kai had said. The crew of young Patrice had taken on a job tracking down and eliminating the cause of a peculiar growth in the northern part of Splinterwood Forest. Strange fungi had been spotted overgrowing the trees and killing off the plant life. It wasn't until the party had discovered the nest of a demon beneath an old great oak that they'd determined it to be the cause.

"And as it turns out his family is pretty well connected," Kai continued after washing down the last of their bread. "So this Patrice was in it for the thrills. Though I don't imagine his family were too pleased about it."

Tal swallowed her mouthful. "You're not suggesting that his family had him killed, are you?"

Kai shrugged. "Noble folk don't think like us. If you've got enough coin to make a problem go away then the laws don't apply to you." They adjusted their hair pins, pulling a few stray locks into place. "Maybe being an adventurer brought shame to his family. At least with him dead they could save face."

"Save face?" Tal couldn't believe this was the cause of a young man's demise. "If they wanted him to stop adventuring there are much better ways to do it aren't there?" Tal racked her brain for alternatives. "Cut off his funds? Have him brought home by force?"

"Those would be cheaper options, I'll admit." Kai waved at Tess who was busying herself at the other end of the bar, doing her best to ignore them.

"Cheaper?" Tal scoffed at the notion. "Do you honestly think coin would be the deciding factor?"

Kai gave a stern nod. "In my experience the upper classes tend to prioritise their appearance and income above most anything else."

"And what experience is that?" Tal had a feeling there was a story behind Kai's disparaging view of nobles.

But Kai had stopped paying attention to her, now solely focused on getting Tess's attention. "You can't ignore us forever!" They shouted down the bar.

"I can and I will," Tess growled back, not bothering to turn to face them.

Tal looked back and forth between Kai and Tess. "Is she mad at us?"

"Yes!" Tess barked.

"She's just hungry," Kai smiled as they leaned across the bar trying to grab an empty mug. "If you won't do it then I guess we'll have to serve ourselves!"

That got her attention. Tess stormed down the bar like pale lightning, kicking the mug from Kai's hand and slamming her palms down on the bar top. "You touch my barrels and elfy here won't be the only one missing a hand," Tess shot a glance towards Tal, "Sorry sweetie."

Tess grabbed another mug and angrily filled it, banging it down hard in front of Kai, spilling most of it. "And yes I'm mad and yes I'm hungry. I'm here all day and you two swan off to get food from Davros, don't get anything for me, and then have the gall to eat it in front of me?"

"In our defence…" Kai trailed off. "No, I've got nothing. How about you Tal?"

Tess turned her glare back upon Kai. "Don't you go blaming our sweet innocent girl. She doesn't know any better. You should!" Tess pushed off the bar, muttering under her breath as she began cleaning various mugs.

An awkward silence followed while Kai drank and Tal's glowing cheeks began to cool down as the tension subsided. Upturning the empty mug onto the bar Kai stood up and stretched.

"I suppose we should be on our way," they declared after a brief glimpse out of the window, "It's always better to be a little early."

⌁⊙⌁

Walking through the quiet evening streets, a chill ran down Tal's spine. Nothing to do with the weather, it had been quite a nice summer's day. It was the anticipation of the meeting the pair were on their way towards. Tal hadn't had much experience with back alley dealings. In fact she'd had none. And as prepared and confident as Kai seemed to be in any given situation, Tal's nerves were starting to get the better of her.

It was really starting to hit her how much she'd relied on magic for most of her life. Now that she was without it Tal had never felt so defenceless.

Hopefully after tonight Tal would be one step closer to her old self.

The meeting spot arranged, either by Jasper or whoever had her spellbooks, was at a spot along the river Kai called 'the north bridge'. The only bridges Tal had seen in the city were the two that led across to the Island District, and they were both on the south-west side of the city.

"I think it's best you hang back," Kai said as the two of them walked, "just in case these are the boys who stole your books in the first place. The last thing we want is them recognising you."

"So you're going to be alone?" Tal didn't feel good about Kai risking theirself for her like this. "Do you think that's a good idea?"

With a nonchalant shrug Kai smiled at her. "It's all part of the job."

The bridge wasn't too far from the Troll's Den, the sun just disappearing past the horizon as the two approached.

"I'm never sure what people mean by sundown," Kai said as they rummaged through their satchel. Pulling out a piece of jerky Kai looked around, chewing slowly. "How about there," they pointed to a house with a cart tied up in front. "You can hide behind that while I meet with our new associates."

"Please," Tal gave Kai's arm a gentle squeeze, "be careful." She turned and quickly made her way towards the cart, kneeling down beside the wheel. From here she had a good view of the bridge. She just hoped she wouldn't be seen.

Tal watched from her hiding spot as Kai leaned nonchalantly over the wall's edge, looking out towards the grand mansions on the opposite bank. She began to wonder how many times they'd done this before, either as a detective or as whatever it was they did for Malachai before. Kai's relaxed attitude to everything made her equally confident and terrified.

A few people passed by their meeting spot while Tal waited crouching behind the cart. Though not one of them paid much attention to either Kai nor Tal, each lost in their own little world.

Just as the pins and needles were beginning to set into Tal's legs she watched as Kai's head turned and their posture shifted. Two cloaked figures approached Kai, leaning back against the wall on either side of them and looking around.

Tal strained her pointed ears to try and make out anything that was being said, but all three were speaking in hushed voices. Kai turned to face the two figures, making various gestures and seeming very confident in whatever they were saying. Leaning forward to get a better look, Tal watched as one of the figures threw back their cloak, revealing a battered looking backpack not dissimilar to her own. Opening it up they removed something just enough to give Kai a glimpse, though Tal couldn't see what it was from her vantage point.

Tal leaned further, propping herself against the cart she could make out what appeared to be a book in the figure's hand. Then the pins and needles kicked in. All of a sudden Tal's legs gave way and she fell against the cart wheel, which in turn creaked as the cart rolled forward.

Unfortunately this did not go unnoticed.

Pushing herself up from the ground, Tal saw the figure with the backpack wrestle it free from Kai, who apparently during her tumble had made a grab for it. The second figure cracked Kai across the back of the head with the hilt of a dagger and the tiefling fell to their knees as the two figures bolted in opposite directions.

Kai stood, shaking the pain from their head. Tal ran up to them to help them up, but Kai pushed her away. "Get after him!" Kai pointed after one of the figures as they began running after the other. Watching as Kai gave chase, Tal summoned up all the will she possessed and ran after the hooded figure as fast as she could, the pain of the tingling sensation in her legs fading fast as the blood rushed through her body.

≈⊙≋

The pain in the back of Kai's head would have to wait, they weren't going to let this guy get away. The cloaked figure was getting away fast, but Kai was closing the distance, their pulse throbbing in their ears.

After darting down a side alley and back out onto the street the few people on the streets gasped as the figure shoved past them, Kai not far behind.

The figure threw a woman in a fine robe to the ground, Kai skipped over her followed by a furious shout from her husband.

Down another alleyway, doubling back on themselves.

Kai ducked and rolled forward as a thin blade was thrown back at them, quickly getting back on their feet.

Into the street once more, following the wall along the edge of the river the figure stopped and turned.

A well-timed punch caught Kai in the stomach, but they grabbed the wrist, bringing their own elbow up to catch the figure in the chin.

Another punch, this time to Kai's chin, knocking the tiefling back against the wall.

Kai grabbed the figure's cloak, pulling the hood back to see the angry snarl of the half-elf lad beneath.

The boy knocked Kai's hand away, shoving them hard against the wall and bolting once again.

The wind knocked out of them, Kai shook it off and pushed on.

As the street turned along the river's edge the boy took a sharp turn down another alleyway, pulling over a pile of sacks.

With a slight tumble Kai rolled to their feet.

A loud clatter erupted from the street as Kai ran out, leaping over two guards that had been pushed to the ground.

"Oi! Stop!" the voices cried out after them.

But Kai didn't have time to deal with that right now.

Seeing the end of a cloak slip down another alley Kai bit their lip through the pain and carried on after the lad.

Kai caught up just in time as the cloaked thief was halfway up the wall that blocked off the end of the alley.

Grabbing his leg Kai yanked the boy to the ground with a heavy thud. The half-elf heaved as the air was forced from his lungs.

As the thief grabbed for the daggers at his hip Kai stepped forward and thrust their foot deep into the boy's groin.

The groan turned to a high-pitched cry, silenced quickly as Kai dropped to their knee and thumped the lad across the jaw.

"That's for throwing a knife at me," Kai growled as they rummaged through the boy's cloak, pulling his bag free.

Kai kicked him in the gut again. "And that's just for me." They looked up as the clanging of two armoured guards blocked the entrance to the alley.

"You there!" they cried, "Stop in the name of the crown!" They both held up crossbows, each aimed at Kai and the boy.

Kai held up their hands and with a flash of their eye darkness filled the alley.

Two bolts pinged against the wall a hair's breadth from Kai's legs as the tiefling quickly scrambled over before the darkness faded away.

"Where did he go?" the voices of the guards echoed from behind the wall as Kai quickly made their escape.

With a groan, the pain in their head, chest, and ankle finally catching up on them, Kai made their way back to the bridge. "Gods I hope you're alright Tally."

ᓚ☉ᓛ

The tingling in her legs grew sharper with each step, feeling more like knives cutting through to the bone, but still Tal'avera ran.

Each breath burned her lungs as she chased after the cloaked figure that had cracked Kai in the head.

Like a cat and mouse, the two ran down the riverside street, the figure frequently looking back to see Tal still in pursuit.

Weaving past a crowd gathered by Davros' food cart, the figure knocked over the makeshift tables, kicking one of the barrels back at Tal.

She skipped round it, nearly falling into a sweaty dockworker.

Turning down a street Tal saw the figure fumble briefly before she herself ran into the couple her quarry had narrowly avoided.

"I'm so sorry," Tal flustered as she pushed off of the overweight gentleman.

The thief was getting away. As much as Tal strained she knew she'd never catch up to him.

But still she ran.

Down an alley they turned, heading towards the city centre.

Another turn, back to the river.

With another peak over their shoulder the figure took a sharp turn into darkness.

As Tal rounded the corner her foot struck something hard, sending her tumbling to the floor. With a wince and a groan she rolled onto her back to see a pale skinned elf with piercing black eyes standing over her, blade in hand.

"Silly little girl," he said in a low hissing voice, "you should learn to stay out of other people's business."

Tal shuffled backwards along the ground. "You stole my bag!" Her shout would have been more accusatory if her voice wasn't trembling.

The elf laughed. "That's my business." He stepped forward, his blade pointed down towards Tal. "But don't worry, you won't be needing it."

A thousand possibilities flashed through Tal's mind as the blade came down towards her. If only she had her magic. If only she had a weapon. If only she had stayed in Rothwood. If only. If only.

One possibility that hadn't flashed through her mind was seeing a large bread roll smack into her would-be-murderer's face.

It hit with such force that the crust split open, the aromatic sauce spilling out across the elf's face and Tal's boots, filling the alley with the fragrances of Davros' food cart.

As the thief looked up a large boot connected with his chest, sending him bowling down the alley.

Tal was pulled to her feet by a thick long fingered hand as Tess stood before her. "Are you ok, sweetie?" she smiled at Tal as if she hadn't just kicked a man like a training dummy.

All Tal could manage was a nod, the fear welling up as tears in her eyes. Tess smiled again, "Good. Let's get you-"

A pained grunt cut Tess off mid-sentence. She slowly turned to face the elf and Tal gasped as she saw the dagger sticking out between Tess's shoulder blades.

"NO!" she cried, the tears flowing from her eyes.

But Tess didn't seem phased. Tal watched as the troll-orc tavernkeep reached back and pulled the blade free, dropping it to the ground with a clatter.

Tess began breathing heavily as Tal backed against the wall, seeing the elven thief draw two more blades. A beastial roar erupted from Tess's throat sending a shiver down Tal's spine.

Another dagger was thrown, this time at Tal.

She ducked but the blade never made it to her, Tess stepping in front of her, the blade sinking into her shoulder.

Pulling it free, dropping it to the floor at Tal's feet, Tess charged at the elf, a third blade plunging into her abdomen.

The elf pulled a thin shortsword from his hip, swinging as Tess.

She caught his wrist and pulled him forward, slamming her fist into his elbow.

A chilling crack, followed by a pained cry echoed down the alleyway as the elf's arm bent in a way Tal never thought possible.

The short sword fell to the floor with a clang.

Not giving up the elf pulled the dagger free from Tess's stomach, jamming it into her side.

She grabbed his hand, holding the blade in, and wrapped her long arm around his shoulder. Throwing her body back she smashed her forehead into the face of the elf.

Blood poured from his crushed nose as he gargled for mercy.

Tess couldn't hear him, the veins pulsing up her neck filling her ears with the beat of rage.

She brought her head back again and flung it hard into the elf's face once again, his body crumpling to the ground.

Tal watched as Tess pulled him up, lifting him off his feet before roaring in his face and flinging his limp body into the wall like a sack of flour.

Towering over him Tess's ragged breathing began to slow. She pulled the dagger free, throwing it to the floor by the unconscious, or possibly dead, elf.

Slowly getting to her feet, Tal walked gingerly toward Tess. "Are...are you ok?"

Her breath calming, Tess looked back towards Tal. "I'm fine," she spat down on the body by her feet. "Are you-" She was cut off as Tal ran towards her, throwing her arms around Tess's waist.

Pulling back quickly Tal began to inspect the stab wounds in Tess's stomach. "You're bleeding! We need to...need to..." Tal stammered as she watched Tess's skin beginning to stitch itself back together, the blood flow already ceased. "What the...how are you...I mean..."

Tess patted Tal on the head, stroking her hair, and leaving a little blood behind. "I told you, I'm fine." She smiled and shrugged.

"Troll blood." She wiped her face, smearing the blood of her foe more than cleaning it away.

Tal sighed with relief. "Thank you," she squeezed Tess again, resting her head against Tess's chest, hearing the pounding of her heart still.

"Don't mention it sweetie," Tess returned the cuddle. "Now come on, we need to clean up," she looked down at the sodden roll on the floor, "and I need to get dinner again."

❧☉❧

Making a brief detour via Davros' cart for the second time that night, the pair noticed that most people gave you a wide berth when you're casually covered in blood.

"So you were getting dinner?" Tal asked as they walked back. She nibbled on a cheese stuffed breadstick that Tess had treated her to.

"Aye," Tess said through her mouthful. "I saw you running down the street on my way back and followed you, and a good job I did too."

"I'm very glad we didn't buy you dinner," Tal smiled, "but I wish you'd let me pay for that, I really do owe you my life."

Tess chuckled. "And your life is only worth dinner? Sweetie, you need to reassess your value."

As they pushed open the doors to the Troll's Den they were greeted by a cry that was both angry and relieved.

"There you are! Why are you covered in blood?!" Kai ran up to them, embracing the two women in a tight hug. "I've been worried sick! Are you ok? What happened?"

After calming the troubled tiefling down with a mug of ale and a bit of Tal's breadstick, the two told Kai about their fight with the pale elf thief. Though Tal's retelling sounded far more dramatic and scarier than Tess felt the situation really was. Nevertheless, Kai hung on every word, their jaw wobbling up and down as Tal's story continued.

When Tal had finished her tale Kai held their mug up to Tess. "If this wasn't your tavern I'd buy you a drink," they smiled at her, "but since it is I'd love another."

Tess rolled her eyes and snatched the mug from Kai's hand. "Sure, I only saved a woman's life, no reason to get excited." She handed the mug back to Kai. "Now are you going to tell us about that welt?"

Kai sipped. "In a moment. Did they have anything on them?" they turned to Tal.

Biting her lip, Tal shook her head. "We didn't really stop to go through his pockets."

"Rookie mistake," Kai shook their head, half in mock disappointment. "You always loot the body."

"I'll remember that next time," Tess poured herself a drink. Evidently this evening was going to be slow business.

"Please don't let there be a next time," Tal winced at the thought of repeating the night's events.

"Speaking of loot," Kai reached into their satchel and pulled out a pair of leather-bound books, setting them on the bar in front of Tal. "I believe these might be yours?"

Like a long-lost love Tal grabbed the books and hugged them to her chest, feeling almost whole again. She'd have recognised that battered leather anywhere. "Oh thank you, thank you, thank you!" For the second time tonight tears filled her eyes. Placing the books back on the bar she began thumbing through the pages. Her notes, incantations, ritual setups. Everything was still there.

"She's so adorable." Tess giggled.

Kai chuckled and winced as the pain in their chest and head now had time to be heard. "And on that note, I think I'll leave you to get reacquainted with your books," they turned to face Tess, "and you...I'll just leave. Good night."

The two women watched as Kai almost hobbled towards the staircase.

Tal stretched and gathered her books. "Thank you again," she turned to Tess, "I really do owe you."

"Don't worry about it sweetie, you'd have done the same for me." She smiled and began tidying up mugs. "Now go get some sleep."

And Tal did just that, curled up in her bed with her spellbooks held close to her chest. There was no way she was losing these again.

CHAPTER 8

The door to Kai's bedroom opened slowly, quietly, the hinges barely groaning at the unexpected activity. What little light was in the hall illuminated the office space and created a long shadow of the hunched figure stepping inside. Just as carefully the door was closed, leaving the room in darkness.

The figure edged themselves forward, feet shuffling along the ground and guiding them around the mess of Kai's room.

With a loud grunt the sleeping tiefling rolled over in their bed and began snoring, oblivious to the presence in their room.

A floorboard creaked. The figure stood still. Kai snorted and continued to snore. The figure pressed on.

Perching at the foot of the bed, looking over the sleeping face of Kaivel Mortzeel the figure placed an open book on the footboard. With one hand held up, the figure muttered a few hushed words, snapping their fingers at the crescendo.

Bright light filled the room, causing Kai to leap up, fumble with their sheets and tumble from the bed with a loud and painful thud.

A string of curses came from the flailing sheet as Kai fought their way free. Finally pulling the bedsheet from their face Kai squinted up into the beaming face of Tal'avera.

"Morning sleepy head," she smiled and waved her hand. The small glowing orb that floated above Kai's bed dimmed slightly and hovered over to Tal's shoulder.

Kai glared at her as they rubbed their face. "If this is what 'helping you' gets me, I quit." They stood up and stretched, their slim frame looking even smaller in the baggy cotton shirt and trousers they slept in. "What time is it?"

"Oh it's quite early," Tal smiled at them, "this is just revenge for last night." She hopped off the bed, the orb following as she almost skipped back to the door. "See you downstairs when you're ready."

"I knew there was a reason I liked you!" Kai shouted after her as the door closed.

Taking their time to get ready, Kai wandered around their office tidying up in their own fashion. While piling related books on top of each other, making sure to leave the relevant ones on their desk, Kai mulled over the information they'd gathered about Patrice Vaskar.

The lad had come from an important, if not good, family. That could have made him a target. But what good did killing him in Belgar achieve?

Then there was the method of murder. How to kill a man without leaving a trace. Poison and magic were the best options. So the question now was when? When was he killed? Sometime between leaving his party to go to his room and Jenah finding his body.

"If we believe Jenah," Kai said to theirself.

One thing Kai knew, much to their regret, is that if you wanted someone murdered in Belgar then Malachai is who you spoke to. Nothing and no one in this city died without his knowledge or influence. Yet their old friend claimed to have no involvement in the boy's death. Malachai was not known to be a liar, it served him no purpose and there was nothing he was ashamed of.

Kai began gathering their clothes, slowly getting dressed as they continued to roam around their office.

Then there was Galen. Tal had seen him being shifty down an alleyway with another shadowy figure. There was no doubt in Kai's mind that Galen was a shifty individual, regardless of their personal feelings towards the intolerant halfling. But being shifty in Belgar was no sign of guilt. There was certainly something Kai didn't trust.

"But does that mean he murdered his friend?" Kai asked theirself aloud as they tightened their tie.

And then there was the family. It wasn't uncommon for noble sons in their prime to take on adventuring as a hobby. A chance to prove themselves to their frequently overbearing fathers. In many houses it was almost a tradition. Was the house of Vaskar so easily embarrassed?

"Maybe a matter of coin?" Kai bit their lip, buttoning up their vest. The barkeep of the Phoenix had mentioned Patrice flashing his coin about. Perhaps he was becoming a financial burden on the family? Killing for coin was also a long tradition of the noble houses.

Pulling their jacket from the back of their chair and giving it a sniff to check for freshness, Kai slung it on with a spin. The pile of books that had just been neatly stacked on their desk thudded to the floor, falling open at Kai's feet.

"Where do you think you're going?" Kai chided the inanimate objects. They knelt down to collect the fallen tomes, casually reading the open pages. Then their eyes caught something. Kai dropped the three books that were already in their arms and stood, staring at a line of text with their eyes growing wider. They grinned mischievously to theirself and slammed the book closed, resting it in pride of place on the centre of their messy desk.

A bang of the door, a click of a lock, and a thunderstorm down the stairs. Tal's eyes went wide as she, mid-bite of a sausage roll, was pulled from her seat by Kai and dragged from the tavern. "What the!"

"Come on," Kai interrupted her protest, "we've got a sword to find!"

Out in the street Tal was released from her grapple. "What's got you so excited all of a sudden?"

"I might have just cracked this case," Kai said proudly, "we just need to find that sword. Where are you going?"

Tal had turned and was walking back into the Troll's Den. "To get my books, and my breakfast. You dragged me out of there like the place was on fire!" She shot a glare at Kai.

Returning moments later with her books in hand, a small parcel balanced on top, and a sandwich in her mouth. She stood before Kai looking back and forth between them and the book, clearly trying to work something out. After a moment her shoulders deflated and a sad look fell down her face.

"You didn't think this through, did you?" Kai asked with a smile.

Tal shook her head.

"Would you like me to help?"

Tal nodded.

Kai took the books and sandwich from her, their smile transitioning into a giggle. Her one hand now free Tal took the sandwich from her mouth and chewed. "I'm getting so tired of this," she almost whimpered.

"I know," Kai gave her a sympathetic pat on the head, "but hopefully it won't be for much longer. Let's stop by Botan's on the way. She might have some news for us, and she definitely has your robe ready."

That cheered Tal up somewhat. With the return of her books she'd been able, albeit with difficulty, to clean and repair her current robes with magic, but it would be nice to have a change. The dress she'd already received from Botan was indeed beautiful, but not very appropriate for daily use.

"That one's for you by the way," Tal gestured to the parcel on top of her books. "Tess insisted you eat something."

"Oh!" Kai slipped the two books into their satchel and began unwrapping the parcel. Inhaling the fragrance from within Kai licked their lips and took an almost greedy bite.

As they walked Kai noticed that Tal had been eyeing their satchel with a look of concern. "They're fine," Kai said between mouthfuls, "it's enchanted."

Tal visibly relaxed. "Sorry, it's just that I've only just got them back and they are already a little damaged."

"Though still usable I see," Kai shot her a sideways glance. "I do hope that won't become a habit."

Tal smiled, remembering the look on Kai's face as she'd scared them out of bed. "It won't, I'd just been practising casting with my left hand and I wanted to try something out."

The pair arrived outside the gleaming white building that was Botan's boutique. Making their way up the stairs they saw the perpetually floating Botan in conversation with the tall red-scaled dragonborn. Floating up to peek over her customers shoulder Botan gave a flick of her wrist and a box floated down from a shelf above, gliding towards Tal.

"Be with you in a moment darlings, changing rooms are in the back." Botan gestured to an archway in the corner of the room. Floating back down, the gnome continued, "My apologies, now you were looking for a ring…"

Taking hold of the box, Tal and Kai strolled across the shop floor to the changing rooms. Tal tried not to stare, but this was maybe the second time in her life she'd seen a dragonborn. He looked very regal, and it reminded her of how prestigious Botan's Boutique was.

"It's rude to stare," Kai interrupted her thoughts.

Tal's cheeks turned their familiar shade of red. "Sorry, it's just…well you never see dragonborn this far south of High Talon."

"Not many tieflings either, are you going to stare at me too?"

Tal shook her head. "No, you're not that pretty."

"Ouch, words hurt you kno-oooh, hello." Kai turned as something floating by on a shelf caught their eye. "You go ahead, I'll wait out here." They reached up and took a small silver rod from the wall.

In the privacy of the changing cubicle, Tal wouldn't have called them rooms, she opened the box and lifted the robe out, shaking it and allowing the material to unfurrow.

A royal purple silk, soft and light, with a dark leather bodice gave the robe a practical yet stylish look. Running her fingers down the silver thread work Tal could feel the hint of arcane that Botan had infused into the robe. Holding it against her body and taking in her reflection Tal was both impressed and terrified. There was no way she could afford this robe, even if she had managed to reclaim her coin purse.

"Are you alive in there?" Kai called to Tal as she gawked. "We're waiting for you out here. Botan insists on seeing you in her work."

"Just a minute," Tal called back, taking a moment to admire the robe a little longer before she slipped it on.

A minute or so later Tal stepped out of the changing area and onto the shop floor where both Kai and Botan waited, each sipping their own cup of tea while a steaming pot bobbed up and down between them.

"Ah! I am a genius!" Botan declared with a wave of her tea spoon. "It is a work of art, and you my dear the perfect canvas!"

Tal blushed, twisting her body slowly to watch the material shimmer in the light.

"It's not bad," Kai nodded and ducked as a spoon flew past their head.

"Not bad? Pfft!" Botan folded her arms, settling a steely gaze on the tiefling. "The clothes you find in the market are 'not bad'. This is an elegant masterpiece of the likes you'd find at court! I wouldn't settle for anything less!" Being spoonless Botan had begun gesturing with her teacup, sending liquid flying in every direction.

Kai smirked, wiping droplets from their cheek. "Yes, like I said, not bad."

"Pah! If you were anyone else I'd throw you out of my shop!" Botan pushed her large spectacles up her small button nose.

"Then I am glad I am me," Kai's smile persisted. "But you do look wonderful," they nodded to Tal, who had taken a few steps back.

Running her finger tips and stump down the frame of the robe once more she took a few steps closer now that there seemed to be no more tea. "It is a beautiful robe Botan, but I'm afraid I can't afford it." She regretted the words as soon as they left her mouth. Botan had clearly put a lot of work into this robe, even adding an enchantment, which Tal knew wasn't something to be done lightly.

"Oh don't worry about that," Botan waved her hand, "I shall add it to your tab."

"My tab?" Tal gave Kai a confused look.

95

"Yes darling," Botan smiled, "you can pay when you can afford to, in the meantime please take it and wear it proudly. That is all I ask."

"Er..thank you?" Tal didn't mean to sound ungrateful, she loved the dress and would have loved to be able to pay for it, but she would also like to not be broke before she had any coin.

"Kaivel was telling me you are still looking for your hand as well, yes?" Botan poured herself a fresh cup, summoning a new spoon with a snap of her fingers.

"Yes, I-" Tal began before being cut off.

"But right now we're looking for that sword we spoke about a few days ago. Has anything like it come by here?" Kai had placed their cup in an empty space in front of them, leaving it to float of its own accord.

Botan sipped her tea, turning back to the tiefling. "Not here darling no," the gnome shook her head, "but a boy did come in here yesterday I believe, asking about where one might sell some unwanted weapons. Though from the way he talked it sounded more like scavenged junk, nothing like what you are looking for, darling."

"Still worth checking out though, right?" Tal asked.

Kai scratched their chin. "Possibly. Could you describe this boy?"

"Oh darling, like any other adventurer. Dented armour, dented face, very uncomely." Botan stirred her tea. "Not usually the kind of clientele I'm used to."

The roll of parchment and ink pen had been drawn from Kai's satchel and they had begun noting down Botan's detailed description. "Why do you think he came in here?"

Botan gasped and spun around on her floating disc. "Why do you think anyone comes in here darling? They want the best and Botan is the best. But the best does not come cheap!" She smiled over to Tal. "Only my very favourite customers get to set up a tab darling. If I let every adventurer that came in here do it I'd never see a coin. They disappear so quickly these days."

"It's a dangerous life," Kai said without much apathy. They folded the parchment and tucked it back into their satchel. "I think that's everything for now."

"Actually," Tal raised her hand as she did during her classes with Master Brum, "if I'm starting a tab, any chance you have some pouches for my books?"

Botan smiled. "For you darling, of course." The little bespectacled gnome floated off and returned a moment later with some leather straps. "Here you go darling. A fine leather belt with a component pouch and two holsters for your books, and space for a third should you need it. And it matches your new robe so nicely."

Tal took the belt and began trying to buckle it around her waist. Hard as she tried, the buckle kept slipping from her stump. She tried holding it down with her elbow too, but that made it difficult to pull the strap. She looked up into the giggling face of Kai. "A little help?"

"Oh gods no, this is too funny." They folded their arms and continued to grin.

A quick clip around the horn came from Botan. "You heartless child," she snapped at them, "there's a special place in the hells reserved for people like you."

Kai just continued to smile. "I know, I have a summer home there."

Botan floated down, muttering something in gnomish, and buckled the belt for Tal. She floated back up and smiled as she admired her work. "Wonderful darling, just wonderful."

Kai sighed deeply, a final chuckle escaping. "Well unless you also need some new shoes, I think we should be going."

"Oh I could actually-"

"We should be going!" Kai grabbed Tal by her new belt and dragged her from the shop to a final course of 'good-bye darlings' from Botan.

☙ ☉ ❧

Back in the street Kai had returned Tal's spellbooks and she had fitted them neatly into her sleek new belt. "What do you think?"

Kai gave her a quick glance as they walked. "You look like a wizard going to a gala."

"Speaking of going, where are we going?"

"To the Phoenix," Kai was already chewing on a bit of jerky.

"Haven't we done this trip before?"

"Yes," Kai smiled, "but you look considerably nicer this time,"

"Thank you."

"And this time I have a theory."

Tal skipped up to match Kai's pace. "What's the theory?"

Kai's broad cheeky smile made a reappearance. "Our boy, the young Lord Patrice Vaskar, wasn't murdered."

Tal raised her eyebrow. "What?"

The pair almost marched across the market square, Kai leading the charge. "I said he wasn't murdered, he just died." Kai pushed open the doors of the Phoenix, giving the room a quick scan.

"What do you mean he just died? People don't just die." Tal followed Kai's eye movements. "Who are you looking for?"

"Our, I mean, My clients. They're not here."

"So should we come back?"

Kai raised an eyebrow. "What? No, I don't want them to be here, they'd never agree to this." Kai began weaving past the tables towards the stairs, with Tal skipping close behind.

"Agree to what? What are we doing here?" Tal was beginning to move from concerned to frightened as they reached the stairs.

Halfway up the flight Kai spun around. "Remember when you asked what I used to do for Malachai?"

Tal nodded, now firmly in the realm of frightened.

"This is it. Come on." Kai led her to the rooms where Patrice, Samara, and Kirtan had been staying. "Four or six?" They pointed to the doors on either side of Patrice's old room.

"How do you know they're still staying here?" Tal didn't know what was about to happen but she was almost certain she didn't want to be a part of it.

"Because they hired me to find out what happened to their friend. Because it's a hassle to change inns, not to mention suspicious. And lastly because if they aren't this is going to look really bad. Now, four or six?" Kai pulled a small leather bundle from their satchel along with another piece of jerky.

Biting her lip and failing to think of any other way to delay the inevitable, Tal let out a heavy sigh. "Six."

"Good choice, one of my top two." Kai knelt down in front of the door and took out three small tools from the bundle. "Keep a look out will you?"

Tal leaned against the wall facing down the corridor, her heart nearly beating out of her chest. This was a terrible idea, why was she helping, how could this possibly end well?

With a soft click Kai pulled their tools free. "We're in, come on." They turned the handle and slipped inside, holding it open just long enough for Tal to follow.

Inside the room was pretty bare. A simple bed like Patrice's, a chair and table against the wall, and a small bedroll on the floor.

"I'd say this is probably the boys room." Kai stated with confidence.

Tal rolled her eyes. "Oh really, what gave it away? Was it the halfling sized bedroll?"

"No, the fact that it's tidy. I think the sword might be in here somewhere." Before Tal could respond they were pulling back the bedsheets and flipping over the mattress. "Are you going to help or just stand there?"

If just standing there was an honest option Tal would have taken it, but she had a feeling that it was a rhetorical question.

For the most part Tal followed behind Kai's search tidying up after them, trying to make it look as though they were never there. It was as Kai started tapping against the walls listening for a hollow spot that Tal's ears pricked up.

"Wait!" she hissed, listening closely as the sound of a key entering a lock sent chills up her spine. "Hide!"

Kai was way ahead of her. Grabbing her wrist Kai pulled her down, rolling the two of them under the bed, pressing as close to the wall as they could.

Tal's heart was pounding. "This is never going to-"

"Shh!" Kai put their hand over her mouth as the door creaked open.

"Huh, I could have sworn I locked up." Kirtan entered, their heavy boots thudding against the wooden floor.

A smaller pair of feet followed, closing the door behind them. "You need to be more careful," Galen chastised the stocky half-elf, "what if someone found it?" The halfling kicked away the bedroll as Kirtan's heavy form sat down on the bed arching the frame so much that Kai feared they may be crushed.

"You mean that detective? Nah, we're in the clear there." Kirtan sounded very smug. "That fool's so focused on that red-head they'll never think to suspect us."

Tal wasn't hearing any of this. Her heart was pounding so hard all she could hear was the blood in her ears, terrified that it sounded as loud to everyone else.

Kai however was glaring at the boots in front of their face, watching as Galen pried open a floorboard and lifted a long roll of cloth out, placing it on the floor beside him. As the scared halfling peeled back the fabric Kai smiled. There it was, the longsword with a rose-gold dragon maw hilt.

"I knew it," they muttered to themselves.

CHAPTER 9

From there under the bed Kai and Tal watched and waited as Galen and Kirtan made their plans.

"So you've got it all set up?" Kirtan's foot tapped against the floor. He was either eager or nervous or most likely a combination of the two.

Galen on the other hand seemed very much at home. The halfling re-wrapped the ornate blade in its cloth and hid it back in the floor, sliding the board back into place and stamping it down.

"Yes, yes, everything is taken care of." Galen leaned back against the wall. "I spoke to my guy yesterday and he's got a buyer for us. We just need to be there." Galen replaced his bedroll over the loose panel and hopped up onto the bed, his feet barely hanging below the mattress.

Kirtan's sigh came from above. "I'll be happy to get this over with." There was a creaking of armour and the stocky half-elf rose from the bed. He began pacing the room, clearly it was more nerves than excitement.

"Not getting cold feet I hope? This was your idea." Galen's feet swung up out of sight.

Tal stifled her surprise. She knew Galen had been up to something, but to find out he'd just been shopping around for Kirtan?

"I know it was, doesn't mean I feel good about it." The pacing increased, Kirtan's armoured boots clanking on the wooden floor. "For a rich entitled prick he wasn't a bad guy."

"Then why kill him?" There was a hint of amusement in Galen's voice.

The boots stopped, slamming down hard. "I didn't kill him!"

"So you keep saying. And yet, he's dead and you have his sword." There was a chuckle. "Don't get me wrong I've got nothing against killing off the noble houses. We'd all be better off without them."

"That's not what this was about." The pacing had restarted. Kai was beginning to get concerned that Kirtan would wear a hole in the floor, fall through and see the two of them hiding under his bed.

"I don't know what happened to him," Kirtan continued. "When we left him he was with that girl, and when I went to get him for breakfast he was dead."

"I said I understand," Galen's feet swung down again. "You see a body, you loot a body. I've been doing it since I was six, I get it." With a grunt and a thud the little man landed on the floor. "What's done is done, let's just get rich and be done with it." He patted Kirtan on the hip and moved towards the door.

With a heavy sigh Kirtan's boots stomped along and opened the door. "So tomorrow night?"

"Yeah it's tomorrow," Galen walked out into the hall, "my contact is meeting us down by the-"

SLAM.

The door closed and the lock was clicked into place. With a slow careful shuffle Kai crawled out from under the bed, helping Tal to her feet as she rolled out after them.

"That was far too close," Tal's heart rate slowly returned to normal.

Kai was more relaxed, giddy almost. "We were fine. How often do people look under their beds?" They dusted themselves off and began removing the bedroll.

"I do. Every night."

Kai just blinked at her. "You know somehow, that doesn't really surprise me." They pried open the floorboard with their fingers while Tal scowled at them. Lifting the bundle and unwrapping the blade, Kai took hold of the hilt and held it up, giving it a few test swipes. "Not bad."

"That looks so…" Tal stroked the flat of the blade with her stump, feeling the cold steel against her skin.

"Yes," Kai recovered the blade.

Tal turned to her horned companion. "Did you really know? And I mean really know that these two were in on it?"

The familiar broad smile stretched across Kai's face. "Of course, I'm very good at my job."

Tal narrowed her eyes at them, sensing they weren't being completely honest, but not caring enough to press the matter. "So what now? We take the blade to Samara and tell her that Kirtan and Galen are responsible?"

Putting the blade back into its hiding spot and pushing the board into place Kai shook their head. "No, that'd be our word against theirs. She's more likely to believe whatever lies her friends have prepared than the truth from you and I." Kai scratched their chin. "No, we know they're meeting tonight, we just need to find out where. Proof is the best evidence. They can't lie their way out of it if she catches them with the sword."

Tal pulled the bedroll back into place as Kai began pacing. "So we follow them?" she asked. It seemed obvious, but the fact that Kai hadn't said anything made her worry there was an idea brewing in their mind.

"No, we want to be there when they're there," Kai tried the door. "Why isn't there a latch on this side?" They sighed and took out their lockpicks once again. "And I don't think Samara will be up for spying on her friends. She seems like the kind of person who sees the best in everyone."

"That's a good thing, isn't it?" Tal crouched down next to Kai, watching them closely as they worked their tools in the lock.

"Nice, yes. Naive also. You're very close." Kai tilted their head, prodding Tal in the ear with their horn.

The elf shuffled back a few steps, still crouched. "What's wrong with wanting to see the best in people?"

"Got it," the lock clicked. Kai rose and opened the door, taking a quick peek to check the coast was clear before gesturing for Tal to leave. "Well her friends looted the guy she was sweet on and then let her pay a detective to find out who killed him. Does that answer your question?"

Tal huffed as she walked out into the corridor. Kai did have a point, but she wasn't about to admit it.

The two carefully made their way down to the tavern floor, taking a quick glimpse around the corner to see if the two opportunists were still in sight.

Tal spotted Galen and Kirtan at the bar, engaged in conversation with the keeper. She elbowed Kai and pointed over to them. "They look annoyed," she whispered.

"Probably want to know if he went into their room," Kai speculated, "got anything to distract them?"

Tal waved her stump in their face. "Yes, but it'll take me a while to cast anything."

"We really should do something about that," Kai took out a piece of jerky. "Right, this one's on me then."

Kai's eyes flashed black and the window shutters began to slam as if caught in a gale. All eyes turned to the noise, including Tal's briefly before she was yanked away by Kai and out into the market square.

ꦸ☉ꦸ

"What was that?" Tal finally asked when they were a safe distance from the tavern.

Kai swallowed their mouthful of jerky. "It's a tiefling thing. Some left over innate magic. It's not much, but good for getting out of a tight spot."

It seemed Tal had a lot to learn about her new friend. She smiled and patted them on the shoulder. "You are full of surprises."

"I know," Kai returned the smile, taking another bite of their dried meat snack. "Right now we need a plan though, and I think I need to have a chat with Jasper."

Tal wondered what attire the fence would be sporting today. "Okay, where do you think we'll find him at this time of day?"

Kai blinked at her. "We? No, just me right now. You have a much more important job to do."

They said it with a tone Tal recognised. It was the same tone her parents used when she was a little girl and they wanted her out of the way or to be quiet. "Oh really?" she pouted in preparation for being sent off on a wild goose chase.

"I need you," Kai began in a slow measured tone, "to find Samara and keep her busy and with you until I can find you."

"Oh," Tal's pout disappeared. She was surprised, this was an actual job, part of a plan Kai had or was working towards. A plan she still had no idea of. "I can do that. Where do you think she'll be?"

Reaching out with both hands and holding Tal by the shoulders, Kai just smiled. "Well, that's where being a detective comes in. Good luck."

Before Tal could protest Kai was already charging off down the street. She sighed to herself, standing alone in the market square. Being a detective. That's what Kai had said to her. Tal had been an adventurer for a time before deciding that life wasn't for her. She'd come to Belgar to get work as an enchanter, though it wasn't her speciality. Becoming a detective was never something she'd thought of or considered. But if this is what being a detective was all about, then she'd definitely give it a go.

Feeling a sense of purpose, helped by the trust Kai was putting in her, Tal strode forward. "If you want to find an adventurer, you start at the lodge."

The adventurers lodge, as it turned out, was a bust. Though Tal had met a very friendly clerk, an elven woman named Cherie, who was more than happy to have someone who wasn't an adventurer to talk to.

Cherie had happened to overhear a conversation with a woman who matched Tal's description of Samara, a list of errands she had to run. She couldn't remember all of them, but Cherie definitely recalled the woman saying she was heading to the Two-Horse Express, a courier service on the edge of the city. After a short goodbye and a proposal to have lunch sometime in the near future, Tal was off again.

Tal wasn't one to so quickly accept such an invitation, she'd done so more out of not wanting to say no. Cherie was quite the insistent elf.

The courier, Tal had been informed, was a large building on the southern gate, but if she reached a stables she'd gone too far. It didn't take her too long to get there, though she did have to stop and ask directions a few times. The streets were busy, but without Kai to talk to and the feeling of responsibility fuelling her, she made good time.

The Two-Horse Express could have quite easily been mistaken for a stable. There were at least half a dozen horses tied up to a hitching post above a long water trough, and two large wagons parked in an alley to the side. Clearly the business was progressing well from its original two horses.

Poking her head inside, Tal gave the place a quick scan. An elderly human woman hunched over a counter making notes in some sort of ledger was the only occupant she could see. One wall was covered in notices, and the other had a long table with a row of ink pots and quills by small stacks of parchment. No sign of Samara anywhere.

"Can I help you, deary?" The shaky voice of the elderly woman called out to her.

Tal stepped inside. "Uh, yes," she said as she approached the desk, "I'm supposed to be meeting my friend here, I don't know if you've seen her?"

The woman closed her ledger and squinted at Tal. "Well that depends, deary."

"On what?"

"On what your friend looks like."

Once again Tal's cheeks flushed. "Of course. She, uh, she's a human woman, tanned skin, long dark hair. Probably wearing armour. Her name's Samara if that helps?"

The old woman looked up to the ceiling as she reached back into her memory. Tal shifted her feet as she stood silently waiting, wondering if the woman had simply fallen asleep.

After a long pause the woman rocked forward with a regretful smile. "Sorry deary, but I don't recall anyone like that popping in today. Why don't you take a seat? You can wait for her here." The woman gestured to the corner, where there was no chair in sight.

Tal smiled politely. "Thank you, but it's a lovely day, I might wait outside."

"Suit yourself deary, I'll be here if you need me." With what looked like great effort the woman heaved open the ledger again and continued her work.

Outside the courier there was indeed a bench, though if that was what the old woman was talking about Tal wasn't quite sure. With no clue on how long she would be waiting, Tal did what any young wizard would do in her situation, she took out her spellbooks and read.

Of the two books she had, one was significantly more weather-worn than the other. This was a book that had been given to her as a gift from Master Brum shortly before she departed from Rothwood for the city. For now it was almost completely useless to her. It was one of many spellbooks her master had saved from his youth, and although he had been her tutor, wizards each wrote their formulas and incantations in their own personal way, making it very difficult or time consuming for one wizard to steal from another. It was a very petty and secretive profession.

So for now she glanced over the pages, recognising the odd symbol here and there, but other than that it may as well have been written in dwarvish. It wasn't, she'd tried that. Master Brum had handed her the book with no instruction, he'd simply said, 'one day dear girl', and that was that.

Master Brum had certainly put this book through its paces. The cover was battered, torn, burnt, and scared. The parchment pages were held together with twine and glue, each treated to an enchantment to protect them from decay. But still she loved it. It was a reminder of home and of her beloved master.

As she perused the delicate pages of the ancient tome, she noticed something that seemed amiss. In three different spots in the book a page had been torn out. Master Brum had instilled many lessons in her beyond the arcane traditions, and one was to never remove a mistake.

107

"Mistakes are how we learn," his voice echoed in the back of Tal's mind, "If we do not make mistakes we do not grow."

Maybe he'd learnt that the hard way, and these pages had always been missing. But something about it didn't sit right. She also had no way of knowing what was on these pages as she couldn't read anything that came before or after the torn edges.

Tal sighed in annoyance, making a mental note to write a letter to Master Brum about this. She then immediately wiped that idea from her mind. If he hadn't torn the pages from the book and thought that she'd damaged it… Tal shivered at the mere thought of his reaction.

"Tal'avera?" A voice broke Tal's concentration. She looked up into the cheerful face of Samara. "It is you, what are you doing here? Is Kaivel inside?" This was the first time Tal had really seen Samara in her adventuring gear. With her battle worn leather armour and her longbow slung over her shoulder she looked quite the intimidating figure.

Tal got up, strapping her books into her new belt. "Hi. No, they're not with me. I was actually waiting for you."

"Oh, is everything ok?" There was a note of excitement and fear in Samara's voice. It was then that Tal noticed the roll of parchment gripped in the girl's hand.

Tal had to choose her words carefully. She didn't want to lie to Samara, but she knew she couldn't tell her everything that had happened since they last spoke. Putting on her best smile, she nodded. "Oh yes, everything is fine. Kaivel is busy sorting out a few things, but they sent me to find you. Are you sending a scroll?" Tal gestured to the parchment.

Samara looked down at her hand with a puzzled expression. "What? Oh, yes! Sorry. In the surprise of seeing you here I completely forgot." She laughed, a sweet melody. "Yes, I'm writing to Lord and Lady Vaskar. I wanted to keep them informed about Patrice," her voice sank as she spoke, "I wanted to let them know it'd be a few more days before we returned. They've not written back to me yet, but I guess they don't know me well enough."

Not knowing what else to do, Tal stepped closer and hugged Samara. It's what she would have wanted were the roles reversed, and from the way Samara held her back she knew it had been the right decision.

"Thank you," Samara said quietly into Tal's collarbone. The pair separated and Samara wiped a tear from her eyes.

"Of course," she smiled back, feeling a little happier herself. "Well why don't you send that and we can head back to Kai's office?"

Getting the scroll sent turned into a quest all its own. After several attempts Samara managed to explain she was looking to send a scroll, not purchase them. It took several attempts to get the scroll addressed to the Vaskar family, as the elderly clerk repeatedly explained that there was no place called Vaskar. A third volley of slowly and carefully spelling out her intentions, the scroll was finally addressed to the Vaskar's in Vallameria, and not the Vallameria family in the city of Vaskar, which the clerk continued to explain was not a place. Tal had to admire Samara's perseverance. After the first five attempts Tal would have given up and delivered it herself.

≈⊙≋

After a great deal of careful, slow, and loud explanations, the scroll was set to depart on the evening wagon to Vallameria and would arrive in a couple of days. There was also an express service, but Samara didn't have the coin for it.

As the two made their way to the Troll's Den they passed the time with idle chit chat, how they each were finding life in Belgar, places that simply must be visited, and where Tal got her wonderful robe. Once at the tavern they didn't quite make it to the stairs before Tess accosted them both, demanding they join her at the bar for a drink.

"Aren't you the tavernkeep though?" Samara asked with some confusion as Tess was seated at an empty table enjoying a bowl of the house stew.

"Good eye," the troll-orc chuckled as she walked behind the bar, "but I'm on my break and I hate to drink alone." Tess returned to the table with another two mugs of ale.

"Thank you," Samara took a seat and held the mug up to Tess.

Tal did the same, tapping her mug against Samara's. "Yes, thanks Tess."

Knocking both the mugs hard enough to spill onto the table Tess smiled at the pair. "Don't mention it sweeties. So Tal, have you finally had enough of our horned friend and traded up?" She winked at Samara.

"Not yet," Tal held up her stump, "I still need them to find my hand."

Samara swallowed her mouthful of ale. "How's that going by the way? Any luck?"

"Sadly, no. But we managed to get these back," Tal tapped the books on her hip, "so if I have enough time and manage to scrounge some coin from somewhere I might be able to make another cuff."

"Well I'm sure you'll find it!" Samara banged her fist against the table. "If you've managed to help me I'm sure of it!"

"Speaking of which, have you two made any progress?" Tess asked with eager interest. Tal hadn't thought Tess was too concerned with Kai's business, but then remembering her comment from the other night about the rent Tal began to wonder; was Kai falling behind on rent?

Tal pulled her mind back into the conversation, putting on her best business smile. "Yes, that's why I brought Samara here. We think we may have found Patrice's family sword."

The thud of two hands slamming against the table made Tal jump.

"Why didn't you say so sooner?" Samara's eyes brightened and she was almost jittering with excitement. "That's amazing! Shall I go get the boys?"

"No!" Tal caught herself too late as she practically yelled in Samara's face. "It's just," her mind panicked as she searched for an explanation to her outburst. "Kai's getting them. Yes, I just wanted to be the one to tell you." She nodded and gave a guilty smile. "Sorry, it slipped my mind."

"She'd lose her head if it wasn't screwed on," Tess jumped in, "you've seen what happened to her hand!"

Even Tal managed a laugh at her own expense, Tess's joke breaking the tension in the room.

The three chatted for a while longer, Tess's break extending longer than probably necessary as she refilled their mugs a few more times. Tal was beginning to wonder how the Troll's Den was still in business. Besides the three of them the only other patrons of the tavern were the five old men, each sat at their own separate table in grumpy silence as they nursed the same mug of ale all evening it seemed. Maybe that's why Tess was so keen for Kai to get paid, they must have been the tavern's main source of income.

The girls had moved to the bar, making Tess's refill trips much shorter. As their mugs were being refilled for the fourth time, a disappointed tutting joined them.

"Starting without me again are you?" Kai patted Tal on the shoulder. "Everything is prepared. Good afternoon Samara, you're looking...tipsy."

"And you're looking blurry, Kaivel. Are we going to meet the boys now?" Samara pushed back the mug of ale that had been placed before her.

Kai shot a look at Tal. "You told her?" Their voice was level, but Tal could hear the knife edge in their words.

Keeping a smile on her face, Tal gave a nod. "Yes, I told her you were off sorting a few things and that you were telling the boys where to meet us later." She raised her eyebrows with each word, hoping Kai got her subtle message.

"Ah, yes, of course," Kai said bluntly, "yes, they're going to meet us there later. I thought it best that we take you personally. I could tell that you were clearly the closest to Patrice."

Samara smiled, hints of a tear welling up in the corner of her eye. "That's very sweet of you, I really do appreciate it."

Kai took the mug that Samara had pushed away, taking a long drink. "Since we've got some time to kill," they said, taking up a stool, "how did you all meet?"

Samara leaned back, then forward again after realising there was no back to the stool, and smiled at her own thoughts. "At the lodge actually, Patrice and Kirtan had a bet to see which one of them I'd let buy me a drink. Stupid really but we had a fun evening. Lots of drinking and gambling. That's how Galen joined us. He lost a hand of cards and didn't have the coin to settle his debts, so he joined us for a quest." Samara chuckled. "I always thought Galen just used that as an excuse. He'd been loitering around the lodge for days looking for work."

"It sounds like the four of you were fast friends?" Tal brushed hair over her ear.

"We were," Samara sighed, "it's a shame our time together was so short."

"Won't you continue on with Kirtan and Galen?" Kai spoke half into their cup as they were mid sip.

There was a long pause where Samara just stared into Kai's eyes, as if she were trying to read their very nonchalant expression. "I don't know," she finally said. "I mean they're great guys and all, but...it just won't be the same without Patrice." She drummed her fingers against the bartop. "I think I might just return to the lodge and see if anyone is looking for an archer."

Hearing Samara's backup plan gave Tal a ray of hope. At least they weren't leaving the poor girl completely alone.

Draining the last of the ale Kai flipped the mug onto the bartop and rose to their feet. "Speaking of the boys, we best be going. Are you ladies ready?"

Samara's hands were in tight fists, her knuckles nearly glowing white. With a flex of conviction, she slipped off the stool onto her feet and gave a confident nod. "Yes, let's do this!"

CHAPTER 10

B y the time the trio arrived at their destination the sun was beginning to make its way towards the horizon. It had been quite the pleasant walk for the most part, their journey taking them up the river walk towards the docks where the meeting was scheduled to be taking place.

Kai took the time to explain their plan, which they assured Tal and Samara would work perfectly as long as nothing went wrong. Kai's contact had informed them that the meeting was taking place in one of the boathouses on the north end of the dock, at some point after sun down.

The plan was for the three of them, or five of them, Kai corrected when Samara asked, to take hiding spots in the rafters and lay in wait.

"So, we ambush them?" Samara asked as they moved stealthily up the docks, trying to stick to the shadows and stay out of sight.

"Shh!" Kai held a finger up to their lips as they pressed their body against the wall of a building. Tal and Samara followed suit just in time as two guards of the city watch wandered by discussing their plans for after work.

In silence they waited, Kai's hand held against their lips the whole time. "Yes, an ambush is our best tactic," they finally replied. "We have the numbers and the element of surprise." Kai poked their head around the edge of the building and gave the women a quick signal. "Let's move."

Keeping low and moving fast, the three of them stepped from shadow to shadow as they drew closer to the northern boat house.

"How do you know this place isn't guarded?" Samara whispered when their destination was in sight.

Kai gestured to the empty docks. "Do you see any guards?"

"No, but-"

"Then let's go before some arrive!" Kai stepped out of the shadows and made their way towards the building.

Tal patted Samara on the shoulder, giving a gentle nod. "Let's go."

Side by side they followed Kai into the boathouse, up a web of ropes and ladders and onto a shelf in the rafters. With piles of planks, coils of rope, and crates filled with all manner of fixings, there was no shortage of hiding spots.

"This way, over here." Kai led them over to a spot they had deemed best. From the barricade of timber the three had good cover from below, while giving them the best vantage point of the large open doors and the smaller back door. There was also a pulley system hanging not five feet away should they need to engage, and the window behind looked out onto the waters below, should retreat be their best option.

"So now we just wait?" Tal asked as she struggled to find a comfortable sitting position. Kai and Samara seemed to have no trouble squatting, but even the thought of that made her calves ache.

"Unless you're got a deck of cards on you, yes." Kai took out a few pieces of jerky, offering one to each of the girls.

As always Tal refused, giving Samara a strange look as she took a piece without question. "What is it with you and jerky?" she asked while the pair chewed. "And how much do you have in that satchel of yours anyway?"

"Enough," Kai said as they chewed, "and it helps me think."

"When are the boys getting here?" Samara asked. "Shouldn't they be here by now?"

"Oh, I'm sure they'll be along soon." Kai rested against a crate behind them. "They know where they're going, probably just hanging back to keep watch from the docks."

"Since they know we're in here that's probably a good idea," Tal went along with Kai's charade. The more relaxed they made

114

Samara the better, the last thing Tal wanted was for Samara to be on edge.

The minutes dragged by like hours. Tal was grateful for her books, she could at least pass the time by brushing up on her spells. Kai and Samara however had their eyes glued to the open doors for any sign of movement. There was a brief moment when a cat wandered in and Samara nearly leapt through the roof, but other than that the evening was quiet.

Kai's ears perked up and their head snapped towards the large open doors. "Shh! Someone's coming." Kai gestured for the two of them to duck down.

Tal and Samara scooted close to the edge, just enough to peek over the edge of their timber cover. A low mumbling grew slowly louder as rhythmic footsteps drew closer. Long shadows entered the boathouse, gradually getting shorter and shorter, until two silhouetted figures were in full view, a long bundle held under the taller figure's arm.

"They're here," Samara smiled and began to rise. But Kai's hand found her shoulder, holding her in place. She stared into Kai's eyes as their finger pressed against her lips, and then gestured for her to watch.

Tal watched as Samara's eyes widened and confusion covered her face. This was it, the moment Samara would find out who her friends were.

Kirtan and Galen paced separately back and forth across the open floor, sighing heavily and kicking dirt.

"You sure this is the place?" Kirtan asked, his voice hushed and agitated. "Maybe it was one of the other boathouses?"

Galen shook his head. "This is the place, he's probably just running late."

"Or he's not coming. I told you we should have just sold this bloody thing and split." Kirtan dropped the bundle to the floor with a muffled metallic thud.

"Oh sure, just pop down to the blacksmith and trade it for a few gold coins? Real smart." Galen prodded himself in the side of the head a few times. "This thing is worth thousands!"

"It's worth crap if we can't sell it!" Kirtan barked back. "And your guy screwed us!"

"You don't know that!" Galen's hand was already twitching. "He'll be here. Sundown isn't an exact time, you know?"

A heavy thud interrupted the discussion as Kirtan and Galen looked into the shadows below where the three of them were hiding. Two of them.

"Oh hell," Kai breathed as they looked over their shoulder to see the empty space where Samara had knelt. They looked to Tal who was just as surprised at how swiftly the girl had slipped away. Kai pointed to the rope and the two of them moved slowly.

"Big guy, that you?" Galen called out into the shadows.

Samara stepped forward, arrow notched, string drawn. "Tell me I'm not seeing this." Her words were shaking with rage or sadness, or perhaps both.

"S-Samara…" Kirtan's jaw opened and closed as words failed to reach his lips.

Kai gestured to the rope behind them, moving slowly as they lowered theirself into the shadows behind Samara.

"I said tell me I'm not seeing this Kirtan...Tell me this is a bad joke and that we can just go back to the tavern and laugh about this." Samara had stopped still, her arrow firmly pointed at Kirtan's chest.

"Samara, just put the bow down and let me explain…" Kirtan's hands were up, but his legs were frozen in place, half turned to the doorway.

Tal stumbled as she slid down the rope, moving behind a beam to keep as out of sight as possible.

"Tell me why you killed him? He was your friend! Your friend!" Samara's hands were shaking as she gripped the bow tighter.

"Ha! He was a prick!" Galen spat on the ground between him and the furious archer.

Kirtan shot a look at the halfling. "Shut up you idiot!" He turned his gaze back to Samara. "If you'd let me explain," he took a cautious step forward, "it's not what you think."

He stopped short as an arrow sunk deep into the wooden floorboards, the shaft just inches from his toes.

116

With another arrow already notched, the tears streaming down her face, Samara returned her aim to Kirtan as he took a step back.

"You'd never be able to do it," Galen drew two daggers from his hips, "you're not the type."

Samara's attention turned to her shorter friend. "You think you mean more to me than Patrice? You think I won't drop you where you stand?"

Spinning his blades in his hands Galen smirked. "I think there's two of us and one of you." He looked up to Kirtan. "It's us or her. Let's get this over with."

Samara's eyes flicked to Kirtan's face, as did Tal's. The half-elf closed his eyes for a moment, his face contorted with internal struggle. Biting his lip Kirtan drew his broadsword. "I'm sorry Samara, but I can't let you ruin this."

"Such big, strong men." All eyes turned to the shadows as Kai stepped out giving a slow clap. "Threatening a crying woman all on her own. What heroes you must be."

Galen cursed under his breath. "This freak again. Just get lost already, isn't there a child you need to eat somewhere?"

Tal stepped forward too, her spellbook open in her hand.

"It seems we have the numbers now," Kai ignored the comment. "So how about we all put down our weapons and nobody has to get hurt."

Kirtan and Galen looked at each other, then back to the three figures in front of them. "You think you can intimidate us?" Kirtan gripped his sword tighter. "After everything we've done, you think we'd just give up and walk away?"

"We still have the numbers," Galen laughed. "An unarmed freak, a one-armed spell flinger, and a little girl who couldn't hit the broadside of a barn?" He laughed again. "Pathetic."

Samara drew her bow tighter, the arrow now firmly focused on the halfling. "I will kill you Galen, I promise you that."

Kai held their hands up in the air as they strode next to Samara. "How about we all calm down and nobody kills anybody?" Putting their fingers between their lips Kai gave a short loud whistle.

A sudden clatter of boots and chainmail filled the otherwise silent evening as a half dozen guards encroached on the boathouse.

"Drop your weapons!" One of the guards in a heavy breastplate shouted as he moved into the room, a spear and shield held up towards Kirtan and Galen. "You two are under arrest for the murder of Lord Patrice Vaskar."

The two looked around at the crossbows aimed in their direction, exchanging glances with each other.

Seeing all the guards, Samara lowered her bow.

"I told you there was a plan," Kai put their hand on her shoulder, giving an affectionate squeeze.

Tal was just as shocked as everyone else. Was this the errand Kai had been running all afternoon? Kai must have been far more connected than she'd thought.

With the guards edging closer Kirtan and Galen backed against each other, looking back and forth from the guards to the trio. They were surrounded. Kirtan's leg began to wobble, his grip on his blade loosening as their chances became less certain.

But Galen's stance didn't change. "I'll take the guards, you finish off those fools," he said as his blades turned in his palms.

"No," Kirtan dropped his sword, "coin's no good if we're not around to spend it." He raised his arms above his head.

"We can take them!" Galen's eyes now jumped from guard to guard.

"It's over Galen," Kai shouted to the halfling, "no one needs to die here."

A snarl of a laugh burst from Galen's throat. "That's another point where you and I differ." With a practiced fluidity the halfling kicked out Kirtan's knees, dropping him down and using him as a half-elf shield from the guards. Three daggers flew out from Galen's silhouette. The first embedded itself with a heavy thud into the beam Tal hid behind. An arrow sunk into the ceiling of the boathouse as Kai swept Samara's legs and pinned her to the ground, Galen's other two daggers clattered into the shadows.

A cry of pain filled the air as the guards released their bolts, many pinging off Kirtan's plated chest piece, but one sinking into his abdomen.

Tal dropped to her knees, her spellbook open on the floor as she began an incantation.

Three guards fell, daggers protruding from their bodies as Galen unleashed a second volley.

"Stay down," Kai barked at Samara as they rolled off her and sprinted towards Galen.

Drawing two more blades the scared halfling leapt at Kai, who rolled to the side avoiding the lightning fast slashes.

"Swords!" A guard cried. Crossbows were dropped and the shiiiing of blades being drawn caught Kai's attention.

"No, no!" Tal panicked as just a few embers sprouted from her fingertips and she began her incantation again.

The guards moved in on Kirtan who had collapsed on the ground, groaning in pain as blood pooled at his knees.

Kai's height was proving to be a disadvantage in their fight. Galen dodged and ducked past every blow, but neither could the halfling's blade find their target as the tiefling nimbly slipped just out of reach at the last moment.

Releasing one dagger into the leg of an approaching guard, Galen rolled between Kai's legs, grabbing their tail and pulling them back.

With a thud and a gasp Kai fell to the ground, the wind knocked out of their chest.

Galen stepped on Kai's throat, his small foot pressing down as he held the blade up. "Back to hell with you!"

"*Maskan!*" Tal cried, a bolt of flame flying from her hand and soaring across the boat house, catching Galen in the face, pushing him away from Kai.

The halfling snarled, his face red and scorched. "Soith tu!" he yelled in halfling as he hurled his last dagger at Tal.

Like a deer she froze as the blade flew towards her. Bracing for the pain Tal felt the daggers point press into her chest before bouncing off as an arcane shimmer rippled out from the impact.

The distraction was all Kai needed. With a deep breath they rolled to their feet, bringing their knee up and connecting it with Galen's jaw.

119

With a grunt Galen tumbled across the ground. Spitting blood across the wooden slats he looked up to see one of his daggers just feet away from him. In a flail of arms he scurried forward and grabbed the hilt.

A heavy plated boot pressed down on Galen's wrist, and a loaded crossbow pushed against the back of his shaved skull. "Try it little man," the guard in the heavy breastplate glared down on him.

Gripping the hilt so hard his knuckles turned white, Galen let out a sigh and released the blade.

The guard kicked the dagger into the shadows while two of his men lifted Galen to and then off his feet.

Kai knelt down next to Samara and helped her up as Tal approached. "You ok?" Tal asked the pair of them as they dusted themselves down.

Kai simply nodded before looking back towards the guards as they wrapped the wound around Kirtan's stomach and locked a pair of heavy iron shackles on his wrists.

"I'm fine," Samara's voice was filled with a mixture of emotions. "Just bumped my head a bit."

Kai turned back to her and shrugged. "Sorry about that. Didn't want that little prick to turn you into a pin cushion." They patted Samara on the shoulder and turned to Tal. "Thank you as well, that was a very impressive shot."

Pride washed over Tal. It wasn't her first time in a fight, but it was her first time in a fight with her left hand. "I only wish I could have been more helpful." She looked at her stump.

"You were amazing Tal," Samara gave her a tight hug, "I don't know what I'd do without the two of you here." She held Tal's stump in her hands, stroking it softly. "And now you've caught these two I'm sure you can both focus more on finding your hand."

"Speaking of which," Kai wandered across the floor and gathered the bundle that Kirtan had dropped. "I believe this is for you."

Samara took a deep breath, her hands reaching shakily for the bundle Kai held out to her. Slowly unwrapping the material, as if she expected another horrible surprise to complete the night,

120

Samara's eyes filled with more tears as they beheld Patrice's sword once again. "Thank you," she choked on the words, "thank you so much."

Kai gave her shoulder another squeeze. "All in a day's work. Why don't you head back to the Phoenix, you've had a long night. We can deal with the guards from here."

"Yes, thank you," Samara rewrapped the sword and handed it to Kai. "Will you hold on to this for me? I'd feel better knowing it was safe with you."

"Of course, we'll see you in my office tomorrow." Kai slung the wrapped blade over their shoulder.

Giving both Kai and Tal a final hug, leaving both their cheeks damp, Samara left the boathouse, not once looking at either of her former companions.

Kai patted Tal on the back, giving her a proud yet still cheeky grin. "You did good, kid."

"Thanks. So did you. I was honestly shocked when you tripped Samara and fought with Galen on your own."

Kai shrugged. "Really? If she died we wouldn't get paid."

An explosion of laughter drew the attention of all in the boathouse as everything that had been bubbling up inside Tal throughout the night was released in one go. "Oh, oh, oh. I'm sorry," she said through giggles, "I didn't expect that."

"Glad to see someone is having a good time," the guard who had been shouting all night approached the pair, a stern look on his tanned and weathered half-elven face.

"Always," Kai shook the meaty hand that was offered. "Tal'avera, I'd like to introduce Sergeant D'Clos of the Belgar City Watch."

The Sergeant's stern expression looked to be his resting face, as now that he stood before the pair Tal could see the hint of a smile tweaking the crows feet in the corners of his bright eyes.

Tal awkwardly shook the sergeant's hand, watching the embarrassment peak on the Sergeant's face as he noticed her missing right hand. "A pleasure to meet you, and thank you for coming, your timing was perfect."

The sergeant smiled as he looked around the room, scratching the side of his head where the first hints of grey were beginning to peek through. "I don't know about that, but thank you Miss Tal'avera."

"And thank you for all your help here," she added, "I don't know what we would have done if you and your men hadn't arrived when you did."

The Sergeant gave a soft chuckle. "Well from what I saw of you I'd say we'd be taking those two away on carts and not in shackles." He cleared his throat and put on a more serious face. "Speaking of which I should attend to them. Thank you again Kaivel, I'll make sure you're mentioned during the arrest report." With that he turned on his plated heels and began shouting orders at his men as they hauled their captives out of the boathouse.

Kai and Tal stood in silence for a moment, watching the guards walk Kirtan out, and carry Galen, who was still struggling to free himself.

Left alone in the boathouse the two shared a sigh. "What do you think will happen to those two?" Tal asked when the silence had started to make her feel uncomfortable.

Kai shrugged and took out a piece of jerky. "If I know D'Clos, they're going to spend a long time chained to a wall to think about their lives." They chewed for a moment as they tucked the fabric wrapped blade under their arm. "Or he'll ship them off to Vallameria and let the Vaskar family deal with them." They gave Tal an affectionate pat on the shoulder. "Let's get back home, I think we need to celebrate completing our first case together."

Tess had drinks waiting for them, and a bottle of the Blue Stuff ready on the side. As soon as the pair walked through the tavern doors the troll-orc was begging them for details, not taking no for an answer. Kai and Tal took it in turns to regale their favourite tavernkeeper with their perspective of the evening's events, calling each other out on embellishments.

Tess continued to refill mugs, but each time her long arm reached for the leatherbound bottle Tal flicked embers at her, not wanting a repeat of her last experience.

"Sounds like you two had one hell of a night," Tess gathered the mugs for another refill. "I'm glad you both made it back safe though. It's difficult to collect rent from the dead," she chuckled as she handed over the mugs once again.

"Yes, sounds like you had quite the adventure," Jasper's voice broke into the conversation from across the tavern floor.

Tal and Kai spun on their seats to see Jasper, once again in his cleaner apparel, walking towards them with a large figure following behind.

A flash of fear shot like lightning up Tal's spine. The figure she didn't recognise, but his frame was familiar. This was Galen's contact, the man in the alley. But it wasn't a man. Walking towards them was an orc, a full orc. His thick hair woven into plaits decorated with bone and wood, matching his long goatee. Hunching over Jasper at almost nine feet tall, his arms about as thick as Tal's body. Tal was amazed no one had seen him strolling the city.

As far as Tal knew, orcs lived in nomadic herds, raiding caravans and small towns or villages before moving on. They never came close to cities or even fortified towns, so to see one so casually standing in a tavern was unsettling to say the least.

Even Tess seemed on edge as the imposing figure strode towards them behind Jasper.

"And you've started the party without us," Jasper continued as he pulled a chair out, either not noticing or caring about the sudden tension in the air.

Kai cleared their throat. "Well if you'd told us you were coming we would have waited. Tess, maybe another two mugs for my friend Jasper and his...companion."

Tess groped around for another mug, not taking her eyes off the orc as she spilled ale over the bar.

"Ah, my apologies," Jasper gestured to his friend, "this is Tiny, he was the one meeting with your two thieves tonight."

"Tiny?" Tal raised an eyebrow. "Is that supposed to be ironic?"

"No," the heavy rumble of Tiny's voice almost echoed off the walls, "I am smallest of my herd." He grinned, the large tusks making the friendly expression very threatening.

"He's the best smuggler I know," Jasper took the two mugs Tess eventually offered. "I figured something as fancy as that would be difficult to get out of the city, so Tiny is the only one I know who could do it."

"I could." Tiny nodded as he took the mug from Jasper. It looked more like a shot glass in his massive meaty hand. "You ones who help Tiny?" The orc pointed to Kai and Tal.

"Er…" they both murmured in unison.

"These are the ones," Jasper gave a small clap. "I told Tiny that you heard about the guards being after the thieves, and that the meeting was a setup." Jasper winked very obviously at the pair.

"Oh yes," Kai followed suit, "yes, that was us."

"We're happy to have helped," Tal gave an awkward smile as Tiny began to walk towards them.

The large orc leaned over them, placing the mug gently down on the bar. He then swooped his massive arms around both Kai and Tal, pulling them off the stools and lifting them up against his chest. With their feet dangling off the floor, both Kai and Tal coughed and wheezed as the air was squeezed from their lungs and every gasped breath was tainted with Tiny's thick sweaty musk.

Just as Tal felt she was about to faint, Tiny lowered them to the ground. Even Kai staggered a little, holding theirself up with the bar top.

"You do Tiny a kindness. Tiny do a kindness for you." As intimidating as his voice and physique were, his words and expression were incredibly soft.

"Thank you...Tiny…" Kai said between breaths, giving the huge orc a gentle pat on the arm.

"And I'll just add this to the list of favours you owe me," Jasper emptied his mug and rolled it down the bar. "Anyway, I just came to see if you were alive, now I've got to get back to work. Come on big guy." Jasper patted Tiny on the arm. Taking a moment to give both Kai and Tal a more sympathetic look, Jasper gave them both a squeeze on the shoulder. "Seriously, I'm glad you're both ok." He gave Tal a little smile before turning and leaving.

"Thank you," Tiny's deep rumbling voice sent a shiver down Tal's spine as he gave a low bow before following behind Jasper. Tal smiled and gave a little chuckle watching the huge orc squeeze himself through the tavern door, which wasn't that small.

Tess released a breath she'd been holding since her visitors walked in, some colour returning to her already very pale complexion. "It's never a dull moment with you two around, is it?"

"That's why you love me," Kai chuckled as they finished their mug. "I think that's about all the excitement I can handle for one night." They stood up and gave Tal a tight hug, though nothing compared to the last hug she'd received. "Good work today." Kai turned to Tess. "You too, no one pours an ale quite like you."

"Get lost," Tess threw a cloth at Kai as they walked away.

Tal spun her empty mug around on the bar, the events of the day still replaying in her mind over and over again. They'd done it, they'd helped Samara get justice. The feelings of pride and joy mixing with the alcohol in her system was an amazing sensation. Maybe this is why she was here, in this city. She could help people. Not as an adventurer, fighting off monsters and bandits in the forest. Not spend her days toiling in the back of an enchanters' shop making toys for the rich. She could be a detective, work with Kai and help people in need.

"Yuhu," Tess waved a hand in front of Tal's eyes. "Aldera to Tal'avera, come in."

Tal shook her head, bringing her consciousness back into the room. "Sorry, I was thinking. What did you say?"

Tess raised an eyebrow. "I said, do you want another? But I think it's kind of my job to cut you off and send you to bed."

With a sigh and a grin Tal pushed her mug towards Tess. "I'm fine, I was just lost in thought. You don't need to send me to bed like a child."

"Yes I do sweetie," Tess took the mug, "trust me, thinkin' and drinkin' don't mix well. Now off with you."

With a few playful flicks of her cleaning cloth Tess managed to chase Tal away from the bar and up the stairs to her room.

Alone in her chambers, the light from her candle flickering in the cool breeze from the open window, Tal began to relax. Her eyes closing and her breath softening, she fell asleep with a smile on her face.

CHAPTER 11

Morning came all too soon, but also not soon enough. Tal's body ached with the strain of the previous night's adventure and a nice warm bath would not have gone unappreciated. However the job was not yet complete, and she was eager to see it through, so the bath will have to wait.

Almost skipping down the stairs Tal joined Tess at her breakfast table, the troll-orc once again hiding her book as Tal approached. "Good morning!"

"You're in a good mood I see," Tess chuckled, "I hope you're hungry."

"Very," Tal smiled and licked her lips. She looked around the empty bar with confusion. "Is there food or were you just curious?"

Tess gave a laugh and kicked the chair opposite her away from the table, gesturing for Tal to sit. "There will be food, Kai is making us breakfast. Yern isn't going to be happy someone is messing up his kitchen, but he'll just have to live with it."

Thoughts of concern and intrigue fluttered within Tal, she'd never seen Kai eat anything other than jerky and food from street carts, so the fact that they were now cooking for the three of them was either going to be a treat or an assault on her digestive system.

"I didn't know Kai knew how to cook," Tal said with a smirk.

"Oh it's a very rare occasion," Tess smirked too, "and there have only been a few fatalities."

The pair laughed and chatted while they waited for the mystery meal to be prepared by their tiefling companion. Tess poured them some 'breakfast ale', which she admitted was just regular ale drunk in the morning.

127

A loud wooden thump came from behind the bar, startling Tal as a few seconds later the familiar horns of Kai peaked over the bar top, followed shortly by the rest of Kai's body and a large wooden tray with three plates of piping hot food resting on top.

"Good morning ladies, breakfast is served." They placed the plates down gracefully on the table and stepped back, clearing their throat.

Tal looked down at the plate of food before her with wide eyes and wide nostrils.

Kai began, "I have prepared for you; crispy bacon," Tal would have described it as burnt, "seasoned roast potatoes," they looked pretty raw, "and devilled eggs."

"Devilled eggs?" Tal raised her brow.

"Yes," Kai nodded with pride, "they're just fried eggs, but made by me." They gave their familiar cheeky grin.

Tess sniffed the air and gave Kai a concerned look. "Is something burning?" A small stream of smoke floated up from behind the bar.

"Oh crap!" Kai stumbled and slipped as they scrambled over the bar top and clunked down what sounded like a lot of stairs.

"What's back there?" Tal asked as she absently pushed the plate of food away from her.

"Trap door to the kitchen," Tess was looking seriously concerned, "if I still have a kitchen that is."

"Everything's fine!" Kai's voice echoed up into the bar, "nothing to worry about." Footsteps climbed the hidden stairs and Kai once again appeared before them, something black stacked on their palm. "I forgot your toast," they said as they placed a cremated piece of bread on each of the plates.

Both Tess and Tal stared at the plates of inedible food before them, Tal with significantly more surprise than Tess. Tal's attention turned to Kai though, who had begun to tuck in to their breakfast.

As Tal picked up her knife and fork, wondering if politeness was worth what she was about to do to herself, the tavern door swung open, and an armour-clad Samara strode in.

"Good morning everyone, I hope I'm not too early?" She seemed like a different person, like the events of the previous night had washed away a darkness that had been consuming her. The cheerful smile plastered across Samara's face was a welcome change to the concern and sadness Tal had seen previously.

"Not at all," Tal pushed off from the table and embraced Samara in a tight hug. "How are you feeling?"

Samara sighed, her smile shaking for just a second. "Relieved? Happy? Sad? I don't know, this has all been a lot." She walked with Tal back to the table. "Oh, I'm sorry, I'm interrupting your...breakfast?"

"It's fine sweetie," Tess got up from the table, "I'll fetch you a drink, yes?"

"Oh, yes please," Samara was still staring at the plates of food that only Kai was eating.

Wiping their chin clean Kai rose from the table. "Excuse my manners," they smiled at Samara, "I was just finishing my meal. I'll collect the sword from my office and be back in the flick of an imp's tail." They gave a gentle bow before hurrying off up the stairs.

"Quick, now's our chance!" Tess barked in a hushed voice, gesturing to the plates from behind the bar.

Tal grabbed the two plates and rushed them over to the bar, where Tess was already grabbing for them. Quickly dumping the contents into a bucket before handing them back to Tal. The two of them then made haste back to the table, where Samara's eyes and jaw were wide open.

"What in the hells was that about?" She asked as the pair caught their breath.

Tal ignored the question and threw an angry finger in Tess's face. "I thought you said they could cook!"

Tess shook her head, finishing the ale in her mug. "No, I said it was a rare occasion. Now you know why."

"So that was food?" Samara looked equally as concerned. "Thank the gods they're a better detective than they are a cook."

Tess laughed. "If they weren't I'd have kicked them out a long time ago."

129

Moments later the sounds of heavy footsteps came bounding down the stairs and Kai reappeared with the fabric wrapped weapon and a large leather-bound tome.

Dropping them both down on the table Kai smiled at Tal and Tess. "I'm so glad you enjoyed your meals." Unwrapping the sword Kai handed it hilt first towards Samara. "I believe this brings our case to a close."

With a shaking hand Samara took hold of the hilt, swallowing hard as Kai released it, the full weight of the sword now held by her alone. Taking a deep breath Samara placed the sword down on the table in front of her, running her fingers over the detailing of the guard and the smoothness of the blade. "Thank you," she almost whispered, "I still can't believe they killed him for this though."

"Ah..." Kai held up a finger, "there I can offer some clarity. They didn't kill Patrice."

All heads turned to Kai with an equal look of bewilderment.

"What are you talking about?" Tal was almost aggressive in her tone.

Samara was more confused. "Yeah, the guards arrested them for murder. They had his sword. You're telling me they were innocent?"

"Yes and no," Kai opened the tome and flicked through its pages. "Does this look familiar to you?"

All three of the women leant forward, examining the illustration of a rather grotesque looking fungus.

"Yes," Samara nodded and tapped the page, "those were growing in the demon's cave, where our quest took us."

Kai ran their finger down a passage. "This fungus releases a particular spore when disturbed. At any point in your battle with the demon did one of them get damaged?"

Samara bit her lips as her eyes lost focus and her memory churned. "Uh...yes...Patrice...I mean, the demon got hold of him and threw him across the cave. He landed on one of those and crushed it."

"This spore is deadly if inhaled," Kai tapped the book once more. "No symptoms or signs of disease other than a slight cough, which you'd get from being hurled across a cave I imagine."

"He was coughing..." Samara trailed off, lost in the memories of the fight.

"If you go untreated -and who gets treated for a cough?- you expire sometime within the next two or three days." Kai closed the books. "I'm sorry Samara, but there was nothing you could have done."

A tear fell from her cheek, splashing against the blade. "Then how did Kirtan and Galen know?"

Kai shook their head. "They probably didn't. Just found him dead the next morning and took his sword. A crime of opportunity."

Tal was just as shocked and surprised as Samara was. "How did you figure all this out?"

Kai smiled at Tal. "With your help, of course." They cleared their throat and began the explanation. "It was when the boys told me of their time spent in the Dancing Dryad, after we spoke to its proprietor and the girl who Patrice had engaged the services of-"

"He what?" Samara gasped.

"-that I knew something was amiss. If she had something to do with the demise of the boy Malachai would have never let us speak to her, and she would have denied being present at all."

"He had a girl in his room?" Samara continued, the tears now gone from her face.

Kai pressed on, ignoring Samara's outbursts. "They themselves told us that no one else had entered Patrice's room. They probably did suspect the girl had killed him and stolen his coin, so what was the harm in making a profit themselves and placing all the blame on her?"

"So how did I help?" Tal rested her chin on tented fingers as she pieced together all that Kai was saying.

"You my incredible assistant," Kai patted her gently on the back, "spotted that tiny fiend Galen skulking about in town, confirming our suspicions that they had more to do with the case than we first suspected."

Kai began to pace around the table, forcing the women to become owls in order to follow their revelation.

"Then the other morning, whilst doing some research into the demon you and your companions most heroically slayed, I came across this fungus. From there all the pieces just fell into place, and it was a simple matter of laying a trap for our thieves."

Kai returned to their seat, leaning back and looking very proud of theirself.

"But how did you get the guards to the boathouse?" Samara looked back and forth between Kai and Tal.

"Ah," Kai rocked forward once again. "I've done some work for D'Clos, the Sergeant, in the past. I informed him that Kirtan and Galen had murdered a Lord in cold blood, and that I knew where they'd be."

"And he just believed you?" Tal added.

Kai nodded in a very matter-of-fact way. "Yes, he was satisfied with my work previously, and apprehending those two would be a big boost to his career."

"But you just said they didn't murder Patrice." Confusion once again marred Samara's face. "You lied?"

Kai shrugged with their usual nonchalance. "Looting the dead is not a crime," they said with a scoff. "Never let the law get in the way of justice."

Samara sighed again. "I suppose," her brow furrowed, "I guess they did lie to everyone about their part in all this, so they're not really innocent."

"You're forgetting they were willing to kill us all to keep their secret." Tal added as her stump absentmindedly brushed against her stomach where Galen's dagger had struck.

"Attempted murder is as good as regular murder in my books," Tess tilted her mug at Samara.

"Yeah, to hell with those guys!" Samara tapped her mug against Tess's. Taking a gulp of ale she slammed her cup down on the table. "Thank you," she smiled to all three in turn. Samara loosened a purse from her hip and placed it on the table in front of Kai. "You've been worth every coin."

Kai took the purse and tucked it into their jacket pocket. "That's very kind of you, we're happy to help." Kai patted Tal's hand.

"If it's not asking too much," Samara suddenly became rather sheepish, "I do have a favour to ask."

"Of course," Tal said with a note of excitement, "as Kai said, we're happy to help."

"Would you both mind coming with me? To the temple. To return Patrice's sword to him before I take him back to his parents." Her eyes were almost pleading. "I'd just feel safer having you with me. And I'm sure Patrice would appreciate it."

Tess chuckled under her breath. "Well how could you say no to that?"

Kai stood from the table and gave Samara a deep bow. "It would be my honour to escort you to the temple and see this through to the end."

Samara's face lit up like a bonfire. "Oh thank you. Well I'm ready to leave as soon as you are."

Straightening up, Kai gave her their usual cheeky smile. "Well we've all had a fine breakfast, so let Tal'avera and I gather our things and we shall be on our way. Come on," they gave Tal a pat on the back and headed on up the stairs.

≈⊙≈

After gathering her books from her room Tal went to retrieve Kai from their office, wondering why it was taking so long to grab a jacket and satchel. She found them hunched over their desk pushing coins into two separate piles.

"What are you doing?" She sat down on the edge of the desk, leaning in over the piles giving Kai a puzzled look.

Kai looked up and smiled. "Just checking it's all there, you'd be surprised how often people try to stiff me." They scooped one pile into their satchel and the other back into the pouch Samara had given them. "Here," they plopped the pouch into Tal's hand.

She blinked in surprise. "What's this for?"

"It's your cut," Kai smiled as they pulled on their jacket, "for the job. Like I said, I couldn't have done this without you."

"You didn't say that," Tal blushed as she shifted the purse in her palm.

Kai blinked at her. "I didn't? Well it was implied. Let's get going." They practically shoved Tal off the desk and out the door. "Besides," Kai added as the pair walked down the stairs, "if you don't have any coin Tess will kick you out eventually and I need you around."

∾☉∽

It didn't take too long for the trio to make their way from the Troll's Den to the temple of Caledoughn where Patrice's body was being kept. Tal thought that the three of them looked almost official, with Samara practically marching the entire way and Kai and Tal flanking her as they tried to keep pace.

The temple itself stood grandly looking out over a large market square, its tall spires casting long shadows at this time of day, and a beautiful stained-glass window picturing the goddess Caledoughn bathed in light.

Tal was not religious per se, after all it was hard to deny the existence of beings many had physically met, but she didn't feel her life would have changed greatly if they weren't around.

Inside the large stone hall the air was cool and calm, their footsteps echoing off every surface. Tall columns and wide pews lined the way towards the altar where a marble statue of the goddess of adventure and luck looked down upon them as the three marched towards the elderly cleric who sat on a bench in deep slumber on the dais.

Samara sat down next to the sleeping cleric, an elderly elven man with a long pointed nose and eyebrows so thick he could have been mistaken for an owl. Placing her hand on his shoulder Samara gave him a gentle shake. "Father Roderic?"

With a loud snort the Father jolted to life. "What-wha-why-who-huh!" The elderly elf spluttered as his eyes blinked out of sync. His long pointed face turned to the source of the noise and his milky grey eyes slowly adjusted. "Ah hello my child, I was just communing with our Lady," he cleared his throat and sat with a more graceful posture.

Tal and Kai both suppressed a snigger.

"Father Roderic, it's me Samara Kalmar, do you remember me?" Samara spoke like she was addressing a grandparent after one too many bottles of wine.

The old cleric narrowed his gaze on her for a moment, and Tal thought she could almost hear his memory churning over. "Ah yes, how are you my child? How can I help you today?"

She smiled sweetly, still speaking with the same slow soft tone of voice. "I'm here for Patrice, Father, I've come to get ready to take him home."

Father Roderic nodded a few times like his head was coming loose, probably giving the words time to filter in. "Ah yes, Patrice, how is that dear boy?"

"Not well I imagine," Kai muttered to Tal, who gave them a sharp kick to the shin.

Samara sighed. "He's at peace, Father, thank you. Could you take us to him?"

"Oh yes, yes, yes," Father Roderic pushed himself up from the bench but began groaning as his knees took on the strain. The three youngsters helped him to his feet to a chorus of "don't make a fuss" and "I'm fine". Slowly...very slowly...the old cleric, guided by Samara, led them through the halls of the temple, down a series of winding stairs lit by arcane flames, to a cool chamber where two large stone doors stood before them. A guard dressed in temple attire, save for the spiked mace at his hip, stood to the side of the door. As Father Roderic approached the guard gave a gentle bow and stepped to the side.

Tal stepped forward, jaw agape, as her fingers traced the intricate carvings in the doors design. "What is this?" She turned to the old cleric as the tingle of arcane energy spread down the arm.

"This is our preservation room," Father Roderic spluttered as he fumbled around in his robe. "It is where we keep our recently departed." He pulled out an old looking talisman and tapped it against the doors.

A shimmer rippled out from the door and filled the room as with a scraping groan the large stone doors opened before them, the temperature dropping to an uncomfortable chill.

Kai visibly bristled as their breath became visible, pulling their jacket tighter around them. "Why is it so cold down here?"

Seemingly used to this sudden drop in temperature the elderly cleric slowly walked forward into the room.

"It feels like an abjuration spell," Tal explained as she rubbed her arms for warmth, "with a little bit of transmutation, I think. Though how it works I have no idea."

Samara blinked at her. "You can tell all that just by the feel of it?"

"Yes," Tal nodded as they followed behind. "It's the sort of thing my master used to teach."

Kai's jaw began chattering. "That's all very impressive, but why is it so cold?"

"Simple, cold stops the decay." Father Roderic turned his head as led them into the room, and for a moment Tal feared it may turn completely around, proving he was in fact a large owl. "And the divine magic of this room slows the passage of time."

"Satisfied?" Tal smirked.

Kai simply glared as their teeth continued to chatter.

Inside the chilled room there were a half dozen long stone slabs, all but one unoccupied. A long ornate coffin, golden filigree and gemstone decorating the polished dark redwood, sat alone at the far end of the room. Their footsteps echoed off the bare marble walls as they walked towards Patrice's temporary resting spot.

Glancing at Samara, Tal could see the anxiety building in her eyes, reaching down and holding her hand. Samara smiled, mouthing a thank you as her nerves began to settle.

Standing before the beautiful coffin Father Roderic stepped back, giving Samara some space to be with her friend. Kai handed her the wrapped sword with a bow, suddenly feeling very official. Unwrapping it and letting the material fall to the floor at her feet, Samara took a deep breath.

"This is for you, my friend. May you find the rest you deserve."

Samara bowed to the coffin and then gave a simple look of gratitude to both Kai and Tal. She reached forward and unclipped the latch on the coffin lid, lifting it slowly with bated breath.

There was a long silence as the three of them stared into the coffin. The empty coffin.

Samara turned to Father Roderic, who looked just as confused and shocked as she did.

The clearing of Kai's throat broke the anxious silence. "If you need some help, I know an excellent detective agency."

Chapter 12

Tal sat with Samara on one of the cold empty slabs in a deep silence. The poor girl hadn't managed a word since the lid of Patrice's empty coffin had been opened. She'd just stared at the emptiness where her friend should have been. She was still staring, her eyes glazed over as Tal attempted to comfort her as the murmurs of an interrogation echoed around them.

"It's only myself," Father Roderic was explaining, "and the two other High Clerics of the temple. We are the only ones with access to protected rooms."

Kai had taken out some parchment and an ink pen from their satchel, along with a strip of jerky, and had begun taking notes. Samara had yet to officially hire them for the job, but they felt getting a head start wouldn't hurt.

"So not even the guards are able to access this room?" Kai turned their attention to the guard, Tomas, who was looking increasingly abashed.

Father Roderic spluttered in irritation before the guard was able to respond. "That's what I just said. Weren't you listening?"

"I was indeed, these aren't just for decoration," Kai ran their fingers around their ears, pulling back a few loose hairs. "But I wanted to hear it from Brother Tomas."

The guard cleared his throat. "No, we do not have access to any of the sealed rooms, sir, and we don't let anyone other than the Fathers in." Tomas spoke like he was reciting a script.

Kai narrowed their eyes at Tomas, making another note on their parchment. "We, we, we. You keep saying 'we', who is 'we'?"

"We the guard, sir." Tomas clarified, his gaze twitching between Kai and Father Roderic.

"I'm not a sir." Kai said as they added another note. "How many guards are there? And how many of these sealed rooms are there?"

Tomas took a moment, his eyes looking up into his memory as his fingers absently counted. "There are six guards for each room, ma'am, and five rooms in total."

"I'm pretty good at maths, so I'll say that's a lot." Kai smirked. "And I'm not a ma'am." They turned to Father Roderic, leaving Tomas with a puzzled look on his face. "Are any of the sealed rooms ever unguarded at any time?"

"Heavens no, they are guarded day and night." Father Roderic stamped his foot, not that it made much sound or had any affect on Kai's next question.

Turning to Tomas again, Kai's gaze narrowed further, their eyes flashing black for a moment. "Is that true, Brother Tomas, is this door guarded day and night?"

Tomas took a half step backwards, suddenly cowering from the horned figure in front of him. He looked to Father Roderic for either support or aid, but the elderly cleric was just as stunned by Kai's sudden intensity.

"I...er..." Tomas swallowed hard, "I...take a bathroom break about an hour into my shift, si-...ma-...detective."

Father Roderic's mouth hung open, his eyes wide and his eyebrows bristled in shock and anger.

But before the Father could deliver his chastisement, Kai moved on to their next question. "How long does this break take you?"

"I have a weak bladder, but I'm only gone about a minute, maybe two. I go before my shift too, but I can't help it." Tomas stared down at his boots, not daring to look up at Father Roderic.

Kai nodded along. "OK, so now the question is how do you break into a sealed room and steal a body in two minutes."

"You mean two hours..." Father Roderic said through gritted teeth. "They would have had two hours."

Kai looked down at their notes, then up at Brother Tomas, then to Father Roderic, before going back to their notes. "I might have missed something…"

"It's the enchantment." Tal approached with Samara still holding her hand. "I've been trying to feel it out, and there's something strange in the air."

"The young woman is quite right," Father Rodeic sighed. "Since necromantic preservation is no longer an option as it used to be, the divine enchantment in this room slows the passage of time."

Kai made another note on their parchment. "That is wonderfully convenient…" They sighed and pinched the bridge of their nose.

"Every minute spent in this room," the elderly cleric continued, "a second passes outside."

Kai sighed again. "That would give them plenty of time. I'm going to need to speak to all the guards and anyone else who was here in the temple for the last…" They turned to Samara. "When was he brought here?"

"Four days ago," Samara said after a moment of counting to herself.

Kai audibly groaned.

Tal put her arm around Samara's shoulder, shooting a stern look at Kai. "Don't worry, we'll find him, Samara, won't we?" The look on Tal's face told Kai there was only one correct answer.

Sensibly they nodded, rolling up their note parchment and putting it away in their satchel. "Of course, you hired me to return Patrice's sword to him. Technically I haven't done that yet." They smiled their familiar cheeky yet comforting smile. "Why don't you head back to the Phoenix? I'm sure you could use a drink after all this."

Samara nodded, placing her hand on Tal's with a smile of gratitude. "Thank you, both of you." She smiled at Kai as well. "A drink sounds good, and now I need to write another letter to Patrice's parents."

With some polite goodbyes to Father Roderic and the guard Samara made her way back up the stairs. Slowly. Kai and Tal watched as the moment Samara stepped out of the aura

140

emanating from the open doorway her movements slowed to almost nothing.

"That is incredibly off putting." Kai noted with a shiver.

Tal merely shrugged. "Magic is unsettling for a lot of people."

"Is there anything else you need from me?" the elderly cleric asked, already making his way back towards the stairs.

"Yes," Kai was still staring at Samara's painfully slow movements. "If you could stop whatever this is from happening I'd feel a lot better."

Grumbling under his breath Father Roderic shuffled towards the large doors. Holding up his pendant the doors began to scrape closed and the aura filling the room washed away until the retreating footsteps of Smara were all that could be heard.

"Much better," Kai's shoulders slumped as they exhaled. "Thank you Father, that'll be all."

Tal had already turned her attention to the doors themselves, Tomas standing to attention at his post as Father Roderic retreated back the way they had come.

"Anything interesting?" Kai asked as they sidled up to Tal as if they were in an art gallery inspecting a particularly abstract painting.

Tal nodded like an excited child. "Very interesting, if we've got time I'd like to spend some of it inspecting the enchantment. I think it might help us if we understood it a bit more."

"Knock yourself out," Kai shrugged. They wandered away, leaning against the wall next to Tomas and chewing a piece of jerky.

The excited elf plopped herself down on the floor in front of the doors and unclasped her spellbook, flipping through its pages until she found the spell she was looking for.

As she began casting Tomas's face became increasingly concerned. "What's she doing?"

"Hell if I know. Wizard stuff." Kai slid down the wall onto the cool stone floor and stared off into space.

"Is she allowed to be doing that?" Tomas seemed very unsure of where he stood on current matters.

"I'm not going to stop her. What do you make of this body stealing business then?" Kai was mulling some ideas in their mind and needed someone to bounce them off.

"There's a body stealing business?"

Tomas was clearly not the person for this job. Kai chose thinking out loud instead, maybe something useful would echo back to them. "Why steal a body? And why go to the effort of sneaking into a temple to do it?"

"Maybe it was about this body in particular." Tal replied without looking over at Kai, her eyes still transfixed on the door as her fingers slowly traced symbols in the air.

Kai tilted their head towards her. "I thought you were busy with that door?"

"I can multitask," a sly grin curled her lips. "Maybe Patrice's body is what was needed."

"It would have had to have been personal. Some sort of vendetta against the boy or his family." Kai continued to chew.

Tal turned a page in her book. "So who knew he was dead? Just Samara, Kirtan, and Galen."

"Are we sure there was even a body in there?" Kai waved a finger in the air, trying to pin down an idea in their mind.

"You think someone stole his body before he made it to the temple?" Tal faltered over her casting. "Damn it, hold on."

"If you need to concentrate, stop answering me," Kai rolled their eyes. "And it's a possibility. Or he was never dead to begin with." They looked over to Tal, who had begun recasting her spell. "I said or he was never dead to begin with!" Kai shouted and smirked.

"I heard you the first time." Tal's tone was not amused.

Kai chuckled and pushed theirself off the floor and wandered over to Tal, crouching over her shoulder. "How long is this going to take?"

"Longer if you keep bothering me." Tal growled between chants. Several minutes of chanting went by as Kai paced impatiently, pressed random sections of the walls, tapped their foot against floor tiles, and huffed and sighed nearly consistently.

142

With a breath of relief Tal closed her book. "Sometimes I want to strangle you," she looked up at Kai, who had returned to loitering over her shoulder popping their lips.

"Only sometimes? I'm impressed." They sat down next to Tal. "So did you learn anything useful?"

Tal closed her book. "Not much that we didn't already know," she admitted with a pained expression. "The spell does pretty much what Father Roderic told us it does, but the protection side only affects the outside of the door."

"Excellent. What does that mean?" Kai's head tilted to the side. Tal was beginning to understand that Kai knew next to nothing about magic and the arcane, but they seemed eager to learn.

"It means that the protection spell stops anyone from opening the doors from this side without the crest Father Roderic has." Tal cleared her throat. "It doesn't stop anyone inside from getting out. And it doesn't stop anyone from translocating in or out."

Kai's eyebrows took it in turns rising in surprise. "Then what good is it?" They scooted around to face Tomas. "Seriously, what good is it?"

The guard "um'd" and "ah'd" a few times before Kai waved them of, scooting back to look at Tal.

"That kid is going places..." Kai rolled their eyes. "I guess we're done here then." They hopped to their feet, offering a hand to pull Tal up. Turning to Tomas Kai gave a wink and a smile. "Thank you for your time, and don't worry, we'll show ourselves around."

Kai and Tal spent the rest of what seemed like an eternity, but was merely the afternoon, questioning other members of the clergy and temple guard. Many of them gave the impression, either by looking put out or saying so outright, that they had better things to do. The answers they gave were short and often followed by "anything else?". All in all no one knew anything about Patrice's body, or at the very least didn't want to be connected with the events, and almost certainly all of them didn't appreciate the investigation intruding into their place of worship.

As Kai and Tal stepped out into the evening air, the orange sky giving the streets a warm glow, the elven girl finally released the gasp of frustration that had been building in her chest over the past few hours.

"Feel better?" Kai asked with a smirk of recognition.

Tal puffed out her cheeks and kicked a loose pebble down the cobbled roads. "Are people always that unhelpful?"

"Usually only those that have something to hide or have something to lose." Kai offered a piece of jerky, which was rejected. "In this case I think it's the latter. The last thing the clergy here want is a reputation for misplacing the dead."

"They probably should have thought about that before they lost a body." Tal regained her composure with a deep breath. Then something popped back into her mind. "What was that you were saying before?"

Kai's eyes rolled back as they racked their memory. "That Tomas is about as useful as a sundial at midnight?"

Tal chuckled for the second time at that comment. "No, the bit about Patrice not being dead?"

"Oh that," Kai led the way down the street, heading nowhere in particular, just not wanting to stand still. "It was just a passing thought. I don't think anyone is incompetent enough to put a live man in a coffin unintentionally."

"Even Tomas?" Tal chuckled again. "Poor boy, he really had the worst luck."

Kai scratched their chin, weaving past two lightly armoured people arguing over something very loudly. "I wouldn't say the worst luck. He's not dead and no one has misplaced his body."

"That's a good point. Poor Patrice." Tal sighed. "So about him not being dead. What was that about?"

Kai held their arm out across Tal as a four-horse-cart sped by with very little care for anyone else using the street. "Just a thought, like I said. It would explain why his body wasn't there."

Tal chewed on her lip as they continued across the street. "But why? And how?"

144

"Where, what, and when, just for good measure." Kai added. "Like I said, it was just a passing thought." Kai chewed their jerky as they looked up and down the cross-street. "That is a good question though."

"Which one?" Tal tried to follow Kai's eye line, on extra alert for carriages and wagons.

"The why and how. Getting into that chamber would be no difficulty." Kai snorted a laugh. "Father Roderic seems to get very deep into his communing. I'm sure even you could swipe that pendant without waking him." Kai cleared their throat. "As for Patrice being dead, technically my theory for the cause of death is just that. A theory." Kai eventually chose a direction and began moving again. "Without his body I can't prove a damned thing."

The pair came to a halt on the edge of a crowd surrounding what sounded like a very physical debate outside a tavern.

"Magic and medicines," Tal said as the words came to her mind. "That could be the how."

Kai turned away from the brawl to face Tal, blinking at her. "You're going to need to keep talking."

She took a moment to arrange her thoughts, wincing as she saw a chair splinter over the back of an already very bruised dwarf's back.

"If you wanted people to think you were dead, you'd either use magic or medicines. Can we walk around this?"

A cheer came from the crowd as the bruised dwarf rallied and had leapt onto the back of the burly man who'd hit him and was now holding him in an aggressive looking choke hold.

"But it's just getting good!" Kai complained as Tal grabbed them by the collar and was already pulling them away from the scuffle.

"Fine," Kai conceded when they were finally released, "so what magic and what medicine would make someone a passable corpse?"

"I don't know," Tal's cheeks reddened. "I mean, any spells like that would involve necromancy, and I'm no expert on alchemy, but I'm sure there's some kind of potion that could do that."

"So, what you're saying is, if Patrice wanted to fake his death convincingly he was either involved in illegal magic, or illegal drugs?"

Tal chewed her lips but said nothing. She knew it was wrong to speak ill of the dead, but was he dead? How else would you explain his body disappearing without a trace?

"Well I'd say one thing is certainly clear. We need to know more about Lord Patrice Vaskar." Kai smiled at Tal. "Whether he's dead or alive it might help us work out where he'd go." Then their smile dropped. "We need to speak to Kirtan and Galen again, they found him dead after all."

"Aii…" Tal winced at the thought of having to be in a room with those two again. "Do you think they'll want to talk to us?"

"Probably not, but they've not got anything better to do." Kai stopped suddenly, looking up and down the street. "But I don't want to deal with them again so soon."

"Then what do you think we should do?" Tal was beginning to wonder exactly what they were looking for.

"I suggest we combine business with dinner. Let's find a tavern." Kai headed off confidently back the way they'd come.

Tal groaned as they drew closer to the tavern where the brawl was still going strong, and had now included two gnomes and a halfling grappling each other on the floor.

"This place, really?" Tal pleaded as Kai stepped over a gnome. "Can't we just go back to Tess and try to stay sober for a night?"

"We're not staying, come on." Kai held the door open and gestured for her to follow.

Inside the tavern was nearly as rowdy as the brawl outside. The place stank of stale ale and body odour. Tables and chairs had been knocked over, presumably in the process of moving the brawl outside. Tal stayed close to Kai as they made their way to the bar, every person they passed appeared drunk and wanting to fight.

"What do you want?" The barmaid matched the aggressive tone of the rest of the tavern.

"Give us your cheapest bottle of wine." Kai winked at Tal as they leaned against the bar, removing their arm very quickly once they noticed the puddle of presumably ale they'd stuck their elbow in.

The barmaid scoffed at them and turned to Tal. "You could do so much better love," she said as she walked away, coming back a few seconds later with a brown glass bottle with a wax sealed cork.

Kai paid the woman, and very quickly made a retreat as a heavyset tattooed sailor walked towards them, cracking his knuckles.

"So we're drinking in the street now?" Tal was very confused by Kai's apparent plan, just following on and hoping life would eventually make sense.

"Of course not, I do have some class." Kai handed her the bottle. "Can you do something magicy to make this look more expensive?" They wiggled their fingers at the bottle, imitating Tal's casting.

With a raised eyebrow Tal took hold of the bottle. "Look, yes...taste? No."

"That's fine, it doesn't need to taste good. What do you need?"

Tal looked around. "Somewhere to put this down and a few minutes to try and cast the spell."

"Perfect." Kai looped their arm around hers and led her down through the street until they were at the river's edge, looking out over the northern end of the Island District.

Tal set the bottle down on the wall along with her spellbook, holding the pages down with her stump. "Do you want to tell me the plan or is this amusing to you?" She flipped through her pages until she found the right spell.

"Yes, and yes." Kai gave her their usual grin. "The plan is to make that bottle look very, very expensive, and then go to dinner."

"Why do we need an expensive bottle of wine to go to dinner?" Tal slowly traced arcane symbols against the bottle surface, whispering an incantation.

Kai was busy dusting theirself off and adjusting their suit. "Because it's rude to turn up to dinner and not bring a gift for the host."

147

Tal traced the final symbol above the bottle and gave it a tap. "We've been invited to dinner?"

The air around the bottle shimmered as the glass took on a polished sheen, the wax around the cork extended down the neck of the bottle and embossed itself with a vineyard stamp. As a final touch a square of parchment materialised against the surface of the bottle with a beautiful drawing of a ship cresting a wave upon it.

Kai whistled. "That does look very expensive. Good work."

"Thanks," Tal smiled. "It's a bottle I've seen on my old master's shelves. He said it was very old and worth more than my life." Tal was never sure how true that was or if Master Brum really did value that bottle so highly.

Kai nodded as they held the bottle in their hands, inspecting every detail. "That should do the trick then. How long will this last?"

"About eight hours I should say. Why?" Tal was getting increasingly concerned now that she was beginning to think things through. Kai hadn't broken her trust yet, but there was always a first time.

"That's fine, we'll be gone by then. Let's go." Kai began walking, following the river north.

"Who's invited us to dinner?" Tal repeated the question, hoping for an answer this time.

"We've not been invited to dinner, that's why we needed the gift."

"So, we're bringing a gift...to be polite...to a dinner we've not been invited to?" Tal was struggling to understand what was going on, but she felt that no matter what the plan was, they were turning up to someone's home uninvited.

"Yes," Kai nodded. "It's rude to turn up uninvited, yes, but it's ruder still to turn up uninvited and empty handed."

"And with a fake bottle of expensive wine." Tal added with a note of disapproval.

"See, you're getting it. Now try to look like you're better than people." Kai straightened their posture and tilted their head back as they looped their arm again through Tal's.

"Like I'm what? Wait, where are we-"

148

Tal suddenly realised that they were walking directly towards two guards standing either side of the gated bridge across to the Island District. She also noticed the guards noticing them and stepping forward.

"Good evening," the first guard said as they approached, "Do you have business here this evening?"

This was far more polite than Tal expected from guards assigned to standing in front of a bridge.

"Yes, my good man, we do." Kai took on a snobbish tone, over-enunciating each word. "We are guests of Lord Uth'ill, he is expecting us and I doubt he'd like to be kept waiting much longer."

Tal wasn't sure if this was just another of Kai's character disguises or if they really were trying to talk their way into the gated noble district.

"Certainly," the guard gave a slight incline of the head, though his eyes never left Kai. "I shall accompany you, guests of residents are required to have an escort. I'm sure you understand."

Kai blew air from their nose and gave their hair a gentle toss. "If you must, but please, don't dawdle."

The gate was opened and the pair, followed closely by the guard, made their way across the bridge to the Island District.

Compared to Belgar, Tal's hometown of Rothwood was little more than a few wooden huts in the forest. Compared to the Island District, she may as well have been living in a bog.

Each home they passed was a manor, towering into the sky. Beautiful gardens locked behind spiked iron fences and personal guards standing by each gate. It even felt like the cobblestone street had been dusted, not a leaf or piece of gravel in sight. Tal felt she could have worked her entire lifetime, which to most other races was a considerable number of centuries, and not come close to the wealth that she was walking past this evening.

That thought alone was unsettling, add the guard not five feet behind them and Tal's nerves were rattling. She could feel the anxious sweat on the back of her neck and brow as her mind jumped from scenario to scenario for what would happen when it turned out Kai had lied their way into this place. Could she feign innocence? Say she's been coerced or kidnapped? Threatened and held against her will? Tal began to turn to see if they were still being followed.

"Don't look back," Kai whispered sharply. "Just act like you belong. That means not paying attention to people that work for a living."

Tal took a deep breath, steadying herself and tried to follow Kai's lead.

Making their way confidently down the streets, Kai stopped at the gate of a tall slender manor. "Wonderful, thank you for your company, good sir, you may return to your post." Kai waved off the guard.

"Not quite yet, if you don't mind." It didn't sound much like they had much choice in the matter as the guard stepped up to the cast iron gate and pulled the chain that hung to the side. A series of bells rang in a multitude of notes, dark and melodic, Tal wondered if the tune had been composed by someone intentionally.

The door to the manor opened and a finely dressed balding man walked slowly towards the gate. "May I be of assistance?" he spoke with an accent Tal didn't recognise as he eyed the three figures standing before him with the look of a man who had been disturbed against his will.

"Begging your pardon," the guard began, but Kai stepped up, forcing theirself in front of the guard.

"Kaivel Mortzeel and the lady Tal'avera for Lord Uth'ill, if you please." Kai smiled politely, avoiding the angered look from the guard.

The balding man gave a bewildered look. "I shall see if his lordship is expecting you. One moment." Without another word he turned on his heel and walked slowly back towards the house. The minutes seemed to stretch on and Tal's nerves working their way into her joints. She could feel the blood draining from her body and filling her legs as her knees started to shake.

It didn't help that the guard was resting his hand quite comfortably on the hilt of his sword, eyeing Kai with an intensity, ready for any slight movement.

Just as Tal felt her heart was about to rupture with the stress, the door to the manor opened once again, and the balding man approached.

"Lord Uth'ill welcomes you, Master Mortzeel and Lady Tal'avera." He opened the gate and gestured for the two of them to enter.

Kai gave a gentle yet cocky nod to the guard as they stepped through the gate and made their way to the house. Tal's heart once again collapsed inside her chest as relief washed through her and the blood returned to her body.

Inside the manor, the door closed behind them, Tal's jaw hung in wonder at the beautiful decor of the entrance hall. Blue flamed candles danced in ornate candelabras. Deep silks draped the shuttered windows, and beautiful paintings hung from the walls. Having never been inside a noble's home before, Tal didn't know what to expect, but she was certainly not disappointed.

"This way, if you please." The bald man, who Tal suspected was the butler, though she could not be sure, directed them towards a pair of large double doors, which he opened and guided them through.

"Kaivel, Kaivel, Kaivel, what an unexpected pleasure." A cheerful voice, with the same accent as the butler, greeted them from behind a tall armchair before a blue-flame fireplace. "And through the front door this time, how times have changed."

The elven figure rose and approached them, his short silver hair and golden eyes contrasting with his midnight blue skin. Standing before Kai and Tal, for the first time in her life, was a drow.

Chapter 13

Lord Drascus Uth'ill turned out to be quite the gracious host, even if that had not been part of his evening plans. After introductions and accepting the bottle of wine, which he seemed surprised more by the vintage than the gift itself, their host sent his butler, Leejoy, to prepare the dining room for his guests.

Then came a tour, which left Tal speechless. Every room in the manor was dimly lit with the blue arcane flames that flared to life when they entered a room. Lord Uth'ill, though he insisted she call him Drascus, explained the reason for such flames was twofold. Firstly they helped to illuminate their home while not afflicting his natural sensitivity to bright light, a trait of the drow. Secondly it meant no candles went to waste if he forgot to extinguish them.

Although dimly lit, each room was decorated to compliment the lack of light. Soft furnishings with shimmering silk throws and polished hardwoods helped to disperse what little light was available, but also gave the rooms a cosy relaxing feel. The sheer size of the manor was what impressed Tal the most. The grandeur she'd expected, even the expensive art and furnishings, but that Lord Uth'ill lived here alone with his staff was really what she found unbelievable.

"It's true," Drascus sighed at Tal when she questioned his living situation. Leading them upstairs to the final floor he continued, "for all my successes it seems my life is not one that was meant to be shared."

"I'm sorry," Tal didn't know what she was apologising for, but the compulsion came nevertheless. She did feel rather embarrassed at putting their host on the spot in such a way, but the thought had come to her lips before she'd realised.

Drascus waved the sympathy away. "Please, it's been many years and I'm quite happy with my life the way it is." Opening the double door at the top of the stairway corridor he gestured into the room. "And finally, my personal study, and the room where I met young Kaivel."

Unlike the other rooms in the manor, the study was not illuminated by arcane candles, instead the ceiling and west facing wall were made up of triangular window frames with glass of varying thickness creating a disjointed and magnified mosaic of the evening's sky. The remaining walls held shelves with all manner of rock, stone, and crystal. A large table covered in maps of regions Tal didn't recognise, sketches of tools and mechanisms that she found fascinating.

Drascus stayed in the doorway, using his hand to shield his eyes from the last rays of the setting sun. "Usually I don't come up here until much later. Since moving to this city I've become somewhat nocturnal."

"It's a beautiful office." Tal had wandered inside and was spinning around like a child taking in wonders for the first time.

A small bell rang above the doorway and Drascus clapped his hands together. "And it seems dinner is served. Come now, I'm sure you're both starving and if you're not, I am."

Leading them back down the winding staircase to the ground floor, Drascus took them into a long dining hall, which could have easily seated twenty to thirty people. A grand chandelier hung above the ornate mahogany table laid with elegant silverware. This was all wonderful, but what really had Tal's attention, and what made her realise how hungry she was, were the plates laden with food.

Evidently Lord Uth'ill didn't do things by the half measure. The plates were piled with roasted vegetables, steamed rolls, fresh salads, and various grains.

"I do hope you enjoy," Drascus smiled at the two of them, "and I hope you don't mind. I don't eat meat, save for special celebrations."

The three of them occupied just one end of the long dining table, making the room feel quite empty. A small chuckle echoed in Tal's mind as she imagined the three of them spread out across its length.

"This is delightful, thank you." Tal tried to control herself as she spooned polite portions onto her plate, when inside her stomach told her to dive in face first.

"Yes," Kai gave a cheeky smirk, "though it's nice to know my visiting doesn't count as a special occasion."

Drascus laughed, covering his mouth just a second too late as a grain of rice flew from his lips. "Well the fact that you used the front door this time is something we should commemorate."

"If you don't mind my asking," Tal fought the compulsion to raise her hand, "but that's the second time you've mentioned Kai using the front door. How do they usually enter?"

Still chuckling as he dabbed his mouth with a serviette, Drascus looked over to Kai. "I see you haven't told your friend how we met, have you?"

Kai was in the process of breaking up pieces of jerky and mixing them into their salad. "I mentioned you in passing." When Tal raised an eyebrow Kai continued. "You remember. Broke into the wrong home. Did a favour instead of rotting in a cell. That's basically it." They smiled as they chewed their meaty salad.

Drascus chucked. "That is basically it, and the ocean is basically a puddle." He rolled his eyes and cleared his throat. "As I said before, I met a young Kaivel in my office, going through the designs of one of my new mechanisms." Drascus rested his chin on tented fingers. "One of my competitors had hired Kaivel's former employer, who in turn sent Kaivel, to steal the designs so that they might build it before I could."

"How in the heavens did you manage that?" Tal's mouth was agape. Having seen the number of guards casually strolling this district, and the fact that it was an island was quite impressive.

Kai merely shrugged as they stabbed at some rice with a fork. "I was very good at my job."

"Not good enough, fortunately." Drascus chuckled. "You weren't expecting anyone to be awake at that hour of the night." He leaned back in his chair. "So that night, Kaivel and I made a deal."

"What was the deal?" Tal felt like a child at story time. If she'd been any closer to the edge of her seat she'd have been sitting on the table.

"I gave Kaivel the designs for my new mechanism, slightly altered of course, to take back to my competitor. Kaivel in turn, would steal something for me."

"Still have no idea what those were," Kai helped themselves to a heavily buttered corn-cob.

"That's not the point though," Drascus smirked. "The point was they needed those designs to complete a contract, and my designs to keep me out of business." The drow took a sip of wine, screwing his nose up at the taste. "I believe that the wine you brought has been corked. Such a pity." He pushed the glass aside with a disappointed sigh. "Anyway, I'm not normally one to play dirty, but I also won't stand for being cheated."

"And here we are today," Kaivel raised their glass in the air. "Now if you'll excuse me I must use the little tiefling's room." With a polite bow to both Tal and Drascus Kai slipped out of the room, leaving the two of them alone in awkward silence.

It was usually in these situations when Tal would stare at her plate or make a poor attempt at small talk, but questions were busy fighting their way to the tip of her tongue.

"What is it?" Drascus's eyes were locked in on her. "I can tell there's something brewing behind those eyes. So tell me, what is it?"

Tal cleared her throat. "I was just curious, when you found Kai, erm, Kaivel, breaking into your home, why didn't you just call the guards? Why hire them and then pay them enough to be free of a thieves guild?"

Drascus leaned back in his chair, taking a breath as he reached for his wine glass. "I suppose because I knew how it was to be in their position." He lifted the glass to his lips, then quickly lowered it as the memory of the taste came back.

"You used to be a thief?" Tal's expression of surprise brought a laugh out of their host.

"Heavens no," Drascus said once the chuckles had subsided, "I used to be a miner, a long time ago. What I mean is..." He sighed as he leaned forward again, elbows on the table and fingers tented towards Tal. "I'm a drow, I'm sure you noticed, your expression certainly said so."

Tal blushed. "I'm so sorry, I didn't mean-"

Drascus waved her off. "No need to apologise. It's not the first time and it won't be the last. But that is what I mean." He relaxed back a little. "I am a drow. Kaivel is a tiefling. Two peoples you do not often see on this continent. One of many things we have in common that also makes us nothing alike.

"People have done, and will continue, to see what we are before who we are. And why? Because that is nature. What Kaivel and I have in common is that millenia ago our ancestors made some choices. Kaivel's ancestors made a deal, or a bet, or a commitment to a devil, demon, or fiend. Thus they were born with red skin, horns, and a tail."

Drascus gestured to himself. "My ancestors would have been close to yours. Then one of them chose to place their faith in a spider-goddess and now my skin is blue and I can't see in the daylight."

Tal hadn't realised her mouth was hanging open, or she would have closed it.

"The point is, neither Kaivel nor I had anything to do with it, yet here we are, dealing with the consequences of someone else's decision." Drascus smiled at Tal. "I chose to believe that Kaivel could be more than what was expected of them." He sighed at the memories passing through his mind. "And I was right." He reached for his wine again before quickly putting it down, scowling at himself for the compulsion.

Tal took a moment to digest Drascus's words. It was true. So often people were expected to live up to their stereotypes that they almost had no other option.

"Let's not get the evening down with such serious conversation though," Drascus rang a small brass bell that was resting on the table and seconds later Leeroy appeared through the doorway. "Please could you fetch us another bottle of wine, Leeroy?"

Without a word Leeroy gave a gentle bow and returned through the door he came from.

"Tell me how you came to be stuck with our horned friend." Drascus once again relaxed back into his chair, still holding the foul-tasting glass of wine but keeping it a safe distance from his lips.

With a deep breath and a heavy exhale Tal recited, once again, her experience of coming to Belgar, losing her hand and belongings, meeting Kaivel, and the cliff notes of their investigation together. All the while Drascus sat silently, nodding along, his eyebrows shifting from curious to sympathetic, then to surprise and delight.

"That is quite the adventure in your short time here," Druscus said when Tal had concluded her tale.

Leeroy had returned during the story with a new bottle of wine and had served the two of them. The butler appeared completely unmoved by what little he heard before returning to what Tal suspected was his storage cupboard.

"Thank you," Tal sipped her wine. Fruity and soft, just what her throat needed after all that talking. "If you don't mind my asking as well, you said before you were a miner. How does someone go from working in a mine to all of this?" She gestured to the grandeur of the room.

Drascus swirled his wine and smiled at Tal. "Laziness," he said quite simply. "I was and still am an incredibly lazy person. Working in mines requires a lot of physical effort. So I designed devices to make the work easier. My devices turned out to not only be useful, but surprisingly popular. Now they're used in almost every mine on the continent and have been for the last seventy-odd years." Drascus was so casual about the whole thing that Tal felt almost embarrassed for being impressed.

The door swung open again and Kai strolled back into the room.

"Not having too much fun without me I hope?" They chuckled as they took their seat.

"To be honest I had forgotten you were here. Tal'avera is such good company." Drascus winked at Tal with a smirk. "What took you so long? I hope the meal didn't disagree with you."

"It does," Kai said with a shrug, "but only for the lack of meat. No, I was looking for a bathroom I hadn't used before." Kai poured theirself a fresh glass from the new bottle at the table.

"Did you manage to find one?" Drascus asked.

A broad smile crept across Kai's face. "I believe so, but there were a number of robes hanging in there."

Tal screwed her nose up at the thought of Kai fouling one of Drascus's cloak rooms. "Please tell me you're joking."

Kai grinned. "Okay, I'm joking."

Drascus just chuckled at the two of them. "So tell me, as I doubt you were merely seeking my company tonight, what is it that brought you to my door?"

Kai threw back their head, downing the wine in their glass. "I was hoping you could tell us anything you know about the Vaskar family out of Vallameria."

Again Drascus leaned forward, resting his chin on a fisted hand. "This has something to do with your work, I take it?" He waved a hand towards Tal. "Tal'avera mentioned you're investigating a murder." His eyes glittered with sudden excitement. "Has the boy been getting up to mischief?"

"Possibly. He's either been murdered or faked his own death." Kai said it with such nonchalance it could have been simple gossip, which is something Drascus appeared to be in search of.

"Oh, well that is interesting." Drascus took up his glass of wine once more. "What do you want to know?"

"Anything you could tell us would be helpful," Tal smiled across the table. "We don't really know anything about the family or Patrice."

Drascus flicked his tongue against his teeth, still smiling as the wine glass swung between his fingers. "The Vaskar family are what you might call 'Old Coin'. One of the oldest families in the country, and one of many who claim to be direct descendants of the Nine."

"Is that true?" Tal burst out. During her time in Master Brum's library she'd read many tales of the Nine, the heroes who saved the world from the Lords of Ash. Her master had never approved of those volumes though, calling them drivel and outrageous over dramatic lies that give youngsters delusions of the adventurer's life. But Tal didn't care, she enjoyed them just the same.

"Who knows and who cares?" Drascus puffed at Tal's question. "Adventures in those days. If they couldn't mount it above or in their beds they didn't care for it. Hells, you two could be descendants for all it's worth." He took a moment to wet his palate. "The point is they do nothing. They provide no service nor contribute to society. Just collect the coin that comes rolling in from whatever land their forefathers purchased for a pittance in days far gone." The expression on the drow's face made his feelings on such nobles very clear.

A moment of silence passed, interrupted only by the sound of Kai chewing.

"But I digress," a smile returned to Drascus's face. "From what I do know of them the family is well connected within the temple of Maival. Martice Vaskar is a rather…" Drascus felt around in the air as he searched for the right word, "direct person. Never says more than one or two words, and never shows interest in the lives of others.

"His wife, by great contrast, Lady Astrid Vaskar, is a delight. She almost makes up for being stuck in her husband's company." Drascus took a sip of wine. "As for their children I know very little. Patrice is the youngest of four, and the third son, so unlikely to be reaping the benefits of his father's fortune. Which is probably why he turned to adventuring."

Kai had taken out their roll of parchment and pen, making notes and nodding along as they did.

With a sigh Drascus threw his arms wide and shrugged, a few drops of wine splashing across the marble floor. "Sadly I don't think any of that is of much help, but if I hear anything down the grape vine I shall be sure to pass it along."

Kai rolled up their parchment and stuffed it back into their satchel. "You've been helpful in a way," they smiled at Drascus. "Now we know Patrice had nothing really to gain from faking his death."

"Unless he wanted a clean start?" Tal suggested, causing Kai's smile to drop as they hadn't considered that point of view.

"Other than that, yes…" Kai sighed. "I'd say it's unlikely though. There are far easier ways to make a break from your former life."

Tal raised an eyebrow but held her tongue. Kai normally spoke in a rather nonchalant tone, but that comment felt far more personal than she thought Kai would have intended. Although she had only been with them a few days Tal already felt as if the two of them had been friends for a long time. Nights like tonight reminded her how little she knew about Kai.

With his glass raised Drascus stood up from the table and looked down to Kai and Tal. "Well my friends, both new and old, I wish you luck in your investigation."

After the spontaneous toast the three continued with the meal, Drascus pushing for more details from the investigation and other news from the city. Evidently the drow lord didn't get out much apart from seasonal events and the occasional party thrown by the other lords in the district.

Much wine was consumed. Much jerky was sprinkled across salads. All in all a pleasant evening was had, and as the impromptu dinner drew to a close Drascus walked his guests towards the door.

"It is always such a pleasure when you drop by Kaivel," Drascus embraced his tiefling friend, "and a wonderful surprise to see you using the front door!"

"I'll try not to make a habit of it," Kai smirked as they patted the drow on the shoulder.

"Please do." Drascus turned to Tal. "And you my dear are welcome anytime." He gave Tal a strong hug, lifting her onto her toes. "You can leave the riff-raff at home next time."

Tal chuckled as Kai stuck their tongue out at the two of them. "Thank you Drascus, but they are so entertaining." She turned and winked at Kai. "Maybe next time we can go for a stroll in the moonlight?"

"Uh!" Drascus nearly swooned at the suggestion. "Kaivel wherever you found her you need to go back and find one for me!" He took Tal's hand and kissed it gently. "Thank you my dear, that sounds delightful."

A few more goodbyes and promises to do this again soon and Kaivel and Tal'avera were out the door into the cool night air.

The two walked back in relaxed silence, being joined by a guard as they stepped into the main street. The stoic armoured man escorted them at a distance back to the bridge where they were allowed to cross back into the city proper and left to fend for themselves.

"So what's the plan?" Tal asked once she was sure they were alone. With the aid of the wine she had fully slipped into the guise of a couple, her arm still looped in Kai's and her head resting on their shoulder as they walked.

"I think," Kai said in a firm measured tone, also still enjoying the guise of a stuck-up noble, "that we should head back to the Den, and see if Tess has any wine."

Chapter 14

There were a few things Tal'avera expected that morning. The headache that came from consuming too much wine was expected. Missing the door handle because she'd forgotten about her missing hand was expected, and had become almost a ritual. Tess hiding her book the moment Tal appeared at the bottom of the stairs was expected.

What was not expected was the thundering storm that had overcast the city and began flooding the streets.

As for things that were unappreciated, Kaivel insisting that they went to the Hall of Justice to question Kirtan and Galen was definitely top of her list.

Wrapped up in a cloak borrowed from Tess, making it far too large for Tal's slight frame, she followed behind Kai through the heavy downpour and into the city.

Kai was relatively unbothered by the sudden storm, the rain splashing off their suit and soaking their hair. They simply carried on as if today was just another normal day and their boots weren't slowly filling with water.

Much to Tal's indignation, the Hall of Justice stood north of the docks overlooking the ocean, where the waves crashed against the high walls added to the flooding of the street.

"Why couldn't we stay in the tavern until the storm passed!" Tal cried into the air as a wave broke against the wall as she passed, spraying saltwater across her face. "And why did you go this way!"

Kai turned to face her, their hair matted against their face and neck making them look like a drowned rat with horns. "This is the shortest route." They shrugged. "I thought you'd want to be out of the rain sooner."

"I wanted to stay inside!" Tal shouted back, a roll of thunder echoing behind her for well-timed emphasis.

An infuriatingly casual shrug was Kai's response. "You didn't have to come with me. I've got work to do."

There was nothing Tal could say to that. She didn't technically work for Kai so there was nothing but her own stubborn curiosity forcing her out into this weather. She really did only have herself to blame for her discomfort. But yelling at herself wouldn't help, so yelling at Kai would have to do.

The Hall of Justice definitely stood out amongst the other buildings Tal had seen in the city. More of a thick tower, its tall arches topped by weather worn gargoyles and decorative stonework that had seen better days. This was possibly, at least based on what Tal had seen thus far, the oldest building in the city. Though whether or not that was true, it was definitely in need of some restoration.

Pushing open the high wooden doors, the looks the pair received from the guards inside the Hall of Justice were exactly what you would have expected. Surprise mixed with amusement.

"Wet out?" one guard snorted at the two of them as they squelched into the building.

Kai blinked flatly, their face an expressionless mask. "No, why do you ask?" They continued walking as the guard's jaw flapped with no witty response available.

In contrast to the outside, the interior of the building was beautifully done. Tall columns rose up to the ceiling, where a mural of Kalborn, the blind God of Justice and Wisdom, looked down upon the guards and clerks. Standing between the columns were statues of the Dukes and Duchesses of Belgar.

Approaching the high marble counter where the clerk sat organising papers, Kai very loudly cleared their throat as they dripped a puddle around their feet.

"Can I...help you?" the clerk leaned over the edge of the table, looking down with disapproval at the two sopping wet figures before him.

Kai beamed up at the pinched face before them, wiping their wet hair from their face. "Yes, we're here to see Sergeant D'Clos. Tell him it's Kaivel here to speak with the two men linked to the Vaskar murder."

The clerk sat back, turning a page in a logbook that sat on the side of his table. "Sergeant D'Clos is not here," he said, tapping the book. "I believe he is at the central guard house."

"Oh I know where that is," Tal smiled. She had been hoping to return there, she wanted to return the clothes loaned to her and payback the coin the guard had lent her.

"Good for you," the clerk didn't attempt to hide their lack of interest. He shifted though some papers before finding what he was looking for and tapping his finger against the page. "He has however left a note that you should be cleared to interrogate the two prisoners." The clerk waved over one of the guards. "I'll have Roger escort you."

Feeling very out of place Tal raised her hand, evoking a puzzled look for the clerk. "Can you give us a minute?" She pulled out her spellbook, shaking rain water from its cover, and handed it to Kai. "Hold this."

Kai held out their hands and Tal placed the book across their palms, using Kai like a tiefling podium. She flicked to the page she needed and began casting. Within seconds the water soaked into Tal's clothes and hair was swept from her body, pooling at her feet, leaving her perfectly dry and clean.

"Now I really don't know why you were complaining." Kai smirked at her. "Can you do me now?"

"Yes, I could." Tal smirked back as she closed the book and tucked it away again. "We're ready," she looked up to the clerk.

Roger, the guard who had been summoned as their guide, led the two of them through a series of gates and staircases to the holding cells, Kai's soggy feet slapping down all the way as Tal followed behind. She did feel a little bad about leaving Kai so damp, but it was also kind of funny.

The path to the holding cells was certainly designed to be as confusing as possible. They took several turns, travelled up and down different staircases, each with a heavy iron gate blocking the way. If it weren't for their guide Tal was certain they'd be trapped down here.

"Gods, this is going on forever." Tal huffed as they walked up yet another flight of steps, her thighs now beginning to burn.

"Mmm…" was all the response that came from Kai.

Tal huffed at them. "Not grumpy about being wet are you?" She really didn't think it would have upset them so much.

"Mmm…." Kai said again.

It suddenly caught Tal's eyes that Kai had their hand inside their satchel, and their wrist was moving around with precision.

"What are you doing?" she leaned forward to ask.

"Shh!" Kai shot a glance at her. "I'm taking notes…"

"Notes about what?" Tal's eyes widened as things clicked into place. "Are you drawing a map?" She covered her mouth just a fraction too late, the look on Kai's face telling her that shutting up was recommended.

Coming to another large iron gate their escort, Roger, took out a set of thick keys and unlocked it. "They are through here, shout if you need anything."

"Much obliged," Kai gave the man a nod and continued through the gate, Tal following suit.

They entered a long corridor lined with cells, only some of which were empty. Miserable faces looked up at them briefly as they walked past. Only two faces looked at them with surprise.

"Oh here we go," Galen spat as he sat up from the suspended wooden plank that was his bed.

Kirtan just sat and stared, his jaw hanging loose. The two looked far less threatening now, their armour and weapons stripped away and replaced with ill-fitting garments made of old hessian.

"Good morning boys," Kai beamed at them. "And how are we feeling today?"

Galen grunted. "Better than you from the looks of it. Someone finally try to drown you?"

"I'll fix that…" Tal said as she dropped to her knees and opened up her book.

"Just a lovely stroll in the rain," Kai smiled as the water was swept from them. "And now good as new. Thanks," they winked to Tal.

"What do you want?" Galen hopped down from the plank and approached the bars. "Just here to make our lives miserable?"

"No, no. You don't need my help with that." Kai pulled a piece of jerky from their bag. "Hungry?"

"Get lost!" Galen spat at Kai.

Wiping the spittle from their thigh the tiefling looked to Kirtan, unphased by Galen. "What about you? Care for a bite?"

Kirtan winced as he shifted against the wall, his arm pressed against his waist where the crossbow bolt had pierced him. "I'll pass if it's all the same."

"It is," Kai took a bite theirself. "As for why I'm here, I believe we can help each other out."

Galen scoffed. "And why the hell should we help you? You're the reason we're here!" The little halfling kicked the bar, grunting as he limped a step back, now regretting the action.

"Because the four of us are the only people in the world who know you're not murderers," Kai almost whispered it, looking back and forth down the corridor.

Kirtan's eyes widened. "If you know then get us out of here. Tell the guards this was just a misunderstanding."

"But then I'd have nothing to bargain with." Kai leaned against the bars, acting far too casually for the conversation or location. "How about it? You scratch my back, I'll scratch yours."

"I'll do more than scratch your back when I'm out of this place!" Galen paced and limped, looking eager for a flight. "I'll pull your tail until I rip your spine out, filthy devil-spawn!"

Kai blinked at him, lips pursed in genuine thought. "I'm not entirely sure that they're connected..." they curled their tail up and held it in their hand. "You've given me something to think about."

Galen climbed back up onto the plank, muttering in halfling.

"What have you got to lose?" Tal remained kneeling, but tilted her head to catch Kirtan's eye. Galen was a lost cause in her mind, anyone who threw a dagger at her deserved to be locked up. But Kirtan was just a victim of circumstance, pulled in too deep by someone he thought was his friend.

Shifting uncomfortably again, the expression on his face betraying the pain moving caused him, Kirtan gave in. "What do you want from us?"

"Everything," Kai said, a serious expression fixing on their face. "I want to know everything you know about Patrice Vaskar."

There was a look of confusion on the faces of the two incarcerated men, though Galen's face remained more suspicious.

"What do you want to know about him for?" Kirtan shifted to a more comfortable, or at least less painful, position.

Kai merely shrugged. "A passing interest, this whole thing has me curious. If you've got nothing then I'll happily wish you well and see you at the execution."

Tal tried to hide the shock that rippled up her spine. For such a charming friendly face, the cold casualness of Kai's threat was unexpected.

"What's your angle, huh?" Galen's eyes narrowed in on Kai. "Why would you offer to get us out of here after you put us in? This all smells like a stable on a summer's day."

"I never said I'd get you out little one," Kai levelled a dark stare at the halfling, "you attacked the guards and tried to murder three people in front of them. You're screwed." They turned back to Kirtan. "But you, however, I can help."

Galen spat a few more halfling curses in Kai's direction, laying back on his plank of a bed.

Kirtan swallowed hard. "I can't say I knew him well," the half-elf began, his eyes twitching from Kai to the floor. "I mean we was friends I guess, but he never really talked about anything."

A fresh piece of parchment rolled out, Kai squiggled in the corner with their pen to get the ink flowing. "What did he talk about? I can't imagine he was silent the whole time."

Kirtan chuckled and flinched. "Nah, he weren't the silent type. He was always going on about the next job, the hunt. He was in it for the thrills, you know?" He sighed, the memories of his friend flooding back. "And it weren't about the money neither. He didn't give a rat's about that. He was always paying for stuff for us lot, even when we told him not to."

"He was a flash prick showing off how rich he was." Galen growled without looking. "He didn't care about the money because he didn't need it. It was just pocket coin to his lot."

Kirtan barked back. "No he weren't! He did good by us."

Kai ignored Galen's outburst. "Did you do anything together that wasn't a job for the guild? Besides visiting the Dryad that is."

"Yeah, we did a few things." Kirtan scratched his beard as he thought back. "We gambled in the odd card game. Or bet on the fights at the Stonejaw tavern. Though to be honest Patrice preferred taking part in them to betting on them."

Galen laughed. "Yeah, I always liked watching him get his pretty face kicked in."

"He won more than he lost!" Kirtan jumped to the defence of his friend. "And when we lost betting on him he covered us, said it was his fault for not trying hard enough."

Kai's pen was dancing across the parchment. "Seems like he liked getting into scraps. You know if any of his fights spilled outside the pits?"

"Not that I saw." A thought came to Kirtan's mind, his face screwing up. "Some nights he went on his own though. One night he came back looking like an owlbear had stormed over him though. He didn't say nothing about it though, just held up this little pin and told us he was going to be the champion."

"This pin, what did it look like?" Kai turned the parchment over.

"Just this little gold pin thing," Kirtan held his thumb and forefinger up, "with a bobble about the size of a gold piece at one end, just kinda strange. Can't rightly remember it that well, and he didn't go showing it around to people."

"Was he trying to hide it?" Tal asked. She didn't have any parchment to take notes, and she certainly wasn't going to use a page from her spellbook, but she had questions all the same.

"I dunno," Kirtan shrugged slowly, "maybe? He didn't wear it or nothing. Think that's the only time I ever saw it or he mentioned it."

Kai jotted down some notes. "And did he take part in any fights after that?"

Kirtan just shook his head.

"A week later and he's going mouldy and we're in here." Galen added, still staring at the ceiling.

"Going...mouldy..." Kai said out loud as they made a final note. "That's charming." They rolled up the parchment and stuffed it and the pen back into their satchel. "Anything you'd like to ask?"

It was the first time Kai had asked Tal for her input, and it took a few seconds for her to realise they were talking to her. "Oh!" Tal cleared her throat, feeling flustered at being put on the spot. "The only real question I have is...why? Why steal your friend's sword and then hire Kaivel to find it?"

Kirtan opened his mouth to speak, but Galen swung down from the plank and stormed up to the bars. "They were going to bury him with it!" It was a shout of anger as well as disbelief. "That's what nobles do, they get buried with their swords. That blade is worth more coin than the hut I grew up in, and they were going to stick it in the ground!" Galen spat at Kai's feet. "If we'd just been able to shift it we'd have been set!"

"Then why hire someone to find it?" Tal repeated. For the first time she actually felt bad for Galen. She'd not grown up with much herself, but she couldn't imagine going to the lengths those two had.

"That was Samara's idea," Kirtan said, "she wanted to get it back for him and it would have been pretty suspicious if we'd not gone along with it."

Galen grunted at the mention of Samara. "She was a fool, thinking it made a difference. She honestly thought that the son of a lord would have gone for a coinless wretch like her."

The hair on the back of Tal's neck bristled. "That's pretty harsh."

With a shrug and a grunt Galen turned his back to her. "The world's harsh, just got to do our best to stay alive."

Tal stood, a sour expression on her face. She knew the world could be harsh, but she felt staying alive wasn't the best that people could do. If anything, she wanted to do her best to leave the world in a better place.

"As always a pleasure talking to the two of you." Kai gave Tal's shoulder a squeeze. "Now we must be going, we've got a busy day ahead of us and I'm sure you do too."

Galen cursed under his breath as he went back to the plank again.

"Are you going to get us out of here then? That's what you said." The pleading in Kirtan's voice was almost heart-breaking, if you didn't know why he was in a cell that is.

Kai was already walking away, but they turned back briefly. "If what you told us turns out to be helpful, sure." They waved for Tal to follow and the two of them headed out the gate, where Roger was half asleep against the wall.

ॐ☉ॐ

After waking their guide, Kai and Tal were led back out through the maze of staircases, corridors, and gates until they emerged into the open foyer of the Hall of Justice.

"You've not got anything in that book of yours to keep us dry, have you?" Kai asked as they pushed open the door, seeing that the storm had not calmed during their time inside.

Tal just shook her head. "No, that's why I borrowed this cloak...And why I wanted to stay at the Den!"

Kai looked back out into the rain as a flash of light followed almost immediately by the roaring roll of thunder emphasised Tal's point. "Well looks like we're going to get wet. Come on, and try to keep up."

The pair dashed out into the street, the cobblestones slippery underfoot making the sprint rather comical for anyone who happened to be looking out of their window. Kai tried their hardest to stick to the alleyways, the buildings on either side of them giving some small degree of cover from the downpour. With all the twists and turns Tal was completely lost. She just hoped Kai knew where they were going.

Running back out into the main street Tal's foot slid straight out from under her and she began tumbling forward. Reaching out to the air, Kai's hand grabbed her by the stump and pulled her forward, yanking her off balance enough to counter the slip. They continued to hold on to her, dragging Tal along as they ran towards a building she recognised.

All eyes turned to the doors, and hands grabbed hilts as Kai and Tal burst into the central guardhouse. The moment of panic subsided as the two guards on duty watched the two of them panting and dripping in the entrance.

"Can we help you?" A voice Tal recognised called over to them.

Kai held up a hand. "Just a moment..." They reached up and pulled their hair pins free, letting their wet locks fall with a heavy slap. Coiling their hair up Kai began to wring it out like a towel, water splashing and puddling at their feet.

"You remember I can take care of that right?" Tal was already opening her spellbook.

Kai blinked at her. "Promise?"

"Just hold this and stand still." She sighed and began casting, once again drying herself and Kai as the guards watched on in bewilderment.

"Ah, much better." Kai rolled their hair back into place, fastening it with the pins. They approached the two guards at their booth, who were staring unhappily at the puddle Kai had left behind. "Now you can help us. We're looking for Sergeant D'Clos, is he in?"

"Yeah," the first guard replied, still looking past the two of them at the puddle on the floor, "what do you need with the Sarge?"

"Are you going to clean that up?" The second guard asked, a knowing frown on his face. The knowing being that if they weren't, he was going to have to.

"He should be expecting us," Kai smiled. "Kaivel Mortzeel and Tal'avera..." Kai stopped short and turned to face his elven friend. "You know I don't think you've ever told me your last name."

"And you haven't asked," Tal rolled her eyes and stepped forward. "Arcanist Tal'avera Liwood." She gave a soft curtsy.

The first guard nodded. "Alright, I'll see if Sarge is available. Micky, can you?" He nodded towards the puddle.

171

"Yeah…" Micky sighed and disappeared into the back with the other guard, appearing a moment later with a mop and bucket, and a sour expression on his face.

"Arcanist, eh?" Kai gave an impressed grin, their eyebrows raising in slight astonishment. "When did you get a fancy title?"

Tal's cheeks flushed. "Well technically I'm still a student, but if I say it enough people might start to believe it."

Kai nodded, the same impressed expression on their face. "A title and a last name all in one day, not bad."

The first guard returned. "The Sergeant is quite busy at the moment," he said with a scowl, "but he said he can spare a moment for you. Follow me." He gestured for them to follow and headed into the back once again.

As the pair followed Tal whispered over Kai's shoulder. "I thought you said he was expecting us?"

"Well," Kai whispered back with a smirk, "he always says to expect the unexpected. It's not my fault if he doesn't take his own advice."

The guard rapped against the oak door where a brass plate with 'Sergeant Aaran D'Clos' engraved into it.

"Enter," the Sergeant's deep voice called from within.

The guard ushered the two of them inside before closing the door behind them.

D'Clos' office was miraculously tidy. The wood clad walls were mostly bare, save for a large board which had a calendar and schedule pinned to it. On his simple desk sat two neat piles of parchment, one significantly larger than the other, and a small flowerpot which now held a variety of ink pens and quills. The most unusual thing about the office was the suit of armour that rested on its stand in the corner looking menacingly into the room. Then there was D'Clos himself, sitting quietly at his desk finishing off some last bit of paperwork. As his armour stood in the corner behind him, the Sergeant looked far less intimidating than the last time they'd met, dressed in a simple linen shirt and studded leather trousers.

D'Clos signed his name with a flourish at the bottom of the parchment and placed it on the smaller of his two piles, making Tal feel a great amount of pity for him.

"To what do I owe the pleasure of this visit, Kaivel?" D'Clos leaned back in his chair, folding his hands behind his head after gesturing to the two chairs in front of his desk.

"Nothing in particular," Kai joked as they and Tal took a seat, "we just missed your charming face."

The half-elf cracked a smile. "Well as much as I appreciate the flattery and the visit, I've got a mound of work to get through. So out with it."

"Patrice is gone." Kai said, cutting to the chase.

D'Clos nodded and took up the next piece of parchment from his stack. "I'm aware. That's why we arrested his murderers. It's a terrible shame and I'm sure the family will hold a ceremony for him, but that's got nothing more to do with me."

"No, he's gone. His body." Tal felt the need to clarify as she had a feeling Kai wouldn't. "We went to the temple yesterday to return his sword with Samara, the woman from the boathouse, and someone has taken his body."

The Sergeant pinched the bridge of his crooked nose, closing his eyes as he digested this new information. "If there is no body…" he began with a heavy breath.

"Then you can't prove the crime. Getting away with murder lesson one." Kai finished off. "The thing is, I don't think the two you've got locked up have anything to do with it."

"How so?" D'Clos raised an eyebrow.

Kai grinned and leaned back in their chair. "Call it a detective's intuition. There's no need for you to get involved, I just wanted to keep you in the loop."

The smile on D'Clos's face was very reluctant, but he nodded to Kai in agreement. "Thank you. I'll let you take care of this one then, last thing I need is another missing person."

Tal's ears twitched. "What do you mean 'another'?"

D'Clos slapped his hand down on the pile of parchments. "We've got over two-dozen missing persons reports in the last month.

Most of them from out of town so it's been a nightmare getting any information."

Kai and Tal looked at each other, a thought sparking between the two of them.

"We wouldn't be able to get a list of them, would we?" Kai asked as they pulled their own roll of parchment out of their satchel.

The Sergeant raised his other eyebrow this time. "Not got enough work on your plate?"

"We have, but this might be helpful to us." Kai nodded. "Besides, I've got an assistant now. We should have this solved in no time."

CHAPTER 15

I t took almost an hour for Sergeant D'Clos to gather all the information Kai requested. The names were easy, but then the tiefling detective asked for addresses, then their last known locations, then their occupations. In the end it probably would have been quicker just to hand over the files. All the while Tal sat staring out of the window at the storm that ravaged the city.

The rain battered against the glass and the dark clouds continued to roll and growl, illuminated only briefly by the odd flash of lightning somewhere in the distance. This sort of weather always made her arm ache, and her fingers gently caressed her stumped forearm, massaging the scar.

Normally she wouldn't notice the aching this much, her prosthetic keeping her warm and the mage hand making her forget her missing limb, but over these past few days she was becoming more and more aware of it.

"Right," D'Clos pushed a roll of parchments across the table to Kai, "that's everything I've got. You'll keep me up to date with anything you find?" The Sergeant's tone heavily implied that this wasn't always the case.

"Don't I always?" Kai's grin confirmed that it definitely wasn't always the case.

With a sigh and a smile D'Clos pushed himself up from the table, his joints popping and cracking as he stretched out. "I'll see you guys out, I've been sitting in this damn chair too long already."

Locking his office behind them, the Sergeant led the two of them down the hall. "Do you think there could be a connection?" he asked quietly as they walked.

175

Tal looked to Kai, if there was a connection she didn't see it, but a missing person was a missing person. Maybe Kai had been mistaken in their theory about Patrice's death.

"Seems unlikely," Kai replied, though their words carried less of the confidence they usually did. "We'll know more once we talk to a few more witnesses."

"How do you witness someone go missing?" Even as Tal asked the question she could hear how much it sounded like the opening to a bad joke.

D'Clos chimed in before Kai could make some witty remark. "The witnesses in this case are the ones who reported the missing persons. Not exactly helpful but we have little else to go on.

They emerged into the main entrance, where the two guards very quickly put on a show of looking busy. It was then that the notice board caught Tal's eye.

She'd seen it before on her first visit here, where the young lad was hanging wanted posters. Though now that she was less distracted with her own problems her eyes took in what was really in front of her.

Missing. Dozens of posters with the word 'missing' written above various sketches of people. She approached them, her eyes darting from face to crudely drawn face. "Oh my gods…"

"It is tragic." D'Clos said as he and Kai stepped up behind her. "You always hope you'll find them alive, but…" He gave a heavy sigh. "Even if we don't, as long as they're found their families can move on."

Kai patted Tal on the shoulder. "Come on, I know it's dry but we can't hang around here all day."

"I wish you both luck," D'Clos shook their hands. "And try to keep us informed. Even just a note on some parchment would be kind."

The Sergeant returned from whence he came, and Kai and Tal pushed open the door, rain splashing at their boots already.

"Here's the plan," Kai raised their voice over the howling of the wind, "I'll check out the people on this list." Kai tore a section of the scroll D'Clos had given them and handed it to Tal. "You head

176

to the adventure's lodge and check out these three. I'll meet you back at the Den later on. Okay?"

Since this plan involved the least amount of getting wet, Tal was as close to happy as she was going to get. She nodded and took the parchment, tucking it in between the pages of her book.

"One more thing...can I have the cloak?" They held out their hand with a wide grin. "You can use your spells to dry off whenever. Do you want me to catch a cold?" The grin quickly turned into a pathetically sad puppy face, complete with wide eyes and quivering lip.

"You're ridiculous, you know that?" Tal huffed as she gave in and removed the oversized cloak, thrusting it into Kai's arms with all the force she could muster.

"I've been told that before, yes." Kai billowed the cloak out as they wrapped it around theirself. "Ok, let's go!" Throwing the hood over their head Kai bolted out into the street, quickly disappearing behind the sheets of dark heavy rain.

Tal gritted her teeth and took a deep breath before doing the same, the doors of the guardhouse slamming shut behind her.

Tal's journey was not pleasant for many reasons. Firstly, and most obviously, was the vicious downpour that was assaulting the city and anyone foolish enough to be outside in such weather. Secondly, and possibly most embarrassingly, she did not know the way to the adventure's lodge. Yes she'd been there once before with Kai, but then they had come from the Phoenix Down. Now it was miserable and grey making one street look like another and the buildings look all blurry and the same

She eventually managed to get directions from the third unpleasant thing that happened to her.

As Tal rounded a corner leading only the gods knew where, a grocer rescuing their canopy from collapsing under the weight of its watery load heaved what felt like a small lake out of the bulging cloth just as Tal ran past. If there was any part of her that had remained dry this had certainly resolved that.

By way of apology the grocer directed her back the way she'd come towards the adventurer's lodge. It wasn't much of an apology mind you, but she'd take what she could get. So squelching with every step, feeling heavy and chilled to the bone, Tal retraced her steps back to the adventure's lodge.

The doors to the lodge swung open with such force that all heads turned and hands reached for nearby weapons as all eyes fell on the dripping elven woman, the thunder cracking behind her. There was a brief silence before chatter continued, people returning to their conversations and a few laughs came from the tables still looking over at her.

Tal huffed over to the counter where another elven woman sat staring at her over the thick rim of her glasses. Taking out her spellbook, wiping down the cover and silently thanking Master Brum for enchanting it against such marring, Tal began for the fourth time that day casting the water from her body. Dry she now was, but the chill in her bones could not be cured so quickly.

"Can I help you?" the nasal voice of the lodge's clerk finally addressed her, the thick glasses now resting tentatively on the tip of a thin pointy nose.

Tal was beginning to get fed up of hearing this question in the tone it was always being delivered. No one who asked 'can i help you' ever really sounded like they wanted to help. More like they wanted to know how they could get you to leave as soon as possible with as little disruption to their day as possible.

"Yes, hi, hello." Tal flustered for a moment, trying to gather her thoughts and stop her teeth from chattering. "I was hoping you could answer some questions for me? About some of the adventurers that have come through here."

The elven clerk rolled her eyes and sighed. "If you're with that meddlesome tiefling then you can tell them I don't know anything more about that Patrice kid, and sending someone else won't change that."

Tal flushed. Clearly Kai's brand of charm had left an impression. "I am with them, but this isn't about that. Well it is, but not just. I mean it might be, I'm not sure yet. But I'm here to find out if it is." The words just kept coming and Tal nearly bit her tongue to stop herself from continuing.

The clerk stared at her, sucking her teeth while she waited for the barrage of words to come to an end. "You must be new."

Tal nodded, brushing some hair over her long pierced ear. "Yes, I'm not really good at this, but hopefully it'll get easier."

Giving a wry smile, the clerk began speaking in elvish. "In all things, repetition is key."

Hearing her own language spoken washed away any anxiety Tal had been feeling. It brought her home to her village, to her parents. Though common was the language of the country, her parents always made sure to speak their own tongue at home. Tal smiled as the warm feeling washed through her.

"My thanks to you," Tal replied in kind, enjoying the feel of elven words on her tongue once again. "I am called Tal'avera, and I seek your aid with regards to a number of adventurers who may have come here. Have you the time?"

The clerk nodded gently, her glasses not shifting from their spot. "I am called Cherie, and if I can be of aid I shall. Whom are these adventurers that you seek?"

Tal unrolled the strip of parchment Kai had given her. "They are; Luther Ironpelt, Olifer Barkin, and Ellis Wanda. Any information you could provide would be of great interest."

Cherie scraped her chair back from her desk with a high-pitched squeal that made Tal's spine shiver. Taking out a tome and riffling through its pages, muttering to herself, until she found what she was looking for. Slapping the book shut and returning it to its shelf, the clerk moved to a cabinet full of scrolls, pulling three of them out without needing to examine their contents first.

"These are the ones you are looking for." Cherie handed the scrolls to Tal. "They became members of this lodge over the last two months. Though it has been some time since they, or any of their party, took a job from us."

179

Tal unrolled the scrolls. Cherie was clearly a very detail oriented person. Each scroll had the name of each member of the party, in beautiful calligraphy, along with the party's moniker, the date they joined, and jobs they had taken. As impressive as it was, it also added a disturbing notion to Tal's mind.

"You say that not one of these people have returned to the lodge? Were they perhaps on a job when they went missing?" Tal chewed her lip as she re-rolled the scrolls.

Taking them back one by one, Cherie shook her head. "No on both accounts. They had all recently completed jobs before their disappearance. This is not uncommon. Adventuring parties move on rather frequently, I doubt it is anything of concern."

As right as Cherie was, in regards to the migration habits of adventurers, Tal had a nagging feeling in her gut that this was most definitely something to be concerned about.

"My thanks to you, Cherie." Tal went to hold out her hand, then remembering it wasn't there opted for a nod of gratitude.

Cherie nodded back and pushed her glasses back up her thin nose. "You are most welcome, Tal'avera. If there is anything else that you need from me I shall be here."

With a smile Tal turned towards the door and sighed, knowing what was out there waiting for her.

"You don't have a cloak?" Cherie asked, switching back to common now that less official business was being discussed.

Tal shook her head. "I had one, but Kaivel borrowed it...said since I could dry myself with magic that they needed it more."

"Hmm." Cherie wrinkled her pointed nose, again having to reposition her glasses. "You're welcome to stay until the storm passes. I'm in need of a break anyway." She rose from behind her desk and Tal found herself almost craning her neck to meet the clerk's eye. Tal was by no means short, but Cherie stood head and shoulders above her. With her slender frame, simple beige work robe and angular features she resembled a pencil more and more.

After placing a small sign on her desk which read "gone to lunch" in five different languages one beneath the other, Cherie took her through to the main room of the lodge. It was loud and boisterous, with scrappy looking adventurers crowded around tables engaged in conversations or games of chance. Running along the far side stood a bar with a raised platform behind it, and a gnomish woman running back and forth pouring drinks.

"Two glasses of the Balcatin when you have a moment, Dorith." Cherie waved to the barmaid as she scurried passed. The clerk shifted a stool into place and sat down, her height not dropping by much. "Take a seat, you don't want to go near any of the tables, trust me."

Not wanting to know why, Tal quickly pulled her own stool out and sat, her height raising slightly. "Thank you. Is it always like this here?" she gestured to the rowdy crowd of adventurers behind them.

"Not always. Sometimes it gets noisy."

Tal couldn't tell if the flat expression on Cherie's face was meant to be sarcastic or honest.

"How did you come to work for Kaivel then? I've never known them to have a colleague before. You must be a skilled detective." Cherie held out her hand as Dorith the barmaid ran past and placed a glass filled with a deep crimson wine between her fingers, a second glass being placed in front of Tal before the gnome hurried off to serve a half-drunk half-orc.

"Well…" Tal took a sip of the very fruity wine, feeling the warmth of the alcohol run straight to her chilled bones, sending a shiver up her spine, and began to recite her story again.

As she spoke her mind began to wonder why it was people were so intrigued by her working with Kai, and what it was about the tiefling that drew such strong opinions from everyone she'd met. She couldn't believe it was simply Kai's fiendish heritage, the opinions were both good and indifferent, with the only aggressive opinion being that of Galen.

Throughout Tal's story Cherie sat quietly sipping her wine, only glancing at Tal's stump during the explanation of her lost hand.

"I was going to ask," the clerk said as she placed her empty glass to the side, apparently waiting for it to be refilled, "was it an accident or have you always had just the one?"

181

Tal chuckled. She'd never heard it put like that before, and most people who asked left the question hanging in the air, usually with a "how did you…?" or they just never asked. Cherie's direct personality was refreshing.

"Well it certainly wasn't intentional." Tal held up her arm, showing off the burn scar that sealed her wrist. "When you are told not to fool around with spell scrolls beyond your power, I'd advise listening."

Cherie just nodded in agreement. "A sage piece of advice for sure."

"So how is it working in a place like this? Do you see a lot of different people?" Tal waved to Dorith as she scuttled by, the gnome giving her a nod in response.

Cherie pushed her glasses up her nose, the light of the sconces shining up Tal's face. "I have been working here for nearly two decades. I have seen more faces than most people do in their lifetime."

"Wow, that is quite impressive. I guess you were right about parties moving on then, it's probably just my mind over reacting with everything that's happened to me the last few days." Tal took a sip from her refilled glass.

"What you need is some down time." Cherie gestured to the room of adventurers behind them. "These people, though crude and unwashed, spend their time risking their lives for adventure, fortune, and glory. That takes a toll on the body and the mind. Drinking, gambling, just passing out in an inn somewhere helps to calm the nerves. Hells, if they didn't they'd be jumping at shadows." Cherie turned her attention back to Tal, pointing a long thin finger between her eyes. "What you need is a hobby. What did you do for fun before you came to this city?"

Tal thought for a moment, chewing her lip. All she'd ever done, even as a child, was study magic. She'd once seen an illusionist who was passing through her town put on a show for the locals in exchange for whatever coin they could offer. From that day she'd been obsessed. It was only after meeting Master Brum that she'd learned about the various schools of magic that were available.

182

But that was it. Studying. Tal's cheeks grew hot as she didn't want to admit what a colossal bookworm she was.

Cherie sighed. "I knit."

This didn't surprise Tal one bit. Cherie definitely looked like the type of person who knitted. "Well when this is over, my next job is to find a hobby I guess."

"Then to your quick success." Cherie held up her glass in a toast. Tal smiled, tapping her glass against Cherie's with a satisfying 'ching'. Wiping a droplet from the corner of her mouth Tal suddenly remembered something that Kirtan had said in the Hall of Justice. "Does 'the champion' mean anything to you?"

The elven clerk's brow furrowed. "Yes...strange that you should be mentioning it. You're not the adventuring type."

"What do you mean by that?" Tal suddenly wished she had her own pad of parchment and something to write with like Kai. She added that to her mental to-do list. Get parchments and an ink pen, find a hobby. A short list but she had to start somewhere.

Again Cherie gestured to the riot going on behind them. "I've heard the word here over the past few weeks. I never thought much of it. Does it mean something to you?"

"Not yet. If you hear it again from anyone, would you let me know? It might be connected to the investigation with Kaivel."

"I'll do what I can." Cherie pushed her glass away. "But for now I must return to my desk." Standing up and patting down her dress for wrinkles she held out her left hand to Tal, and in elven said. "It has been a pleasure meeting you, Tal'avera. Fare well and far."

Tal smiled and shook her hand, replying in kind. "It has been a pleasure meeting you, Cherie. Fare well and far."

Tal finished her glass, stepping carefully up from her stool as she felt her head wobble. In her first week in Belgar she had drunk more than the rest of her life combined. The warmth that still clung to her stomach though helped as she prepared to face the storm outside. Wrapping her arms around her waist and taking a few deep breaths, Tal stepped outside once again.

᷂⊙᷊

183

"You look terrible." Tess looked as sympathetic as she sounded. "Did you lose my cloak?"

Tal slapped her book down on the bar, dripping onto the floorboards as she gave the troll-orc tavernkeep a miserable look. "Kai took it. Are they back yet?"

Tess shook her head. "Not seen them since the two of you left this morning."

Tal finished casting and sat her dry self down at the bar, slumping forward with a heavy groan. Running her hand through her hair, pushing it back from her face as she looked up at Tess. "Am I boring?"

A belt of laughter exploded from Tess's throat. "Where did that come from?"

Tal sat up. "I was talking to the clerk at the adventurers lodge, and she asked what I do for fun." The red returned to Tal's cheeks. "And I couldn't think of anything. Not a thing. Does that make me boring?"

Tess whistled as she put away mugs. "Nothing? Seriously?"

Tal shook her head. "All my life I've just learned spellcasting. Then I did odd jobs in my village. And then I came here looking to find work as an enchanter. My whole life has been about magic."

"That's a passion." Tess pulled an empty barrel out from the wall. "Passionate people can't be boring. A little one track sure, and yeah that can be boring to some people..." she rolled the barrel down the bar, "I mean, everyone needs a hobby, a little variety...I've forgotten what my point was..."

"You were trying to convince me I'm not boring." Tal smirked as she slumped back down onto the bar.

"How am I doing?" Tess opened the trapdoor and kicked the barrel down, bouncing thuds echoing up.

"Not great."

Tess kissed her teeth. "Ok, let me start again." She cleared her throat and stomped down the steps. "Maybe what you need is a little..." her voice trailed off into muffled echoes as she disappeared below the floor. The muffled noise continued,

184

interrupted by loud thuds and banging. A dark oak barrel began moving up through the hole as the mumbles became clearer. "...and sooner or later it'll be something you enjoy. You know what I mean?" Tess reappeared, kicking the trap door closed.

"Oh yes, definitely." Tal did her best to keep her laughter internal.

The door swung open as a rumble of thunder peeled over the tavern, Kai's drenched form standing in the opening.

"Look what the hellhound dragged in." Tess beamed across at the soaked tiefling as they plodded into the tavern.

Kai stuck their tongue out as they pulled up a stool next to Tal. "I am cold. I am wet. And I am thirsty. I trust the two of you to fix all of that."

"You're such a child." Tess rolled her eyes. "Give me back my cloak, I'll get you a drink." She dragged the soaked garments from Kai's body and walked off into the back.

Tal took care of the drying, waving her hand over Kai's form as the rain drained from their body. "Do you want me to take care of the cold too?" She smiled as embers began to glow from the tips of her fingers.

Kai blinked at her. "Are you seriously asking if I want you to set me on fire?"

"Maybe."

"Another time maybe," Kai smirked as they took the glass Tess put in front of them. "So how did it go?"

The two of them exchanged notes on their sides of the investigation, though Kai actually had notes to refer to. From what Kai had gathered from the seven homes they managed to get to, most of the missing people had visited the fighting pit at least once, but wasn't in the adventuring line. They worked at the docks, or in the markets, nothing that would make them targets for abduction. Nor were there people knocking down their doors looking for gambling debts to be repaid. These were modest working folk, living day to day.

"I think our best lead is going to be the Stonejaw." Kai said after a long pause and a longer drink. A shiver ran through their body and they stretched out. "So unless there's anything else we need

185

to do this evening I'm going to curl up in a blanket and warm up." Kai pushed theirself up from the bar.

"I do have one thing…" Tal already felt stupid as the question travelled from her mind to her lips, "What do you do for fun?"

Kai stood staring at her for a moment, eyes narrowing as they tried to read her face. A smile crept across their face and Kai threw their arms wide. "This. This is fun, no?" They walked up to Tal and put their arms around her, giving her a tight hug. "Relax. I'm going to bed. Please don't set me on fire in my sleep."

Tal followed on shortly, heading to her room and throwing herself down on her bed. It had been a long, horrible day, and the storm sounded like it was going to carry on through the night. After getting ready for bed and brushing her hair out she wrapped herself up in the blanket and closed her eyes. "What do I do for fun?" She whispered to herself as she drifted off to sleep.

Chapter 16

This place looks...nice?" Tal said as she and Kai stood outside the Stonejaw Alehouse. The storm from the day before had worn itself out through the night, leaving the sky clear and the air fresh and crisp.

The lack of heavy rain made the morning's walk through the city much more pleasant than the previous day, however it meant they had time to stand before the unusual building.

"It has a certain charm, for sure," Kai added.

Charm was one word for it. The windows were smashed, the twin doors hung at odd angles, and the roof had more holes than a warren.

"But we're not writing a review of the place, we're here to find out what Patrice was doing here. Come on." Kai pushed the door aside and with a horrible creak it fell off its hinges. "I...er...just come on." They continued into the tavern.

Tal bit her lip to hold in the laugh as she followed on, making sure not to touch anything.

The inside of the tavern wasn't so much inside. The damaged roof only covered the first ten to twelve feet in and around the edges of the tavern, the central area being an open courtyard dotted with tables surrounding a large sunken sandpit. The tavern was busy and loud, the patrons looking to be mostly sailors and off duty guards, drinking and arm-wrestling at their tables. Of the establishments she had visited thus far, this one ranked the lowest.

Kai made their way up to the bar where a heavily tattooed goliath leaned back against the wall behind the bar, laughing and drinking from a mug larger than Tal's head with a couple of battered looking dwarves.

"Biday, and what can I get you, my well-dressed friend?" The goliath slammed his mug down, ale sloshing over the edge. Even as he leaned against the bar he was still taller than either Kai or Tal.

Kai learned against the bar, looking up into the face of the broken-nosed goliath. "Two of your finest brews, and one for whoever runs the pit."

"That's mighty kind of you little red one," The goliath poured out three mugs of a golden yellow ale, putting two in front of Kai and pouring the third into his own large mug.

"Ah, so this is your place huh?" Kai handed over a few coins and passed a mug to Tal.

"I am that," The goliath slammed a fist against his chest. "The name's Philip. What can I call you?"

"My name is Kaivel, and this is my good friend Tal'avera." Kai resisted the urge to copy the chest thumping gesture.

"I'll never remember those." Philip admitted. "I'm going to call you...Red. And you can be...Not Red."

Tal and Kai exchanged a look that needed no words.

"I like your hair. Pretty colours." Philip rubbed his own bald tattooed head. "Can't do much of that myself. Maybe I'll call you Ribbons."

Tal smiled, twisting a strand of hair around her finger. Most people ignored it, so it was nice to get a compliment. "Thank you. I like your tattoos. Do they mean anything?"

"The mark of my herd." Philip said with pride, standing tall and rolling up the sleeves of his dirty brown linen shirt, flexing his arms to show off his toned muscles.

"So do you run the pit too?" Kai asked, their eyes tracing the intricate lines of Philips tattoos.

Philip nodded, then shook his head, and then scratched his chin. "Well yes, and no, and well, yes." He took a drink from his mug. "You see I owns the pit and this place, but my partner is in charge of arranging the fights. He's good with coin so I let him deal with all that."

188

Tal sipped the golden ale in her mug. Sharp and crisp, with a nice citric aftertaste. Not as nice as wine but it'd do. "Are the fights a regular thing here?" She looked around at the tables full of people. It looked like a fight might break out at any second.

Philip chuckled into his mug, wiping his mouth clean on his forearm. "That's what we do, ha!" He looked Tal up and down with a bit of surprise. "You looking to go a few rounds, Ribbons?"

Tal's jaw flapped and her brow furrowed. She definitely didn't want to get thrown into a fight, especially when she was already a hand down.

"I'm...er..." Kai stepped forward and straightened their jacket. "I'm actually here to see the...Champion." They learned forward across the bar, an eyebrow raised and about as subtle as a minotaur in a potter's workshop.

Philip looked Kai up and down in the same manner he'd inspected Tal. "You Red, really?" With an explosion of laughter the goliath slapped both hands against the bar. "Excellent. Bertrand!"

Kai and Tal both covered their ears at the bellowing roar from the goliath.

Moments later a voice came from behind the bar. "Yeah buddy, what is it this time?"

"See if you can find the champ. Tell him we've got someone here looking for him." Philip was looking almost straight down at his feet. If Tal hadn't heard a voice she would have sworn he was talking to himself.

"All right, he shouldn't be too hard to find. Back in a flash." There was a burst of purple light and a pop from behind the bar, and Philip looked back up to the two people standing before him.

"He'll be back shortly, no pun intended." Philip chuckled. "Is there anything else I can do for you while we wait?"

Kai's hand dipped into their satchel and pulled out the roll of parchment. "Well if you don't mind answering a few questions, that would be a help."

"Sure. You doing a quiz or something?" Philip settled back against the wall again.

189

Tal felt like this was not going to be the most impressive or in-depth interrogation she'd been a part of, but Kai's expression remained optimistic.

"Close enough. You get a lot of people coming here for fights, yes?" Kai waited for the goliath to nod. "Excellent. By any chance do you remember a noble named Patrice? Human man, blonde hair, average looking."

Tal frowned at Kai, her face twisted in puzzlement. "That's your description of him? Blonde average human man?"

Kai shrugged. "I never thought to get a description of him. I was paid to find his sword, not him. We thought we knew where he was. It's not like we expected his body to walk off."

Philip was still scratching his chin, apparently thinking back over the people that had come into his tavern that were blonde and human. "You know, I'm not good with the names," he said eventually, "but we get a lot of people coming in. If I see a blonde human I'll let him know you're looking for him."

Both Kai and Tal turned to him. Clearly Philip was a one-thing-at-a-time kind of goliath, thinking and listening had to be performed separately from one another.

"If that does happen please do. He's dead so that would be rather impressive." Kai choked down a chuckle. "He would have been in one of your fights, maybe even a champion?"

Now it was Philips turn to hold the laughter down, which he dramatically failed to do. A loud infectious bellow of a laugh, fists banging on the bar too, and his huge tattooed body shaking. Even Tal had to bite down on her lips to keep from joining in the hilarities.

When he'd finally calmed down, and after a good portion of the surrounding patrons had ceased their conversations to turn and see what exactly was so funny, Philip took a deep breath, sighing with the effort of his laughter.

"Oh if that's what he's going around telling people then that is very, very funny." Philip took a long drink from his mug. "There's only one champion around here, and he's not been taken down in years, except by yours truly." Ha added the last bit with a note of pride in his voice.

"No one has beaten him? Not even outside the tavern?" Tal turned to Kai, with a puzzled expression. "Are there any other fighting pits in the city that Patrice could have gone to?"

"Well now hold on!" Philip folded his arms and Tal suddenly felt very intimidated. His hulking form reminded her of Boa, the goliath that carried Kai and her through the Dancing Dryad when they interrogated Jenah. "There ain't nowhere else the champion fights in this city, and there ain't no one who would try taking him on without my says."

Kai held up their hands, waving Philip down. "Of course, of course. This is all just theory."

"Theo-what?" Philip blinked.

"Conjecture. Speculation. Postulation." Kai knew the words would mean nothing to the goliath, but distracting him from his frustration was the best plan they had.

Philip rubbed his bald head squinting at Kai in utter confusion.

"We're just saying," Tal leaned in against the bar, putting her hand out towards Philip, "That someone might have tried to fight your champion when he wasn't expecting it. Maybe someone your champion had beaten in the pit?"

Philip looked down at Tal, placing his huge meaty hand on top of hers, covering most of her forearm as well. "If anyone had tried that they'd be sorry. No one beats up my friends but me."

Tal opened her mouth to speak but thought better of it, choosing instead to pat the giant man's hand with her stump.

Wanting to move the conversation back to something that might be useful Kai cleared their throat to interrupt the hand-holding. "Do the people that fight in your establishment get anything for winning? A little gold pin perhaps?"

"A little gold, yeah." Philip nodded. "Or a lot of gold. Depends how the crowd bets. Winner gets a piece of the action."

"Nothing else?" Kai pressed. "Nothing that shows off that they fought here?"

"Well if you count black eyes and broken noses, yeah." Philip turned to Tal and gave her a smile he meant to be reassuring. "We've got a cleric here that fixes people up best she can. No one's died here in…" He counted off six fingers, "at least two years."

"That's good to know." Tal gave an awkward smile. "I don't think this is the place," she said to Kai with a defeated sigh. "What now?"

"Well I still think we should talk to this champion," Kai tucked away their parchment and pulled out a few strips of the bag jerky, "he might know something that could help us." Kai offered out a piece to Philip who took it with a smile.

They weren't kept waiting long, which was fortunate as Philip wasn't much of a conversationalist.

The one remaining door was pushed aside as a bare-chested half-orc was led in by a finely dressed gnomish man. "I've found him," Bertrand called out as the two of them approached, "who was looking for him?"

"This one!" Philip pointed down to Kai, hovering his thick finger just inches above Kai's horns.

"Excellent! We'll be over here when you're ready." The gnome and half-orc wandered over to an empty table next to the sunken fighting pit.

Kai nodded to Tal and then to Philip. "Thanks for your help. Let's go see if this champion can give us a lead."

"Bye Red, bye Ribbons. Good Luck!" Philip gave a wave as they walked away, then re-joined the two dwarves he'd been chatting with beforehand.

As they approached the table where Bertrand and the shirtless half-orc were sitting Tal couldn't help but notice the gnome making notes of his own on a scrap of parchment, muttering back and forth with his companion.

"Afternoon." Kai greeted the two of them as they pulled a chair out for Tal and theirself. "You must be the champion I've heard so much about."

"Hey, buddy, friend, over here." The gnome waved his hand to grab Kai's attention, not that the interruption hadn't already done that. "You talk to me here, I manage this pit and those who fight in it." Bertrand was standing on his chair, still only at chest height to the table.

192

Kai raised an eyebrow but held their tongue. "Okay, sure. I've just got a few questions if you and your...associate, don't mind?"

"Yeah, yeah, yeah. I'm sure you have. But me first. What's your name?" Bertrand held his own pen at the ready above his parchment.

"Kaivel Mortzeel," Kai negated their usual flare of introduction as this was clearly a gnome who didn't have time for the eccentric.

"Odd name, but ok. Where are you from?"

Kai kissed their teeth. "Why does that matter?"

"Ok, moving on." The gnome was clearly working down some sort of check sheet. "Occupation?"

"I run a private investigation service." This was beginning to get tedious.

"Mm-hmm, okay, okay. I think that's all I need. I shall leave you two alone for a minute while I see to some things." Bertrand hopped down from the chair and sauntered off into the crowd.

"That was strange." Tal muttered just loud enough for Kai to hear. She was beginning to get a bad feeling about all of this, and was not looking forward to being carried off into a store room again for asking too many questions.

"Indeed," Kai took out their parchment and laid it out on the table. "So, as I was saying, you must be the champion?"

The half-orc nodded. "Aye, that I am. You can call me the Cannon, everyone else does." He folded his thick arms across his chest, his olive-green skin pockmarked and calloused from the tips of his fingers to his biceps.

"Is that a nickname?" Tal asked, her eyes taking in the various scars that covered his arms.

The Hammer snorted. "No, my parents named me 'The Cannon'. Of course it's a nickname. I'm the gunner for the Hurricane Mary."

Tal did not expect the disdain and sarcasm that came her way, and immediately turned bright red, sinking back into her chair.

Kai cleared their throat, suddenly taking on a sterner tone. "Are you familiar with Patrice Vaskar? Human lad, frequented here a few times in the last few weeks."

The Cannon shrugged, leaning back in his chair and looking down his broken nose at the pair of them. "I don't bother remembering the names of the fools I beat into the sand. That's the little man's job. He keeps track of that stuff. I'm just here to get paid and break some faces."

"Charming..." Tal said under her breath. This wasn't an interaction she was enjoying, and a part of her secretly hoped that the half-orc was somehow responsible for Patrice's disappearance.

"Right," Kai jotted down the word 'useless' on their parchment, "Do you know when he'll be back? Or perhaps where he's gone?"

An unsettling smile crept across the half-orc's tusked face. "Let me go find him for you. I'm sure he's not gone far..." He pushed off from the table, knocking his own chair onto the floor and making his way into the crowd in the same direction as Bertrand.

As soon as he was out of sight Tal leaned into Kai. "I've got a bad feeling about those two, they're definitely up to something."

"Same. They might also just be horrible people, but they're definitely up to something." Kai took out another piece of jerky. "Keep your eye out for anything that doesn't look right."

Tal didn't need to be told that, but it was good to know that Kai and she were thinking along the same lines. Her eyes were well and truly peeled, scanning the crowd for any sign that something wasn't right. Carefully taking in the various folks that were scattered about the tavern, Tal was surprised by the variety. Humans, elves, half-orcs, gnomes, and dwarves all coming together to watch people beat each other unconscious. Or by the looks of some of them, beat people unconscious. She focused mostly on those that were worse for wear, the bruised and the broken, they were the ones most likely to have some kind of information for them.

As her eyes skimmed over the crowd they caught something shiny, her head quickly darting back in its direction. Kneeling down to a gnome with his head mostly bandaged up was a hooded figure handing over something small that briefly glinted with a golden hue. Reaching back to get Kai's attention, Tal

194

opened her mouth to speak before a loud voice roared out from the crowd surrounding the pit.

"Ladies and gentlemen!" Bertrand's voice bellowed out from the centre of the court yard. "If I could have your attention please!"

"This doesn't sound good..." Kai got up from the table. "Stay back a bit, make a scene if things get out of control."

Tal nodded as she unclipped her spellbook in preparation, watching from the table as Kai walked towards the gathering crowd of people. She gave a quick glance back and cursed as the hooded figure she'd seen a moment ago had vanished.

"Gather round, gather round, for a grand spectacle to enchant your afternoons!" Bertrand continued, standing on a chair on top of a table so that his small frame could be seen over the crowd that was moving towards the centre of the courtyard.

"We have a wonderful show for you today! With a very special guest! Now where are they-AH!" Bertrand pointed his short arm out towards Kai. "There you are! Ladies and gentlemen, and gentlethem, please give a big hand, or a small one if that's all you've got, for Detective Mortzeel!"

Kai stood in bewilderment as the crowd turned to them and cheered, patting them on the back and pushing the tiefling through the crowd towards the table.

"And welcome back, the big green smashing machine! Your favourite and mine. The champion of the Stonejaw fighting pit, Verr, the Cannon!"

Kai looked out across the sunken sandpit they had been pushed towards to see the half-orc standing on the opposite side, arms in the air and the crowd cheered and chanted, "Cannon, Cannon, Cannon...". With a wink the half-orc, Verr, leapt down into the pit. Sand and dust exploded from his weight as he landed, roaring up at the crowd who cheered back with all the more intensity.

"Oh...oh..." Kai looked down at the half-orc grinning up at them. "I think there's been a misunderstanding," Kai began, turning to face Bertrand. "When I said I was looking for the champion, I didn't mean th-OUF!"

A foot from someone in the crowd kicked Kai right in the stomach, shoving them over the edge. Kai's body slammed into the sand, the wind forced from their lungs as the dust cloud settled around them.

"Ouu…" was all Kai managed as the cheering was quickly replaced with laughter.

"Kai!" Tal rushed to the edge, dropping to her knees as she leaned over. "Are you ok?"

"No…" Kai groaned back, sitting up slowly and coughing. "I think things might be out of control." They pushed theirself up, standing and dusting off their trousers.

"Want me to make a scene?"

"I don't think you could out do this…" Kai turned to face the Cannon, who was busy stretching and flexing for the crowd. "Just keep your eye out, I'll try and stay alive."

Bertrand's voice boomed out over the crowd once again. "All bets are in! So let the brawl…begin!" The little gnome clapped his hands together and a loud bell rang out.

The Cannon didn't waste any time. He charged at Kai head on, arms spread wide ready to tackle the tiefling to the ground.

As the half-orc's arms slammed closed, Kai rolled forward, ducking past him and retreating as fast as they could to the other side.

"Not very sporting," Kai shouted across the pit, "at least let me get ready." Kai removed their jacket and tie, pulling out their hairpins and tying their long hair up into a knotted bun. "Ok, let's dance."

With another roar the half-orc charged again. Kai turned and ran at the wall, kicking off as the Cannon's body slammed into the wall with a heavy thud.

A cry of "oooh!" erupted from the crowd, but the chants for the half-orc continued.

Kai landed in the sand and rose just in time to push away the fist that came flying at them. The Cannon was in full swing, throwing blow after blow at the tiefling. All Kai could do was parry and back up.

"Come on Kai!" Tal cried from the edge.

Backed against the wall again Kai ducked as a fist crashed where their head was a moment before. Giving two short jabs to

196

the half-orc's abdomen, Kai gave a groan of pain. It felt like punching solid stone.

The air was knocked from Kai's lungs as the half-orc's elbows were driven down into their back, pounding them into the sand.

With a mouth full of sand Kai rolled to the side, dodging the foot that slammed down next to them.

Things were not looking in Kai's favour and Tal had no idea what to do. She looked around the crowd of people cheering on the violence beneath them, searching for the hooded figure she'd seen before. Her eyes moved from face to face, expressions of excitement and bloodlust smeared across each of them. Fists pumped in the air, imitating the blows being thrown below.

A bracer. A brass bracer. Tal would recognise it anywhere, after all it had been attached to her for nearly fifteen years.

Across the pit, the hood of his long dirty cloak thrown back, stood a slender man with ruddy skin and a half-shaved head, wearing her prosthetic as jewellery. Tal's heart was caught in her throat. She didn't know what to do or how to act, all she knew is she was somewhere between frightened and furious.

The crowd cheered as Kai scurried around the Cannon, kicking the half-orc in the back of the knee and sending him tumbling forward.

Tal saw that the man with her hand was the only person not celebrating the fight, he was just watching, staring, his focus solely on the brawl below. This could be her chance. Tal began to carefully move between people, keeping her eyes locked onto the man as best she could.

Kai leapt onto the Cannon's back, wrapping their arms around his thick neck and their legs around his chunk of a torso. The tiefling locked their wrists in, tightening their grip around the Cannon's muscular neck.

"Go to sleep! Go to sleep! Go to sleep!" They muttered as they squeezed as best they could.

A roar ripped from the Cannon's throat as he leaned forward, his head almost touching the sand, before throwing all his weight backwards, smashing himself and Kai into the ground.

197

Tal slipped between a pair of dwarves who were busy yelling suggestions into the pit. Her quarry remained focused, not noticing her approaching as the fight continued.

Kai groaned, their grapple around the half-orc lost as the Cannon stood up and lifted Kai up by the scruff of their shirt. Kai grabbed his wrists in an attempt to pry theirselves free, but was quickly hurled across the pit, their body crashing into the wall again.

Coughing blood into the sand, Kai wiped their lips clean and pushed theirself to their feet.

The Cannon roared, and Kai couldn't do anything but roar back. They charged at one another, the Cannon's fist already winding back. The half-orc swung as Kai dropped, sliding between his legs and rolling back onto their feet.

Kai was out of here. They ran at the wall, jamming their foot into a dent left from a previous fight and pushed off, reaching for the edge.

Fingertips touching the rim of the pit Kai let out a chilling high-pitched scream as they were pulled back to the ground by their tail.

Tal's attention was torn back to the fight, seeing her friend's body being thrown to the ground in such a way. "Kai!" she cried out, pushing forward to the edge and knocking a tankard from a cheering half-elf.

"Oi, watch it!" The dunk half-elf shoved her back, almost pushing her over the edge. Steadying herself Tal looked down at Kai and back up at the man she'd been edging towards. Who was now looking right at her.

Tal's jaw hung open, the figure's eyes narrowing on her as he stepped backwards into the crowd.

"Oh no…" Tal struggled her way through, pushing past whoever she could, and getting pushed back a fair bit herself. Out of the crowd She looked around frantically for any sign of the man.

The lone door swung on its hinge and Tal ran to it, looking out into the city to see the edge of a dirty cloak disappear around a corner.

Feet stamped into the sand as Kai rolled over again and again. Twisting their body Kai rolled up onto their feet, grabbing a fist full of sand and flinging it into the Cannon's eyes.

A chant of booing ripped through the crowd as the Cannon swung a fist wildly, his other hand rubbing at his eyes.

Kai darted round the half-orc, jabbing into his ribs as they ducked beneath blind swings.

Dashing around the corner Tal watched the man pulling himself onto a horse, kicking it sharply in the flank. With a pained neigh the beast was off, horseshoes clattering against the cobbled street.

"Stop! Stop him!" Tal cried out as he galloped away, the people in the street only stopping to stare at her. She dropped to her knees in defeat, tears of rage building in the corners of her eyes. He'd gotten away.

Kai was getting desperate. Jabbing with their left and feigning to the right, Kai went for the dirty tactic. If the Cannon was going to rip their tail, Kai was certainly going to return the favour.

Grabbing hold of the half-orcs belt they used all their strength to pull theirself forward smashing their knee into his crotch.

With an anguished whine the Hammer dropped to his knees, eyes watering. Kai threw their fist back, getting ready to deliver a finishing blow.

Two thick arms wrapped around their torso, pinning them in place as the Cannon grinned at them. "Got ya," the half-orc smiled as he arched back and thumped his forehead into Kai's face.

Colour swirled in front of Kai's eyes, and the last thing they saw was that tusky grin as darkness took them.

Chapter 17

So tell me again, how did they end up in a pit fight?" Tess had heard the story twice already, but still couldn't make sense of it.

On her return to the Stonejaw Alehouse, Tal had found Kai unconscious and bleeding in the sand with an ashen-haired female gnome crouching over them. Even after their wounds had been taken care of, Kai remained completely blacked out. The gnomish woman was kind enough to wait with the battered teifling while Tal rushed off to get help. Help in the form of Tess, who was the only person Tal thought would be able and willing to help her collect Kai.

So here they were, walking down the sunny streets of Belgar, with a tiefling slung over Tess's shoulders and odd looks coming from passers-by as they made their way back to the Troll's Den.

"I don't know how it happened exactly, I don't think Kai would have jumped into a fighting pit voluntarily." Tal was nervously twirling hair around her finger, her cheeks glowing as more people stared as they passed.

"I don't know…" Tess hummed a little as she thought, "if they thought it would help the case they might have. That one has done some really stupid things when a case was involved."

Tal wasn't sure if she was surprised or not. Kai definitely seemed like the kind of person who would take chances, but putting theirself in harm's way for a case? "I still don't think so. I think that gnome must have tricked them into it. There was no way Kai stood a chance in a fair fight."

"And those places are anything but fair." The two of them rounded a corner and Tess took a moment to shift Kai's weight to a more comfortable position.

Tal sighed. She hoped at the very least Kai learned something useful from all this. "How long do you think they'll be out of it?" Tal tapped the tip of Kai's horn, hoping for a sign of life.

Tess shrugged, jostling Kai in the process. "No idea. We can just leave them in their room to sleep it off. Maybe pick up a bun for them later."

Just the mention of food made Tal's stomach grumble. "Could we stop and get buns first perhaps?"

"I'm not your mother, if you want food, we can get food." Tess rolled her eyes. "Tell me again about the guy with your hand. Did you recognise him?"

Tal bit her lip as she ran his face through her mind again and again. He certainly recognised her. Perhaps he had been the one to steal it from her in the first place. But then why was he just wearing it as jewellery?

"I don't think he knew what it was…" Tal said half to herself, half to Tess. "I mean he had both his own hands."

"Could you have been mistaken? I mean a brass cuff is a brass cuff. Did you really get that good a look at it?"

Tal gave a stern nod. "I didn't need to get a good look at it, I know that cuff like the back of this hand." She wiggled the fingers on her left hand for emphasis.

"Okay," Tess neither looked nor sounded convinced, "well I guess you've finally got a lead on your case." The troll-orc groaned and huffed, shifting Kai's weight again. "Pwah, for a skinny thing you aren't half heavy." She patted Kai's unconscious butt. "Maybe it's time to start a diet."

A trickle of a chuckle came from Tal. "It's probably all that jerky. I don't know how Kai can eat that stuff, it's so dry and salty." She stuck her tongue out in disgust.

As the pair continued through the streets, heading towards the market square in search of something to eat, a soft hissing sound caught Tal's ear. She looked about, trying to figure where the sound was coming from and why she felt it was being directed at her.

Tess continued on for a few steps before realising she was alone, turning back to see Tal spinning on the spot. "Did you get hit in the head too? I can't carry you both." She looked Tal up and down, doing a quick calculation. "Okay, maybe I could, but I don't want to."

Tal wasn't listening, she was still looking for the hissing that seemed to be coming from all around her. People were walking past her and going about their day, not one of them looking in her direction or moving towards her. The hissing had stopped and was replaced by a short yet tuneful whistle. Tal spun around to face a shop front where a familiar bundle of rags sat waving to her.

"Jasper! It's Jasper," Tal pointed him out to Tess before moving towards the disguised fence. "What are you doing here? And why were you hissing at me?"

The bundle shifted with a muffled clatter. "I've been waiting for you." There was a brief pause before Jasper cleared his throat. "Sorry, that sounded creepy and ominous, which for a change wasn't my intention."

"What does the pile of rags want?" Tess yelled out from the street.

Jasper tilted to the side, staring past Tal. "Is that Kaivel slung over her shoulders?"

"It's a long story, I'll tell you about it later." Tal waved the question away. "Why were you looking for me?"

"We need to talk," Jasper said as he leaned back upright. After another pause he cleared his throat again. "I really do sound creepy and ominous today don't I? Where are you headed?"

"We're heading back to the Troll's Den."

Jasper clapped his hands together and a smile appeared from beneath the thick beard. "Perfect, I'll meet you there." He groaned as he rose to his feet, still clattering like he was wearing a suit of armour inside another suit of armour.

Tal watched him hobble away in confusion before returning to Tess, feeling slightly shaken by the whole interaction.

202

"So what was he doing there?" Tess asked as they continued walking.

"He said he was looking for us."

Tess grunted. "That's kind of creepy. What did he want?"

"He just said 'we need to talk'." Tal rubbed the back of her neck, feeling warm all of a sudden.

Tess grunted again. "That sounds ominous."

"Yes, I know...Can we eat now please? I don't think I can handle more of today without something in my stomach."

Back at the Trolls Den, a bundle of spice-smoked salmon tucked underarm, Tal held the door open as Tess bashed Kai's head into the frame.

"I'm sure they didn't feel that." Tess said with a half guilty expression. She looked across the bar to the staircase and gave a dismissive sneer. "I'm not lugging their boney arse up those stairs. We'll dump them in my room. Come on." Tess pushed forward, once again using Kai's head to open the door to her chambers.

Tal watched as Tess practically body slammed Kai onto her bed. "I'm not sure who's done more damage, you or that Cannon fellow."

Tess shrugged. "I'm sure they're fine. Take a seat, I'll grab us something to eat with." The troll-orc disappeared back out into the bar.

Feeling slightly awkward, as she always did when left alone in someone else's rooms, Tal spun on the spot a few times before sitting herself down next to Kai on the bed, giving the tiefling a gentle pat on the back. "What doesn't kill you I guess..." She sighed to herself.

Tal shifted uncomfortably, feeling something hard and pointy pressing into her butt. She pushed down on the bed sheet and felt the distinctive flatness of a book cover. Tal bit her lip, one voice in her head telling her not to, and another shouting it down telling her to go for it.

She lifted herself slightly, sliding her hand beneath the sheet until she felt the hardened cloth of a book cover against her finger tips. Tal slid the book free and her eyes immediately went wide as her jaw hung open.

A beautifully drawn cover of a muscular male orc, with long flowing hair and an open shirt, staring lovingly into the doey eyes of a female half-orc, her satin dress covering just enough to leave something to the imagination.

"Ok, I poured us a couple of-what the hells are you-!" Tess dropped the plates and goblets she was carrying as she rushed towards Tal, her hands grabbing for the book.

Tal rolled backwards off the opposite side of the bed, narrowly missing landing on Kai. "Tribes and Transgressions?" Tal read the title of the book out loud, her cheeks bright red and a laugh building in her throat. "Is this a trashy romance novel?"

"Give! Me! That!" Tess clambered over the bed as she swiped for the book again and again.

Tal ran to the corner of the room, leaping up onto Tess's armchair and holding the book high above her head, still well within Tess's reach. "Is that why you kept hiding it from me? You read trashy orc romance novels?" The laughter was rippling into Tal's words now, her whole face burning red with embarrassment and joy.

Tess rushed the elf, snatching the book back as she held both of Tal's wrists with one hand. "It's not trashy!" Tess's normally grey complexion was gaining a significant pink hue. "It's a passionate tale of two people desperately in love, yet kept apart by the feud between their tribes." Tess released Tal and held the book against her chest. "It's sweet, and romantic, and charming, and...and....and you shouldn't be snooping around my room anyway!"

Tal continued to giggle as she climbed down from the chair. "I didn't mean to, you left it under your bed sheet. Not exactly a great hiding spot."

Tess stuffed the book under her pillow and grabbed the bundle of salmon. "I'm not sure you deserve this now." She stomped off in a huff back to the bar.

"Hey! I paid for that!" Tal chased after her, leaving the unconscious Kai alone in the room. The chase didn't last long. As Tal stepped through the door her face pressed into Tess's back as the tavernkeep stood stock still.

Rubbing her nose and peeking around Tess's wide frame she saw the rag-pile that was Jasper, sitting at a table with his feet up.

"Thought I'd beaten you here." The fence said as he moved from his comfortable position. "How is our horny friend?"

"She's fine," Tal smirked, "and Kai will be alright too." She danced around Tess as an elbow swung out at her. "Now you're here, what did you need to talk to me about?"

The beard shuffled a little in confusion. "I feel like I've missed something, but no bother." Jasper stood and threw his ragged form over the table before him with a thunderous crash. "And I believe I may have found your missing cuff!"

Tal's eyes lit up and she ran to the table as Jasper continued to shuffle and rustle. After a minute or so Jasper flung his tattered cloak to the side, revealing a huge collection of cuffs and bracers. Brass, copper, bronze, and even a couple of gold.

"Feast your eyes ladies, and don't say old Jasper never did nothing for you." The fence sat back down in his chair as he pulled off his hood, the beard being absorbed into its fold revealing Jasper's clean shaven grinning face.

Both Tal and Tess began searching through the fine collection displayed before them. They were all beautiful, either inlaid with gemstones or detailed with fine filigree. Tal even took out her spellbook, casting a quick detection incantation so see which ones were enchanted.

"Take you time ladies, it's nice to be off the streets for a while. This get-up is great, but not what you wanna be wearing on a day like this." Jasper wiped his face down with his ragged cloak. "I've been sweating from places I didn't know I could!"

"That's disgusting…" Tal turned up her nose as she inspected a silver inlaid brass wrist piece with a strong protection enchantment. As fine as all these pieces were, none of them

205

were her missing hand. "It's not here." Tal sighed in disappointment.

Jasper furrowed his brow and kissed his teeth, leaning forward over the collection. "You sure? This is every piece that's being moved at the moment."

Tal nodded. "I'm certain. I actually think I saw someone with it today, maybe you could help me find them?"

"This is gorgeous!" Tess suddenly explained, holding up a gold bangle with onyx and garnets. She unhooked the clasp and fixed it around her wrist, holding her arm out to examine it.

"That really suits you, strong yet feminine. Do you like it?" Jasper smiled at her. Tess nodded, still staring at the piece of jewellery. Jasper's smile widened. "Wonderful! That one's two and a half thousand gold pieces."

Both Tess and Tal nearly broke their necks with the sudden snap to face Jasper.

"How much?!" The cry came from both women as Tess frantically tried to remove the bangle.

Jasper shrugged. "What can I say? I deal in high end, elusive items."

"Were you going to charge me for giving me back my own hand?" Tal slammed her palm and stump down on the table as she leaned over at Jasper.

With a gasp Jasper stumbled backwards, hand on his chest in an overly dramatic display of being wounded by the accusation. "Miss Tal'avera! What must you think of me? Just some villain looking to make a quick coin by exploiting the less fortunate? I am hurt."

Tal raised a suspicious eyebrow, folding her arms like a disappointed parent. "So you were just going to return it to me?"

"Of course," Jasper shrugged, the smile returning to his face. "I mean in exchange for a favour in kind. The price was simply to let you know how valuable this favour would be to me."

Tess was very carefully placing the bangle back down, backing away from the table to either avoid damaging anything or temptation. "Where did you get all of these? And why are you walking around the city with a king's ransom in your pocket?"

"Ah, ah, ah!" Jasper wagged a finger at her. "We do not ask where they come from, that way we don't have to lie to each other." He began regathering his precious items, sorting them back into place inside his cloaks. "Tal'avera, why don't you tell me who's got your hand? Maybe I can make some arrangements."

"You're sounding creepy and ominous again." Tal said, her eyes following the pretty jewels as they disappeared beneath the layers of rags.

"It seems to be my thing, just go with it." Jasper polished a smudge from the bangle Tess had tried on.

Tal sighed. At least he was being creepy and ominous for her and not to her. "I don't know who he is, I just saw him in the Stone Inn."

"Stonejaw Alehouse," Tess corrected. She'd made her way back to the bar and was tucking into her portion of the now cold salmon.

"Yes, thank you, the Stonejaw Alehouse." Tal cleared her throat, taking a moment to recall as much detail as she could about the unknown figure. "He was tall, a bit taller than you," she held her hand above her own head to demonstrate, "reddish skin, like he'd been running or been out in the sun too long." She began gesturing as she spoke, trying to paint more of a visual image for Jasper. "Half his head was shaved, the right side. The left was sort of long and matted, like he hadn't washed it in a while. I think he was human, I didn't get close enough to get a good look. And he was wearing some really dirty leather, like, caked in mud."

"Tell him about the horse." Tess called over between mouthfuls.

"Oh yes!" Tal slapped her stump down into her palm. "I think he stole someone's horse to get away."

"Get away? From what?" Jasper gave a little giggle, things jingling in pockets as he did.

"From me. I was following him. I think he recognised me, so he must have been the one who stole it."

"Right," Jasper tucked the last bracer away. "Well that doesn't ring any bells, but I can ask around. Would you prefer I make arrangements, or would you prefer to deal with it yourselves?"

Tal felt very uncomfortable about both of those options. "If by 'make arrangements' you mean get my hand back then that please."

Jasper smiled. "Then arrangements shall be made." He pulled the hood back up over his head, the thick beard materialising over his face. "For now ladies, it has been a pleasure, but I have some wares to distribute." He gave a deep clattering bow. "I'll be seeing you."

They watched as he rattled his way out the door, leaving the two of them alone, both suddenly aware of how quiet the tavern was.

"He's an interesting fellow," Tess licked her lips, "wish he'd brought the big guy with him again though."

"Why? Looking to add a chapter to your own novel?" Tal teased her, unwrapping her own food with a sudden frown.

Tess snorted. "Now I don't feel so bad about eating half your food."

"That's the last time I treat you to lunch!" Tal muttered an incantation as she ran her fingers over the fish, little embers tricking off and warming the cold fish.

Tess shrugged. "I know where you sleep."

"Now who's sounding creepy and ominous…"

⮞⊙⮜

The two women finished their meal, Tess making up for snacking on Tal's by pouring out a few mugs of ale. The regular crowd of grumpy old folk slowly began to filter in, taking up their usual spots after collecting their drinks from the bar.

"It always seems to be the same faces in here," Tal noted as she looked around the bar.

"Yeah, it usually is. No one really comes to this part of the city unless the other taverns are full." Tess put away the mug she was cleaning. "I don't mind it so much. I like this place just the way it is. Come on, let's go see if Kai's alive or not. If not, I'll leave you to clear out their room."

Tal wasn't quite sure if Tess was joking or not. Nevertheless, she finished her mug and followed Tess back to her chambers.

"As his strong hands caressed her cheek, Vulcor shivered. 'Please Gruunfa, you must go! My father will return at any moment!'" Kai turned the page of Tess's book, looking to the open door where Tal and Tess stood. "Ah, there you are," they smiled, "well come in, sit down. Things are getting steamy."

Tal could see the hairs on the back of Tess's neck and arms bristle. "Good, you're alive. Now I'm going to kill you."

Kai chuckled, then groaned as they sat up slowly. "Are you sure I'm alive? I don't feel it."

Tal went and sat next to them, gently placing her hand on Kai's shoulder. "How are you feeling?"

Now that Kai had had a moment to rest, the evidence of their battle looked painfully blatant. Heavy black and purple bruises circled both their eyes, along with several on their face and forearms. Their bottom lip was thick with a deep cut down one side, and their nose seemed slightly more crooked.

"Like a warm spring morning in the third hell…" Kai winced as they shuffled away from Tal's touch. "Everything hurts. Even my horns, and I didn't even know that was possible." Kai gently rubbed their lower back where their tail sat curled up. "Oh good, it's still there…"

"What in the name of the gods happened to you?" Tess retrieved her book and began walking around her room looking for a new hiding spot. "I think this is the worst I've ever seen you."

Kai raised a finger. "What about that thing with the enchanted rug?"

"Ha, oh yeah." Tess snorted a laugh. "I'd forgotten about that. Oh beaten up by a rug, ha!"

"You got...what?" The more Tal learned about Kai's life the more confused she became.

"Home security feature, wasn't expecting it, had to throw myself out of a window." Kai gently massaged a tender spot. "I think you might be right, Tess, this could be worse." Slowly lowered theirself back down onto the bed. "Ow…"

"I say again," Tess opened her wardrobe and rummaged around for a moment, "what happened to you?"

"It's kind of fuzzy and painful to think about. I believe I was hit by a small building or perhaps a large wagon." They gestured to Tal. "Ask her, she was there."

Tal cleared her throat. "Well actually I…erm…I left."

Kai shot up. "You what?…Ow…." Quickly collapsing back.

"I think I saw who stole my hand, or who at least has it now." Tal's cheeks were hot, and seeing Kai in pain sent a pang of guilt through her body. Not that there was anything she could have done about it.

"Ok, that's one excuse…" Kai mumbled. "The last thing I remember is being yanked off the wall by that brute. And I think that's just what my tail remembers."

"That's the last thing I saw too." A shiver ran down Tal's spine. Even without a tail of her own, the thought of the sensation alone made her shift where she sat. "I called out to you and this guy saw me and ran."

"Pretty suspicious." Kai opened and closed their mouth in slow, wide movements. "Can you hear that click?"

"No."

"That's probably ok then. So did you catch the guy?" Kai moved on to gently rolling their shoulders.

Tal shook her head, once again feeling the disappointment from her day. "No, he stole a horse and galloped off into the city."

"Even more suspicious. Help me up." Kai extended their arms straight up, waiting for anyone to come to their aid.

"You're such a child," Tess grabbed Kai by the wrists and pulled them up hard with a sudden pop.

"Wah-Urp!" Kai yelped as they were yanked to their feet. Rolling their shoulders a few more times Kai smiled. "Well whatever that was, I think you fixed it…thanks."

"Don't mention it. I'm going back to work, someone here needs to earn a living." Tess muttered a few other things in orcish as she returned to the bar.

Kai wobbled in place for a moment, holding their arms out to steady theirself. "Is the room moving or am I?"

"You're both completely still." Tal's concern for Kai's wellbeing was growing by the second as she watched the bruised tiefling struggle against gravity. "I really think you should lay down."

"Later." Kai took a careful step forward. "So remind me, what did we get from the Stonejaw again?"

"You mean besides a pair of black eyes and a possibly broken rib?"

Kai gently prodded each of their ribs in turn, hissing at the sensation. "I don't think they're broken. Bruised, however..." They turned back to face Tal. "So besides my very pitiful condition, what did we get?"

Tal wasn't really sure how to answer. Obviously they hadn't gotten anything useful, but saying so out loud would mean Kai took a terrible beating for no reason. "I don't think Philip had anything to do with missing people. He seemed friendly enough." She stood up to give Kai some extra support as they tried another step. "The Cannon, I think, is just a brute looking for a fight."

Kai looped their arm over Tal's shoulders. "Thanks. I'll agree with you there. Everything is still pretty blurry."

"That gnomish fellow though," Tal snapped her fingers a few times trying to remember his name. "Bertrand. If anyone is doing something suspicious, I'd say it's him."

Kai closed their eyes tight, trying to push past the throbbing in their head and pull out any memory from the day. "I don't know about suspicious. Unless you consider arrogant and obnoxious as suspicious, in which case I've never known a person more suspect." Kai managed to crack a smile, which made Tal feel better.

Though the feeling didn't last long. She sighed, realising they really had made no progress today. "So what now? What should we do next?"

Kai held up a finger, looking as though they were about to reveal a master plan. "We drink. I need something to numb my face enough that I can stop seeing sounds."

211

As if the mere mention of booze had summoned her from the great beyond, Tess suddenly appeared in the doorway. Though the expression on her face was more fearful than godly. "There's um...someone here to see you."

Tal had never seen Tess nervous before. Seeing a woman of her stature and ferocity nervous filled the elf with a sense of impending dread.

"If it's that gnome expecting me to pay up from the fight he's got another think coming!" Kai hobbled past Tess.

Looking straight into Tal's eyes Tess shook her head, just holding the door open for them to pass. Fearing the worst Tal followed on.

The bar, only moments ago half-full with the contented locals, now stood empty. Just two figures alone at the tavern's more central table, one seated with the larger one stood menacingly behind.

"Oh my graces, Kaivel!" Malachai cried out, mouth agape in shock. "You look terrible! Like someone threw you down a flight of stairs twice just to make sure of it."

As Kai stood before the albino tiefling and his suited mountain of a body guard, they turned back to Tal. "Just knock me out again would you?"

CHAPTER 18

The tension in the Troll's Den tavern was so thick you'd need a battleaxe just to make a dent. Kaivel, Tal'avera, and Tess stood around the table occupied by the imposing presence of Malachai and his large muscular body guard, Bao.

Eyes danced between the two tieflings, all waiting for one or the other to make the first move. A duel of personas.

Tal's nerves were on edge, her blood travelling back and forth between her arms and legs so fast she had begun to feel dizzy. A battle between fight and flight taking place in her own body. She didn't dare abandon Kai, especially not in their current state, but she didn't want to start something by unclipping her spellbook. Even if she had something prepared, there was no doubt in her mind that Malachai's goliath would be on her before she could finish an incantation.

Kai cleared their throat, a sound so sudden in the deathly silence that even Tess jumped. "What are-"

"Would you mind awfully fetching us something to drink, darling?" Malachai flashed a smile at Tess. "I never do business without refreshments. Some spirits of any sorts will do." He swung his booted feet up onto the table, leaning back in his chair as if he owned the place.

Tal could see the vein in Tess's neck twitch, but the tavernkeep just swallowed hard and went to retrieve a bottle.

"What are you doing here, Malachai?" Kai finished their question, their face expressionless.

Casually inspecting the many rings on his fingers, Malachai gestured to the other chairs around the table. "Why don't you take a seat while we wait for our drinks to arrive? No reason we can't mix business with pleasure."

"I'll stand." Kai replied flatly. "You think this is pleasurable?"

The albino's thick forked tongue licked both lips as he smiled. "Please, I must insist. You look as if you're about to collapse."

Kai folded their arms, showing no sign of the pain Tal knew they were in. "I said I'll sta-"

A chair slammed into the floor as Bao towered behind his employer. "The boss says for you to sit."

Tal moved to reach for a chair, but Kai caught her wrist. Their gaze now fixed on the goliath. "You don't frighten me, Bao, you never have."

"Easy, easy," Malachai flapped his arms in his seat. "If they do not wish to sit, Bao, then we must not force them. We are after all guests in this…" He looked down his nose around the tavern. "…this charming little hovel."

Tal was now very glad Tess had been sent away. That one sentence could have been what decided their fate.

Bao relaxed, though his eyes never moved from Kai.

"As for how I find this evening," Malachai continued as if nothing had just transpired, "it may not be as I had originally intended, but a chance to see you and your beautiful friend here is always a joy."

A chill ran through Tal's body as the blood once again rushed to her legs. Even though Malachai was smiling, his words somehow seemed like a threat.

Tess emerged from the back with a slim red bottle and four small mugs. Silently pouring a small amount of the spirit into each mug she placed the bottle in the middle of the table and slowly backed away to the safety of the bar.

Taking a mug, Malachai held it in the air. "To your health," he threw the drink back, not waiting for anyone to join him in his toast. Taking the mug placed in front of Bao, the alabaster tiefling sat straighter, looking intently at Kai. "I understand you recently visited the home of Imis Wikson, is that correct?"

Kai took a mug from the table, sipping carefully and wincing as the liquid stung their split lip. "The name rings a bell," they said with a heavy sigh, "what does it have to do with you?"

Malachai tented his fingers, resting his chin on their tips and glaring up at Kai. "Imis was formally in my employ. He absconded a number of weeks ago, possibly with a large amount of what was due to be my property."

Placing the mug down on the table, Kai opted for taking a seat. Tal watched as with each movement Kai's knees shook violently. It must have been taking everything Kai had left just to stay conscious.

"That is terrible news, but I don't see how this has anything to do with me." Kai leaned back in the chair, looking a bit more alive now they weren't having to hold theirself up.

The two tieflings sat staring at each other before Malachai broke eye contact to look directly at Tal. "My dear, I must insist you sit down. You're beginning to make me feel uncomfortable."

Tal opened her mouth to refuse, but the intensity of Malachai's gaze stunned her to silence. Under the pressure of his burning pink eyes Tal pulled out a chair and sat.

"And do forgive me, but I'm afraid we have not been properly introduced." He held out his hand. "Malachai Vorikz, of Jerau."

Tal placed her arm in front of her on the table, offering her left hand instead. "Arcanist Tal'avera. And I know who you are."

Malachai held her hand, inclining his horned head towards it in a gentle bow, his thumb uncomfortably caressing her fingers. "And I naturally know who you are, Tal'avera Liwood, but introductions are part of polite society. It's important to keep in practice."

As his grip loosened Tal snatched her hand back, feeling the urge to go and wash it.

"I have heard tell of the one-armed wizard who has been escorting Kaivel here, I never realised it was you when we met in my establishment." Malachai sucked the tip of his thumb as he stared at her.

"Because if you had we would have received a warmer welcome?" Kai pulled the attention away from Tal. Finishing their mug they rolled it across the table. "You still haven't told us why

215

you're here. If you could skip the theatrics, some of us have to work for a living."

Malachai sighed. "You used to be so much fun, Kaivel. Living here, doing whatever it is you do, has certainly made you a dreadful bore." He took another sip from his small mug. "But if you insist on getting down to business." Malachai snapped his fingers and Bao stepped forward, untying a bulging purse from his hip and dropping it onto the table. Tal's eyes widened as the sound of a lot of coin tumbling against itself rang in her ears.

"I want to hire you, at your previous rate, of course, to find him." Malachai drummed his fingers across the table, watching the faces of the detectives before him.

Kai's eyebrow was already raised, they hadn't even glanced down at the bulging purse that had transfixed both Tal and Tess. "Find him?" Kai repeated with unusual emphasis.

"Yes, you can deal with him in any way you see fit, I just want my property back." Malachai continued to drum against the table. "So, do we have a deal?"

Tal looked back and forth between the two of them. The amount of coin that must have been contained within that hefty purse on the table before her would be more than she'd seen in her life. Thinking how Malachai had called it Kai's 'previous rate' made her wonder how they'd come to be living in a tavern. Part of her also wanted to accept, thinking about how much the coin could help. Settling her tab with Botan, finding a more permanent residence, not to mention the spells she could craft. But even as the greed inside her edged towards taking the coin, there was another more realistic side that knew that accepting meant Malachai owned them.

Kai flicked the purse, hearing the rustle of coin inside. They sniffed, looking dead on at their pale acquaintance. "What property of yours did Imis have? It might help us to narrow the search."

Tal couldn't believe it. Was this Kai taking the job? A voice in her head screamed in protest, but the cry never made it to her lips.

216

A look of terribly unconvincing innocence came across Malachai's face. "Just some ornamental items, nothing dangerous if that's what you're worried about."

Kai leaned forward and picked up the purse, feeling its weight as they tossed it from hand to hand. "There's a reason I don't work for you anymore." Kai threw the purse back to Bao, who nearly fumbled it in surprise. "I'm not keen to do it again."

The tension that had been gripping Tal suddenly released.

Malachai's expression however didn't change. "Are you sure you won't reconsider? You know I don't make the same offer twice."

Kai smiled. "Good, that way I don't have to reject you twice."

Bao stepped forward, clenching his fists, his knuckles cracking. But Malachai raised his hand, and the goliath stepped back, folding his arms across his chest.

"Oh Kaivel, Kaivel, Kaivel. That foolish sense of honour will be the death of you one day." Malachai sighed as he rose from the table. "Such a shame, I hate to see talent like yours go to waste." He nodded to Bao, who only grunted in response and walked towards the door. Malachai placed two platinum pieces on the table. "For the drink. Keep the change."

With a grin the snow white tiefling turned on his heel and followed the hulking goliath out of the tavern, leaving the three occupants alone in the wake of his imposition.

In the emptiness all three released a heavy exhale, no longer walking on eggshells as Kai had just stamped all over them. Thinking back to the stories in Master Brum's library, the relief in Tal's chest was slowly replaced with fear. People as powerful as Malachai was, appeared to be, or thought of themselves as, were not accustomed to being told 'no'.

"This is going to be bad, isn't it?" Tal voiced her internal fear.

"Probably," Kai nodded.

"Should we be worried?"

"Probably," Kai nodded again.

This wasn't helping Tal's nerves. "What are we going to do?"

"I think I'm going to faint." Kai nodded a third time. "Yes, definitely going to faint."

217

Before Tal could do anything, the wounded tiefling fell to the floor in a crumpled pile, snoring loudly.

Tess let out a sigh. "It was only a matter of time. Come on, you get the legs, I'll get the arms."

With more difficulty than expected, Tal and Tess carried their unconscious friend up the creaking stairs and into their office, where the two women unceremoniously tossed Kai's body onto the unmade bed. The two of them stood there for a moment, watching Kai snore into a pillow.

"Looking around here," Tess said as she examined the mess around them, "I'm very glad I never offered a cleaning service."

"It is quite something in here." Tal agreed. "Maybe when this is all over I'll try and tidy up."

Tess grabbed the elf by the shoulder and spun her around, pressing and prodding at her shoulder blades.

"What in the world are you doing?" Tal tried and failed to shrug Tess's meaty hands off.

"Checking for wings. If you're not an angel then you must just be a masochist." Tess spun her back. "Or just plain crazy to try cleaning this place."

Tal smiled. After the evening they'd just had anything would have cheered her up. "Crazy might be closer to the mark. But if I'm going to be working with this nutcase," she kicked the bed where Kai lay, "then I want to be able to walk around in here without knocking something over or stepping on something."

≈⊙≈

With Kai tucked in their room Tess returned to the bar, hoping her customers would return at some point, leaving Tal to return to her room to contemplate the day's events. Kai had been beaten up, knocked out, thrown about, threatened, and tossed about again. Yet they were still standing, after a fashion. Laying on her bed Tal took a long slow breath.

Her hand was still in the city. She'd seen the man who had it and he was still in the city. There was a chance she'd get it back, she just had to keep holding on to hope. Tal gently rubbed her stump

218

as she drifted off to sleep, the pain of her old wound gradually fading back into memory.

⇜☉⇝

The following morning Kai remained dead to the world. Poking them, yelling at them, even setting off her little light spell had done nothing to stir the tiefling. In a moment of panic Tal held her hand by their mouth to check for breathing. Not convinced by the slight breeze she felt on her palm she then checked for a pulse. After counting Kai's heartbeat for a full two minutes her fear sunk away and she was left sitting on the end of Kai's bed not knowing what to do with herself.

Jasper was out looking for the ruddy-faced man, she hoped, so there was nothing she could do but wait. Kai had chased up the missing people that D'Clos had given them, and she herself had gotten all she could from Cherie. Tal was no detective, that was for sure, but she wanted to try, she wanted to be helpful. Mostly because she really wanted her hand back, but also for Samara. That poor girl had had her heart ripped out again and again. First losing Patrice, then finding out her friends had betrayed her. Then to top it all off, just when everything seemed to be going her way, Patrice's body had been stolen. Or gotten up and walked away.

That last thought sent a shiver down her spine. It wasn't possible, but the idea was enough to chill her bones. Bones. Bodies. Bodies. The word bounced around her mind over and over again. In her short time in the city she couldn't recall seeing a graveyard or cemetery anywhere. People died, that was for sure, and in a city filled with doe-eyed adventures the amount of people dying was probably higher than average. So what happened to the bodies?

"We've been asking the wrong questions," she said to Kai's limp form, "we've been looking for people. We should have been looking for bodies." Tal patted Kai's leg as she got up and paced back and forth in front of their bed. "The only thing we know that connects Patrice to the missing people is that he's missing…"

219

She voiced the thought out loud to make sure it didn't sound as crazy outside of her own head. "...but what if that's not the only thing they have in common? What if they're also dead?" She looked down at Kai and smiled. "You rest, I've got this!"

With a surge of new found vigor Tal took a deep breath and headed out the door, only to return a half second later to grab Kai's satchel. After all, they weren't going to need it today, and she didn't have a bag. She added that to her mental to-do list, buy a bag.

࿐☉࿐

Out in the street Tal took a deep breath, the fresh morning air filling her chest as she looked up at the cloud speckled sky. Now the real question was, where to begin. The temple seemed like the best option. The dead would be brought there first to be cleansed and interred, so logically they should know what happens to the bodies.

Walking alone through the streets Tal had time to take in more of the sights, gaining a bit more of the geography of the city. Hopefully she'd get lost less frequently if she actually knew where she was. It would also have been nice to know where she could go shopping for some of the basics. She'd only packed a modest pack when she'd left home, just the essentials that were light enough to carry and small enough or foldable enough to fit in a backpack. Which turned out to be fortunate since it was stolen on her first day in the city.

Stopping off at a bakery on the corner of the district for a sweet roll, Tal watched a group of children playing in the street with a bundle tied into a ball, kicking it back and forth between four of them while a fifth tried to intercept. She clutched Kai's bag close to her side. Having her own things stolen was bad, losing Kai's satchel would have been the worst.

It only took Tal a couple of hours to find the temple, and she'd only needed to ask for directions twice, which she felt was an improvement. Her directional skills had never been the best in

220

her own small village, the fact that she'd made it anywhere at all was progress.

Entering the cool stone temple Tal stayed close to the back wall as the preacher delivered a deep sermon, the pews mostly filled with people listening to his words or reading through the passage in their own tomes. Tal chuckled quietly to herself as she spotted two children sleeping while their mother bobbed her head along with the words.

Tal moved slowly around the room, not wanting the echo of her footsteps on the stone floor to interrupt or draw attention. Near the raised altar she saw a boy in temple robes replacing candles in the decorative sconces.

"Excuse me, sorry," Tal whispered as she stood close, not wanting to scare him with her sudden approach, "but could you please tell me where I can find Father Roderic?"

The boy turned around, a puzzled look on his face. "If you need someone for confession the booth is in the west corner near the door." He smiled, happy to have been of help.

Tal frowned. She wanted to ask what about her appearance made her seem like someone who needed to confess to something, but she was also certain she probably wouldn't like the answer. "No," she gritted her teeth in a polite smile, "I need to speak with him about a matter regarding Lord Vaskar. The Father is aware of the matter."

"Of course, I will go and find him immediately." The boy bowed and quietly shuffled off up a flight of stairs.

Tal stood quietly, feeling incredibly out of place in the temple as the preacher continued his sermon. He spoke of the power of the gods, Caledoughn in particular, not that he was in any way biassed of course. He talked about their power to aid those who were seeking help, to guide them through the darkness of the world. Tal accidentally scoffed, drawing the attention of an elderly couple nearby. Blushing horrendously she hid behind a pillar, pressing her back against it.

It was almost a reflex and had been ever since she was a child. Her parents had been quite religious, and she'd spent many a morning listening to the local priest go on about the power and will of the gods, shortly before requesting donations. It was partially down to her choice of vocation. From what she knew of the gods and what she knew of the arcane there were very few differences. The gods granted powers, that was true, and she did not deny that they were indeed powerful beings. But Master Brum had also granted her powers in the arcane, or at least helped her unlock their secrets. Did that make him a god? To her the line between deity and wizardry was far more blurred than either side would like to admit.

Tal's thoughts were interrupted as the boy returned with a priest who was very much not Father Roderic. A considerably younger and more portly dark-skinned elven man, with neat cropped hair and a well groomed beard smiled as he walked over to her. "You were looking for Father Roderic, is that right my dear?"

Tal nodded. "Yes, and unless I'm mistaken you're not him."

The priest laughed, a deep rumble that bounced his husky frame. "Not mistaken at all, my dear. I am Father Elaba. Father Roderic is in a moment of deep reflection." With a glance left and right Father Elaba smiled, leaning in closer to Tal. "He's asleep, and at his age he needs it."

Tal placed her hand over her mouth, trying not to laugh herself. "Well is there perhaps somewhere private we could talk? I have some questions in relation to Lord Vaskar."

A sombre look came across the younger Father's face. "Of course, please follow me." Father Elaba led Tal through a large mess hall and into a modest kitchen. "Can I offer you a cup of tea, miss...?"

"Arcanist Tal'avera," adding her self-imposed title sounded out of place inside the temple, but it was too late now. "And yes, I would love one, thank you."

Father Elaba smiled and set a pot to boil, placing some tea leaves into a pair of ceramic cups. "Do you take honey?"

"I've not before," Tal admitted, "so I will if you are."

"I do, sweetness is a weakness of mine." The Father spooned some of the thick golden goo into each of the mugs. "So an arcanist seeking out Father Roderic. Looking to trade one book for another?"

Tal gave a polite smile. "I am quite happy with my book as it is, but if I do you'll be the first I come to." She cleared her throat and slipped her hand into Kai's satchel. "As I said before I'm here to talk about Lord..." She stopped as her hand groped around at nothing. Tal opened the satchel and peered inside. It was empty. Reaching around inside all she felt was the soft leather of the inside of the bag.

"Damn it," she bit her lip and looked up at the priest before her who was pouring out the tea. "Sorry for cursing Father, I thought I had some parchment-" As the word entered her mind she felt something thump into her palm. Pulling her hand out she found Kai's roll of note covered parchments in her hand. "Oh you sneaky..." She put the parchment on the table and reached back into the bag, thinking about Kai's ink pen. Thud. She smiled as she looked at the pen in her hand.

"Everything okay, miss Tal'avera?"

Tal smiled. "Yes, kind of..." It suddenly occurred to Tal that she'd never written a word with her left hand, and right now that's all she had. "Anyway, where was I?"

"I believe you had some questions about Lord Vaskar?" Father Elaba pushed a cup towards Tal. "I'm happy to help in any way I can." He sipped from his own mug, a gentle moan humming in his nose.

Tal took a sip of her honey-sweetened mug and instantly regretted it. She would never be able to drink plain tea again. "I appreciate that, Father." She flipped through the parchments until she found a blank page. "Are you aware of the situation with Patrice Vaskar?" Tal didn't want to say too much in case Father Roderic hadn't shared the information.

Father Elaba nodded. "Yes, most unfortunate for a young man to pass on so soon." He watched Tal's expression for a moment before continuing. "Or are you referring to the loss of his body?"

"It would be the loss that I'm referring to, yes."

The portly priest nodded. "I thought so. I appreciate your choice of words. Father Roderic has informed the senior clerics about what has happened, but the rest of the clergy, guard, and altar boys have been kept in the dark, just told to be extra vigilant. We didn't want to cause a panic."

"That makes sense," Tal scribbled over her chicken scratch handwriting and started again, the words no more legible than before. "I was interested to know about your temple's process of interment, if you don't mind sharing?"

"As I said, I want to be as helpful as I can." Father Elaba straightened his posture.

"Thank you, Father. So…" Tal cleared her throat. "What is your process? I've not seen a graveyard or cemetery in the city so I was curious to know what happens to those who have passed."

Father Elaba took a deep breath. "There is no cemetery or graveyard within the city limits. The cemetery is to the north outside the city, that is where those that are to be buried are buried."

"Those that are to be buried?" Tal jotted a note she hoped she'd be able to read later.

The priest nodded. "Yes. The ceremony for burial is only for those who have donated to the temple. We cleanse and bless the body, which is a costly and timely process. This protects the body from corruption and helps the soul to move on to its final resting place."

"And those that don't make this donation?" Tal resisted using the word 'fee'. A toll on the dead didn't sit right with her.

"Cremation." Father Elaba said flatly. "There is a short ceremony where a blessing is said over a pyre and the body is burned, allowing the soul to travel freely to the afterlife."

"Uh-huh," Tal chewed her lip to stop further comment. "And who takes care of these ceremonies, Father?" Tal had given up on the written word and started making small pictures. They were still messy, but she had a better chance of deciphering them later.

"One of the senior Fathers performs the blessing," he sipped his tea, "but the rest is taken care of by the clergy here or the groundskeeper at the cemetery."

Tal drew a crude sketch of a man in a robe and a man with a shovel. "If I might also ask, how are those for burial transported

224

to the cemetery? Is that again taken care of by the clergy, or do you hire a coach?" Tal had a sudden absurd image in her mind of a pair of priests and a body with its arms slung over their shoulders trying to hail a coach.

"The groundskeeper," Father Elaba cleared his throat. "The groundskeeper collects those to be buried from the temple. He has a cart and horse that he uses and maintains also as part of his duties."

Adding a stick figure horse and cart to the parchment Tal rolled it up and put it away in the satchel. "Thank you, Father. You have been very helpful."

A smile rested upon the priest's face. "I'm glad. Hopefully we can bring this terrible business to an end, and get that poor boy rested properly." Father Elaba opened a cupboard and pulled out a small ceramic pot with a cork stopper. "For you, my dear, as a sign of my thanks."

Cheeks reddening slightly, Tal took the pot from Father Elaba and popped the cork with some difficulty. The sweet scent of honey floated into her nose. "You are too kind, Father."

"No one should be without sweetness in their tea." Patting his round stomach Father Elaba gestured to the door. "I'll see you out, my dear. And when Father Roderic awakens I shall let him know you stopped by."

As she wandered the streets of Belgar Tal examined the notes and doodles, trying to commit as much of it to memory as possible. Her handwriting was awful and her drawings looked like they'd been made by a drunk ogre, but she knew what they meant and hopefully by the time she got back to the Den Kai would be awake and could write everything down for her.

Dipping her hand back into the enchanted satchel, Tal pulled out a piece of Kai's jerky, sniffing it reluctantly. She took a tentative bite, tearing off a strip of the dried meat. The flavour was not as bad as she expected, but the salt! Tal spat the piece out as she walked, feeling like all the moisture from her mouth had been sucked away by the overly seasoned meat.

"How they eat that I'll never know." She said to herself, quickly looking around to check no one had spotted her spitting in the street. She saw a sailor leaning against an alley wall urinating and realised it could have been worse.

The sun had just tipped past noon as she found herself back in that familiar market square, the statue she'd once slept by standing tall and casting little shadow on those sat by its plinth.

Tal smiled, thinking about how much her life had changed in the last few days. When she woke up on those cold stone steps she'd had nothing. No coin, no belongings, no hand, no friends, and nowhere to stay. The lack of hand notwithstanding, since meeting Kai her life had certainly changed for the better. Far more exciting than she could have expected as an enchanter.

Looking around the stalls and noting that she wasn't in any particular hurry, Tal decided to tick a few things off her mental to-do list. She spent a good portion of that afternoon haggling down vendors, not being as tight on funds as before, but also not wanting to spend all her earnings in one day. She managed to pick up a simple yet stylish woven leather satchel, a modest roll of parchments with an ink pen and a few pencils. After reviewing her doodles Tal was considering taking up drawing as her hobby. After all there was a significant amount of artistry in spell crafting, and she'd always enjoyed that.

In a moment of gratitude, still thinking about all they'd done for her, Tal decided to buy a gift for Kai and Tess, feeling incredibly embarrassed as she tucked Tess's gift away in her new bag.

A beautiful hue of red and gold began to spread across the sky by the time Tal made it back to the tavern, where she was happy to see Tess's clientele had not been put off by the events of the previous night. It even appeared to have grown somewhat as there were a few faces Tal did not recognise.

She sauntered up to the bar, making sure Tess got a good view of her new satchel. The troll-orc tavernkeep smiled, pouring a small cup from a small dark wooden barrel. "Looking fancy there sweetie."

226

"Thanks," Tal smiled with pride as she stroked the soft woven leather, "thought I'd treat myself." She took out the parchment wrapped gift and placed it on the bar before Tess. "Speaking of treats..."

Tess beamed at her. "Oh sweetie, you shouldn't have!" She lifted up the gift and began to unwrap it, her usually pale cheeks suddenly turning bright pink. "Untamed Passion..." Tess bit her lip and quickly covered the book again.

"Thought you might like something new to read." Tal smiled, taking the mug from Tess and sipping, surprise lighting up her eyes. "Is this?"

Tess nodded. "Like you said, 'speaking of treats'. I bought a barrel of red wine for you. Since it looks like you're going to be sticking around for a while longer."

The two smiled at each other, both grateful for the gifts they had given one another.

"Has Kai poked their head out yet? Or have you been up to see them?" Tal asked when Tess had returned from hiding her evenings entertainment.

"No and no," Tess shrugged, "surprisingly I've been crazy busy. Word got out about you-know-who's visit last night and now people are flocking in."

That was surprising. Tal sipped her wine, enjoying the fruity taste. "You'd think being threatened and kicked out of here would make people think twice. You've really been that busy?"

Tess nodded. "Apparently he didn't threaten anyone to leave, he paid them."

That wasn't surprising. Though it did make Tal wonder how valuable the items were that Malachai wanted back that he was willing to offer up so much coin. "Mind if I take this upstairs?" Tal tapped her mug. "I should probably check to see if Kai's still alive."

"If they're not, you get first dibs on their room." Tess smiled, grabbing a mug and pouring a drink for a heavy set halfling.

☙ ☉ ❧

Up in Kai's office the battered and bruised tiefling continued to snore, their position unchanged since Tal had last left them. Tal gathered some cushions from around the room and set up a cosy little nook beside the bed, and spent the remainder of the evening talking to her unconscious friend about her day. She even lit a small candle and began sketching Kai's sleeping face, not to any great degree of accuracy, but it helped pass the time until she too drifted off to sleep, the flickering candle burning itself out.

CHAPTER 19

The aroma of bacon filled Tal's nose, her other senses taking their time to awaken that morning. Her mouth watering, her eyes blinking away the sleep, and an aching throb running down her back, neck and shoulders, Tal groaned as the world came into focus. Sitting on her lap was a small plate with a steaming hot bacon sandwich, dripping with butter, between two slices of thick crusted bread.

"Morning sleepyhead," Kai smiled down at her from the bed. They seemed to have recovered somewhat from their day of rest. The bruising around their eyes and jaw had faded a bit, and the cut on their lip had scabbed over.

"Good morning," Tal smiled, happy to see Kai conscious. "How are you feeling?"

They'd clearly been awake longer than Tal. Changed from their dirt and blood covered suit to a simple linen shirt and trousers, with a half-eaten sandwich on their own plate.

"My face hurts, my tail aches, and I can't breathe out of my left nostril," Kai shrugged, "but much better, thanks. What about you?"

Tal shifted to sit up straight, her body protesting the movement. "Achy. A wall does not make for the most comfortable bed."

"I'll bear that in mind!" Kai laughed. "It is sweet that you spent the night there just to keep an eye on me." They took a bite of their sandwich. "Where'd you find that?" Kai pointed to Tal's new bag.

She pulled it towards her, covering her bad drawings of the sleeping tiefling. "Yesterday at the market, I had a little time to kill so I went shopping."

Kai stared at her in deep confusion. "Yesterday? We didn't go near the market yesterday."

"Kai..." Tal narrowed her gaze on them and began speaking in a slow gentle tone, "you've been sleeping for two nights. Ever since Malachai left."

"Huh, well that explains it." Kai shrugged, not phased by this new information.

Now it was Tal's turn to look confused. "Explains what?"

"Why I was so hungry." Kai gestured to her plate. "This is the second round of sandwiches. I ate both mine and yours earlier. Then I felt bad, and still a bit peckish honestly, and got us some more."

Tal lifted the sandwich to her lips, giving it a tentative sniff. "You didn't make these, did you?"

Kai shook their head, swallowing their mouthful. "No, Yern won't let me in the kitchen after last time. Why?"

Tal took a bite, smiling back. "No reason. Who's Yern? Tess mentioned him before but there was so much going on I didn't think to ask."

"Tess's half-brother. He runs the kitchen, and is one hell of a cook." A cheeky smile crept across Kai's face. "If you ever meet him you'll see which side of the family he's from. What are those?"

Tal ignored the fact that Kai implied there was a troll living under the tavern and let herself be taken by the change of subject. "Oh just some doodles. I thought I'd try drawing, as a hobby I mean."

Before she knew it Kai had rolled out of bed and scooped up one of the pages, landing on the opposite side of her. "Huh, interesting." Kai held the page up in front of the pair of them. "An interesting style. Is it some kind of dragon?"

"Kind of," Tal smirked.

"I like it." Kai chucked the page back to the floor. "So, catch me up. What have I missed?"

The pair sat on the floor, finishing off their breakfast, as Tal went through her day in detail, even sending Kai to collect her notes from their satchel. They nodded throughout, asking the odd

230

question here and there, but largely just listened to her theory as she explained.

When she was done, Kai continued to nod, making more legible notes under Tal's scribbles and sketches. "I'm impressed," Kai finally said as they put their arm around her. "You thought of something crazy and went after it. And you didn't wait to be told to." They gave her a squeeze. "You're going to be a great assistant."

"Thank yo...assistant?" Tal's smile of gratitude turned into a frown.

Kai just beamed at her. "Well if your crazy idea turns out to be a good lead, we'll talk about promoting you to 'partner'." With a grin and a wink Kai pushed theirself off the floor and walked over to the wardrobe.

"You're such a pain sometimes," Tal rolled her eyes as she stood up with a groan. "And after I went and got you a present."

Kai spun on the spot, holding two identical white cotton shirts. "Oh a present?" Their smile almost reaching from ear to ear.

Tal opened her bag and pulled out a twine wrapped roll of emerald green material, throwing it over to Kai. "It's a tie. I thought it would go well with your complexion, and add a bit more colour to your outfit."

Untying the roll, Kai unraveled it, draping it around the neck of the shirt they held. "That's far too kind, Tal'avera." Kai turned to her with a smile. "You can't tell, but I'm blushing. Now, unless you want to get your pencils out again, I need to get dressed, so be gone."

"I don't think I'm ready to start life drawing yet!" Tal cried as she scurried from the room, shutting the door behind her.

After making a brief stop in her own room to freshen up and cast a cleaning spell on her own robes, Tal headed down to the tavern, where Tess stood behind the bar checking the various barrels.

231

"Morning sweetie," Tess waved at her, "feeling better now are we?"

"Feeling better? When was I unwell?" Tal cocked an eyebrow as she sat at the bar stool.

"I don't know," Tess shrugged, "but apparently you had quite the appetite. Kai said you polished off those sandwiches like a starved hound."

Tal screwed up her face. "Oh did they now..."

"Ah, speak of the devil!" Tess nodded to the stairs as Kai meandered down.

"And they shall appear," Kai finished, sitting down at the bar next to Tal. "Are you ever going to get tired of that?"

"Probably not. You look nice though. Done something to your horns?"

"Yes, I thought I'd try wearing them up today." Kai rolled their eyes and stood up, giving a spin. Back in their slate-grey suit, hair tied up and hairpins in place, and a shiny new emerald tie around their neck.

"I think you look lovely." Tal smiled, happy to have been right about the complimentary colours. "Are we off to the cemetery today then?"

"That's our best lead for now," Kai nodded, "though I want to catch Jasper before we leave. I want to pick his brain about something."

"Well when you see him," Tess called over her shoulder, "tell him to say hi to Tiny for me."

✿☉✿

Jasper, as it turned out, was incredibly hard to find when he wanted to be. Checking the usual spots with no success, Kai and Tal began searching down every street, alley, and nook for any sign of the sneaky fence. After an hour with less luck than a bull in a house of mirrors, a memory popped into Tal's head.

"He took me to this tavern before," she snapped her fingers together, trying to recall more details. "Near the edge of the city. Or was it just outside?"

232

"Do you remember what it was called?" Kai asked, trying not to get frustrated by Tal's terrible city geography.

"No," she admitted as she chewed on her lip, "but the sign had a rat on it. Or maybe it was a mouse…"

Kai clapped their hands together. "The Mouse Hole. Come on!" Without waiting to see if she'd followed, Kai was off at double pace, their elven accomplice skipping after them.

≈⊙≈

Keeping at Kai's brisk speed the pair made good time as they raced halfway across the city, arriving at the dingy looking tavern that Tal remembered.

"This is the place." She nodded as Kai led them through the door into the small bar area.

Just as dark and uninviting as Tal remembered, and sitting in a booth with a foaming pint of ale at his lips and a look of surprise in his eyes was Jasper.

Not waiting for an invitation Kai and Tal slid into the booth opposite him, waiting for the tankard to be lowered.

Wiping the foam from his lips Jasper sighed. "I knew bringing you here was a bad idea."

"Are you avoiding me, Jasper?" Kai leaned back in the booth and folded their arms.

Looking around to see if anyone was watching the table Jasper nodded. "Yes. The word is out, you're persona non grata." He leaned in across the table, keeping his voice low. "What the hells did you do?"

"They turned down a job from Malac-" Tal stopped short as both Kai and Jasper held a finger to their lips.

Shaking his head Jasper whistled a long low note. "The old snowflake must have been desperate thinking he could pull you back in. What was the job?"

"That's why I'm looking for you. What can you tell me about Imis Wikson?" Kai leaned in too, keeping their voice down.

Not wanting to be left out Tal did the same, making it completely obvious that this table was up to something suspicious.

Jasper scratched his stubbly chin, looking back and forth between Kai and Tal. "He's a thief, well, a lazy thief. Works for you-know-who, or at least he did last I spoke to him. What's he to you?"

"Our pale friend is looking for him. Thinks he's gone off with some expensive goods." Kai said, keeping an eye on the bartender who was unsubtly watching their table.

"What do you mean a lazy thief?" Tal asked, eager to learn more terminology.

"He's a graverobber," Jasper said, "got no skill for breaking in or out of places. But from what I hear he can dig and fill a grave faster than any gravedigger. I suppose that's a skill in itself."

Tal didn't know much about digging graves, but she'd tried to plant a tree once and digging that little hole had taken hours. Not to mention what it has done to her arms.

Kai and Tal exchanged a glance, both sharing the same thought. It looked like her crazy theory might have been right after all.

"When was the last time you saw him?" Kai turned back to Jasper.

"Ooh..." The fence pinched the bridge of his nose as he cast his mind back. "Got to be at least a month ago now. Had this nice little broach he wanted shifting." Jasper stared intently at the pair in front of him. "He got something to do with your dead noble?"

"You've been a great help," Kai patted their friend on the cheek, "let's not get you into any more trouble, eh?" Kai gestured for Tal to get up and the two of them slid out of the booth.

"I've not had any luck finding your red-faced man yet either," Jasper said aloud to Tal as she stood, "but don't worry, I'm still keeping an eye and an ear out for you."

Tal smiled, giving him a nod as Kai made their way to the bar.

Placing two silver coins down on the bar, they said in a very serious voice, "You didn't see us, and you didn't see anyone speak with him all day."

The grubby faced bartender looked over at Jasper and Tal. "What about your friend there?"

Kai placed a third coin down on the bar, their eyes turning black and the small sconces around the bar flickered out and on again. "What friend?"

The bartender took the coin, cowering back into the corner as with a flick of their tail Kai turned, leading Tal out and back into the street.

Not stopping as the doors closed behind them, Kai led Tal at a quick march down several streets before turning a sharp corner and stopping flat against a wall. Tal did the same, not quite sure what was going on but not wanting to be in the way.

"What are we doing?" she leaned over to Kai and whispered, keeping her eyes peeled for anything at all.

"We're leaning against a wall," Kai leaned into Tal. "Why are we whispering?"

The elven woman frowned at the puzzled tiefling. "I thought we were hiding from someone. Why did you rush off like that?" Tal stepped away from the wall and brushed the dust off the back of her robe as best she could.

"Oh, no. I just wanted to put some distance between us and Jasper. No use getting him in trouble too." Kai pulled out a piece of jerky and chewed as they thought. "Looks like we've got a few reasons to be heading to the cemetery today, huh?"

Tal nodded. "Do you think this Imis Wikson has something to do with Patrice's body going missing?"

"Maybe," Kai kicked a stone down the alley and walked back out into the street, moving slowly with the crowd. "It's not a big leap from grave robbery to body snatching. And if he's as strong as Jasper's rumours say it would be easy for him to snatch Patrice and run."

"But surely someone would see a man walking out of a temple with a body over his shoulder?" People could be caught up in their own world sometimes, but Tal honestly couldn't imagine missing that pass her by on the street.

The idea made Kai chuckle as they walked along. "You'd hope so," they said with a deep exhale. "There could be another way out of the temple. We can check that out tomorrow."

Something had been playing on Tal's mind since the meeting with Malachai, and now that they weren't in any particular hurry it seemed like a good time to bring it up.

"The other day, when Malachai came to find us at the Den," Tal was already turning pink as the words formulated in her mind, "when he said to 'deal with' Imis…"

Kai nodded along, waiting for the question to come. "Yes?"

She cleared her throat, suddenly feeling like she was getting involved in something that wasn't her business. "Why didn't you take the job? That was a lot of coin he was offering."

Kai sighed hard, running their hands through their hair and tightening their pinned bun. "To Malachai there's only one way to deal with someone who he thinks has turned on him. Kill them."

Panic returned to Tal's mind. Hadn't Kai turned on Malachai?

"I didn't take the job because I don't, and won't, kill people." Kai continued. "Taking a job from him wouldn't stop there. There's always another job, then another, and another. I'm not going back to that life."

A smile of pride warmed Tal's face, hiding the fear that lurked beneath. "Aren't you worried that he'll come after you? Pay someone else to 'deal' with you?"

Kai scoffed. "Nah. I know everyone he'd try to send after me, and they like me better."

"Even Bao?" Tal remembered the goliath's reaction to Kai's refusal of the job.

"Maybe not Bao, but he doesn't scare me. He's all fire and no spark." Kai laughed. "Don't you worry Tal, we're safe from Malachai for the time being." They patted her on the shoulder.

Somehow that didn't make her feel better. The more she learned about Malachai the less she liked him, and the more she realised her novels played down the realities of such people. "Another thing, why did you and Jasper shush me in the tavern?"

The pair turned onto the north street, the gate not too far off in the distance.

"Places like that," Kai said, "it's usually better to avoid using his name, especially if you don't want him hearing about it."

236

They continued walking towards the gate, where a cluster of guards were examining the contents of a large wagon. A number of heavily armed adventurers clambering about, lifting hides and opening barrels, trying to prove they weren't smuggling anything. Tal remembered her own entry to the city. It hadn't required as many guards, but they'd gone through her belongings and asked far too many irrelevant questions. No one ever paid as much attention to you when you left the city she noticed, as the two of them passed through the gate unmolested.

"Tal! Hey!" a familiar voice broke through the arguing around the wagon.

The pair turned to see a dirt covered Samara standing on top of a large pile of furs on top of the wagon, waving at them as she hopped over people on her way to the ground.

"Samara!" Tal embraced her as she approached them. "What's going on with all of this?" She gestured to the chaos.

Samara wiped a dirty arm across her sweaty brow. She was filthy, but happy it seemed, a bright smile plastered across her face. "I needed to take my mind off of things," she panted as she spoke, "so I joined up with a new party going out on a hunt." She turned to greet Kai and her smile turned to shock. "My gods! What happened to you? You look terrible!"

The tiefling gave a crooked smile of their own. "That's kind of you to say. Nothing to worry about, just took a cannon to the face."

Tal interjected as utter dismay spread across Samara's face. "They got caught up in a tavern brawl, it's not as bad as it sounds."

"Of course you'd say that," Kai scoffed, "you abandoned me to go chase boys."

"Oh stop exaggerating!" Tal huffed and gave Kai a shove. "All that matters is we're ok and making progress with the case."

Samara's face was a mess of dirt and expressions, not following what was going on in front of her at all. So she simply smiled and nodded along. "Have you managed to find out anything more about what happened to Patrice?" Once again Tal saw that glimmer of hope sparkle in Samara's eye.

Wanting to keep that hope alive as long as she could, Tal nodded. "Yes, we're on our way to the cemetery now. We think the groundskeeper there might be able to tell us something."

Joy now beamed through the dirt, a large grin on Samara's face making her doey eyes look even bigger. "That's wonderful! Do you mind if I come along? I promise not to be a bother."

Tal was about to open her mouth to extend the invitation, but stopped short. This was Kai's investigation, and Samara was Kai's client. As much as Tal now felt a part of their world, she was still practically brand new to it, maybe Samara tagging along would interfere with Kai's plans. She turned to face them, trying to read the blank expression on their still slightly swollen face.

Kai shrugged and threw their hands back. "Why not? I don't see what harm it would do. I've already got one tag-along," they playfully nudged Tal, "a second wouldn't hurt."

The two women smiled, an obvious wave of excitement rolling through both of them. "Oh thank you! I will be on my best behaviour." Samara gave a little salute and heel click. "Let me just tell these guys I'm off, I'll catch up with you." She skipped back to her party, who were now haggling the entry fee with the guards.

Tal and Kai continued walking. "You really think I'm just a tag-along?" Tal asked with a note of feigned sadness to her voice.

"Of course not," Kai grinned cheekily, "not just a tag-along."

CHAPTER 20

It was a pleasant afternoon stroll around the city's outer wall. The clouds smattering the sky occasionally passed across the sun, keeping it relatively cool on their uphill hike to the Belgar cemetery. Kai remained mostly silent as they walked, but that was less to do with them and more to do with Samara's constant talking. Tal managed to squeeze in a few words edgewise, but that took up what little room there was.

The excitable archer filled the two of them in on her last few days of activity, which involved a lot of crying, drinking, and writing letters to the Vaskar family. In her words, Samara finally decided enough was enough and joined a small party to help take her mind off things. They'd just returned from hunting down a cursed dire boar that had been tearing through the countryside. It had been good to get out of the city, but she wasn't quite ready to go back yet.

"I received a letter from Patrice's parents just before I left. They're on their way to collect his body, it was sent a few days ago, so they should arrive sometime next week." Samara sighed, staring off at the horizon. "Which means they didn't receive my other letters in time."

"That express charge will get you one way or the other." Kai nodded with recognition.

Tal held Samara's hand, giving it a reassuring squeeze. "Then we've still got time to find him."

Belgar cemetery was almost like a small village of its own, the array of tombstones looking like buildings, and the mausoleums like grand manor houses. A rundown stone wall encircling the area around the cliff edge, it was a beautiful spot for a final resting place. As they drew closer to the wrought iron gates Tal pointed out a building that didn't seem to fit in with the marble and stone architecture surrounding it.

"Is that a house?" She asked as if it wasn't obvious to all of them that it was. A patched thatched roof with a chimney poking out to one side, and ivy-covered red brick walls. It really looked quite quaint if you ignored its macabre location.

"More of a cottage I'd say." Kai pushed the gate open with an ear-piercing screech.

"Wouldn't that make this a graveyard then?" Samara added, waggling a finger in her ear to stop the ringing.

Tal shrugged. "What's the difference?"

"We can ask the groundskeeper if you're that curious, people are still in the ground no matter what you call it." Kai rolled their eyes at the conversation. "It doesn't look like anyone's home though."

Getting closer to the house or cottage that resided in the cemetery or graveyard, it did look like no one was home, and hadn't been home in quite some time. The windows were clouded with dust, dirt, and cobwebs, the ivy was less decorative and more wild. There were sections of the thatching that had become home to a number of bird's nests.

"Either no one lives here or this groundskeeper isn't very good at their job." Kai wiped the window before pressing their face against it, trying to peek inside. "It's pretty dark in there."

"I thought you guys could see in the dark?" Samara said before holding her hand in front of her mouth. "I don't mean to presume, that just always something Kirtan mocked the rest of us for. Our human eyes being useless after sundown."

Kai's face squeaked along the glass. "He's not wrong, you aren't great when the sun goes down." They smiled as they looked over to the two women. "And yes, we can see in the dark, but not perfectly." Kai reached into their satchel and pulled out a familiar little tool pouch.

Tal rolled her eyes. "We could try knocking first?" She walked up to the door, banging her stump against it a few times. "Hello!" She shouted. "Hello! Is anyone at home?"

Only the response Tal got was the sounds of birds flapping out of their nests to escape from the crazy elf making all the noise below.

"Satisfied?" Kai crouched down by the lock and began picking it. "You two just keep an eye out."

Tal and Samara turned their backs to Kai, forming a wall around them as they worked on the lock. Looking around for any sign of movement between the headstones, it seemed they were completely alone. A few short clicks and a groan and the door creaked open. The trio hurried inside, closing the door behind them.

Tal spoke a few words and some small globules of light floated up from her fingertips, hovering around the room casting dancing shadows in strange patterns.

Inside the house was in as much of a state of neglect as the outside. Dust coated every surface, the smell of damp and mould hung in the stagnant air. In the absence of any person sized creature smaller lifeforms had taken residence. Beatles scurried away from the light, hiding beneath furniture and creeping into cracks in the floor. Spiderwebs hung from the ceiling and filled gaps between the cupboards and stair railings, a banquet of dead bugs gathered in the sticky nets.

"Much better, thank you." Samara smiled as she blinked a few times, her eyes adjusting to the sudden brightness of the room. "So what's the plan?"

Kai cleared their throat, having a quick glance around the open living room. "You two search upstairs for anything that looks out of place. I'll search down here. Shout if you find anything, scream if anything finds you."

"Scream?" Tal raised an eyebrow. "Why can't we just shout for anything?"

"Because we need some kind of code to know if something bad is happening." Kai shrugged. "But sure, shout if you find anything, shout if anything finds you, just make the shouts different."

Tal and Samara headed up the stairs, each step groaning under their weight.

Samara laughed quietly as she followed behind Tal. "It's both impressive and unbelievable that Kai is a detective. Every time I've spoken to them it feels like they're making it all up as they go along."

Tal laughed too, trying to hide the awkward agreement she felt. Kai may have been making it up as they went along, but so was she.

The globules floated around Tal as she walked, meaning Samara was stuck following too. Upstairs was in as much of a state of disrepair as below. Tal sniffed the air, screwing up her nose. "It smells so much worse up here."

Samara nodded, holding her own nose as they entered the dank bedroom. "Let's get this done as quickly as we can and get out of here."

They began searching opposite sides of the room, Tal taking the bed and desk. She pulled draws and moved books, blowing clouds of dust around her, not sure what she was looking for. Everything seemed normal if not a bit depressing. The draws contained dates for burials and plot locations, which Tal grabbed to compare the names with Kai's list of missing people. There was nothing particularly special about the book, though they might have been interesting reads. A book on masonry repair had a number of bookmarks sticking out of it, and another on floriculture had a few dog-eared pages.

Putting those back into place out of habit Tal called over to Samara. "I've got some papers, have you found anything?"

Rummaging through a chest of drawers she turned and shook her head. "This guy needs some new socks, but I don't feel like that's relevant."

Moving on to search the bed with a smile on her face Tal threw the covers back and yelped. Samara turned, hand reaching for the dagger at her hip as the large rat that had been nestled beneath the covers scurried off with a few agitated squeaks.

The two women released a breath of relief as Kai's voice from below called up. "Did you find something or did something find you?"

"Both." Tal shouted back. "We're fine, don't worry."

Checking carefully for more rodents Tal started under the bed, brushing away thick cobwebs. There had been many occasions over the past week where Tal had very much missed her arcane prosthetic, but never more than having to touch cobwebs.

Bugs, spiders, and a warrenful of dust bunnies now called this section of the house home, along with a pair of well eaten shoes and a few pebbles of which Tal assumed were rat droppings. Nothing that stood out to her as unusual. Disgusting, yes, but not unusual.

An actual scream came from above, and in Tal's hurry to be of aid she cracked her head on the bed frame. With spots dancing in her eyes and her pulse roaring in her ears Tal knelt up, looking across the bed to see what had startled Samara.

"Did you find something, or did something find you?" Kai's new catchphrase echoed from downstairs.

"Er...we definitely found something." Tal's eyes were wide as she watched Samara wrestling with a long dead body that had fallen out of the closet.

Pushing the corpse to the floor Samara dusted herself down and tried to regain her composure. "I'm okay, I'm okay," she said to herself as well as Tal. "It just surprised me, that's all."

After a rush of footsteps Kai appeared at the door, looking from the body to the women and back again.

"He was like that when we found him," Tal held her hands up defensively.

Kai nodded. "Good to know. Let's see who he is." They crouched down next to the body and began examining it with ruthless efficiency.

Tal crouched down next to them, watching as they examined the hands, went through the pockets, sniffed the dirt on its bug-eaten clothes. Kai didn't even flinch as a large beetle scurried out of the empty eye socket while they examined the rotten teeth. It made Tal wonder how many dead bodies Kai had seen that they were this comfortable.

Finished with their investigation of the body they stood up and cleared their throat. "I think we've found the groundskeeper."

"What makes you so sure?" Samara asked as she climbed over the bed, giving the body a wide berth.

"Firstly," Kai held a finger up, "his clothes and finger nails are covered in dirt. Secondly, his body was stuffed in his closet."

Samara didn't look convinced. "Why does his body being here make him the groundskeeper? That could be anybody."

"It could, but if you were going to hide a body, would you do it in your own bedroom?" Kai raised a curious eyebrow. "Add the fact that someone has been staying here and hasn't bothered to tidy the place makes it all the more likely."

Now it was Tal's turn to be curious. "What do you mean someone's been staying here? There was a rat sleeping in the bed."

Kai led the two of them back downstairs and into the kitchen where the remains of a plate of food sat on the table, not going mouldy, and a bedroll was folded up by the fireplace. "I think whoever killed the groundskeeper has been squatting."

Tal nudged the plate of food, wrinkling her nose once more. It may not have been mouldy but it certainly stank. "Even if you were squatting, who could live like this?"

"The kind of person who leaves bodies in closets?" Samara suggested. "Maybe even the kind of person who steals bodies from temples?"

Kai shrugged. "Well unless you two want to go back upstairs with the groundskeeper, you can help me search down here."

Not wanting to spend any more time in a room with a dead body than necessary, both Tal and Samara joined in the search. They began checking in cupboards and draws, moving things as little as possible, trying to put things back exactly as they found them when they did move something. Everything was as Tal expected, which was not what she expected. There were no bloody weapons hidden with the brooms. No poisons or potions mixed in with the spices and herbs. Not even a bag of coin tucked behind the flour. Everything was unordinarily ordinary.

"Where would you even hide a body here?" Samara called from the living room.

"There is a cemetery out there." Kai replied from the pantry. There was a clutter and a bang, followed by some curses in infernal. Tal added 'learn basic infernal' to her mental to-do list. That may only include the curses, but it was always good to know when you were being insulted in another language.

She leaned against the pantry door, looking down at Kai who was buried under a half-dozen hessian sacks. A grin crept across her face. "Did you find something, or did something find you?"

Kai blinked up at her, looking unimpressed and uncomfortable. "Both." They shoved aside a large sack that had landed on their chest, holding their hand out to Tal. "Are you going to just stand there or are you going to be helpful?"

Tal scratched her chin in mock thought. "Are those my only options?" She stuck her tongue out as Kai glared back at her. "Oh alright," she laughed and held out her hand, helping Kai to their feet. "Careful, it's the only one I've got left."

Kai snorted as they dusted theirself off. "Thanks. I think there's more in these sacks than flour and oats." Opening the nearest one Kai sifted through the loose grain and pulled out a small porcelain raven. "Start emptying bags."

Like children on Winterscrest the two of them began tearing open sacks, tipping them up, pouring their dusty contents all over the place. Oats and grain covered the floor of the small pantry so deep that the pair were almost wading through it. All manner of peculiar oddity rested on the oaty floor as Kai kicked about to reveal as much as possible. Jewellery, clothing both fine and simple, the odd weapon, and a very unusual picture frame. Kai continued to sift through their discovery, watched by Tal and Samara, who had heard the commotion and come to investigate.

Dusting their hands off on their already dusty trousers Kai surveyed the mess around them. "Can you do your thing?" Kai wiggled their fingers

Tal folded her arms and raised an eyebrow. "My thing? I'm not just here to be your utility wizard."

"Fair enough, you can pick the next lock then, deal?" Kai grinned.

Rolling her eyes, but refusing to admit defeat, Tal rolled up her sleeve, which was only half as effective as she'd hoped, and pulled out her spellbook. After spending a couple of minutes casting Tal's eyes flashed with arcane light. "The raven and the picture frame are enchanted, as well as that dagger. But the rest is pretty mundane."

"Thank you," Kai continued to grin. They waded through the oats and grain, gathering the items Tal had pointed out. "If there's a chance these were what Mala-" They shot a glance at Samara, "What you-know-who was looking for then I think we should hang on to them."

Watching Kai slide the tall frame into the void of their satchel gave Tal an uncomfortable feeling in her stomach.

"So does this prove that whoever is staying here is the one who took Patrice?" Again there was that glint of hope in Samara's eye.

"Well," Kai made their way out of the pantry, shaking off the dust from their trousers, "I think we should stick around to find out."

꙳☉꙳

One of the wonderful things about summer is that the evenings never grow cold. Even as the sun begins to set and the shadows grow long the wind carries warmth from beyond the horizon. Tal was especially grateful for this as she sat back against the cold marble of a mausoleum a hundred or so yards from the house.

Kai and Samara were sitting nearby enjoying a bite of Kai's satchel jerky. Smiling at a thought in her head Samara chuckled. "We are starting to make a habit of late night stakeouts."

"Ha, true." Kai patted her on the shoulder. "Let's hope this one works out as well as last time." They stretched out against the wall, their horns making a high-pitched squeak as they scratched against the marble. "Oops," Kai grinned awkwardly.

Tal sighed as she watched the oranges and reds of the evening's sky slowly fade into deep purples and blues, the first speckle of stars beginning to shine through. "And hopefully we don't have to wait as long. " She hugged her stomach to muffle the bubbling groan.

Kai held up a hand to silence them, tilting their head to the side and staring into the middle distance. "I think our wait might be over."

Tal listened carefully, a quiet drumming sound getting slowly louder to the rhythm of galloping horseshoes.

The three of them peeped around the edge of the mausoleum, the last rays of the day just shining over the horizon, to see a man on horseback half-silhouetted racing towards them, a large bundle bouncing behind the saddle. As he drew closer Tal was able to pick out a few details. In his speed the hood of his cloak had blown back, revealing his half-shaved head. Slowing to a canter and then a trot as he approached the house, she could better make out the bundle. It was long, dropping down on either side of the horse's hindquarters, wrapped in many layers of cloth and tied tight with rope.

The three continued to watch, Samara held back by Kai when she tried to engage, as the man hoisted the bundle off the horse, dropping it to the floor with a heavy thud and a cloud of dust. He proceeded to drag it towards the house, stopping only to unlock the door, before continuing inside. They waited for a moment for a candle to be lit but the house remained dark.

"Do you think he saw the mess in the pantry?" Tal asked. For all their tidying as they searched etiquette, there was no way to clean up what they had done in the pantry. Even magic had its limits.

"Let's move in, but be quiet and careful." Kai held a finger to their lips and crouched down, moving quickly yet silently towards the house.

Tal and Samara followed suit, staying low as they moved. Tal began to trail behind, sneaking around wasn't her forte and she didn't want to make a noise by rushing.

When she caught up with them Samara nodded to Kai and drew her bow, moving around towards the other side of the house. Kai turned to her now, speaking in a low soft voice. "I'll get the lock, you just be ready to run in case things go sideways. Get back to D'Clos, tell him what we know."

Tal didn't like the idea of running while her friends were in trouble, but she knew Kai had a point. While she was still handless she wouldn't be much help if things turned violent in such a small environment.

After waiting a few moments for Samara to get into position Kai took out their lock pick set and carefully inserted them into the door. Though it didn't appear to be needed. As Kai moved the pick the door eased open with an unwelcome creak.

With eyes wide Kai quickly moved into the darkened room. Not knowing whether to stay or follow Tal gave into instinct and slipped in behind them, carefully closing the door behind her.

The room was much like it had been on their first visit, apart from the large bundle in the middle of the floor. Looking at it clearly now, it's shape and size, Tal feared she knew what was inside.

There was no sign of the man though. No little flickering candles coming from the kitchen or the stairs. No sound of footsteps from above or from the other rooms. It was as if he'd simply vanished.

Kai knelt down by the bundle, taking the dagger they'd found in the pantry and carefully cutting through the material at one end. Tal stood next to them, looking down with sadness at the face of a young half-elf lad.

Kai held their fingers under his nose, then against his neck before shaking their head. "He's dead." Kai whispered.

"Yes, dead." A voice echoed around them, seemingly coming from nowhere.

Kai shot up, the dagger now held in a more aggressive manner. Tal stood at their back, embers glowing from her fingertips as she quietly repeated the first part of the cantrip over and over.

"Dead indeed," the voice continued, "dead like you will be, should be." There was a chuckle. "I knew I should have killed you little elf girl, when I found you sleeping under that statue. But foolish as I am, wanting to take my time got the better of me and we had company."

Tal and Kai began to spin on the spot, keeping back to back as their eyes searched the room. The voice sounded like it was coming from the very shadows.

"We've never tried a caster before," it continued. "My master only wanted the strongest, but I think taking you could have been the key to what the little ones were after."

A chair toppled over, Kai and Tal spinning to face it.

"But now you're here, you've come to me." The voice came from behind them and they turned again to see nothing. "I don't know how you found me, you and your devilish friend, but I am glad."

The window beside them slammed open and shut, glass cracking with the sudden impact.

"A wizard and a devil," the voice hummed with satisfaction. "We will see what we can do with you."

Tal had had enough of being taunted like this. Quickly changing the incantation to the only other spell she'd had time to practice, Tal threw out four floating globules of light.

With the room suddenly illuminated Tal let out a cry as the man leapt down at her from the corner of the ceiling.

Knocking Tal to the floor and landing on her he swung with his scimitar. But Kai got there first, their dagger deflecting the blade as they kicked him in the chest, pushing him back away from Tal.

"Go!" Kai shouted at her as the man slashed at them, the blade just missing Kai's throat.

She lunged for the door, pulling the handle as hard as she could. But it was locked.

Kai's legs were swept out from under them, the man flinging a dagger at Tal. She fell to the floor, the small blade embedded in the door just where she had been.

Kai rolled to their feet, swiping left and right, but having their blows expertly deflected each time. Kai ducked a swing from the scimitar, but was caught in the chin by a rising knee. They stumbled back, dazed, still not quite recovered from their last fight.

Tal scrambled for the corner, quickly throwing out a bolt of flame in the general direction of the fight but afraid of hitting Kai.

The tiefling was on the back foot. Dodging and parrying slashes from the swordsman, suddenly pressed up against a table.

Glass shattered as two arrows blasted through the front window, one sinking into the man's shoulder. He turned, giving Kai enough time to dodge past him as Samara fired twice more through the broken window.

He knocked the arrows aside with ease and continued after Kai, a cackle of bloodlust ringing from his throat.

Sparks flew as blow after blow was deflected and each riposte was parried, the chimes of blade against blade almost rhythmic.

Another short volley of arrows shattered the window in the kitchen, narrowly missing both Kai and their combatant.

Shoving Kai against the wall, shaved-head thrust his knee into their gut before drawing a dagger and flinging it through the broken window in the entrance. There was a cry from outside and fear prickled Tal's neck.

Kai was back up, though gasping for air, swinging dagger, fist, and foot at the swordsman. The chime of steel, the groan of a hit connecting, and the cackle of a battle enjoyed, shaved-head span, grabbing Kai by the horns and slamming them to the ground.

Panic running through her veins, Tal released two quick bolts of flame, the first extinguishing against the wall, the second finding its target, knocking shaved-head off balance.

A smile on his face as he rolled to his feet and hurdled two daggers at Tal. Both hit, the first catching her corset and ricocheting off, but not without forcing the air from her lungs. The second embedded firmly in her shoulder, blood running down her one full arm. In her shock Tal's concentration of her orbs was lost, the three of them plunged back into darkness.

Kai was up, leaping onto shaved-head's back, wrapping their arms around his neck in a tight hold. Gritting their teeth as blood ran from their nose and lips, Kai squeezed as tight as they could.

In the struggle their attacker had dropped his sword, the blade sticking out of the floor. Shaved-head tugged at Kai's arms as he reached for his scimitar, the brass cuff dangling from his wrist.

Tal saw her chance. Pushing passed the pain in her shoulder she scrambled forward and wrapped herself around his arm, digging her fingers beneath the cuff, trying to pull it free.

With a roar of frustration shaved-head kicked Tal in the back, arching her spine and sending her tumbling, the cuff slipping from his wrist and her fingers, rolling towards the stairs.

Panting and in pain, Tal began to drag herself towards it.

Another roar came, followed by the sound of smashing wood as Kai was thrown forward, their body crashing through the table sending splinters of wood flying. Their arms falling lifelessly to the ground.

More glass scattered as Samara pulled herself through the broken window, arrow notched and bow drawn. She blinked around in the dark, unable to focus. "Where is he?! Where are you?!" She cried.

Tal turned as the shadowy shape slipped from the kitchen. "Watch out!?" She called out to Samara.

The archer turned and released the arrow with a cough and a splutter. She coughed twice more as a dagger was plunged again and again into her stomach.

Tal scrambled for her cuff, her bloodied fingers locking around it.

"Well now," shaved-head spoke softly between heavy breaths. "You put up quite the fight." Tal looked over her shoulder as she pulled the cuff close to her chest. He approached slowly, his arm around Samara's neck, the dagger still held into her abdomen.

"Why don't you be a good little elf girl and give up, eh? I might even let this one live."

"Run, Tal." Samara coughed blood as she tried to call out, her voice hushed as the arm around her neck tightened.

"Or I could cut you up like your little friend here?" He twisted the knife as he moved Samara a step closer.

Fighting back tears of pain and fear, Tal curled up on the floor, slipping the cuff around her stump.

"Though it would be a shame to waste a body," he continued, "even a damaged one like yours. I'm sure my master will have a use for you."

Keeping her back to him Tal pushed herself onto her knees. "When I'm through with you, there won't be a body to waste!" The tears were flowing freely now, streaming down her cheeks.

He chuckled, pulling the dagger from Samara's stomach and pressing it to her neck. "I like your spirit little elf girl," he pressed the blade in, a trickle of blood running down its length.

Samara let out a whimper, her hands clutching against the gushing wounds in her stomach as she tried not to breathe.

Keeping her arm behind her back, the tingling in her stump increasing as her prosthetic came back to life, Tal pulled her spellbook free, her thumb searching for a page she knew too well.

A broad grin spread across shaved-head's face. "Oh I see," he chuckled and pulled Samara closer to his body, using her as a human shield. "An old fashioned duel then is it? What fun!" Keeping the dagger against Samara's neck he flicked his cloak aside, loosening another dagger from his hip. "Let's see what's faster, yes? Your spells or my blades."

Biting her lip, Tal let out a groan as she tore a page from her book. "Let her go, I won't ask you again."

He let out a loud burst of a laugh. "Now we're having fun!" With a twist he dragged the blade across Samara's throat, throwing her body to the ground, before flinging the second dagger at Tal.

Tal screamed as she watched Samara fall, crushing the page in her hand as the purple glow of her arcane prosthetic lit up. The page disintegrated into green dust, the energy travelling quickly up her arm and around her shoulders. With a well practised gesture, and her right hand returned, the energy flew from her purple fingers, a green beam shooting out, passed the dagger that travelled towards her, and into the torso of the cackling man.

The dagger sunk into Tal's thigh and she fell to her knees, but her eyes never left that man in front of her. His cackling turned to cries, his body crumbling into a pile of fine grey dust.

A moment of silence passed, the fight over.

Tal let out a scream, hunching over on the floor. Pulling the dagger from her leg and throwing it to the side she crawled towards Samara's body, blood pooling around her. The girl's

252

eyes were wide, my mouth open and the wound at her neck had stopped bleeding.

"Samara! Samara!" She pressed her head against the girl's chest, willing her to answer. "Kai! Kai! Get up! We have to-" her voice broke as she stifled a cry. "We have to help her! Please Kai! Get up!"

She looked over to the tiefling, but they weren't moving. Here in the darkness she was alone.

Sniffing, Tal tried to wipe the tears from her face, only managing to smear blood across it. She began crawling towards Kai, hoping she hadn't lost them too.

"What a mess," a deep voice came from the doorway. Tal turned just in time to see a large silhouetted figure, and the heavy boot that came down on her face.

CHAPTER 21

Pain.
That was the only sensation Tal could feel. The throbbing pain rippled through her body with every beat of her heart. She couldn't open her eyes, she didn't even know if she wanted to. Her face ached, a pounding in her head like a thousand dwarves beating drums with warhammers, and a burning pain in her shoulder and thigh. All this pain that racked her body was nothing compared to the pain in her mind.

Samara was dead. She'd watched that man slit her throat and toss her aside like garbage. Tal had watched the life fade from her friend and there was nothing she could have done to stop it.

A tear ran down her cheek, stinging her skin.

All the pain she felt told her one thing; she wasn't dead. That was a start.

Carefully letting her body and mind wake together, Tal's other senses slowly came to life.

Cold. Her body was laying against something cold, and hard. A floor, a stone floor. So she wasn't in the groundskeeper's house anymore.

Nothing. Tal tried to breathe through her nose but she could smell nothing, and the effort made her headache worse.

Iron. The bitter sharp taste of blood filled her mouth. Not a good sign, but at least she could taste something.

Drip. A slow, rhythmic dripping, somewhere in the distance, echoing off the stone floor and walls. A basement maybe?

Finally Tal opened her eyes, letting them adjust to the darkness. She saw the floor she was laying on. Then thick dark iron bars. Pushing herself up slowly, her head spinning, Tal looked around to see the bars that surrounded her. She was in a cage, a cell. She was a prisoner. Feeling dizzy she dropped her head into her hands. Hands. The memory came back to her as she looked into the purple haze of her translucent arcane hand. A smile parted her lips as she wiggled her fingers. So whoever had imprisoned her let her keep her hand?

"Good morning," Kai's voice rasped at her from behind.

Tal turned sharply, her head spinning with the sudden movement. Sitting back against the wall in a cell of their own, their suit covered in dirt and dried blood, was Kai.

"Do you feel as bad as I feel?" They asked with a smirk. Kai's black eyes had returned, accompanied by a new cut on their lip and a large bruise across their cheek.

Tal smiled. Even after everything that had happened, how could Kai still be smirking and making jokes? "Probably, but not as bad as you look." She ran her hand over her face, wincing as she touched her nose. "I think my nose is broken."

"We can fix that," Kai sighed, "at least you've got your hand back." Slowly they stood up, wincing and groaning with exertion.

"Yeah, it's the only part of me that doesn't hurt." Tal looked up at Kai, tears pooling in the corners of her eyes. "Kai...Samara...she's..."

Kai nodded, their smirk fading to a solemn frown. "I know, I saw them dragging her away."

"Them? You saw them?" Tal crawled to the edge of her cell, pressing herself against the bars as if she could somehow melt through them to get to Kai.

"Yeah, two halflings." Kai shook their head. "What is it with halflings these days? They're known for being such merry folk. Now we've got Galen in prison, and whoever they were stealing dead bodies."

That wasn't the question on Tal's mind. "Two halflings? Are you sure?" Although slightly foggy from having her face stomped on, Tal had a very vivid memory of a large figure standing before her. She may have been crawling along the floor, but even from that vantage point it was certainly larger than a halfling.

255

Kai nodded. "Yes, they were surprisingly friendly given the circumstances. Asked how I was feeling and if I wanted any tea." They snorted with amusement, then screwed up their face as a jolt of pain filled their head. "Whatever is going on here, I don't think it's got anything to do with Patrice Vaskar."

"I saw someone, or something, big." Tal rubbed her temple, her head aching with the strain of thought. "Definitely bigger than a halfling."

Kai shrugged. "Bigger than two halflings?" A small chuckle was all they could manage without groaning. "I haven't seen anyone. The last thing I remember is being on that guy's back and then I woke up in here."

Tal looked around her small cell again. "Speaking of here, where are we?"

Kai's and her cages were not the only ones. Another three cells lined the stone walls up to curved stone stairs that disappeared past the wall, leading up to a faint flickering light source. The dark smear of dried blood led out from the cage next to Tal's and along the narrow corridor to the stone steps.

"I'm not sure," Kai tapped the bars of their cage. "I don't think the groundskeeper had a dungeon under his house, but at this stage nothing would surprise me." Using the bars Kai pulled theirself to their feet, wobbling and taking deep breaths. "I haven't seen the fellow with the bad haircut yet, but I'm guessing since you've still got your hand that he's not feeling too great."

Tal took a deep breath. She wasn't proud of what she had done, but she also didn't regret it. Telling Kai what she had done, however, made her sick to her stomach. "He's dead. More than dead..." she stared straight at the floor, not wanting to see Kai's reaction.

"What's more than dead?" Kai's tone was flat, which didn't make Tal feel better or worse.

"He's dust...I disintegrated him... I only meant it as a threat, but when he killed Samara..." Thinking about it made her tremble, anger and sadness dancing around her head.

Tal felt a hand press down on her shoulder as Kai reached through the bars to offer what comfort they could. "You did what you had to. If you hadn't, who knows where we would have woken up, or even if we would have."

With a sigh of relief Tal placed her hand on Kai's, the gentle tingle in her arcane fingers more comforting than she'd expected. "So you're not mad or disappointed?"

A blast of laughter came from Kai's throat. "I'm not your mother, and you didn't just break a lantern." They squeezed her purple fingers before pulling their hand back. "I'm not going to lie, touching your hand feels very strange." Kai smiled. "And if you're talking about what I said earlier, about not killing people, that's my personal thing. I'm not going to force my views on you, especially if your life is at stake."

Tal pulled herself up to face them, no longer weighed down by the stress she'd imposed on herself from worrying about Kai. "Thank you," she smiled, "and you get used to the hand eventually."

"I hope so." Kai stared at the faint purple glow for a moment before pacing around their cell. "If I'm not mistaken that was a pretty powerful spell. How are you still a student?"

"It was a prepared scroll Master Brum had had in his study. Last time I tried to use it this happened." Tal held up her glowing prosthetic. "The rest of me would have been dust too if he hadn't walked in and countered the spell. I kept a copy as a reminder of the dangers of playing with high level magics."

"Good reminder," Kai tapped the wall, listening to the sound of their knuckles against the stone. "Do you know any spells that could get us out of here?"

"Sadly no, and I don't have my spellbook either so I'm pretty useless right now." Tal began pacing her cell as well, tapping the bars as if it would help. "I'm guessing you don't have a lockpick stashed somewhere?"

Kai shook their head. "The little ones must have searched us before locking us in here." They slumped down against the wall. "Hopefully they'll be back soon, it's been a few hours I think. Hard to tell time when there's no light and you're fading in and out of consciousness."

"You should have said yes to the tea."

257

Kai laughed and groaned. "Maybe I should, I'd probably feel better." They gently rubbed their bruised face, a thought rolling around in their mind. "How real is your hand?"

Tal was genuinely confused by the question. She'd never thought about her hands as real or unreal, they were just her hands. One might have been magical, but did that make it less real? Tal wriggled the fingers in both her hands. "What are you thinking?" This seemed like the easiest way to answer Kai's peculiar question.

"Do you think you could...put your fingers inside the lock to open it?" Kai said, gesticulating with their own fingers as they spoke as if that helped.

It was an interesting idea that was for sure, and not something Tal had ever thought about before. "At this point I'll try anything." It sounded crazy, but it was all they had. Tal crouched down next to the gate of her cell, but there was no key hole. "I don't see a lock on this side."

Kai cursed. "That's ok, can you reach through the bars and get it from the other side?"

"I'll try." Tal slipped her arm through the bars, walking her arcane fingers along the iron frame searching for the lock. Although she had full control of the magical appendage, the sensation of touch always felt numb, like her hand had just fallen asleep. Now was one of those times when Tal felt like she was taking blind stabs in the dark. Trying a new technique of stroking her fingers up and down, Tal suddenly felt a dent in the metal.

"I think I've found it," she called over to Kai, "now what?"

Kai released their held breath at this sign of hope. They pressed theirself against the bars between the two cells to get the best view they could. "Right, now if you can squeeze or shrink your fingers down, you should be able to feel the tumblers on the inside."

"Okay." Tal took a deep breath, concentrating her mind, focusing on making her fingers long and thin. It didn't seem to be having an effect, so opting for plan A, she tried to squeeze her fingers into the keyhole, awaiting the uncomfortable sensation.

As she pushed, the iron gates creaked open.

258

"You did it!" Kai began to celebrate, stopping abruptly as their body protested the movement.

Tal was confused, she'd not felt anything and barely touched the lock. Standing up she pulled the gate wide open and stared at the other side. "There's no keyhole…"

Kai blinked at her. "What do you mean there's no keyhole?" Walking up to their own cell's gate Kai gave it a pull, the bars swinging open with a high-pitched squeak. "Huh…"

"Are you kidding me?!" Tal raised her voice as her cheeks grew bright red, throwing her arms up in the air in utter dismay.

Kai just stood there, slowly opening and closing the gate. "I umh…Well I just umh…"

"You've been awake for how long and you didn't think to try opening the gate?!" Flailing her arms around was painful, but Tal felt the situation required dramatic movements. "What kind of detective are you!"

An injured look took over Kai's face, making them look more pathetic than they already did. "In my defence, who leaves people in a cell with no lock?" Kai stepped out, closing the gate behind them. "Besides that I've spent most of the last two days unconscious, so forgive me if my head is a little scrambled."

They made a good point, and all the dramatics had worn Tal out, so she wasn't in the mood to argue her case further. "The important thing is that we're out," she said with a smile. "Now we just need to find our things and get out of here."

"Wherever here is," Kai added, adjusting their tie.

Moving slowly and quietly the pair made their way up the stone steps towards the light. Peeking around the edge of the wall when they reached the top they saw another long stone corridor. This one however had torches burning in sconces along the walls, and alcoves built into either side where aging coffins rested.

"I think it's safe to say we're still in the cemetery." Kai stepped out into the corridor when it was clear that no-one else was around.

"I thought it was a graveyard?" Tal added, watching Kai inspect a coffin.

259

They turned, giving her an unamused look. "You're really going to make that distinction now instead of asking the important question?"

She smirked, getting a rise out of Kai definitely made her feel better. "Well what's the important question?"

"What happened to the bodies that were in these?" Kai patted the coffin.

Tal walked around the room, staring in shock as each of the coffins had been cracked open and its occupant removed. The pair continued down the hall of disturbed coffins, splinters of rotting wood littering the floor, bent rusted nails here and there. Someone, or from what Kai had seen, two someone's, had gone to a lot of effort to gather a large number of remains.

Reaching the end of the hall their path split into two, and neither Kai nor Tal were interested in dividing themselves to cover more ground. Staying together, and alive, was their main concern.

Taking a moment to investigate the stone slabs at their feet, Kai noticed a series of drag marks and scuffs leading down the right-hand path. Following these signs of wear, the two came to the edge of a well-lit chamber. Pressing themselves up against the wall Tal opted to follow Kai's lead.

Carefully the tiefling poked their head around the opening, giving the room a quick once-over before pressing theirself back out of sight with a gasp.

"What is it?" Tal whispered, her nerves beginning to build.

Kai leaned in close, keeping their voice low. "It's an empty study." They whispered back with a grin. "Come on, no one's in there." Throwing caution aside, Kai stepped into the chamber, followed by the rolling eyes of Tal as she muttered something unflattering.

It was as Kai had said, an empty study. Empty of people, that is. The low built desks that Tal initially mistook for benches were covered in various parchments and scrolls, bits of leftover food, and a wide variety of spell components. She also noted two hay stuffed cots nestled in the corner, partitioned off by a series of crates. The whole room made Tal feel like a giant. She'd spent very little time with halflings, and never had she been in the home of one. The miniaturised version of furniture was quite adorable, or it would have been given better circumstances and location.

Kai began rummaging through the more human sized sacks and crates. Various provisions and components that they couldn't make heads or tails of, but they made a mental note of each of them before moving on to the next box.

Tal was more focused on the parchments. Halfling wasn't a language she spoke, and she guessed that was what was written across many of the documents. Handwritten notes that Tal guessed concerned anatomy based on the crude sketches that accompanied them. Not being much of an artist herself she tried not to judge, but everything had the air of a child's work about it. Unless oversized letters that didn't follow a particular line were part of written halfling, the notes and drawings looked far worse than what she'd attempted with her left hand.

After a few minutes of sifting through pages Tal noticed an immediate change to the style and quality of a series of parchments. As well as a change in language. A good half-dozen arcane scrolls were bundled together, next to a small pile of golden pins. Tal sat cross-legged on the floor, the halfling table now at a usable height, and spread the scrolls out in front of her. The scrolls appeared to be quite old, the aged parchments hard and stained. They also each had a rough torn edge, as if they had been ripped from some ancient tome.

"Hey, come check these out," Tal called over to Kai without looking over to the sounds of banging and clattering.

"Not until you check this out." Kai slammed down Tal's spellbook on top of the scrolls she'd laid out. "Not bad for a semi-conscious detective."

Tal tilted her head backwards, looking up at Kai at a very unflattering angle as they chewed on a piece of jerky. "You found our things," she smiled at them, "were they just in those crates?"

Kai nodded. "Along with Samara's weapons, and other clothing and equipment. Most of it far too large for a halfling." They tilted over Tal, examining the scrolls from above. "What have you got there?"

261

Tal rocked herself forward again, moving her spellbook to the side. "They're scrolls, or possibly pages from a spellbook. The symbols are strange though, they have a very transmutationy feel about them, but something isn't right."

Kai raised an eyebrow at her as they looked over. "I know what scrolls are, Tal'avera. I meant the little gold things." Kai reached down and picked one up. "This could be one of those pins that Kirtan mentioned."

Tal picked one up, rolling it between her fingers. Crudely made, looking like it had been hammered out of a gold piece, the small pin resembled a tiny spiked skull with the pin pointing down from the jaw.

"It's not very pretty," Tall screwed her face up.

Kai tucked one away in their satchel. "People that enjoy beating each other up for coin don't usually concern themselves with things being pretty."

A familiar tingling tickled the tips of Tal's fingers. "This doesn't feel right..." She opened her spellbook, turning to the correct page. "I want to try and identify this thing, I think it might be magical."

"How long is that going to take? I don't know how long we'll be alone. Can't you do it back at the Den?" Kai tapped their foot impatiently, looking back towards the hallway.

"It'll take ten minutes or three seconds," Tal flipped back and forth between two different spells. "Maybe I'll just find out if it's magic? If they are, I can take longer when we're somewhere safer."

"Compromise, the cornerstone of all healthy partnerships. Quickly please." Kai edged towards the hallway, looking up and down.

Taking a deep breath, Tal uttered the incantation and her eyes flashed with arcane light.

Kai's attention was quickly dragged away as the sound of a table being thrown across the floor was almost drowned out by Tal's cry. Kai ran to her side, the crying elf holding her head in agony as she rocked back and forth. "You're okay, you're okay, you're okay." Kai wrapped their arms around her head, holding her

262

close as they quickly looked her over for any physical damage. "Take a deep breath, it's okay."

Breathing heavily through the sobs, the pain in Tal's head slowly became a dull moan before fading altogether, leaving her feeling drained. She sunk into Kai's arms, looking back at the table with wide tear soaked eyes. "The scrolls..."

Kai looked over at the toppled table and the scattered pages, then back down to Tal. "What happened? Do you need the scrolls? Or did they do this to you?"

Tal could hear the questions and the concern in Kai's voice, but no other words would come to her.

Leaving her on the floor hugging her knees to her chest, Kai gathered the parchments Tal had shown them and tucked them away in their satchel. "Come on, let's get out of here before a chair attacks us too." Kai put Tal's arm around their shoulders and lifted her to her feet, the elven woman still dazed by the shock that had riddled her mind.

As they guided her towards the doorway Kai noticed a shift in the light, and a mumbled echo of voices slowly getting louder. "Oh hell," they muttered, hurrying Tal back to a corner of the room and lowering her down.

"I'm certain, brother, it definitely came from over here," the first voice grew clearer, accompanied by the scraping of footsteps.

A second voice, not too dissimilar to the first, replied. "Unlikely, brother, your ears are playing tricks on you."

Kai stayed crouched next to Tal, awaiting the arrival of their two small captors, ready for whatever was about to come.

Two almost identical halflings entered the room, a large lantern held between them. On second glance, the lantern was perfectly normal, but being carried by two halflings made it seem significantly larger. Dressed in the same simple leather tunics, their scruffy sand-brown hair and puffy sideburns leading down to badly trimmed beards, the two halflings smiled as they laid eyes upon Kai and Tal.

"See, I told you, brother, I told you. Did you change your mind about the tea?" The first halfling looked very proud of himself.

Ready though they were, this show of simple hospitality took Kai off guard. "What? I uh...no."

"Oh, well that's disappointing." The first halfling approached, still smiling, leaving the lantern behind. "She doesn't look too good. Would she like some tea?"

"Brother, no one wants your tea. It tastes terrible." The second halfling called over.

Tal was still silent, she hadn't even looked up at the bizarre conversation that was taking place around her.

"My tea is fine, brother, it's the leaves that are terrible." He turned back to look up at Tal. "Some tea might help you know."

Still crouched, Kai shifted around Tal, shielding her from whatever this weirdness was. "Who in the hells are you two? And what are you doing here?"

"I'm Poppy," the second halfling introduced himself. "And that tea obsessed fool is my big brother, Spring."

"I know my own name, brother." Spring snapped back. He paused for a moment, staring at the mess that Kai and Tal had left. "Oh my, brother, did you do that?"

Kai began to suspect that these two were not the criminal masterminds behind the corpse abductions. "That would have been me, I'm afraid." Kai stood up and gave an apologetic shrug. "Got my tail caught on it and I tripped. I was just about to tidy up when the two of you arrived."

Poppy tutted, shaking his head in disappointment. "Tails always get in the way. I'll sort this lot out, brother, you just keep our guests company."

"I could make tea?" Spring suggested with a broad smile.

"Enough with the tea, brother!"

Tal sighed quietly and took a long deep breath, the aching in her mind now completely gone. Taking a moment to brush herself off, and giving Kai a nod to show she was okay, Tal pulled her feet round and sat cross-legged on the floor, keeping her roughly at eye level with Spring.

"We're sorry to have made such a mess," she said to the scruffy halfling. "I noticed you had been making notes, what have you two been up to down here?" Tal kept a sweet smile on her face,

264

hoping her politeness and Spring's apparent childlikeness could get them some answers.

Spring's grin exceeded that of his excitement over tea. "Oh yes, we have been quite busy here. My brother is the one who makes the notes, I can't really read or write." He cleared his throat. "We've been working very hard on a secret project for mister Hannon." Pressing his fingers to his lips Spring turned to his brother. "Should I have mentioned mister Hannon?"

Poppy was busy shuffling through his pages of notes, trying to put them back into order. "I don't think so, brother. He said not to talk to anybody."

"Okay, brother." Spring turned back to Tal. "Forget I mentioned mister Hannon."

"Already forgotten," Tal smiled. Not that it would matter if she did forget. Out of the corner of her eye Tal could see Kai leaning against the wall taking notes of their own.

"Thank you. So like I was saying," Spring continued, "we've been working on this project. We're trying to help people get better."

"Get better?" Tal raised a confused eyebrow.

"Could you give me a hand here, brother?" Poppy called over as he struggled to lift the long desk.

"Of course, brother." Spring turned back to Tal. "If you'll excuse me for a moment, I need to help my brother." With a gentle bow he scampered off.

Tal slowly stood, aided by Kai, and leaned back against the wall. "Thank you, I still feel a bit dizzy." She gently massaged the side of her head as she watched the two halflings try to right the table.

"What happened to you?" Kai whispered, also watching the two halflings with utter fascination.

"I was doing a quick spell to see if the pins were magical, and they are." She kept her voice low. The halflings didn't seem like a threat, but right now her nerves were teetering on the edge of breaking entirely. "They are, divination magic. That means-'

"That means they're for locating someone or something." Kai finished. They frowned at the look of surprise on Tal's face. "I'm not completely new to this stuff."

265

"Right," Tal smiled. "Well while I still had the spell going, I glanced over at the scrolls." Her blood ran cold as the feeling once again rippled down her spine. "It was like the scrolls were alive. I could feel their pain, like a thousand souls screaming in my ears."

"That doesn't sound pleasant."

"It wasn't. I think there's a protective charm on the scrolls, I couldn't even tell the school of magic." The second part annoyed Tal almost as much as being rendered stupefied.

"Well I've got them now," Kai patted their satchel, "so we can deal with all this later. Now we need to get out of here in one piece."

The two halflings rejoined the pair, having righted the table and organised most of their papers. "Sorry for the interruption," Spring apologised, "where were we?"

Before Kai or Tal could speak Poppy folded his arms and raised his voice. "Either of you two see some old parchments on that desk before you tripped over it?"

"Can't say that I did," Kai shrugged and feigned ignorance. "And my friend didn't go near it, did you?" They smiled at Tal, who shook her head.

Another sigh of disappointment from Poppy. "That's unfortunate. Mister Hannon won't be happy about that."

"Shh!" Spring held a finger to his lips and flapped at his brother. "We're not supposed to talk about him, brother."

A thought popped into Tal's head, not a good one, but a thought nevertheless. "Maybe you could introduce us to mister Hannon? We'd love to meet him, wouldn't we?" She turned to Kai and raised her eyebrows in a 'play along' kind of way.

"Uh, yes...of course. It would be rude not to, wouldn't it?" Kai smiled back and forth to the three of them.

The two halflings beamed at them, looking far too delighted. "That sounds like a wonderful idea. Doesn't it, brother?" Spring said cheerfully.

"That it does, brother." Poppy replied just as cheerfully. "Help me with the lantern, I think mister Hannon should be awake by now."

266

Chapter 22

Moving at a halfling's pace, the four dawdled down the long stone corridors of what Poppy confirmed was a tomb. Kai and Tal followed behind as their two small guides tried to remember the way to mister Hannon's chambers.

"You were saying you were trying to make people better," Tal tried to rekindle the conversation, "what did you mean by that?"

Spring half looked up over his shoulder as they walked, the shadows cast from the lantern giving his tiny face an ominous appearance. "There are lots of sick people around here. Our ma got sick too, so if we can help these people we can help her."

"That's what mister Hannon says anyhow," Poppy added, not bothering to look up as he was the one directing the four of them.

"I'm so sorry," and Tal genuinely was. She knew how upsetting it could be to have a parent be taken unwell, and as a child there's nothing you can do about it but hope. "What made her sick?"

"She died," Spring said very flatly, as more of a fact without an emotional connection, "and we're going to make her better."

"What?" Both Tal and Kai said in unison. Kai had again been trying to write as they walked, but that statement nearly made them drop their pen.

"Death is just a sickness," Poppy said, "that's what mister Hannon told us, isn't it, brother?"

"That's right, brother," Spring smiled. "And all these people here," he gestured to the rooms they passed filled with empty sarcophagi, "they're sick too, and we've been making them better."

A pit was forming in Tal's stomach. Her brain demanded more answers, but the words kept sticking in her throat.

The four headed up a staircase, for the first time in a while, though the well laid stonework had been replaced. Bare mud and rock walls now made up the passage, with damp-rotting planks covering just enough of the corridor to walk down single file. Either the city or family had been extending this tomb, or these halflings and their mister Hannon were far more capable than they appeared. A tall plank of wood blocked the end of the tunnel, flickering light shining through the nicks and knotholes.

"These are mister Hannon's chambers," Spring said as he and his brother left the lantern behind and began shifting the makeshift door. "Mister Hannon, sir, it's Poppy and Spring. We've brought your guests from downstairs." They led the way into the candle lit room

"If we're guests, I'd hate to see how they treat prisoners." Kai muttered to Tal, approaching slowly.

"They probably lock the cells…" Tal said sarcastically.

The room was illuminated by about two dozen candles scattered haphazardly around the place for no obvious aesthetic reasons. Though they did give off a pleasantly warm glow, as well as a calming aroma. A dark open tunnel dug into the far wall slipped down and out of sight. The room itself was barely more furnished than the brothers' room. A mound of hessian sacks with a tattered blanket over them serving as a bed and a number of repurposed coffins made up the large central table that was drawing both Kai and Tal's attention.

It wasn't that the table was made of coffins that was so eye-catching, it was the amount of dried blood and viscera that covered it. Tal's jaw hung loosely as she approached. The reason for the scented candles became quickly apparent as she got closer, the stench of the rotting flesh filling her nostrils. The elven woman covered her mouth, her body wretching, warm bile stinging the back of her throat.

Kai looked around the room, either unfazed by the smell or unable to smell at all through their battered nose. Wherever this mysterious mister Hannon was, if indeed he existed at all, he wasn't in his chambers.

"What exactly is it you do in here?" Kai asked as they approached the table, running their fingers over its damp and dusty surface.

"This is where we make people better," Spring said cheerfully, "like your friend. She's feeling much better."

Tal swallowed the viscous liquid building in her throat, turning to face the halflings. "Samara? The human girl with the dark skin? Where is she?" The questions came fast and frantic.

Poppy scratched his scraggly beard. "Sounds like her. She was the one that was sick in the cell, wasn't she, brother?"

"I believe so, brother." Spring turned to Tal. "You can see her if you like, she's in the recovery chamber at the moment."

Tal's jaw just flapped, her mind caught between disbelief and terror. If she understood what these two were talking about, they were doing the impossible.

"Take us to her." Kai said, their tone harder than Tal had ever heard, making it very clear that this was not a request.

Either unphased or unaware of the change in tone the conversation was taking, both Spring and Poppy smiled. "Of course," they both said in almost perfect sync. They returned to collect their large lantern, lifting it between them as they marched towards the dark tunnel.

Kai and Tal followed behind at a half-step, Tal fighting the urge to run on ahead. "Do you think…?" She whispered to Kai, but couldn't find the words to finish her thought.

"I don't know if these two are crazy or serious," Kai whispered back, their eyes never leaving the backs of the small heads in front of them, "but we need to find out what's going on here."

The tunnel was even more bare than the one leading to the chamber. Soft mud made up the walls and floor, well-trodden though it was, with no timber or stone to support it. The burrowed-out nature of it made Tal think of the great worms of the underdark. A shiver ran down her spine imagining one such beast coming towards them. With everything that had transpired lately it wouldn't have surprised her.

"What's that?" Kai asked as they continued down the path, a flickering light growing brighter.

269

"Mister Hannon!" the halflings called out, picking up the pace as they ran to their master.

"Boys!" The figure called back. As the light of the lantern revealed the approaching man, Tal and Kai both stopped in their tracks. Walking towards them, a flickering candle in his hand, was a portly middle-aged human man. A cheerful face, mud-stained clothes and a heavy cloak, a mop of greasy white hair resting on his shoulder. He looked like everyone's uncle rolled into one.

Tal's mind raced, trying to match him with the blurred memory of the figure standing over her in the groundskeeper's house. But something didn't quite fit.

The halflings ran to him like children welcoming their father home.

"Mister Hannon, we've brought your guests." Spring looked up at him. "They want to see their friend."

"We told them how we're making people better," Poppy added, his voice filled with pride as Hannon rustled his hair.

With a belly shaking laugh Hannon looked up at Kai and Tal. "So I see boys, so I see." His eyes were by far the most striking thing about his appearance. Unnaturally bright, a shifting mix of blue hues that could have been a trick of the candle light.

"Mister Hannon," Kai stepped forward, extending a hand, "I am Kaivel Mortzeel, and this is my partner, Tal'avera Liwood." The slow measured tone of their words made this simple introduction sound like a challenge, the extended hand a weapon drawn for a duel.

Wiping his dirty hand on his even dirtier trousers, mister Hannon met Kai's gaze, his meaty fingers enveloping the tiefling's smaller digits. "Oggi Hannon," he said with a firm shake. "So you want to see your friend, huh?" His eyebrow raised as those pearlescent blue marbles scanned over his two guests.

"If possible, yes." Tal said from over Kai's shoulder. This was all far too casual for the location or situation, and Tal began to wonder if there was some kind of mental game going on that she wasn't aware of.

Hannon smiled, his teeth too unnaturally bright for the rest of his greasy and unkempt appearance. "Of course, I'm sure she's eager to see you. Why don't you follow me? You boys can get back by yourselves, yes?" He placed his hand on Spring's head, ruffling his hair as he gave the halfling a little push forward.

"Yes mister Hannon," Spring scurried up to Kai. "It was a pleasure meeting you both. Come see us again."

"Yes, do come see us again." Poppy added as he joined his brother. The two picked up the lantern and slowly returned down the path they'd travelled down.

"You can be sure of it," Kai muttered, turning back to their new guide.

Still smiling, though in the light of the single flickering candle the expression took on a more sinister appearance, Hannon turned and began to walk back the way he had come.

"So what is it you do?" Kai asked as they followed his silhouette down the tunnel by his flickering candlelight.

Hannon did not look back over his shoulder as he replied, or even slow his pace. He just continued forward, his voice seeming to echo even against the soft mud walls. "Oh I tend to the needy." Even though neither Kai nor Tal could see his face, there was a certain tone to his words that made his smile clear. "I help to guide those two poor boys. As you can see they're rather helpless."

The tunnel began to slope, heading deeper into this extended tomb.

"The world is incredibly sick," Hannon continued as they walked, "and it's only going to get worse as long as the cause goes unchecked."

"What cause?" Kai's hand moved to their satchel for reassurance, a sense of unease tickling down their neck.

"We had a cure once," Hannon ignored Kai's question, lost in his own thoughts, "but people have forgotten."

Tal wrinkled her nose, which hurt, but the sudden change made her instincts jump. "What's that smell?"

"I have no great talent myself, though I do have some small skill in the arcane." Hannon looked over his shoulder now, the bright

271

blue of his eyes seeming to give off its own light. "But those boys, my gods. Their innate talent goes far beyond anything I could have hoped for."

"What talent? Where is our friend?" Kai opened the satchel and slipped a hand inside, thinking of the dagger they had found before. But nothing came.

"It's getting stronger." Tal held her hand over her mouth and nose, the taste of bile once again building in her throat. It smelt like Hannon's chamber.

The tunnel levelled out, a dark void untouched by the candle light approached them. The stink of rot and decay now overwhelming.

"Your friend is here." Hannon turned, his smile twisted into a toothy grin, his eyes shining on them. He gestured towards the void and faded away into a fine mist, the candle falling to the ground, extinguishing.

Kai lunged forward. Even without the candle they could see well enough in the darkness, but Oggi Hannon was gone.

Creeping forward Tal quickly created her small floating orb of light, letting it hover above her palm. "Where did he go?"

"Shh." Kai's hand was up, as they looked towards the void. "Can you hear that?"

Tal stopped, straining her long ears in the sudden silence. Footsteps. Slow, shuffling footsteps. He was close. Tal looked around the muddy floor, checking for any new footprints that appeared on their own.

"It's coming from down here." Kai pointed towards the void.

Letting her orb float away, Tal could see clearly. It was a pit. A large open pit.

"Those boys have been very useful to me," Hannon's voice came from all around them. "Necromancers are so hard to find these days."

A heavy shoulder slammed into Tal's back, the sudden impact making her lose control of her orb. Plunged again into darkness, Kai turned as she yelped but not fast enough, and the two of them fell into the black pit below.

≈⊙≈

Kai groaned, the wind knocked from their lungs first from the impact of hitting the packed soil, and then from the elf who landed on top of them.

"Oww..." Tal pushed herself up to her knees, looking down at Kai. "Are you ok?"

The look she received clearly marked that as a stupid question.

Kai sat up, almost pushing Tal off of them. "No. No I'm not." They rubbed their head and horns. "We need to get out of here fas-" Kai stopped suddenly. "There's someone here."

The two of them looked into the blackness around, but saw nothing. Kai gave Tal a gesture that she quickly recognised as the hand motion she made when creating her lights. She was impressed, she hadn't realised how much attention Kai had been paying her. With a word and a flick of her fingers the four globules of dancing lights orbited around her.

The pit suddenly illuminated around them, the bare soil walls marked with the occasional stone or root. More tunnels led away from the pit, though the light did not extend enough to see down them. Not that either Tal or Kai were looking. Something far more urgent drew their attention.

There was a woman standing not a hundred feet away from them. Dark soiled hair draping down her back. She wore bloodied leather armour that glistened in the light as she rocked back and forth in place. As the light cast shadows about her she turned, her dark skin offset by the milky white eyes that stared at the two people on the ground.

"Samara?" Tal almost whispered it, not fully believing what she was seeing. She stood up, taking a step forward and passed Kai, her eyes locked on her friend.

Reacting to her name, the milky eyed Samara opened her mouth, and growled. She rushed at Tal, arms extended and snarling.

Like a deer in torch light, Tal froze. She felt the tip of Samara's gnarled finger stroke her throat before it was dragged away.

Kai tackled the corrupted woman to the ground, the two of them rolling away and coming to a stop with Samara on top. Gripping her wrists Kai wrestled with her, holding her back as Samara snapped at their face, coating them in spittle.

"A little help here!" Kai shouted over to Tal, frantically trying to stay unbitten.

Tal was still frozen, her eyes wide as she watched the fight unfold. "Undead..." The word finally left her lips. "She's undead..."

"Oi! Magic girl! Do something!" Kai was getting frantic as Samara's teeth grazed their chin.

Tal twisted her fingers into arcane patterns. "I'm sorry!" She cried to Samara as the bolt of flame flew from her hand and blasted the undead husk of her friend. The impact was enough to knock her from Kai, giving the tiefling enough time to roll free.

As if the blow had been nothing, the undead Samara pulled itself up, the body contouring unnaturally as if being pulled up by invisible strings. It came at Kai again as they got to their feet.

Two more bolts of fire came in quick succession, the first blasting through its shoulder and the second separating the knee from its body.

With a final gassy breath the body of Samara fell limply to the ground, unmoving.

Kai and Tal stood silent for a moment, their eyes locked on the body, waiting to see if it got back up.

"Is she dead?" Tal asked in a breath, her voice low and shaky.

Kai knelt down next to the corpse. "For the second time today, yes." They rose, returning to Tal with a look of concern. "So this is necromancy?"

Tal nodded. Then shook her head. Then shrugged. "I don't know, I never studied necromancy. It's forbidden magic, lost for centuries, destroyed, why would I need to?"

Kai just pointed at the body.

"How was I supposed to predict this?" She flailed.

With a sigh Kai returned to Samara, rolling her over carefully. "I'm sorry for this, you deserved better." Brushing their fingers down her face, Kai closed her eyes. "Let's get out of here. Help me."

274

Kai lifted Samara up, looping her arm over their shoulders. Tal leaned forward to get the other arm before stopping, her ears twitching. Looking around the pit she saw nothing. Waving her fingers the four floating orbs each darted off to the mouth of a different tunnel.

"K...Kai..." Tal's eyes widened again as standing in each dugout archway were more milky-eyed figures, jaws open and walking towards them.

Dropping Samara's corpse to the ground, Kai backed up, their eyes moving from tunnel to tunnel, quickly calculating. "Oh hell."

"What do we do?" Tal was still moving back, only stopping when she hit the edge of the pit.

The undead creatures let out a cry one after the other, a shrill harmony of hunger and agony. As one the horde rushed towards them.

"Stay alive!" Kai barked. Reaching up they grabbed the long hairpins and pulled them free, their mess of dark hair tumbling down. Holding them out Kai flickered their wrists and a series of arcane sigils lit up down their length.

Tal's jaw hung even lower. "Wands! You've been wearing wands!"

"They're for emergencies." With another flick of their wrists six arcane bolts flew from the tips of the wands, flying haphazardly through the air and severing the legs of three creatures. "And this definitely feels like an emergency!"

Tal agreed. Her spellbook open Tal began to send her own bolts of fire out, knocking back the creatures as they charged.

Flashes of red and blue illuminated the pit as creature after creature fell to the ground, quickly replaced by another as the horde of undead descended on the two living beings.

"What about your 'no killing' rule?" Tal grunted the question, sending out a blast of frost and freezing an undead orc, before following up with a bolt of flame, shattering its torso across the mud.

"Now's hardly the time!" Kai sent out a volley of bolts. "But I think being undead counts as an exception!"

275

Another flurry of bolts from Kai knocked back a skeleton in ceremonial armour, another dressed in fine robes stepping over it and clawing at Kai.

The tiefling shoved it back, placing the tip of the wand against its chest with a flourish and blowing a hole through it. Their second wand flicked towards Tal and the arcane bolts swirled passed her, delimbing an undead half-orc that was bearing down on her.

Quickly flipping a page in her spellbook Tal pulled moisture from the air, a dagger of ice forming in her palm. She hurled it into the horde, the frozen blade exploding into shards and shredding through the walking corpses.

Dozens had fallen and dozens more came. Skeletons, partially rotten corpses, and recently deceased. It appeared the halflings had raided half the graveyard.

Kai ducked the swing of a corpse, kicking it back against the wall as they fired another series of bolts into the crowd. The corpse turned around and Kai faltered with their wand. It wore a tabard with a crest that they had become relatively familiar with.

"Lord Vaskar, I presume." Kai gave it a nod before flicking the wand towards its face. The corpse of Patrice Vaskar lunged forward, mouth agape, and fell as the back of its head exploded out. "Sorry about that."

More bolts of ice and fire flew out from Tal as she tried to push the creatures back. She fell, tripping over a re-dead corpse. Two elven undead, their faces half decayed away, bearing down on her. A blast of blue tore through their chests, the corpses falling lifelessly either side of her. Tal got to her feet, standing back-to-back with Kai.

"Thanks. How are you doing?" Tal panted over her shoulder as she sent out another bolt of flame.

Kai held up the two wands, the numerous glowing arcane sigils now reduced to just two and one. "I'm nearly done here." There was a nervousness to their voice that Tal had not heard before.

"I've got something," Tal turned a page, "stay behind me!"

Kai didn't ask questions, they just followed instructions as Tal moved around them. Beginning her casting Tal released the book, the tome floating on its own, and placed her thumb and

276

fingers together. A ghoulish looking creature leapt at her and was quickly turned to ash as with a cry Tal released a burning wave of fire that tore out from her palms, arcing out across the pit.

The brightness of the flames fading with the spell, beads of sweat pouring down Tal's forehead, as one lone undead dwarf continued to move towards them.

Kai stepped around Tal, surveying the charred corpses and sending the last of their bolts towards the final corpse with a casual flick. It fell to the floor with a heavy thud, leaving the two of them in silence, surrounded by mounds of charred and dismembered bodies.

Both breathing hard, hearts still beating violently in their chests, Kai and Tal just looked at each other, lost for words.

Kai coiled their hair into a bun and replaced their wand hairpins. "Well..." They released a deep breath. "I think I know what happened to all those missing people." They had a bittersweet grin on their face, but Tal knew there was more going on in Kai's mind.

"We need to find Hannon and those halflings before they make more of these things." Tal wiped her hand down her face. This was all far more than she'd ever signed up for, especially since she never really signed up in the first place.

A deep chuckle echoed from the tunnel and around the pit. "That was quite the show. I'm going to have to make those boys work harder if these creatures can be stopped by the likes of you two." Oggi Hannon's voice sounded so close, but so distant at the same time. "No matter though. We have a whole cemetery at our disposal."

"I believe it's a graveyard!" Tal shouted into the air. It wasn't an important point to make given their current situation, but she hoped irritating their captors might help locate him.

A rumbling, arrogant laugh echoed from the tunnels around them, slowly fading as it focused on a single spot. Oggi Hannon, still wearing his simple muddy clothes and long cloak, had now acquired a long heavy-looking glaive. For a man of his age he must have possessed incredible strength, the fierce looking weapon being nearly twice his size yet he carried it like a simple staff. Hannon walked towards them, slow casual steps as his gaze passed between the tiefling and the elf that had just destroyed months of his work.

"I've got nothing," Kai whispered to Tal as they watched the stout man approach, "what about you?"

She took a deep breath, her spellbook still in hand. "I'm getting pretty tired, but I'm not giving up yet."

Kai chuckled. "That's the spirit."

With a deep thrust, Hannon planted one end of the glaive into the mud and began to untie his cloak. "Your bravery in the face of all this is commendable," Hannon said as he tossed the cloak aside, "but ultimately foolish. You adventurers bit off more than you can chew."

"Erm," Kai cleared their throat and raised a finger, "we're actually just detectives."

The smirk on the middle-aged man's face turned to surprise. "Well then, detectives, you can consider your case closed." His grin returned as his form began to swell and grow. The rolls of fat on his arms and legs tightening into thick muscle, his skin changing from its pasty tone to a vivid shade of blue. Limbs and body elongating until the once portly man now resembled a hulking ogre. Pulling the glaive free from the mud and spinning it around with the grace of a performer, Oggi Hannon's pointed black teeth grinned. "Good bye, detectives."

CHAPTER 23

Tal and Kai stood frozen, the hulking beast that was Oggi Hannon sauntering towards them, savouring the moment.

"Ogre mage," the words escaped Tal's lips in a breath. She turned to Kai, swallowing hard. "Ogre mage, he's an ogre mage." Tal kept repeating it, not knowing what else to do.

Kai's eyes were busy assessing the pit around them, scanning the various corpses and flicking from one tunnel to the next. "We need to get out of here." The determination in their voice helped shake Tal from her panic. They looked back towards the ledge the two of them had been shoved from and then gave Tal a quick once over. "I'll boost you up to the ledge, ready?"

Tal looked up at the ledge some fifteen feet above their heads. "Wha-? Ho-? Wh- no!" She stammered.

A frightening seriousness took over Kai's face as they stared directly into Tal's eyes. "Get out of here, find D'Clos, bring the city watch back here." They glanced back at Hannon. "I'll be alright."

Kai wasn't going to be alright, Tal couldn't think of a way they could possibly be alright. This wasn't a plan, this was a sacrifice, and she wasn't ready to lose another friend.

"I can't just leave you here." Tal tried to match Kai's intensity, not coming anywhere near the mark.

Kai shrugged. "I'm not giving you a choice and we don't have any time left." They braced theirself against the wall. "Get a run up, it'll be easier."

This was madness, but Kai was right, they were out of time. Tal took a few steps forward and turned back to face them, holding

279

the tears of sadness, anger, and frustration back as best she could. "I'm coming back for you."

Kai grinned. "I know. Now go!"

Tal ran at them, taking the steps quickly as Kai laced their fingers together and crouched down. Tal skipped and as Kai caught her foot they flung her up, the elven girl kicking off as hard as she could. But it wasn't enough. Tal felt time slow as she saw the distance between the edge and her outstretched arms.

In a moment of panic and instinct Tal thrust her arms to her sides, her fingers making the now well practiced gestures, and released short bursts of fire. The blasts of arcane flames launched her higher, sending her rolling over the edge.

Not taking any time to catch her breath, Tal crawled on her elbows to the edge of the muddy path, looking over the side to where Kai had been.

Seeing the attempted escape Hannon had charged, roaring as he held the glaive high.

Kai turned to face the giant of a man as the blade came down. The tiefling's eyes flooded black, an explosion of dark cloud filling the side of the pit.

The thud of a blade hitting soil was all Tal heard. A moment later her companion came rolling out of the dark, a fresh cut on their cheek.

"What are you staring at, get going!" Kai shouted to her, backing up as bladed tips sliced through the cloud with frustrated grunts.

Forcing herself not to argue, Tal got to her feet and began running back up the path Hannon had led them down. She was going, but she wasn't going far.

Back in Hannon's chamber she searched wildly, no longer caring about being tidy. There must have been something, anything, in this room that could help Kai.

With all her strength she pulled apart the bed made of heavy sacks hoping to find a weapon tucked away discreetly. Nothing.

She barged the large table of coffins, sending them tumbling over and badly bruising her arm and shoulder. The wood splintered, but whatever had once occupied the coffin had been completely removed.

With a cry of desperation Tal grabbed a piece of broken wood and flung it across the chamber. Her ears pricked up at the sound of metal hitting stone.

ॐ☉ॐ

Watching Tal flee up the tunnel and out of sight, Kai readied theirself for Oggi Hannon's next move. The darkness they had created wouldn't last long, and the ogre mage was unlikely to stay in that one spot for much longer.

The bladed edge of the glaive sliced left and right, chunks of soil flying out of the cloud.

Kai looked over their shoulder towards the tunnels. They could try running too, but Kai didn't know where these tunnels led, if they led anywhere at all. If any more of the undead were skulking down there Kai would be done for.

No, this was their best chance. The longer Kai could keep Hannon occupied the better chance Tal had of getting out.

Appearing from the cloud of oily blackness, Hannon looked around, his shining pupils widening as they caught sight of their prey.

"It'll take more than some devil-blood magic to save you." Hannon cackled, rolling his meaty shoulders and dropping his stained cloak to the floor. He kicked a corpse aside, spinning his long weapon around and spraying out drops of mud.

"Do you have to talk?" Kai cocked an eyebrow.

Hannon smiled, his blackened teeth dripping as he ran his pale tongue over them. "So eager to die, are we?" Not waiting for a response Hannon thrust the blade forward.

Kai barely moved in time, the sharp blade tearing through their soiled jacket. Pushing off, the tiefling did the only thing they could do, evade.

They stepped left and right, ducking down and rolling backwards, reacting to each swing of the heavy weapon. Stepping forward just a fraction too late Kai caught the staff, feeling blood running down their hip.

281

Drawing the blade back, having just sliced the skin, Hannon backhanded Kai across the face, sending the lithe tiefling spinning to the ground.

Using the momentum Kai rolled away across the muddy floor, pushing theirself to their feet and pressing a hand to their ribs. A deep cut, but nothing fatal.

The two circled each other, eyes locked together waiting for the other to make a move.

Kai feigned right, dropping to their knees as Hannon threw his weapon like a javelin.

The blade flew over Kai, so close they felt the air rushing past them, and sunk deep into the wall.

Using the pole to pull theirself up Kai rushed around the edge of the pit, Hannon waving his hands in a way they'd seen Tal doing many a time.

A chill filled the air as a blast of freezing wind erupted from Hannon's palm, frost suddenly covering the ground and wall where Kai had been just seconds ago.

Stopping to look back at the ogre mage Kai turned their attention to the numb sensation in their tail. The tip had turned deathly pale, bright pink with small crystals speckling the skin.

"Kai!" Tal's voice called from above, drawing the attention of both tiefling and orge.

They looked up at the muddy elf, frustration building. "I told you to go!" Kai yelled, trying to keep Hannon in their sights.

"Catch!" Tal yelled back, either not hearing or not caring about what Kai wanted. She hurled two long pointed objects towards them, and Kai had to skip back to avoid getting skewered.

Looking down with confusion to see Tal had tossed a large two-pronged fork and carving knife at them. With a smile Kai picked them up, giving Tal a nod of gratitude. If this is where it ended, they were going out swinging.

Hannon pulled the blade from the wall with ease, looking between Tal and Kai with a grin. "It's so much more fun when your prey has-"

A bolt of flame hit the pontificating ogre in the face, knocking him back in surprise.

282

With a roar Hannon charged forward again, but this time Kai didn't flee. Using the oversized cutlery Tal had thrown their way Kai parried the blade, rolling between the ogre's legs and slicing at their calf.

Turning to grab for Kai, another bolt of flame pushed Hannon off balance and his hand clutched nothing but air.

The detectives were on the offensive now. Tal flung bolt after bolt of flame at Hannon, not caring where or even if she hit the hulking man. She was just keeping him distracted enough to keep Kai safe.

Hannon was now forced to choose between attacking the tiefling before him, or repelling Tal's barrage of flames.

Kai dodged the spinning glaive, sinking the fork deep into the back of Hannon's knee. With a cry the orge fell forward, dropping his heavy weapon with a thud. He pulled the fork free, snarling and gripping it tightly.

Tal tossed another bolt of flame, but in the brightness of the fire she missed seeing the bloodied fork being thrown her way. She screamed as the prong pierced her collarbone, dropping back against the wall.

"Enough!" Hannon yelled as he reached for his weapon again. But Kai was there.

Using all their meagre weight Kai slammed the blade into Hannon's hand, piercing through and slicing away two fingers as they rolled forward.

Clutching his gushing hand, Hannon gritted his teeth, spittle spraying from his lips as his breathing got heavier.

"Fine!" He grunted. "It's over! But mark you, devil, I'll be returning the favour!" Hannon snapped his remaining fingers and vanished, bloody footprints appearing on the ground fleeing towards the tunnels.

Tal looked down towards Kai, the tiefling dropping to their knees with exhaustion. "Are you okay?" She called down.

"No," Kai dropped the knife, "are you?"

Wincing as she tried to pull the fork free, Tal shook her head, opting for leaving it where it was. "No."

283

With a nod Kai smiled. "Okay, as long as we're on the same page. Let's get out of here."

⩘⊙⩗

Using Hannon's bed sheet as a rope, along with some sacks to weigh it down at the top, the two eventually got Kai out of the pit. Taking their time to recover, Tal even enjoying a piece of Kai's jerky, just grateful for some form of nourishment, the two slumped down at the edge of the pit. The dozens of bodies below looking up at them with vacant eyes and gaunt expressions held an eerie calm over the events of whatever time of day it was.

Bruised, bloodied, and exhausted they made their way back through the tunnels, finding Poppy and Spring happily working away in their own chambers. The two brothers were more than eager to help Tal, Poppy pulling the fork free slowly while Spring used healing magic to close the wound. If it wasn't for the last hour of her life Tal thought she might have liked the two of them.

After another short rest, while Kai carefully explained what mister Hannon had asked them to help with, the halflings led Kai and Tal out of the maze-like tunnels of the tomb and into the early morning light. Excited to see the city, Spring and Poppy followed behind, singing away on their journey home with their two new friends.

⩘⊙⩗

Many strange and terrified looks were thrown towards Kai and Tal as they headed towards the guardhouse and D'Clos. Their blood-stained clothing and battered bodies caused people to either stop and stare or give them an incredibly wide berth as they hurried past. Even the duty guard was initially hesitant to let them inside in their current state.

The Sargent was eventually called down, and after hearing Kai recounting their night the two halflings were calmly led away, unaware of what was happening, and a unit of guards

284

dispatched to the graveyard. D'Clos refused any further explanations from either Kai or Tal, insisting they sought aid before either of them dropped dead in the reception hall. Furthering this point D'Clos, along with two more armed guards, escorted the unkempt and soiled pair back to the Troll's Den personally, sending word for a cleric to be called for as soon as possible.

Tess's tirade as Kai and Tal were escorted into her tavern was pulled up short once her eyes managed to take in the state of her two most regular patrons. She watched with her jaw hanging open before quickly filling two large tankards with ale and following the train of people up the stairs.

Left alone in her room Tal's mind and body slowly collapsed with exhaustion, grief, and relief. Her emotions overflowing and her spirit broken, the elven woman passed out, a tear rolling from her eye and soaking into her pillow.

Tal didn't know how long she'd slept for, or even what time it was when her eyes opened. Laying in bed in silence she stared at the ceiling breathing deep and slow. Everything ached, though not as much as before. Looking herself over, mild confusion and concern set in. Her wounds had been cleaned and dressed, and her clothes had been changed. On the table next to her bed she saw three plates with remnants of food stacked on top of each other, as well as a couple of tankards. So someone had been spending some time with her.

The sight and thought of food made her stomach twist and groan, providing enough motivation for her to get up and face the world.

Down in the tavern a bandaged tiefling sat in a fresh three-piece suit at a table with an armed and armoured half-elf.

"Good morning, Arcanist Tal'avera." D'Clos greeted her with a nod and sombre smile. "You're looking well."

Tal smiled back out of politeness, she certainly didn't feel well. "Thank you. Good morning Sargent," she said, pulling out a chair next to Kai.

The tiefling put a hand on her shoulder and gave a gentle squeeze. They said nothing, but the look in their eyes conveyed everything Tal was feeling and more. Gesturing to D'Clos, Kai put on their cheerful expression. "Our good friend here was just about to fill me in on the details. Thank the god's you came down when you did or he'd have to repeat himself."

D'Clos snorted, rolling his eyes at Kai's attempt at levity. "Quite." He cleared his throat. "Well firstly, my congratulations to you both. It appears you have saved the city from a plague it never knew existed."

Tal raised an eyebrow at that, but before she could interrupt with questions the half-elven guard continued.

"Upon arriving at the cemetery," he coughed, "-sorry, graveyard- we searched the tomb where you were held. Following the blood trail down the tunnel system my guards eventually emerged in the sewer system beneath the city." A look of serious concern furrowed the sergeant's brow. "Whatever they were planning was being directed to an attack against Belgar."

Kai remained silent, listening carefully without even making a single note. Tal opened her mouth to speak, but D'Clos answered her question before it passed her lips.

"There was no sign of this Oggi Hannon you mentioned, though his description is being circulated to nearby towns and a scroll has been sent to Vallameria." D'Clos tented his fingers with a sigh. "Though if he is indeed an ogre mage then I doubt that description will be useful. Unless he's arrogant enough to use the same disguise elsewhere."

"I don't think he'll be gone for too long," Kai drummed against the table. "He didn't seem happy to leave partially handed."

"Yes, quite." D'Clos pulled out a scroll from his belt and unrolled it across the table. "As for his two accomplices, I doubt they will be much help."

"Are they not willing to cooperate?" Tal asked with a small amount of surprise. The two halflings were eager to join them on

286

their return to the city, but perhaps the sudden change in circumstance had altered their opinion.

"Willing, yes. Able? No." The look on D'Clos's face was a mix of frustration and defeat. "The brothers are what I suppose you would call, 'savants'. Neither is able to really read or write, but they both possess incredible innate abilities."

Tal looked at Kai, who seemed just as baffled as she did. "You mean they were just...born necromancers?" The thought alone worried her. A school of magic not taught or practised in over eight-hundred years just appearing out of nowhere in the minds of two innocent halflings. Could there be more people like them?

"That appears to be the case." D'Clos sighed. "The brothers are from a small farming community to the far East of the country, a community that was sadly ravaged by a pestilence. They are all that's left of their family and somehow they fell into the service of an ogre mage who sensed and exploited their abilities."

Kai cleared their throat. "What's going to happen to them? Will they be tried and sentenced?" While little was known about necromancy itself, the punishment for those found using it was clear. Death.

"That's currently to be decided. We have the unique situation of two necromancers who do not know what necromancy is." The sergeant sighed and scratched his chin. "It's a complicated situation, but I think they will more likely be collared."

D'Clos's words both relieved Tal and set a lump in her throat. While she was glad the brothers were not to be executed, collaring was a punishment reserved for wayward mages. A permanent steel ring locked around one's neck that absorbed magical essence, making it impossible for the collared mage to cast even the most basic of spells.

For a wizard it was torture, but for the brothers it might not have been so bad. Magic was not an integral part of their being, so they should have a more simple life safe from exploitation.

"That brings us to a more interesting matter," D'Clos cleared his throat again as he ran a finger down the scroll before him. "As you are both aware there was a large number of missing persons cases mounting up on my desk."

287

The pair nodded.

"Twenty-seven of the thirty-two people were discovered in the piles of corpses you left in the tomb, including your young Lord Vaskar." D'Clos signalled to the guards that Tal suddenly noticed sitting off to the side. They both rose, carrying a small wooden chest between them and placing it down in the centre of the table where Kai and Tal sat.

"Twenty-three of these cases had a reward for their discovery. Thus, I hereby present you with twelve-hundred gold pieces and forty-two silver. Thank you for your help."

Tal's eyes went wide. Kai simply gave a smile and nod. "All in a day's work," they said with a chuckle. "I'm just glad we managed to give these people closure."

D'Clos chucked too. "You're either the best or the luckiest investigators I've ever met. Though I have a feeling that it's the latter." The sergeant stood up, his chair scraping behind him. "Either way, thank you both. I look forward to working with you again."

As he turned to leave Kai raised their hand. "One last thing, if you don't mind." They stood up as well, stretching slightly as their joints cracked. "The two you arrested for the murder of Patrice Vaskar. They didn't kill him."

D'Clos frowned, pinching the bridge of his nose. "I suppose you would like me to see about their release?"

"Oh, no," Kai shook their head, "just Kirtan. The little one still tried to kill us and injured a number of your men. Let him serve out his time." A wicked grin crept across Kai's face.

With a smirk to match it D'Clos nodded. "I'll see to it. Now unless there's anything else, I've got some reports to complete." D'Clos and his men gave a gentle bow before leaving the two of them alone with the coin laden chest.

As the two of them stared back and forth between the chest and each other, a loud throat clearing broke the silence.

"If you're wondering what to do with all that coin," Tess called over from behind the bar, "may I remind you that you both have quite the tab to cover."

Tess's room and board fees were not the only tabs the pair had run up, nor were they particularly high. With the coin divided almost evenly, Kai taking a cut from Tal since, as Kai put it, "you did hire me after all", the pair settled their debt with Tess, along with securing their place for the next few months.

The next stop was the temple of Caledoughn, as Kai still had Patrice's sword to return. Tal was initially surprised that the guards had managed to retrieve and identify so many corpses overnight. She was less surprised when Kai informed her that she'd been asleep for four days.

There was a notably high number of guards roaming the streets of Belgar, the city was definitely on alert. Tal and Kai made their way to the temple, where the guard presence was even higher, though there was also a shift in the uniforms. A small detachment of guards armed with spears and dressed in half-plate with purple tabards stood watch by an ornately armoured carriage.

"This looks to be interesting," Kai muttered as the pair walked through the doors under their watchful eyes.

Inside the temple was cool and quiet, not a worshipper in sight. Most likely scared off by the loiterers outside. The two approached the Dias and Kai began calling out, hoping to attract the attention of any of the clergy.

Footsteps echoed from a nearby staircase and a young friar appeared. After taking their names he smiled with relief, they had been expected and apparently couldn't have arrived a moment too soon. The friar led them down to the chambers below, where Patrice's body had been stowed previously. The dull echo of conversation grew louder as Kai and Tal emerged into the open chamber, the time-slowing aura not in use, just the cold air of the marble storage room stinging the tips of Tal's ears.

Inside the chamber stood Father Roderic and Father Elaba, along with a finely dressed human woman Tal judged to be in her thirties, and a pair of the purple clad guards.

The friar announced their arrival before hurrying away, keen to get back to whatever he was doing in the first place.

"Lady Amelia," Father Elaba spoke to the serious looking woman as he gestured to Kai and Tal, "these are the detectives that I mentioned, the ones responsible for recovering your brother."

As much as the woman and her guards drew the attention of the room, Tal couldn't help but let her eyes wander. Whereas the last time she had been in this chamber there was only the single occupied slab, now the room was at full capacity.

"Finally," Lady Amelia Vaskar said with the heavy sigh of a woman who had been waiting longer than she'd wanted, "do you have it?"

Kai stepped forward, being the more practised at political politeness of the two. "If by it you are referring to his sword then yes." Kai opened their satchel and drew the blade free to the surprise of all but Tal, holding it flat across their palms.

With a nod in the tiefling's direction one of her guards stepped forward and took the sword, carrying it over to Patrice's coffin and placing it inside.

"My family has been receiving communications from a girl named Samara, is she among your organisation?" Amelia asked flatly. She was either well versed at concealing her emotions or the death of her brother didn't bother her as much as Tal would have expected.

Clearing her throat Tal answered her. "Samara gave her life to reclaim your brother. She was his friend and companion in battle."

"Her body rests in another chamber of our temple." Father Elaba said in a sombre tone. "Alas, she has no family to claim her." The portly cleric spoke directly to the noble woman, his implication subtle as a temple bell.

Amelia grunted and nodded to her guards again. Another one stepped forward and handed a coin pouch to the cleric before stepping back into place. "See that she receives the proper rites and a marked burial."

"It shall be done," Father Elaba gave a humble bow to Amelia and shot a quick wink towards Tal. Clearly he has been thinking the same as her, and had experience with drawing blood from stone.

"I believe that concludes our business," Amelia said, nodding to her guards for a third time.

Tal was unable to distinguish one nod from the next, but her guards had been well trained in the subtleties of such a gesture. The two armoured men took either end of Patrice's coffin and marched out of the chamber, with Lady Amelia Vaskar in tow.

"She seems pleasant," Tal sneered when the sound of retreating footsteps had faded.

Father Roderic sighed. "Nobles have priorities far above that of us mere mortals."

Kai snorted a laugh. "Well at least she was kind enough to help attend to Samara. Thank you Father."

"It is the least that dear girl deserved." Father Elaba nodded to Tal, "I shall keep you updated with your friends rites and arrangements."

"It may take some time," Father Roderic interjected, "we have the business of replacing the sanctification of our graveyard. I never thought I'd see this again in my lifetime." He sighed.

"That's what you get for living so long," Father Elaba patted his elder on the back gently with a laugh. "Thank you both," he turned his attention back to Kai and Tal, "may our Lady guide you safely."

꙰⊙꙰

Declining Father Elaba's rather insistent invitation to tea, Kai and Tal left the temple and returned to the late afternoon air of the city. The detachment of purple garbed guards and the armoured carriage had departed and people had begun to return to the temple for the evening's sermon.

"Can we stop by Botan's?" Tal asked as they began their journey back to the tavern. "I need to pay for those clothes while I can and there's something I want to talk to her about."

Kai was staring into the light orange sky, seemingly worlds away from the conversation. Blinking back to reality they stared blankly at Tal for a moment. "Sorry, what did you say?"

"Botan's. Going there. Are you coming?" Tal raised an eyebrow as she spoke slowly. "Are you ok?"

Kai shook theirself, plastering a smile on their face. "Sorry, still feeling a little drained. I'll be fine. Say hi to Botan for me, I'll see you back at the Den."

Narrowing her gaze on the tiefling, Tal rested her hand on their shoulder. "Are you sure?"

"You're far too pale to be my mother," Kai joked, waving her off. "Go, go, I'll see you later."

With a frown Tal gave them a final squeeze on their shoulder before heading off down the street. Kai stood in place, watching her leave and waiting for her to be out of sight. Reaching into their satchel Kai took out a piece of jerky and chewed, turning on their heel and heading off down the street. They would see Tal back at the Den, they just weren't heading there straight away.

Moving at speed, taking shortcuts down alleyways and pushing through crowds, Kai made their way to a small antiques shop near the north-eastern wall of the city.

They opened the door, a small bell ringing above their head, and approached the counter where a young human woman sat reading an old dog-eared book. The shop was filled with all sorts of oddities, furniture and artwork, all decorated with a thin layer of dust.

"How can I help you?" The girl asked, putting a bookmark in place before giving Kai her full attention.

"I'm a collector of fine wood cabinets," Kai recited a phase they had not used in years, "do you have anything I can see?"

The girl looked them up and down for a moment. "We may have a piece in pine," she said slowly, "would that interest you?"

"Only if the grain is subtle."

Finishing the exchange the girl walked Kai to a corner where a pine cabinet rested against the wall. Rapping against its surface there was a brief pause before it swung open, an armed half-orc waiting behind it.

Kai was guided down a spiral staircase, the soft hum of music getting louder, to another door. Led into the secret room below the antique shop, Kai looked around, a number of relaxed patrons diverting their attention from the elven singer to them. Sitting in a pile of soft velvet cushions, a girl on either side and the towering form of Bao behind him, was Malachai. The ivory horned tiefling grinned as Kaivel approached, taking a long drag from his pipe and blowing a thick white cloud over his shoulder.

"Kaivel, Kaivel, Kaivel. I knew you'd come back to me one day." Malachai's grin of self-satisfaction looking all the more ominous with ribbons of smoke still escaping between his teeth.

"Don't get your hopes up, I'm just here to settle something." Kai opened their satchel and reached deep inside.

Bao took a step forward, cracking his knuckles.

"Easy mutton-mits," Kai rolled their eyes, "don't make things more difficult than they need to be." With a heave, Kai lifted the mirror they had taken from the groundskeeper's home free from their bag.

Malachai's normal calm confident demeanour melted immediately, the look of excitement and expectancy rippling through his body almost childlike. "Oh my, oh my, oh my! Kaivel my sweet you never fail to surprise me." He held out his hands greedily grabbing for the piece that Kai held close to their chest.

"Needless to say," Kai handed the mirror across, the snow-white tiefling snatching it away, "but your man Wikson is dead. And before you ask, it wasn't by my hand."

Malachai was too busy staring at the mirror to ask questions, his pink eyes taking in every intricate detail of its design. "Methods matter not, only results." Without looking back Malachai snapped his fingers at the goliath behind him. "Bao, be a dear and fetch Kaivel's payment."

"I didn't bring you this for payment," Kai interrupted before Bao moved, "I told you before, I don't work for you."

Resting the mirror to his side, Malachai's grin intensified. "Well now, you are still full of surprises." He tented his fingers, staring over the tips at Kai. "Tell me, what do you want?"

"Information. Oggi Hannon, an ogre mage that's been busy beneath the city. What do you know of him?"

Malachai frowned. "The name is not familiar, but if I do learn anything you'll be the first I tell." He stroked his chin as he leaned back into the cushions. "So this was your plan, to get me in your debt? I'm so proud of you."

Kai simply shrugged. "As they say, better the devil you know."

Kai's return to the Troll's Den had been bombarded with questions about where they'd been, what they'd been doing, what they were up to. All these questions however were easily dissuaded by the suggestion of drinking. The case closed, their wounds healing, and a large amount of coin to boot, Kaivel and Tal'avera decided to celebrate, and celebrate they did! Tess filled tankard after tankard, even opening another bottle of the blue stuff to raise a glass to the partnership and the many adventures to come.

჻⊙჻

After a night of heavy drinking the last thing Kai expected was to be awoken by Tal bashing about in their room. Pulling a sheet around their dehydrated body Kai staggered into their office.

"What in the nine hells are you doing?" They slurrily demanded of the elven woman who was piling books on their desk.

"Well," Tal took a breath and rolled her sleeves back up, "if we're going to be working together then we need to tidy this mess up." She shifted a pile of scrolls over to the corner of the room. "I want to be able to find things, and I'll need a desk too."

Kai opened their mouth to protest when a loud knock at the door stole Tal's attention. Skipping over to the door Tal opened it to see an elderly gnomish woman dressed in a heavy woollen cardigan.

"Mortzeel's Lost and Found," Tal smiled at her, "how can we help you?"

294

GLOSSARY

Bao
Male – Goliath
Bodyguard and right-hand
to Malachai Vorikz.

Master Cornelious Brum
Male – Human
Librarian. Tutor in the
arcane to Tal'avera.

Seageant Aaran D'Clos
Male – Half-elf
Sergeant of the Belgar
Crown's Guard.

Bertrand DuPont
Male – Gnome
Manager and bookkeeper
for "The Stonejaw Inn &
Fight Pit".

Father Dewyn Eleba
Male – Human
Senior priest if the temple of
Caledoughn.

Kirtan Farvel
Male – Half-elf
Adventurer. Companion of
Galen, Patrice, & Samara.

Davros Granitebrand
Male – Dwarf

Chef, food cart vendor. 'The
best meal in town".

Samara Highsworn
Female – Human
Archer, adventurer.
Companion of Galen,
Kirtan, & Patrice.
Client of Kaivel Mortzeel.

'Jasper'
Male – Human
Fence and smuggler.
Member of the "Hall of
Whispers" thieves guild.
Kaivel's connection to the
underground market.

Jenah
Female – Elf
Performer at the Dancing
Dryad.

Cherie Le'Claire
Female – Elf
Manager of the
Adventurer's Lodge.

Tal'avera 'Tal' Liwood
Female – Elf
Arcanist in training from the
town of Rothwood.

Client of Kaivel Mortzeel.

Tessandra 'Tess' Melelea
Female – Troll-orc
Owner and tavern keeper of
"The Troll's Den".
Landlord to Kaivel Mortzeel.

Kaivel 'Kai' Mortzeel
Non-binary – Tiefling
Detective and proprietor of
"Mortzeel's Lost & Found".

Father La'Quil Roderic
Male – Elf
High priest of the temple of
Caledoughn.

Philip Stonejaw
Male – Goliath
Owner of "The Stonejaw Inn
& Fit Pit".

Galen Tanner
Male – Gnome
Adventurer. Companion of
Kirtan, Patrice, & Samara.

Tiny
Male – Orc
Smuggler. Member of the
"Hall of Whispers" thieves
guild.

Brother Bartholemew
Tomas
Male – Human
Guard within the temple of
Caledoughn.

Botan Turi
Female – Gnome
Enchanter and proprietor of
"Botan's Boutique".

Lord Drascus Uth'ill
Male – Elf, Drow
Nobleman. Owner and
founder of "Blue Moon
Mining".

Lord Patrice Vaskar
Male – Human
Youngest son of the Vaskar
family.
Matrice (Father), Astrid
(Mother), Amelia (Sister)
Adventurer. Companion of
Galen, Kirtan, & Samara.

Malachai Vorikz
Male – Albino Tiefling
Master of the "Hall of
Whispers" thieves guild.

Printed in Great Britain
by Amazon